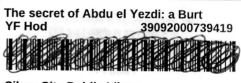
THE S
ABDU

DATE DUE			
MAY 1 4 2014			
JUN 1 0 2014			
JUN 1 0 2014			
JUL 3 1 2014			
AUG 0 5 2015			
JUL 2 7 2016			

Library Store #47-0108 Peel Off Pressure Sensitive

D0207755

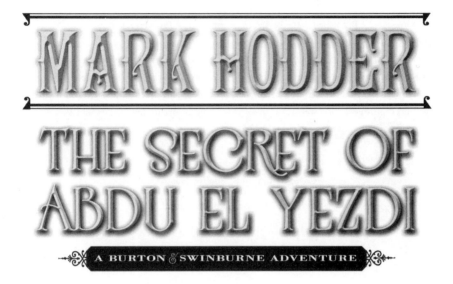

MARK HODDER
THE SECRET OF ABDU EL YEZDI

A BURTON & SWINBURNE ADVENTURE

an imprint of **Prometheus Books**
Amherst, NY

Published 2013 by Pyr®, an imprint of Prometheus Books

Cover illustration © Jon Sullivan
Cover design by Jacqueline Nasso Cooke

Inquiries should be addressed to

Pyr
59 John Glenn Drive
Amherst, New York 14228–2119
VOICE: 716–691–0133
FAX: 716–691–0137
WWW.PYRSF.COM

17 16 15 14 13   5 4 3 2 1

Library of Congress Cataloging-in-Publication Data

Hodder, Mark, 1962–
    The secret of Abdu El Yezdi : a Burton and Swinburne adventure / By Mark Hodder.
        pages cm.
    ISBN 978-1-61614-777-8 (pbk.)
    ISBN 978-1-61614-778-5 (ebook)
    I. Title.
PR6108.O28S43 2012
823'.92—dc23
                                                                        2013010096

Printed in the United States of America

Dedicated to

Venus Speedwell

ACKNOWLEDGMENTS AND DISCLAIMER

Writing is a solitary business at the best of times, but when deadlines draw near, one is forced into prolonged seclusion. During these periods, on the infrequent occasions when I've emerged from my study, bearded, unwashed, and with a crazed glint in my eyes, my beautiful partner, Yolanda, has fed me and talked soothingly until the twitching has stopped. What small measure of sanity I still possess must be credited to her. I give her my thanks and my love.

My gratitude, also, to Lou Anders and the Pyr team in the US, and Michael Rowley and the Del Rey team in the UK. Your faith in me and your continued support are hugely appreciated.

Many of the characters featured in this novel bear the same names as—and similar personalities and histories to—people who actually lived. However, as will quickly become apparent, the 1859 of this story is not the 1859 you'll discover in history books.

If a person whose life is well documented had been presented with completely different opportunities and challenges, would they have turned out the same? In *The Secret of Abdu El Yezdi*, the answer to that question is a resounding, "No!" Thus, though my characters are intended to evoke their famous counterparts, their portrayal is not in any way biographical. In an attempt to compensate for any disrespect I may have shown them, I've included brief factual information at the end of this book, which I hope will encourage my readers to explore the real histories of the truly remarkable and admirable men and women featured herein.

BURTON

"Unjust it were to bid the World be just
And blame her not: She ne'er was made for justice:
Take what she gives thee, leave all grief aside,
For now to fair and then to foul her lust is."
—A THOUSAND NIGHTS AND A NIGHT,
TRANSLATED BY SIR RICHARD FRANCIS BURTON

CHAPTER 1

THE SUMMONING

"When one creates phantoms for oneself, one puts vampires into the world, and one must nourish these children of a voluntary nightmare with one's blood, one's life, one's intelligence, and one's reason, without ever satisfying them."
—ELIPHAS LEVI, *AXIOM XI OF LA CLEF DES GRANDS MYSTÈRES*

Captain Richard Francis Burton leaned on the basin, looked into the mirror, and saw Captain Richard Francis Burton glowering back. He scowled into the black, smouldering eyes and snarled, "I'm sick of your meddling! I'll live by my own choices, not by yours, confound you!"

His tormentor's glare locked aggressively with his own.

At the periphery of Burton's vision, behind the devil that faced him, the cabin door opened and a slim young man stepped in. He was prematurely bald but sported a very long and bushy beard.

"You're awake!" the newcomer exclaimed, leaning his silver-topped walking cane against the wall.

Burton turned, but when he stopped the room didn't—it continued to spin—and the other jumped forward and took him by the elbows. "Steady on, old chap."

There was something rather repellent about the man's touch, but Burton was too weak to shake him off, so submitted meekly as he was guided to his bunk.

The visitor shook his head disapprovingly. "I don't know what you think you're doing. Sister Raghavendra will have your guts for garters. Back into bed with you, sir. You need rest and plenty of it. You're not out of the woods yet. Not by a long shot."

Burton managed to shrug free from the other's grip and slurred, "Did you see him? Why won't he leave me be?"

"To whom do you refer?"

"Him!" Burton shouted, flinging a hand toward the mirror and almost overbalancing. "Dogging my every step, the old fool! Interfering! Always interfering!"

The younger man chuckled—a sound that inexplicably sent cold prickles up Burton's spine. "It's merely your reflection, and you're hardly old; just worn out, that's all. The fevers have taken their toll, but I'm sure you'll regain your looks once you've shaken off the malaria. Now come, lie down, I'll read to you awhile."

Burton shook his head, his knees buckled, and he sat heavily. "Reflection, be damned. If I ever meet the dog, I'll kick him all the way to Hades!"

The visitor gave a snort of amusement, and the odious nature of his presence finally registered in full. Burton looked up at him, his jumbled senses converging, bringing the man's penetrating blue eyes into focus, noting the wide and rather cruel-looking mouth and the polished, overdeveloped cranium.

Dangerous. The fellow is dangerous.

A tremor ignited in Burton's stomach and raced outward through his body, causing his question—"Who are you, anyway?"—to come out more as a teeth-rattling moan.

"Four times I've visited your room, Captain," the man replied, "and four times you've made that very same enquiry. The answer is as ever. I am Laurence Oliphant, Lord Elgin's private secretary. He and I joined the ship at Aden for passage to London."

Burton frowned and struggled to clarify his thoughts. Memories eluded him. "Aden? We're not at Zanzibar?"

"No, we're not. The *Orpheus* departed Zanzibar two weeks ago. It spent five days at Aden, has just departed Cairo, and is currently en route to London via Vienna, where it will pick up the foreign secretary, Lord Stanley."

"What day is it?"

"Night, actually. Wednesday, the thirty-first of August. Tomorrow, your long expedition will finally be over. You'll be glad to get home, I expect. I understand you have a fiancée waiting for you."

Burton lifted his legs onto the bed, waited for Oliphant to arrange the pillows behind him, and lay back. His limbs jerked and his hands began to shake uncontrollably. He felt himself burning, sinking, disconnecting.

He could sense the eyes of the Other Burton upon him.

Go away. Go away. Leave me alone. I haven't time for you now. I have to watch this fellow. There's something about him. Something wrong.

Oliphant went to the basin, wetted a flannel, returned, placed it on Burton's forehead, and sat beside him. "You've been out of commission for nearly a month, but Sister Raghavendra says you're through the worst of it. She thinks the fever will break within the next few hours." He tapped his finger on Burton's shoulder. "Why do you do it, Captain? Why push yourself so hard? First in India, then your mission to Mecca, and now Africa—what drives you to such endeavours?"

Burton whispered, "The devil. He's inflicted upon me a mania for exploration."

"Ha! Well, this time Old Nick took you to the brink of death. You were lucky you had one of the Sisterhood of Noble Benevolence with you."

Sister Sadhvi Raghavendra. Her beautiful face blurred into Burton's memory then swam away.

"It wasn't luck," he murmured. "Is she aboard? I want to see her."

"She was here but half an hour ago. I'll call her back if you wish it."

Fragments. Broken recollections. Cascading water falling from the great lake—almost an inland sea—to begin its long journey to the Mediterranean. Standing on a hill overlooking it, his companion at his side.

Burton sucked in a deep, shuddering breath, feeling his eyes widen.

"John! My God! How is John?"

Oliphant looked puzzled. "John?"

"Lieutenant Speke."

"I'm afraid I don't know him. Half a mo! Do you mean the chap who was with you at Berbera back in 'fifty-five? The one who died?"

"Died?"

"I was in the Far East at the time, but if I remember the reports rightly, he took a spear meant for Lieutenant Stroyan. It pierced his heart and killed him outright. That was four years ago."

"Four years?" Burton whispered. "But Speke and I discovered the source of the Nile."

"The fever has you befuddled. As I say, Speke copped it during your initial foray into Africa. It was you, William Stroyan, George Herne, and Sister Raghavendra who solved the puzzle of the Nile. You'll be remembered among the greatest of explorers. You've made history, sir."

The information fell between Burton and the Other Burton and they fought over it. The Burton here, now—the *real* Burton, blast it!—knew the fact to be true. Lieutenant John Hanning Speke had been killed in 1855. The Other Burton disagreed.

That is not when he died.

It is. I was there. I saw it happen.

He died later.

No! He died defending Stroyan.

He sacrificed himself for you.

Get away from me! Leave me alone!

You need me, you dolt.

The argument melted into Burton's overheated blood and raged through his body. He felt his limbs thrashing and heard a wail forced out of him. "I've made history, you say? I've made history?" He started to laugh and couldn't stop. He didn't know why it was funny, but it was.

Funny and agonising and terrifying.

I've made history.

Dimly, he felt Oliphant rise from the bed and—through tear-blurred eyes—watched him cross to the speaking tube beside the bureau. The young man pulled the device free, blew into it, and put it to his ear. After a brief wait, he placed the tube back against his mouth. "This is Oliphant. Can you have Sister Raghavendra sent to Captain Burton's cabin? I think he's having a seizure." He clipped the tube back into its bracket, turned to face Burton, then raised his right hand and made an odd and complex gesture, as if writing a sigil in the air.

"You say you have a mania for exploration, Captain Burton, but to me, you appear to possess all the qualities of a fugitive."

Burton tried to respond but his vocalisation emerged as an incomprehensible bark. Flecks of foam sprayed from his mouth. His muscles spasmed.

"Perhaps," Oliphant continued, "you should consider the possibility that, when a man struggles to escape his fate, he is more likely to flee along the path that leads directly to it."

Burton's teeth chattered. The cabin skewed sideways, righted itself, and suddenly he could smell jasmine and Sister Raghavendra was there—tall and slim, with big brown eyes, lustrous black hair, and dusky skin burned almost black by the African sun. Eschewing—while she still could—the corsets, heavy dresses, and multiple petticoats of the civilised woman, she was wearing a simple, loose-fitting Indian smock.

She said, "Has he been at all lucid?"

Burton closed his eyes.

She's here. You're safe. You can sleep.

Oliphant's voice: "Barely. He was in the midst of one of his delusions. It's just as you told me. He appears to believe himself a divided identity—two persons, thwarting and opposing each other. Will he be all right?"

"Yes, Mr. Oliphant, he'll be fine. It's a normal reaction to the medicine I gave him. The stuff brings the malarial fever to a final crisis and burns it off with great rapidity. This will be his last attack. In an hour or two, he'll fall into a deep sleep. By the time we arrive in London, he'll be weak but fully recovered. Would you leave us, please? I'll sit with him for an hour or so."

"Certainly."

The creak of the cabin door opening.

The bunk shifting as Sadhvi sat on the edge of it.

Her hand removing the flannel from his forehead.

Oliphant whispering, "As the crow flies, Captain Burton. As the crow flies."

Oblivion.

Burton opened his eyes. He was alone. Thirst scratched at his throat but something else had yanked him from his sleep. He lay still and listened. The *Orpheus* thrummed beneath him, the noise of the airship's eight engines so familiar he now equated their background rumble with silence.

There was nothing else.

He pushed the sheet back, struggled out of bed—*Bismillah! So weak!*—and tottered over to the basin where he gulped water from a jug.

The mirror had been waiting. Hesitantly, he scrutinised the fever-ravaged countenance he saw in it: the sun-scorched but yellow-tinged skin, still marked with insect bites; the broad brow, beaded with sweat; the angular cheeks, the left furrowed by a long, deep scar; and the wildly over-grown forked beard that ill-concealed a forward-thrusting, aggressive jaw. He peered into the intense eyes.

My own. Just my own reflected.

He sighed, poured water into the basin, splashed it over his face, then closed his eyes and tried to concentrate. Employing a Sufi technique, he withdrew awareness from his trembling legs, from the ague that gnawed at his bones, from every sense but the auditory.

A few minutes passed before it impinged upon his consciousness again, but—yes, there it was, extremely faint, a distant voice, chanting.

Chanting? Aboard the *Orpheus*?

He gave the mirror a second glance, muttered an imprecation, then crossed to a Saratoga trunk, opened its lid, lifted out the top tray, and retrieved a small bottle from one of the inner compartments.

The label read: *Saltzmann's Tincture.*

Five years ago, when an inexplicable impulse had led him to first purchase the cure-all from a pharmacist named Mr. Shudders, his good friend and personal physician, John Steinhaueser, had warned him off the stuff. Its ingredients were a mystery, but the doctor was certain cocaine was principal among them. Burton wasn't so sure. He knew well the effects of cocaine. Saltzmann's offered something entirely different. It imparted the exhilarating sense that one's life was ripe with endless options, as if all the possible consequences of actions taken were unveiled.

"Richard," Steinhaueser had said, "it's as insidious as opium and almost as addictive. You don't know what it might be costing you. What if it permanently damages your senses? Avoid. Avoid at all cost."

But Saltzmann's Tincture had cured Burton of the various ailments he'd brought back from India, saved him from blindness during his pilgrimage to Mecca, kept malaria at bay throughout his ill-fated penetration of Berbera, and had—despite Sister Raghavendra's seconding of Steinhaueser's opinion—sustained him while he led the search for the source of the Nile. For sure, in the final days of the expedition, he'd succumbed to the fever that was currently burning through his veins, but it wasn't half as bad as those experienced by the members of the Royal Geographical Society who scorned Saltzmann's and relied, instead, upon quinine. Livingstone, for example, was very vocal in his opposition to it and suffered as a consequence. In his most recent dispatch, sent from a village near the headwaters of the Congo and received at Zanzibar four years ago, Livingstone had reported himself "terribly knocked up" and predicted that he'd never see civilisation again. *If only I had my faith to sustain me*, he'd written, *but the terrible things I have witnessed in these wicked lands have stripped it from me. I am no better than a beast.* He hadn't been heard from since, and was now presumed dead.

Saltzmann's. If Livingstone had taken Saltzmann's, he'd have maintained his health and seen a way out of whatever predicament he was in.

Burton broke the bottle's seal, popped out the cork, hesitated a moment, then drank half of the clear, syrupy contents. Moments later, a delicious warmth chased the ache from his joints.

He turned and lurched across the room to the door, lifted his *jubbah*—the loose robe he'd worn during his pilgrimage—down from a hook, wrapped it around himself, then pushed his feet into Arabian slippers.

A walking cane caught his eye. It was leaning against the wall. Its silver grip had been fashioned into the shape of a panther's head. He picked it up and realised it concealed a blade, which he drew and examined: an extremely well-balanced rapier.

Sheathing the weapon and using it for support, the explorer opened the door and stepped out into the passageway beyond, finding it warmly illuminated by bracket-mounted oil lamps. His cabin was on the lower of the *Orpheus*'s two decks, in the middle of the mostly unoccupied rear passenger section. William Stroyan's was a little farther along, closer to the stern observation room. He hobbled toward it. The corridor wavered around him like a mirage, and for a moment, he thought himself trekking across African savannah. He shook off the delusion and whispered, "Fool. You can barely stay upright. Why can't you just leave it be?"

He came to Stroyan's cabin and found its door standing partially open.

"Bill?"

No reply.

He rapped his knuckles against it.

"I say! Stroyan?"

Nothing.

He pushed the door open and entered. The lieutenant's bed was unmade, the room empty and lit only by starlight glimmering through the porthole.

Burton noticed his friend's pocket watch on the bedside table. He picked it up and angled its face to the light from the passage. Eight minutes to midnight.

Perhaps Stroyan was having trouble sleeping and had left this quiet area of the vessel to join the crew on the upper deck.

No. The bedsheets. The lieutenant is as neat as they come. Army training. He'd never leave his bedding twisted and trailing off the bunk like that.

And—

Burton grunted, took a box of lucifers from the table, lit one, and applied the spitting, sulphurous flame to a lamp, which he then lowered over the thing he'd noticed on the floor.

A pillow, darkly stained.

Blood.

He straightened, looked around again, saw the speaking tube, crossed to it, whistled into the mouthpiece, then put it to his ear and waited for a response.

A tinny voice said, "Yes, Lieutenant? What can I do for you?"

It was Doctor Quaint, the ship's steward and surgeon.

"It's not Stroyan, Doctor. It's Burton."

"Good Lord! I thought you were incapacitated."

"Not quite. Do you know where Stroyan is?"

"I haven't seen him since dinner, sir."

"I think someone struck him on the head and dragged him from his bed. Would you have the captain come down here, please?"

"Struck? Bed? Are you—?"

"I'm not delirious, I can assure you. Will you—"

"The captain. I'll tell him at once, sir."

"Thank you."

As he returned the speaking tube to its housing, the muted chanting touched his senses again. He cocked his head and listened. It was louder now, a single voice, generally low and rhythmic but occasionally increasing in volume, as if impassioned and unable to fully contain itself.

Curiosity got the better of him, turned him around, and drew him back out into the passage. His balance was off and he stumbled along as if drunk, but pushed himself onward, spurred by a growing impatience with his own weakness and an almost vicious determination to conquer it and discover the origin of the mysterious sounds.

As he passed the passenger cabin doors, each summoned a splintered recollection, as if they opened onto memories rather than empty chambers.

Number 35: Lieutenant George Herne. Like Burton, down with fever. He'd been left at Zanzibar, where, when he recovered, he'd be taking over as the island's new consul. Burton would miss him. Herne was a good sort. A little stolid and unimaginative, perhaps, but loyal. Unflappable.

Number 36: Gordon Champion. The airship's chief rigger. Dead. He'd crawled out along one of the engine pylons to investigate the inexplicable power failure that had immobilised the vessel just north of Africa's Central Lakes. He'd lost his footing. The slightest of misjudgments and—snap!—gone. That's how quickly, easily, and apparently randomly a life could be extinguished.

Number 37: John Hanning Speke. A beetle had crawled into his ear and he'd permanently deafened himself while trying to extract it with hot wax and a penknife.

What?

No.

There was no door 37.

That last never happened.

Burton reeled as a wave of dizziness hit him. He slapped a hand against the wall and rested for a moment. Why did he keep thinking about Speke? He'd hardly known the man.

This was a mistake. He should get back to bed. He was beginning to hallucinate again. He could see Speke's face as clear as day, the lieutenant's pale blue right eye contrasting starkly with the dark lens of his mechanical left.

Except Speke never had a mechanical left eye.

What is happening to me?

A voice pulled him back into reality. He looked up. The double doors to the observation deck were just ahead. The chanting was coming from behind them. It had just risen in pitch.

He wiped sweat from his eyes, closed them, and concentrated on the sweet tingle of the Saltzmann's Tincture as it oozed honey-like through his arteries. He felt it climbing his neck and easing into the back of his skull.

I've made history.

He would be accepted; offered an official position; hopefully, like Herne, a consulship. Damascus. He could marry Isabel and settle there; start his translation of *A Thousand Nights and a Night*. No one would again accuse him of being "un-English." No one would dare to call him "Blackguard Burton" or "Ruffian Dick." His years of exclusion and exile were over.

He tottered forward, holding tightly to the swordstick.

The chanting had greater clarity now. A man, repeating the same phrase over and over. Burton was an accomplished linguist, fluent in nearly thirty languages, but the incantation was utterly unfamiliar; a pulsating jumble of outlandish sounds and syllables, unfathomable, even to him.

He placed his left hand on one of the doorknobs, became aware of a pungent odour, paused, then twisted and pushed.

The door swung open. The explorer took two steps forward and stopped.

Laurence Oliphant halted in mid-recitation. His eyes met Burton's. He was standing in the middle of a pentagram painted on the floor. Clouds of foul-smelling smoke billowed from small brass censers positioned at its points. William Stroyan, obviously dazed and with blood dripping from a wound on his forehead, was kneeling at Oliphant's feet, facing away from him and toward Burton. Oliphant was gripping the lieutenant's hair and holding a large curved knife to his throat.

He sneered and slid the blade sideways.

Burton gave a cry of horror as blood spurted and his friend collapsed to the deck.

Oliphant raised his arms into the air. His eyes blazed triumphantly. "It is done! The way is open! I await thy coming, Master! I await thy coming! Thou shalt endure until the end!"

Barely aware of his own actions, Burton lifted the swordstick and drew the blade.

"That's my cane," Oliphant said.

The statement, so mundane amid such extraordinary circumstances, strengthened Burton's growing conviction that he was caught up in a fever-fuelled fantasy. He levelled the weapon at Oliphant—its tip shook wildly—and quickly glanced around, hardly comprehending what he saw. The walls of the observation room—three of glass; the fourth, at his back, of wood panels—were painted all over with squares, subdivided, each division containing a sequence of numbers. Beyond the glass, in the clear night sky, curtains of multicoloured light were materialising, shifting and folding, blocking the stars, and fast making the night as bright as day.

"Your cane?" Burton mumbled.

A horrible bubbling diverted his attention back to Stroyan. He saw the lieutenant's life gutter and depart.

Burton's eyes snapped up to Oliphant, who held out a hand and said, "I'll have it, if you please. It is bespoke. The only one of its kind. I had it fashioned in memory of a white panther I once kept as a pet. Marvellous creature. Don't you admire the single-mindedness of the predator, Captain?"

Uttering an inarticulate yell, Burton hurled himself forward, but his left knee gave way and his charge instantly became an uncoordinated floundering. He stabbed at Oliphant's shoulder, intending a disabling wound, but his opponent slashed his knife upward and deflected the rapier, sending Burton even more off-kilter. The two men collided and crashed to the floor. They grappled, Oliphant's weapon tangling in the explorer's *jubbah*, Burton dropping the sword and seeking a stranglehold.

Oliphant cried out, "Get off me! It's too late! It's him you should worry about now. He knows who you are, Burton. He'll come for you! He'll come for you!"

Burton punched him hard on the left ear, then, as the knife came free of the cloth, caught the man's wrist and strained to prevent the weapon from being thrust into his chest.

Who does he mean? Who's coming for me?

Without loosening his grip, Burton jerked his arms to the side and gouged his elbow into the other's eye.

Too fragile for this. Too damned fragile.

Oliphant twisted. The knife sliced through cloth and scraped across Burton's ribs. The explorer yelped, rolled over until he was on top of his foe, then slammed his forehead into the man's face, hearing the back of the other's skull clunk loudly on the deck. Lord Elgin's secretary went limp. Burton pushed himself up, sat on Oliphant's stomach, and with all the strength remaining to him, sent his fist crashing across the man's jaw. His opponent became still.

There. That'll keep you quiet, you bastard.

Falling to the side, he flopped onto his back and blacked out.

The distant coughing of lions.

The soothing songs of his bearers as the safari settled for the night.

The jungle, as red as blood.

Red?

The Other Burton's voice: *Parallel all things are; yet many of these are askew; you are certainly I; but certainly I am not you.*

"Burton! Captain Burton! Captain Burton!"

He opened his eyes and saw Nathaniel Lawless looking down at him. The airship captain's eyes were of the palest grey, his teeth remarkably straight and white, his snowy beard tightly clipped. Second Officer Wordsworth Pryce and Doctor Quaint were standing to either side of their commander.

Burton moistened his lips with his tongue. He said, "The sky."

"I know," Lawless responded. "It's the aurora borealis. But this bright and this far south? In all my days, I've never seen the like. Are you all right?" He stretched down a hand and helped the explorer to his feet.

"Comparatively speaking, yes."

"You're covered in blood."

"Most of it is William's. I have a scratch across the ribs, nothing more."

Doctor Quaint interjected, "Let me see it."

"Later, Doctor."

Burton turned and saw that rigger Alexander Priestly and engineer James Bolling—both big, beefy men—were holding the unconscious Laurence Oliphant upright.

Lawless asked, "He killed Stroyan?"

"He did."

"Why? And what are all these scribbles on the floor and walls?"

"It was some sort of ritual. A summoning, I think. William was the sacrifice."

"Summoning? Summoning of what? From where?"

"I haven't a notion."

Burton picked up the rapier and its sheath, slid the one into the other, then supported himself on the cane and waited for his head to clear. The Saltzmann's was causing a ringing in his ears and had put a strange glow around everything he saw. Or was that caused by the rippling illumination outside?

He took a deep breath, blinked, and addressed the second officer. "Pryce, would you mind fetching my notebook from the bureau in my quarters? I'd like to make a record of these diagrams and numbers."

Pryce gave a nod and departed.

Lawless jerked a thumb toward Oliphant. "I suppose I should lock this lunatic in one of the cabins."

Burton slipped his hand into his *jubbah* and gingerly touched the laceration running down his left side. His fingertips slid through warm wetness. He winced, and nodded. "Strap him down onto the bed. Make sure he can't move. We'll give him to the police when we reach London. I'll have a word with Lord Elgin."

"I can do that," Lawless objected. "You should go back to bed. You look sick as a dog—your skin is jaundiced."

"I'm over the worst of it, Captain. The excitement appears to have jolted me back to my senses. I'd rather see Elgin myself, if you don't mind."

"As you wish."

A couple of minutes later, Pryce returned and handed over Burton's notebook. Oliphant was hustled away. Quaint bandaged the explorer's wound then summoned a couple of crewmembers and helped them carry William Stroyan's corpse off to the ship's surgery.

Burton pushed to the back of his mind the misery he felt at his friend's death. He sketched. Each wall, he noted, had been divided into a seven-by-seven grid, the outer squares of which were densely filled with numbers. The next squares in—five by five—contained fewer numerals. They surrounded three by three, in each of which only four-figure numbers were painted.

Burton couldn't work it out, but he felt sure some sort of mathematical formula was in operation, which led to what he guessed was the "sum" in the central square of each wall. Behind him, on the wood panelling, this final number was ten; on the wall to his left, eight; on the wall in front, one thousand; and on the right-hand wall, nine hundred.

He was aware of Lawless looking over his shoulder until the diagrams were copied, then the captain crossed the deck to one of the glass walls and stood beside it, gazing out at the sky. "You surely don't expect me to believe he magicked up the aurora?"

Burton shook his head. "He referred to someone he called his 'master.' As for the lights, perhaps Oliphant somehow knew they were coming and timed his ritual to coincide with them."

Lawless ran his fingernails through his beard. Over the course of the past year, he and Burton had become firm friends, but the airship captain still observed the proprieties and nearly always called the explorer by his rank. Now, though, he let that formality slip.

"Damnation, Richard! After all we've been through, I wanted to get us home quick sharp! Instead, we had to lay over in Zanzibar until Herne's position was confirmed, wait in Aden for Elgin, and now bloody Oliphant goes batty just as we're about to land in Vienna. I swear, if our new passengers demand yet another delay because of this, I'll get off the confounded ship and walk home."

"Passengers?" Burton asked. "Who's with Lord Stanley?"

"Only His Royal bloody Highness Prince Albert."

Burton's eyebrows went up.

"I know," Lawless said. "Quite a surprise, eh? I was informed less than an hour ago. Disraeli obviously considers the *Orpheus*—as the flagship of the fleet—the most suitable vessel to escort the prince home, no matter that we've been in Africa for over a year and are all sick and exhausted." He pulled out his chronometer and clicked open its lid. "We'll be landing in fifty minutes but our precious cargo won't come aboard until daylight, so I suggest you get some more sleep. You look done in."

Burton nodded. "I am. But when Elgin shows his face in the morning, send someone to wake me."

"Righto." Lawless glanced around at the floor and walls then out at the rainbow colours that shimmered from horizon to horizon. "Hell and damnation!"

CHAPTER 2

HOMECOMING

ETERNAL REST
IN LOWER NORWOOD CEMETERY
Home to the Finest Sepulchral
Mausoleums and Monuments in London.
Privately Landscaped Memorial Gardens.
Rural Setting. Protected from Resurrectionists.
Uninterrupted Interment Assured.
Episcopal and Dissenters' Churches.
Extensive Vaults and Catacombs
for Added Peace and Security.
Consecrated by the Bishop of Winchester
West Norwood Cemetery, Norwood Road, Lambeth.

Sir James Bruce, 8th Earl of Elgin and 12th Earl of Kincardine, was a short and stout man, whose hair, despite his being just forty-eight years old, was as white as snow. He was bright-eyed and clean-shaven, though thick muttonchop whiskers framed his deceptively good-natured countenance.

"I suspected something had gone wrong with the lad," he said, "but to such an extreme? By heavens!"

"In what way wrong, sir?" Burton asked. They were seated in armchairs in the airship's plush smoking lounge. Elgin was puffing on an after-breakfast hookah. Burton had opted for a Manila cheroot. They each had a cup of coffee on the table between them.

"He was appointed my secretary two years ago and accompanied me to China, where we've been overseeing the Arrow War. For the first few months, he was perfectly efficient in his work and perfectly innocuous in his private life. He had, however, brought with him a book entitled *The Wisdom of Angels*, with which he became increasingly obsessed. He read it over and over. When I asked him about it, he became oddly reticent and refused to discuss it."

"The author?"

"I don't recall. Thomas something. I'm not sure why, but I associate that volume with his subsequent behaviour, which, I'm bound to observe, left a lot to be desired. In fact, I was set to dismiss him upon our return to London."

Burton ground the stub of his cheroot into an ashtray and immediately lit another one. After five hours of sleep and a hearty breakfast—it was now nine o'clock in the morning—he was feeling a little stronger. The laceration across his ribs was stinging but it wasn't a serious wound and hadn't required stitching.

"On what grounds?" he asked. "What did he do?"

Lord Elgin breathed out a plume of blue smoke and watched it curl toward the ceiling.

"There are a great many complications in our dealings with the Qing Dynasty," he said. "I'm returning to London to brief the prime minister and our Navy—and to request military support from the French. We must quell those Chinese forces that oppose the opening of the country to improved trade, and I fear there's no choice but to negotiate not with a handshake but with a fist. The *Sagittarius* will be a fist like no other."

"The *Sagittarius*?"

"A rotorship, Burton; a war machine of fearsome power. Its construction is almost completed, and it will be sent to China before the year is out."

"Very well, but how does this involve Oliphant?"

"China will only accept payment for tea in silver. This has caused a serious trade deficit, which we have countered by exporting opium there from India."

Burton threw his hands out in a gesture that made it clear he didn't get the point and was confused by Elgin's obfuscation.

"Opium, Captain!" Elgin barked. "Highly addictive! We exported it as a medicinal ingredient but the Chinese immediately started puffing on the stuff like it was cheap tobacco. Now half the damned country is enslaved by it. The Qing Dynasty isn't happy. Not at all."

"So?"

"So to hell with them! We'll pump enough opium into China to make addicts of the entire nation, if necessary. We'll even force them to legalise the trade so our private companies can profit from the poppy industry, too. By

God, we'll bring the bloody dynasty to its knees unless they give us a better deal on the export of tea."

"Dirty politics, Lord Elgin."

"All politics is dirty. It has to be. Trade is warfare and warfare is trade. That's the way of the world."

"You still haven't told me how Oliphant fits into this distasteful picture."

Elgin pushed his hookah aside and reached for his coffee. As he sipped it, his eyes met Burton's above the brim of the cup and the explorer saw amusement in them. He realised that Elgin was purposely provoking and prevaricating—that it was the man's technique in negotiations and he'd employed it so frequently, it was now habitual.

Elgin leaned forward, placed his emptied cup onto its saucer, and jabbed a finger at Burton.

"The opium trade is but one factor among a great many in our dispute with China, but it's the one Oliphant was responsible for. I relied on him to assess the situation as it developed, to communicate British demands to the emperor, and to summarise and bring to me the Chinese counter-demands—all of which would have been well and good were it not for one thing."

"It being?"

"That the bloody fool himself became an addict."

"Ah."

"It came to my attention at the start of April this year. We had briefly returned to London during the latter half of March, and while there, Oliphant joined some sort of gentlemen's club. He was rather secretive about it—never told me its name—but I gather its members share his fascination with that damned book. A mere week after we returned to China, I went to his rooms to collect some papers and found him in an opium-induced stupor."

Burton pursed his lips and thought for a moment. "You associate his taking of the drug with the club?"

"I do. A week or so later, I demanded an explanation for his behaviour. He babbled a great deal of nonsense, but from what of it I understood, I gather *The Wisdom of Angels* hypothesises multiple levels of existence—beyond even the Afterlife—and the club encourages the exploration of these through the use of mind-altering drugs. Oliphant told me, in all seriousness, that he'd established communication with a being from one of these other worlds. Absolute rot, of course."

"I take it your confronting him had little effect?"

Elgin leaned back and grunted an agreement. "None. He became thoroughly unreliable. In the end, I took over the duties I'd assigned to him, and I'll confess, it's been more than I can comfortably cope with. Thus my determination to replace the fellow."

A few minutes of silence fell between them. Burton finished his coffee. He looked out of the porthole and saw the rooftops of Vienna.

"Would you object to me searching his quarters?"

"Not at all."

"Thank you, Lord Elgin. You've given me much to think about."

Elgin flapped his hand dismissively.

Twenty minutes later, Burton had retrieved the key to Oliphant's cabin from the steward and was letting himself in.

The Wisdom of Angels, its leather spine cracked, its pages worn and creased at the corners, was on the bedside table.

"Thomas Lake Harris," Burton said aloud, reading the author's name. He flicked through the pages, looking at the chapter titles, digesting random paragraphs, gaining an overall impression of the subject matter. It was just as Elgin had summarised, with the addition that Harris reckoned his noncorporeal beings were influencing human history. Bizarrely, he also claimed to be married to one of them—an angel known as the Lily Queen.

Burton muttered, "Utter claptrap!"

He pushed the book into his jacket pocket and started to search through Oliphant's belongings. He found a daguerreotype showing the man posing with a white panther—the animal had moved during the exposure and its face was blurred. He opened a chest to reveal a large collection of daggers and flintlock pistols. He lifted three books down from a shelf. Two were travel journals written by Oliphant: *A Journey to Katmandu*, published in 1852, and *The Russian Shores of the Black Sea*, from 1853. The third was a thick sketchbook. Three-quarters of its pages were filled with pencilled illustrations of landscapes, buildings, and people—obviously a record of Oliphant's various travels—but they petered out, leaving a thick section of blank paper before the sketching resumed toward the back of the volume. These pictures, which Burton guessed were more recent, were far less accomplished and appeared to be the unconscious scribblings of a meandering mind. Mostly they took the form of diagrams and sigils, many of which the explorer recognised as occult in nature. There were also rapidly made drawings of a panther and, on the last page, a bizarre self-portrait in which Oliphant had combined his own face with his pet's, giving himself feline eyes, a projecting muzzle, and a mouth filled with canines. Above the portrait, he'd written the word *Predator*, and beneath it, the sentence: *What better way to transcend human limitations than by quite literally becoming something a little more than human?*

Burton shuddered. He closed the book but kept hold of it as he continued his search of the room.

He found a bag of opium and a number of pipes.

There was little else of interest.

He was turning to leave when something glittered and caught his eye. He crossed to an occasional table and looked down at a pair of white gloves folded upon it. A tiepin had been placed on them. He picked it up and examined it. At its top, a small disk of gold bore two symbols, one looking like the letter C but with two small lines extending outward from the left edge of its curve, the other like a mirror-image number seven. Letters, Burton was sure, but—again!—from a language he was unfamiliar with.

He pocketed the pin and sketchbook, left the cabin, and found Sister Raghavendra standing in the corridor.

"Hello, Sadhvi. Have you been waiting for me? Why didn't you knock?"

"I didn't want to interrupt. But what are you doing running around? You should be in bed. You're not well."

"I'm shaky, I'll admit. Gad, that potion you gave me certainly brought the fever to crisis! Really, though, I'm thoroughly fed up with my bed. Don't worry—I won't overdo it. I want to visit Oliphant, then I'll settle in the library and I shan't move until we're home."

"You've already overdone it, Richard, and there's no point in seeing Oliphant. The captain called me to attend him an hour ago. The man is a raving lunatic. Apparently he screamed and babbled his way through the early hours then lapsed into a catatonic trance. He's neither moved nor said a word in the past three hours. Poor William! He was such a good soul. Why in heaven's name was he killed?"

"That's exactly what I'm trying to find out."

Burton looked the Sister up and down and gave a broad smile—not something he did very often, for he knew it looked as if it hurt him, and fully exposed his overly long eye teeth. Indeed, Raghavendra blanched slightly at the sight of it.

"Bound and smothered, I see," he said.

She glanced down at her voluminous bell-shaped skirts, tightly laced bodice, and frilly fringes, then reached up and patted her pinned hair.

"Woe is me," she said, "a genteel woman of the British Empire, which spreads its civilised mores across the globe and slaps its shackles on every female it encounters. Are we really so dangerous?"

"None more so than you, Sadhvi," Burton replied. "Such beauty has, in the past, caused empires to fall."

"No, no, I'll not have that. It is men who create and destroy empires. Women are just the explanation they employ to excuse their ill-disciplined passions and subsequent misjudgments. History is proof enough that your so-called superior sex is utterly inferior and wholly lacking in common sense."

"Thank you kindly, ma'am," Burton said, with a slight bow, and it struck him that—though it was Isabel Arundell he loved and would marry—he possessed few friends as loyal, true, and forthright as Sadhvi Raghavendra.

"And the reason for this bondage," the Sister said, gesturing down at her clothes, "is that our passengers are about to board, so I thought it prudent to sacrifice my comfort and liberty, especially after having so shocked Lord Elgin with my thoroughly practical Indian garb. That's why I'm here, Richard: to fetch you. We're to greet the newcomers in the ballroom. After that, you can—and you will—take to the library."

Burton grunted his acquiescence and followed her along the corridor.

"Have they told you who our passengers are?" he asked.

"Lord Stanley," she replied. "And who? His secretary?"

"Prince Albert."

"Prince Albert? *The* Prince Albert? The *HRH* Prince Albert?"

"That one, yes."

"Bless me!"

"Indeed. I feel our homecoming has been somewhat overshadowed. We are eclipsed."

Sister Raghavendra put her hands to her face and exclaimed, "Imagine! I might have met him in my smock! Thank goodness I changed!"

"And there you have it," Burton said. "The fair sex identifies the crux of the matter."

They reached the staircase and started up it. Impatiently, and somewhat ungraciously, Burton was forced to accept Raghavendra's supporting hand on his elbow.

"A bloody invalid!" he grumbled. "Excuse my language."

She giggled. "I've been bloody well excusing it every bloody hour of every bloody day for well over a bloody year. Why must you insist on a display of strength when you know full well you have none?"

"Climbing stairs is hardly a display of strength. And you should wash your mouth out with soap, young lady."

"Don't worry. By the time we land in London I'll be as timid as a mouse, won't speak unless spoken to, and will allow nothing but meaningless platitudes to escape my lips. I may even indulge in a dramatic swoon or two, providing there's a dashingly handsome young man standing close enough to catch me. Let's stop a moment and rest."

"There's no need. It's a small staircase between decks, not the confounded Kilima-Njaro Mountain."

"Be quiet, fathead! I can see your knees buckling. Good Lord, you've had malaria, Richard. My medicine has burned it out of you, but you require time to regain your health. For once in your life, stop trying to be a hero. Rest!"

They halted. Burton fumed. A minute ticked by.

"Can we please scale the remaining heights?" the explorer growled. "What is it? Six or seven blessed steps? I give you my solemn word they'll not have me succumbing to a heart attack."

They continued, and at the top of the stairs entered a smartly decorated corridor leading to double doors of frosted glass. Burton pushed them open and ushered Raghavendra through into the airship's sumptuous though modestly sized ballroom. Most of the crew was gathered inside. Nathaniel Lawless, standing with the tall and bony meteorologist, Christopher Spoolwinder, waved Burton and Raghavendra over. As they drew near, they noticed Spoolwinder's hands were bandaged.

"What happened?" Burton asked.

"The blithering telegraph has gone barmy!" Spoolwinder said in a plaintive tone. "Absolutely gaga! It's been throwing out sparks, setting fire to paper, then—pow!—it sent such a shock through me I practically somersaulted across the bridge!"

"We disconnected it from the ship's batteries," Lawless added, "but it's still operating."

"Eh? How?" Burton asked.

"We don't know!" Spoolwinder exclaimed. His naturally glum face lengthened into an expression of deep misery. "I mean to say—crikey!—it's just not possible. The machine should be dead as a doornail. Instead, it's churning out messages like there's no tomorrow. Messages sent from nobody and nowhere!"

Sister Raghavendra stifled a giggle. She'd often told Burton that she found Spoolwinder's exaggerated mournfulness highly comical, especially when he was overwrought. "Nobody and nowhere?" she asked.

Captain Lawless shrugged. "There's no point of origin, Sister. No source. We don't know who—or where—the messages are coming from."

Spoolwinder added, "But it's always exactly the same gobbledegook.

Have a gander at this." He took a sheet of paper from his pocket, unfolded it, and passed it to Burton. The explorer read:

THE BEAST . . . THE BEAST . . . THE BEAST . . . YOU SHALL BOW DOWN FOR . . . OL SONF VORSG . . . BORN FROM THE WRECK OF SS BRITANNIA AND . . . LONSH CALZ VONPHO SOBRA ZOL ROR I TA NAZPSAD . . . TO REND THE VEIL . . . FROM THE FALLEN EMPIRE . . . NOW . . . FARZM ZVRZA ADNA GONO IADPIL DS HOM TOH . . . FOR THE ROYAL CHARTER . . . WILL DELIVER HE . . . BALTOH IPAM VL IPAMIS . . .

"English mixed with random letters," Burton murmured. "SS *Britannia*? Is there such a ship, Captain?"

"There was an RMS *Britannia*. An ocean liner. We sold her to the Prussians some ten years ago. They renamed her SMS *Barbarossa*. There's no Steamship *Britannia*. Never has been."

"And you say this message has been repeated over and over?"

"Countless times and without variation," Spoolwinder said. "It used up nearly all our paper supply, and the telegraph burned the rest."

"May I keep this copy?"

Lawless said, "By all means," and straightened as the boatswain's whistle suddenly sounded. He muttered, "Look out, here we go," then yelled, "ship's company, attention!"

The crew fell silent, stood with stomachs in, shoulders back, and chins up, and all eyes turned to the second set of double doors at the far end of the chamber. They swung open and Doctor Quaint stepped in, moved aside, and bowed two men through. On the left, Lord Stanley, the secretary of state for foreign affairs—short, stocky, and with a permanently aggressive expression—and on the right, His Royal Highness Prince Albert of Saxe-Coburg and Gotha, widower of the late Queen Victoria, overweight, his long sideburns ill-concealing his developing jowls and thickening neck, and appearing to bear the weight of the world upon his shoulders.

"He looks ill," Sister Raghavendra whispered.

Burton gave a quiet grunt of agreement.

Quaint guided the new arrivals across the ballroom and introduced them to Captain Lawless.

"An incredible ship, *Kapitän*!" Prince Albert declared. He spoke with a heavy German accent. "*Mein Gott, gigantisch*, no? How many crew?"

"Thirty-five, Your Royal Highness. We were thirty-six but lost a man in Central Africa."

"Ach! Unfortunate! I understand you haff quite the adventure. Most successful. You solve the mystery of the Nile."

"Not I, sir. May I present the expedition's leader, Captain Richard Burton, and his medical officer, Sister Sadhvi Raghavendra?"

The prince smiled at Burton, who noticed lines of pain around the man's eyes. "Oh dear. Your reputation goes before you, Burton. I am afraid almost to meet you."

Burton bowed. "I give you my solemn assurance, Your Royal Highness, that whatever calumnies you have heard about me are probably entirely true."

"*Ja!* I expected no less! You are a warrior! A man who must cut his own path through life. We are similar, you and I."

"Similar, sir?"

"It is so! For just as you haff chopped your way through the jungles of Africa, so I haff chopped through the jungles of German *Politik*. We are relentless, no?"

"Then I take it your endeavours have met with success?"

"It is correct. Just as yours. I tell you this, Burton: the union of Hanover, the Saxon Duchies, *unt* Bavaria—the new Central German Confederation—through the middle of Prussia it will slice, so we weaken our opponents, you see? Bismarck is now nothing but bluster *unt* hot air. He haff no power remaining *unt* can offer no opposition to the forthcoming British–German Alliance. We deny him his *Deutsches Reich*. It is *sehr gut* for our countries. *Sehr gut! Unt* now the question of Italian independence haff been settled with Austria, I am confident there will be no more wars in Europe."

The prince turned to Sister Raghavendra. "But forgive me, *Fräulein*, this is disgraceful! I do not wish to bore you with such matters. Europe is a game of chess. One concentrates *unt* concentrates on the next move until one's good manners, they are forgotten completely. For far too long I haff been dealing with the devious men."

He raised Raghavendra's hand to his lips and continued, "I am—what is the word, *Kapitän* Burton: *überwältigt?*"

"Overwhelmed, sir."

"Ach! Indeed. Overwhelmed. Overwhelmed to meet such a courageous young lady. It is true, *ja*, that you accompanied the *Kapitän* around the great lake in the middle of Africa?"

Raghavendra smiled and curtseyed. "Yes, Your Highness, it's true, though the lake is not quite in the middle."

"Remarkable! Remarkable!" Prince Albert released her hand and stepped a pace backward. He pulled at his cuffs, winced, and flinched, as if pain had lanced through him, then said, "Well, to get home you are both eager, no? As am I. Let us delay no longer. *Kapitän* Lawless, will you please haff the ship depart? *Unt* Doctor Quaint, if you would to my chamber now show me? I was up half the night watching the lights in the sky—Ach! Strange, no?—and am in need of sleep. We will meet again at the palace, Burton. I look forward to it."

Burton opened his mouth to ask, "The palace?" but before he could utter the question, the prince turned away and said to Sister Raghavendra, "Excuse my rudeness, I beg of you. The life I chose after the death of my dear wife haff of me made a monster where the women are concerned. No manners, Sister Raghavendra! No manners at all!"

"Not a bit of it, sir," she responded. "You have thoroughly charmed me."

He smiled, flinched again, and followed Doctor Quaint from the room.

Everyone relaxed.

Burton turned to Lord Stanley, who regarded him with hooded eyes and a stony expression.

"Sir—" the explorer began.

Stanley interrupted, his voice clipped. "Captain. I daresay you are keen to be reunited with your fiancée."

"Er—yes. I wasn't aware that—"

"That I knew of Miss Isabel Arundell? Oh, I'm aware of her, Captain. It's very difficult not to be when one's office is bombarded on a weekly basis by letters from her."

Burton was suddenly lost for words.

"Apparently," Stanley continued, "she considers you an ideal candidate for the consulship of Damascus, and is of the opinion that only an idiot would pass you up for the job."

"She—she said that?"

"It was implied. Do I look like an idiot to you?"

"No, sir. Not at all."

"Good. I'm relieved. I can trust my own judgement, then?"

"I'm sorry. I had no idea—"

Stanley's stern countenance softened somewhat. "No, of course not. You were in Africa. But it has to stop. I'll not be browbeaten by a woman." The corners of his mouth twitched upward. "Excepting my own wife, of course; may God bless her and have mercy on my soul."

"I'll have words with Miss Arundell."

"See that you do."

"On another matter, sir—"

"Yes?"

"I have a great deal of information for you regarding the disposition and resources of the Lake Regions."

"Good man. In reports? Properly written up?"

"Yes."

"Excellent. Have them delivered to my cabin. I'll pass them directly to the prime minister when we reach London. Africa is one of those matters about which he prefers to form his own opinions before consulting with me. Your intended, I'm sorry to say, isn't the only one who doubts my ability to make the right choices."

Burton said, "Very well."

"And enjoy the ceremony, Burton."

"Ceremony?"

"At the palace. By George, don't you know?"

"Know what, sir?"

"On Monday, Burton. You're due at the palace. You are to receive a knighthood!"

At four-thirty that afternoon—it was Thursday the 1st of September, 1859—Captain Richard Burton, with his top hat in one hand and Oliphant's cane in the other, stood beside Nathaniel Lawless on the bridge of HMA *Orpheus* and watched through a side window as the vessel's rotors gouged a deep furrow through the top of a sickly yellow cloud. Ahead, four copper towers poked out of the pall, and beyond them, in the distance, the tips of factory chimneys and the dome of St. Paul's Cathedral were visible.

The sunlight, streaming from a clear blue sky, reflected glaringly from the four metal columns as the airship drew alongside them.

"Cut the engines, Mr. Wenham," Lawless said to the helmsman. He turned to his chief engineer. "Out they go, Mr. Keen."

"Aye, sir," Keen replied. He lifted a speaking tube to his mouth and said, "All out!"

"Take us down, Mr. Wenham. As slow as you like."

"Aye, Captain."

Lawless said to Burton, "Just like they did in Africa, our riggers and engineers are now dangling at the end of chains outside the ship, and Mr. Wenham is venting gas from the dirigible, so we'll sink very gradually. This time, though, the men outside won't have to peg us down themselves—the station's ground crew will be on hand to assist with trolley-mounted windlasses. The chains will be attached and wound in, hauling us down until we're secured, and you'll then be able to set foot on British soil again."

The bridge suddenly turned gloomy as the fog swallowed the *Orpheus*.

Ten minutes later, the airship settled in the Royal Navy Air Service Station beside Battersea Power Station, the latter being the well-guarded headquarters of the Department of Guided Science.

The pride of the British fleet was home.

Lawless accompanied Burton down to the main doors, where Sister Raghavendra and Doctor Quaint joined them. They stood and watched as crew unbolted the big hatches and slid them aside before lowering the ship's ramp. Fog rolled in. Lawless coughed.

Outside, two steam-horses—like miniature tall-funnelled versions of the famous Stephenson's *Rocket*—emerged from the murk, pulling a large armour-plated six-wheeled carriage behind them. They drew up to the base of the ramp.

Lawless nodded at Quaint, who turned on his heel and hurried away, only to return moments later with Prince Albert, Lord Stanley, and Lord Elgin.

"Thank you, gentlemen," the prince said. Stanley and Elgin nodded their gratitude. The three descended the ramp and climbed into the vehicle. The steam-horses belched smoke from their funnels, jerked into motion, and dragged the carriage back into the cloud.

Burton squinted into the pea-souper.

"Well," he said, pushing his top hat onto his head and leaning on the panther-headed cane. "It's nice to see London again."

"I can't remember it ever being this bad," Raghavendra remarked.

"And it stinks to high heaven," Lawless observed. "I fear we must re-adjust ourselves after being spoilt by the beauty and purity of Africa."

Burton snorted. "So says the man who enjoyed the luxurious facilities of his ship while Sadhvi, William, George, and I were struggling through methane-bubbling swamps with crocodiles trying to eat us and mosquitoes sucking our blood."

"Point taken. Is that someone approaching?" Lawless jerked his chin toward a shadowy figure that, as they watched, detached itself from the fog and started up toward them.

"Ahoy there, *Orpheus*!" a voice called. "Welcome back to the civilised world!"

"Sir Roderick!" Burton exclaimed and strode forward to meet the man, clasping hands with him halfway along the ramp.

Sir Roderick Murchison, president of the Royal Geographical Society, was a tall and slender individual whose rigid demeanour belied the warmth of his personality. "Well done, Burton!" he effused. "Well done! You've placed a jewel in the crown of the RGS! The Nile is cracked at last!" He slapped Burton's shoulder. "We lost track of you last night—apparently that extraordinary aurora borealis has disabled telegraph systems the world over—but I knew the ship was due this afternoon, so braved the funk to meet you. The rest of our fellows are waiting at the Society. No doubt you're looking forward to the comforts of home, but you'll attend a little reception first, yes?"

"Of course, Sir Roderick, I'd be delighted."

"Good show, old boy! I say, though, you look perfectly rotten. Are you ill?"

"A touch of fever. Nothing I can't cope with."

Murchison peered past Burton, uttered a cry of pleasure, then hurried up to the airship's door—the explorer followed behind—and took Sister Raghavendra's hand. "My dear, *dear* young lady! May I be the first to congratulate you? You are absolutely the talk of the town. And I'm delighted to tell you that, as a mark of respect for your astounding contribution to Captain Burton's expedition, the Society has seen fit to lift its ban on women. You are a member, Sister! What! What! A *member*! The vote was unanimous!"

"Thank you, Sir Roderick," she answered, with a slight bob. "That's splendid news. Simply splendid! A woman member! My goodness! I *am* honoured!"

"Captain!" Murchison said, turning his attention to Lawless. "You and your gallant crew will be granted honorary membership, of course. You are heroes to a man. The RGS holds you all in the highest regard. There will be medals issued by the palace, I guarantee it."

Lawless smiled and gave an appreciative nod.

"Where is Lieutenant Stroyan?" Murchison asked.

Burton responded, "I'm sorry to have to tell you, sir, that he was killed last night."

Murchison slumped. "No! By God! No! An accident?"

"Murder. Lord Elgin's private secretary, Oliphant, went insane and cut his throat."

Murchison slapped a hand to his forehead. "Oh my! Oh my! Insane, you say? Oh, poor William! He was a splendid fellow. I shall have to talk to him.

I'll give him a chance to settle, obviously, but I must offer my condolences, ask whether he has any messages for those he's left behind."

Burton couldn't help himself. His lip curled in disdain. "If you wish it, sir."

"It's my duty, old chap. The dead must be eased into the Afterlife, and as a murder victim Stroyan is no doubt confused and disoriented. A familiar voice will soothe him during his difficult transition."

Burton shrugged non-committally.

Murchison pondered for a moment, then perked up, clapped his hands, and announced, "Shall we be off? Captain Lawless, will you and your crew join us? Should I summon more carriages?"

Lawless shook his head. "Thank you, but we must pass up the invitation, Sir Roderick. I have to summon the police to fetch Mr. Oliphant, and there is much to do aboard ship. We'll be flying up to the RNA Service Station in Yorkshire next week for a refit and will begin preparations immediately." He turned to the others. "Captain Burton, Sister Raghavendra, your luggage will be delivered to your homes within the next couple of days."

Murchison said, "Very well. I shall see you on Monday, then. Medals, Captain! Medals! And well earned!"

Burton and Raghavendra said their farewells to Lawless then Murchison hustled them down the ramp, across the landing field, and into a waiting steam-horse-drawn growler.

"Back the way we came, please, driver!" Murchison called up to the massively built individual on the box seat.

"All the way to the Royal Geological Society, sir?"

"Geographical. Yes, all the way there. Fifteen Whitehall Place."

"Right you are. Geographical, as what I said. Hall aboard? Hoff we bloomin' well go! Gee-up!"

As the conveyance lurched into motion, Murchison said to Burton and Raghavendra, "Incidentally, I have good news. Last month, the RGS was officially sanctioned. The king, in recognition of your discovery, issued us with a royal charter. We are *establishment* now."

Burton put his hand up to his beard and slowly dragged his fingers through it. "A royal charter, you say? You didn't attempt to inform us of that by telegraph last night, did you?"

"No. Why would I when it was just a matter of hours before your arrival? Besides, as I mentioned, the whole telegraph system has been crippled since midnight."

Burton grunted. "Hmm! Peculiar. Our own telegraph went off the rails and churned out a lot of gibberish. There were a few English words mixed in with it—'royal charter' being two of them. Quite a coincidence."

"Stroyan," Murchison said.

"I beg your pardon?"

"Stroyan. He was trying to get through from the Other Side. They say all past and future knowledge is available in the Afterlife. William obviously saw that the king has endorsed our organisation and, through means of the dysfunctional telegraph, tried to tell you."

"If I may," Sister Raghavendra interrupted, "I don't wish to diminish the significance of the royal charter, Sir Roderick, but surely where matters of life, death, and the Afterlife are concerned, it's a comparatively trivial matter? Surely, if William's spirit were to contact us, it would have something more substantial to communicate?"

Murchison crossed his arms. "It was merely conjecture. Should I assume, then, Sister, that you've adopted Captain Burton's skepticism where the Afterlife is concerned?"

"I remain open-minded."

Murchison acknowledged her statement with a hum then addressed Burton. "But you've returned from Africa with your objections intact, I suppose?"

"As before, I neither support nor denounce the idea," Burton replied. "Whether there is an Afterlife or not, I simply do not know, and since I exist in the material world, nor do I need to know. What I oppose is the undue influence in our society of spiritualists who claim to convey messages to us from the departed. In the event that the mediums aren't all charlatans and the communiques are real, I have to ask, what motivates the dead to make the effort? Why are their messages so frequently abstruse? What is their agenda? No, Sir Roderick, I'll not have it. My life is my own and Death will come in due course, but until it does, I'll avoid the Afterlife, will make my own decisions, and will brook no meddling from Beyond."

The three of them grabbed at hand straps to steady themselves as the growler navigated a corner.

"As a non-believer, you are in the minority," Murchison observed.

"Quite so. The majority succumb to blind hope and allow it to compromise their intellect."

"You have no hope?"

"I am realistic. My mind dwells on the lessons of the past and the challenges of the present, not on the unknowable future."

"Ah ha! So you dismiss prognosticators as well as mediums?"

"Of course. They are obviously fraudsters."

Sister Raghavendra patted Burton's arm and said to Murchison, "In expressing his views, Captain Burton is never backward in coming forward. We had many discussions of a philosophical nature during our safari. After each one, I felt as if I'd been savaged by a jungle cat."

"I fear for Miss Arundell," Murchison mused. "Has she any lion-taming skills, Burton?"

The explorer gave a slight smile. "Isabel believes she'll eventually beat me into submission with her ferocious Catholicism."

Murchison shook his head despairingly. "Of all the people to marry into the country's most influential Catholic family, I'd never have predicted it to be you. How do her parents feel about welcoming a stubborn and outspoken atheist into their clan?"

"When she told them, her mother became hysterical and fainted and her father vowed to shoot me. She's had a year to work on them. Perhaps they've calmed down." Burton coughed and moved his tongue around in his mouth. "Really, can this awful stink possibly get any worse?" He fished a handkerchief from his pocket and pressed it to his nose.

"We're next to the Thames," Murchison said. "This time last year, the stench was so bad they had to abandon parliament. Thank heavens for Bazalgette!"

"Who is he?"

"Joseph Bazalgette—a freshly emerged luminary among the DOGS. His designs for an advanced sewer system were approved a few weeks after your departure and he got to work immediately. The city has been in upheaval, but there's not a single citizen who isn't happy to put up with the nuisance of it in the knowledge that, when the tunnels are completed, the air will be breathable and the roads clean. Actually, Burton, you timed your expedition well."

"How so?"

"There's a subterranean river—the Tyburn—that flows through your part of town, under Baker Street, Marylebone, and Mayfair, beneath Buckingham Palace, on through Pimlico, and into the Thames slightly to the west of Vauxhall Bridge. Bazalgette has incorporated it into his system. It was one of the first parts to be constructed, so for many weeks the district where you live was badly disrupted. You avoided much inconvenience."

"It's finished now?"

"That part of it, yes. The Tyburn now runs into one of the system's main arteries—the Northern Low-Level Sewer—which, when complete, will extend all the way from Hackney in the west to Beckton in the east, running parallel to the northern shore of the Thames. By God! You should see it, Burton! Such an undertaking! It's the Strand that's suffering at the moment—and its theatres and hotels are vociferous in their complaints, as you'd expect—but Bazalgette works like a demon. It won't be long before that part of the city returns to normal while he ploughs onward into the Cauldron."

"Gracious!" Raghavendra exclaimed. "He's going into the East End? Isn't that awfully dangerous?"

Her concern was justified. London's East End was the city's poorest, meanest, and filthiest district. A labyrinth of narrow alleyways, bordered by decrepit and overcrowded tenements, overflowing with raw sewage and rubbish of every description, it bred disease and despair in equal measure. The destitute lived amid the squalor in vast numbers and were vicious to such a degree that the police wouldn't go near them. Disraeli had famously referred to the area as "a country within our country, and a damned wicked one at that." When asked how to best solve the problem, he'd replied, "With fire."

Murchison nodded. "Of course, but even criminals and ne'er-do-wells can see the advantage of having their effluence flushed away. The gangs that operate there have guaranteed that Bazalgette's people will be protected and treated well."

"Will wonders never cease?" Burton murmured. His eyes started to water. He took slow and shallow breaths.

Murchison smiled. "You'll adjust, old boy. You'll need to. To a lesser degree, this stench currently pervades all of London north of the Thames."

"Why so?"

"Because until the principal west-to-east artery is finished, all the smaller tunnels running into it, flowing from north to south—the Tyburn included—have had their flow tightly restricted by a sequence of sluice gates. The muck is backing up, and it may well rise into the streets before it can be released into the completed system."

"And south of the river?" Raghavendra asked.

"Tunnels are still being constructed to carry the effluence into the Thames. When they're done, another big west-to-east intercepting tunnel will be constructed, parallel to the river's south bank."

"Incredible," Burton said. "A monumental task!"

"Quite so. Bazalgette is a miracle worker."

Sister Raghavendra, who appeared less affected by the stink, asked, "And what other progress has been made by the Department of Guided Science, Sir

Roderick? Its inventors are so prolific, I fully expect London to be unrecognisable to me once this fog clears."

"Steam spheres," the geographer answered.

"And what are they?"

"Horseless carriages—large ball-shaped machines with a moving track running vertically from front to back across the circumference, giving motive power. They are two-man vehicles. Not much good for the city streets—which are too crowded—but excellent for a run in the country."

The growler swayed and bumped. They heard the driver shout something insulting, probably to someone who'd blocked their path.

"And submarine boats," Murchison continued.

"Vessels that travel beneath the surface of the sea?" Raghavendra guessed.

"Exactly so."

"My goodness. Whatever for?"

"The DOGS have but a single bark, my dear: *Because they can!*"

Burton pushed aside the curtain and peered out of the window. Vaguely, he saw gasworks looming out of the fog, and deduced that the growler had by now traversed the complete length of Nine Elms and was proceeding north through Lambeth.

"Not much traffic," he observed.

"You haven't noticed," Murchison said, "no doubt because you're acclimatised to Africa, but it's very warm for the time of year. We've had the hottest summer in living memory and it's brought with it regular London particulars. In such murk, people fear to set foot in the streets lest they get lost or mugged."

"Or suffocate."

"Indeed."

"Our driver appears to know where he's going."

"He's a reliable cove. Montague Penniforth. I use him a lot. He normally drives a hansom but hires a growler when he has occasion to. I'm convinced he can see in the dark."

Burton let the curtain fall back into place. He wiped his eyes with his handkerchief then pressed it again to his nose. He'd spent most of the day sleeping aboard the *Orpheus*, but although he felt much recovered, his hands were still trembling and his throat was dry. Dropping his left hand to his pocket, he surreptitiously felt the outline of a bottle of Saltzmann's Tincture.

During the course of the next half-hour, Murchison and his companions discussed various incidents that had occurred during the expedition, while the growler took them along Palace Road to Westminster Bridge, crossed the reeking Thames, turned right at the Houses of Parliament, and trundled along King Street and Whitehall to Whitehall Place. Finally, it drew to a stop outside number 15, a many-windowed building situated opposite Scotland Yard.

The passengers disembarked. Murchison paid Penniforth and the carriage departed, its wheels grinding over the cobbles, its engine panting smoke.

"Two or three hours, my friends," Murchison said. "That's all we ask of you. Just time enough to take a drink with your fellows and entertain them with a few tales of derring-do. Then you'll have three days to recuperate before the ceremonies at the palace."

Burton looked at the building's grand entrance.

Knighted! He was going to be knighted!

It would give him influence.

Damascus. Marriage. Books. No more of this. No more RGS. No more exploring. No more danger.

Tomorrow, he'd get back to his half-finished translation of the *Baital-Pachisi*, a Hindu tale of a vampire that inhabits and animates dead bodies. With that completed, he'd be able to commence his great project, a fully annotated version of *A Thousand Nights and a Night*, translated from the original Arabic—an undertaking which, he reckoned, would keep him busy for at least the first couple of years of his consular service.

"Shall we?" Murchison asked, waving Burton and Raghavendra toward the door.

They crossed to it, pushed it open, and entered.

CHAPTER 3

THE WEDDING PROPHECY

"There has always been a world beneath London.
There is more below than there is above."
—JOSEPH BAZALGETTE

By nine o'clock, Sister Raghavendra had already made her excuses and left the RGS, and Burton was eager to do the same. Fighting off the many protests, he extracted himself from the reception party, collected his hat, jacket, and cane from the lobby, and stepped out into Whitehall Place. To his surprise, the fog had been completely swept away by a warm night breeze and the air was clear. Even more amazing, though it was night, he emerged into what appeared to be broad daylight. He looked up and his jaw dropped. For a second night, the aurora borealis was rippling overhead.

A large number of detectives, clerks, and secretaries had forsaken their offices in the Scotland Yard building and were standing in the street gazing at the spectacular illumination. One of them, a gaunt chap with thick spectacles, a red nose, and a straggly moustache, moved to Burton's side and said, "Quite a sight, isn't it? Have you ever seen the like?"

"I haven't," Burton confessed. He was tired, wanted to get home, and felt a little bit drunk. He'd also downed the remaining half of the Saltzmann's Tincture and needed to walk off its effects.

You're driving yourself to collapse. Why do you never know when to call it quits?

"Aren't you the explorer chappie?" the man asked. "Livingstone?"

"Burton."

"Oh, yes! That's right. The Nile man. Congratulations! Pepperwick. That's me. Clerk. Scotland Yard. Ordinary sort of job. Not romantic, like yours."

Burton ran a finger around his collar, feeling the grit that had already accumulated there.

Welcome home.

"The world over, apparently," Pepperwick went on, using a thumb to gesture upward. "The lights, I mean. Fancy that! At this precise moment, right now, there's no night anywhere. Do you think it'll last?"

"I don't know what to think."

Burton examined the crowd, his eyes roving from person to person. He noticed that one man, a thickset individual, was gazing not at the aurora borealis but at him. Burton stared back. The man's eyes widened. He looked shocked. Then he turned and hurriedly moved away.

"I should get home, Mr. Pepperwick."

"You'll not have any trouble finding your way. It's all topsy-turvy. The days are darkened by fog, the nights are lit up by whatever-it-is."

"Indeed," Burton agreed. "Good evening to you." He touched the brim of his topper, strode off, and at the end of the street turned right into Charing Cross Road, heading toward Trafalgar Square.

For the first time since his return, Burton plunged into one of London's throbbing arteries and was engulfed by the cacophony of the world's most advanced city.

The middle of the thoroughfare was clogged with traffic. Horse-drawn wagons, carriages, and omnibuses vied with their steam-powered counterparts, the animals snorting and shying away from the hissing, growling, spluttering, iron-built competition. 'Penny-farthing' velocipedes clattered and bounced between the larger vehicles, their riders shouting and cursing through clacking teeth.

Burton espied one of the new steam spheres, which, he thought, was probably being condemned as a wasted expense by its owner due to it being jammed between—and completely immobilised by—a coal cart in front, a hearse to its left, a landau carriage on its right, and a massive pantechnicon behind. Amid the general hubbub, he could hear the sphere's driver yelling, "Get out of my way, confound you! Get out of my blessed way!"

The sides of the road were lined with stalls and braziers offering jellied eels, pickled whelks, sheep's trotters, penny pies, plum duff, meat puddings, baked potatoes, Chelsea buns, milk, tea, coffee, ale, mulled wine, second-hand clothes, old books, flowers, household goods, shoes, kitchenware, tools, and practically everything else a person could possibly eat, drink, or require for the home; as well as astrological charts, palm and tarot card readings, scrying by tea leaves, and prognostication by numbers, by bumps on the head, by marks on the tongue, and by the throw of a dice. The sing-song tones with which the traders called attention to their wares were almost, to Burton, the master linguist, an entirely unique dialect, barely comprehensible but very, very loud.

Between the stalls and the shops that bordered the street—many of which were currently open beyond their normal business hours—the pavements were packed with pedestrians who thought to take advantage of the peculiar light and the mild weather. There were couples and bachelors out strolling, ragamuffins playing and yelling and begging, dolly-mops touting for customers, jugglers juggling, singers warbling, musicians scraping and plucking, vagrants pleading and wheedling, and thieves as numerous and as persistent as African mosquitoes.

Burton shouldered through them, slapped away the pernicious fingers of pickpockets, and made painfully slow progress into Trafalgar Square and up St. Martin's Lane, where he hoped to find Brundleweed's jewellery shop open. Shortly before leaving for Africa, he'd ordered a diamond ring from old Brundleweed. The man was a craftsman of exceptional ability, and the explorer was looking forward to seeing the item in which he'd invested a considerable sum.

It was not to be. The shop was closed.

He strolled on into Cranbourn Street, followed it to Regent Circus, and traversed Regent Street up to the junction with Oxford Street.

Here, as fatigue gripped him and he realised he'd overestimated his strength, he made the decision to leave the main roads and cut diagonally through the Marylebone district to the top of Baker Street. It was more dangerous—he would have to pass through a poverty-stricken enclave of alleyways and crumbling tenements—but it would be quicker.

Keeping a firm hold of his swordstick, he entered a long side street. Shadows shifted around him as the aurora folded and glimmered overhead. A strange clicking began to echo from the walls to either side. He stopped and looked up. The clicking became a chopping. The chopping became a roar. A rotorchair skimmed over the rooftops and was gone, its noise rapidly receding, its trail of steam hanging motionless in the air, changing colour as it reflected the uncanny light.

Burton pushed on. He turned left. Right. Right again. Left. The maze of alleys narrowed around him. The stink of sewage haunted his nostrils. Mournful windows gaped from the sides of squalid houses. An inarticulate shout came from one of them. He heard a slap, a scream, a woman sobbing.

A man lurched from a dark doorway and blocked his path. He was coarse-featured, clad in canvas trousers and shirt with a brown waistcoat and a cloth cap. There were fire marks—red welts—on his face and thick forearms.

A stoker. Spends his days shovelling coal into a furnace.

Run. He's dangerous.

I'm dangerous, too.

"Can I 'elp you, mate?" the man asked in a gravelly voice. "Maybe relieve you of wha'ever loose change is weighin' down yer pockits?"

Burton looked at him.

The man backed away so suddenly that his heels struck the doorstep behind him and he sat down heavily.

"Sorry, fella," he mumbled. "Mistook you fer somebody else, I did."

The explorer snorted scornfully and moved on. His friend, Richard Monckton Milnes, had once told him he had the face of a demon. Sometimes, it was useful.

Burton continued through the labyrinth. A sense of déjà vu troubled him. Was it because the depths of London felt remarkably similar to the depths of Africa—tangled, perilous, toxic?

He came to a junction, turned left, and stumbled over a discarded crate. An exposed nail gouged into his trouser leg and ripped it. Burton spat an oath and kicked the crate away. A rat leaped from it and scuttled into a shadow.

Leaning against a lamppost, the explorer rubbed his eyes. Last night he'd been in the grip of a fever after a month-long illness and now he was walking home. Dolt!

He noticed a flier pasted to the post:

> *The Department of Guided Science.*
> *A Force for Change. A Force for Good.*
> *Developing the British Empire.*
> *Bringing Civilisation to All.*

"Whether you want it or not," he added.

Pushing himself away, he continued along the alley and turned yet another corner—he wasn't sure exactly where he was but he knew he was heading in the right general direction—and found himself at the end of a long, straight street bordered by high and featureless red-brick walls: the sides of warehouses. The far end opened onto what looked to be a main thoroughfare—Weymouth Street, he guessed. He could see the front of a shop, a butcher's, but before he could read its sign, steam from a passing velocipede obscured the letters.

Burton walked on, carefully stepping over pools and rivulets of urine and filth.

A litter-crab came clanking into view near the shop, its eight thick mechanical legs thudding against the road surface, the twenty-four thin arms on its belly darting this way and that, skittering back and forth over the cobbles, snatching up rubbish and throwing it through the machine's maw into the furnace within.

The machine creaked and rattled past the end of the alley and, as it did so, its siren wailed a warning. A few seconds later, it let out a deafening hiss as it ejected hot cleansing steam from the two downward-pointing funnels at its rear.

The automated cleaner vanished from sight as a tumultuous wall of white vapour boiled toward Burton. He stopped and took a few steps backward, leaned on his cane, and waited patiently for the cloud to disperse. It billowed toward him, extending hot coils which slowed and became still, hanging in the air as they cooled.

Movement.

Someone was entering the alley.

Burton watched as the person's weirdly elongated shadow angled through the mist, writ dark, skeletal, and horrific by the distortion.

He suddenly felt uneasy and waited nervously for the shadow to shrink, to be sucked into the person to whom it belonged when he—for surely it must be a man—emerged from the cloud.

It did shrink.

It was a man.

He was aiming a pistol at the explorer.

"Captain Richard Francis bloody Burton," the individual snarled. "Drop your stick or I'll shoot you in the arm."

Burton dropped the stick.

"Get back against the wall. Take your hat off, put it down, and stand with your hands on your head."

Burton did as ordered, watching the man through narrowed eyes. He recognised him. It was the individual who'd been staring at him outside Scotland Yard—a short, big-boned, and heavily muscled fellow with wide shoulders and a deep chest. He had thick fingers, a blunt nose, and, under a large outward-sweeping brown moustache, an aggressively square chin.

"I've been waiting to meet you," the man said, in a slightly husky voice. His pistol didn't waver. It was aimed steadily at a point between the explorer's eyes. "The moment I saw your likeness in the newspaper, I knew I'd seen you before."

"Who are you?" Burton demanded. "What do you want?"

"My name is—is Macallister Fogg. How old are you?"

"How old? Rather an impertinent question. Thirty-eight. Why?"

"Mind your own business. Where were you on the tenth of June, 1840?"

Burton frowned, puzzled. "The Assassination? I was on a ship from Italy bound for Dover, on my way to enroll at Oxford University."

The other man muttered to himself, "Plausible. But I could swear to it! I could swear!"

"If there's something I can—?"

"Be quiet. Let me think for a moment."

Burton sighed in exasperation and threw out his arms. "What in blue blazes is this about, Mr. Fogg? Do you intend to rob me?"

"Stop moving! Hands on head!"

The explorer shrugged, put his right foot against the wall, and launched himself forward. He chopped his hand down onto the other's wrist, knocking the pistol out of his grasp. As the gun went spinning over the cobbles, Burton sent an uppercut crashing into the man's chin. Fogg's head snapped back and he stumbled, emitting a loud grunt before steadying himself.

His pale blue eyes met Burton's. "So, it's to be like that, is it?"

Burton was astonished. He'd boxed at university and in fight pits in India and had never been beaten. The uppercut had been his best shot. It should have knocked the man cold. Was his strength really so diminished?

"I'll not submit to a mugging," he growled, and took up the fighter's stance.

Fogg grinned, as if relishing the prospect of battle, and mirrored the explorer's posture. "I have no interest in your valuables," he said, and suddenly ducked in and sent a fist thudding into Burton's ribs. The explorer doubled over. Lights exploded in his head as knuckles smashed into the side of it, then into his mouth, then into his right eye. He fell, rolled, and jumped to his feet, stumbling back, suddenly feeling completely sober, horribly weak, and utterly befuddled.

Fogg had recovered his pistol. Burton looked down its barrel and raised his hands.

"Will you please explain?" he slurred. "Has it something to do with Prince Albert?"

"Albert? Why would it concern him?"

"I was with him this morning."

"So?"

"So he was Victoria's husband. He was present when she was shot."

"It has nothing to do with Albert," Fogg said. "Your father—do you resemble him at all?"

"What? My father? Not in the slightest bit."

"By Jove! It has to be you! Except you're simply too young. It's impossible." Fogg scowled, looked at his gun, hesitated, and lowered it. "Confound it! I suppose I should apologise. A case of mistaken identity, Burton, that's all."

"That's *all*? I'd appreciate a rather more enlightening excuse, if you don't mind," Burton said, relaxing his arms.

"I do mind. You'll not get one."

"Then your address, please, Mr. Fogg, for the laundry bill." Burton indicated his dust-stained overcoat and trousers.

Fogg raised his pistol again. "Enough. Get going."

Burton gritted his teeth, picked up his hat and cane, and slowly walked to the end of the alley.

Just as he was about to turn the corner, his assailant shouted after him, "Hey!"

Burton looked back.

"If it's any consolation," Fogg called, "my head is still spinning from that uppercut of yours."

The explorer's eyes locked with the other man's for a moment, then he turned and strode away.

By the time he reached number 14 Montagu Place, Burton was light-headed, shaking, and perspiration beaded his brow. He opened the door, entered the hallway, and saw Mrs. Iris Angell frozen in mid-step halfway along the passage. His landlady, a white-haired, broad-hipped, sprightly old dame—who also functioned as his housekeeper—was gaping at him as if he were a ghost.

He removed his topper and put it on the hat-rack, placed the cane in an elephant-foot holder, and popped open his collar button.

Mrs. Angell let loose a shriek and threw her not inconsiderable weight across the intervening space and into his arms.

"My goodness! My goodness! What has Africa done to you? You're as thin as a broom handle! Your lip is bleeding! Your eye is black! Your trousers are torn! You look as sick as a dog! Isabel has been waiting! We knew you'd be arriving today but thought you'd be home earlier! You found the Nile, Captain Burton? Of course you did! The papers say you're a hero! Are you hungry? What do you think of the light in the sky? Do you know what it is? I'll get you fresh clothes! My goodness!" She raised her voice to a shrill scream. "Miss Isabel! Miss Isabel!"

Burton disentangled himself from her arms. "Slow down, Mother Angell. Calm yourself. I'm quite fine. I've been a little ill and I had a slight accident on the way here, but it's nothing to be concerned about. The comforts of home will soon put me to rights."

"Oh!" she cried out. "Thank the Lord you've returned to us. Such a long time away and every single day of it I worried you were being eaten by giraffes or stung by poisonous monkeys."

"Africa wasn't so bad," he responded. "I've already encountered more danger right here in London. And to answer your earlier questions—no, I'm not hungry, and yes, fresh clothes would be most welcome. Isabel?"

A mellow voice sounded from the top of the stairs. "Dick."

He looked up and saw Isabel Arundell, having obviously just emerged from his study, standing on the landing. She was tall, slender, and pretty—with large clear eyes, a straight Grecian nose, and thick, lustrous blonde hair.

"A pot of tea, please, Mrs. Angell!" he bellowed, and shot up the staircase and into Isabel's embrace.

She held him tightly and sobbed onto his shoulder.

"Isabel," he whispered. "Isabel. Isabel."

He pushed her away a little, so he could lean in and kiss the side of her neck. His split lip left two small spots of blood on her jugular.

"Blanche is here!" she gasped.

"I don't care," he said. "I have to kiss you. You waited."

"Of course I did. You're bleeding. You look all banged-up. Have you had an accident?"

"Yes, just a mishap." He pulled out his handkerchief, wiped the little red stains from her skin, and dabbed the square of cotton against his mouth.

"We can marry," he said. "I'm done with Africa."

"Come and say hello to her."

"Isabel, have your parents given their blessing?"

"Not their blessing, but their permission. They realise I won't accept any other man."

He nodded, checked his handkerchief, put it away, and followed her into the study.

It felt strange to be back. Nothing had changed, but it all appeared dream-like in the shifting multicoloured illumination that streamed in between the open curtains. His three desks were still piled high with books and papers; the swords and daggers still hung on the wall over the fireplace, with spears and guns in the alcoves to either side; his old boxing gloves still dangled from the corner of the mantelpiece; the bureau still stood between the two tall sash widows; the bookcases were still warped beneath the weight of his books; and his comfortable old saddlebag armchair was right where he'd left it.

Isabel's petite younger sister, Blanche, rose from the chair.

He strode to her, grabbed her hand, and gave it a peck.

"Hello, Little Bird. I'm sorry I missed your wedding. How is old Smythe Piggott?"

"Hello, Richard. The sky has lit up to celebrate your return. I'm fine, but do emphasise the *pig* when you say my husband's name. He already has two mistresses. But he's a rich pig, so I can't complain. There are women with worse husbands; the variety of man that remains at home in the evenings and insists on conversation, for instance. The fifth of November, Richard, the fifth of November."

"What about it? Do you intend to throw him onto a bonfire? I didn't think you Catholics celebrated Guy Fawkes Night."

"We Catholics don't. It's the date my parents have set for your engagement party. They'd prefer that my sister's marriage be founded on financial security, as mine is—I think they're rather intimidated by such concepts as love and passion—but they've bowed to the inevitable. Great-Uncle Gerard has agreed to host the party at New Wardour Castle, and if you wish to bring guests, you have his leave to do so."

Burton looked at Isabel and arched an eyebrow. "Have you been doping your parents?"

She laughed. "No, just driving them to the brink of madness by singing your praises at every opportunity. But I think it was the knighthood that finally swayed them."

"Oh. You know about that? Good grief! Was I the last to be told?"

"I heard it from Monckton Milnes. You know what a great depository of knowledge, gossip, and secrets he is."

"Not so much secrets, it would appear."

Burton indicated that Blanche should resume her seat and Isabel take the other armchair. He dragged over a padded chair from beside one of the desks and sat facing them.

Isabel reached for his hand and held it. She said, "You won't object to the party, will you?"

"I'll concede to it," he replied, "but we'll keep the wedding itself a small affair, as we agreed—yes?—for a grand marriage ceremony is a barbarous and an indelicate exhibition."

Isabel first laughed then frowned. "Your face. What was this mishap you mentioned?"

"Yes, brother-in-law-to-be," Blanche added. "You look a hideous mess."

He dismissed the question with a wave. "Thank you, Blanche. It's really nothing to worry about. I tripped."

Blanche giggled. "Months and months in dangerous Africa and as soon as you're home, you fall flat on your face."

"Exactly."

"Was the safari very difficult?" Isabel asked. "Why did it take so much longer than predicted?"

"The *Orpheus*'s engines failed," he replied. "Some five hundred miles north of the lakes, they simply packed up. The engineers couldn't find a thing to explain it. What little wind there was came from the west—the dirigible couldn't even float southward—so Sadhvi, Bill, George, and I left it and continued on foot. We followed the upper Nile through a chain of swamps and lakes until we arrived at its source—waterfalls descending from the Nyanza, which is practically an inland sea. We then skirted around its western shore, past the Mountains of the Moon, until we came to the water's southernmost point. While we were doing all that, the breeze altered direction, allowing Captain Lawless to drift the *Orpheus* over the eastern shores of the Nyanza then southward to an Arabic outpost called Kazeh. He set up camp there and paid natives to spread the news of the ship's location. The information eventually reached us and we rejoined our colleagues. A few days later, we discovered that the engines had miraculously come back to life and immediately set course for Zanzibar."

The door opened and Mrs. Angell entered with a tea tray. She gave Blanche an approving glance, pleased to see that propriety was being observed and Isabel was correctly chaperoned, then set the tray down on a table.

"Shall I pour?" she asked.

"It's all right, Mrs. Angell," Isabel said. "Leave it to me."

"I'll lay clean clothes out in your bedchamber, Captain Burton," the housekeeper said. "Oh, I'm so happy to have you home safe and sound. You'll not be returning to Africa, I hope."

"No, Mother," Burton responded. "I have no plans to go back."

The old woman wrung her hands in satisfaction. "You'll have some beef broth before you go to bed. I insist upon it. You need building up. Ring when you're ready for it. Don't forget!" With that admonition, she left the room.

Isabel said, "Have you satisfied your craving for danger and unexplored lands, Dick? Are you ready to settle? I have petitioned Lord Stanley. I think he's willing to hand us Damascus."

Burton sighed. "I wish you hadn't. The *Orpheus* gave him passage home from Vienna. He made it quite clear to me that your unsolicited recommendations were unwelcome and irritating. You may have done more damage than good."

"There!" Blanche interjected. "I told you not to be so bullheaded. Really, Isabel, mother is right. You are far too brazen."

"I was trying to help!" Isabel protested.

Burton gave her hand a squeeze. "I appreciate that, darling, but in doing so you might have given the impression that I lack the wherewithal to advance my own career."

"It's just that—that—Oh, Dick, I just want to be able to do something for our future together. I so regret that I'm bringing you no money, but Papa simply won't allow it."

"That's no disadvantage as far as I'm concerned, for heiresses always expect to lord it over their lords. A man must be a man, Isabel. He must be in charge of his own destiny, and more importantly, he must be seen to be in charge."

She swallowed and nodded.

"Don't fret," he added. "You may have riled old Stanley, but I'm confident we'll get what we want anyway."

"You forgive me?"

"I forgive you."

Isabel smiled, stood, and crossed to the table. While she attended to the teapot, Burton asked Blanche, "Your parents really want me to bring guests?"

"Oh, yes!" she answered. "You should invite them for the first of the month, so we have a few days to become acquainted before the party itself. Will Styggins be among them? I so want to meet him. I hear he's absolutely utterly!"

"Steinhaueser? Absolutely utterly what?"

"Just utterly! Isabel tells me you've known him forever."

"Since India," Burton corrected. "Utterly, hey?"

"You must admit," Isabel said, returning with a filled cup and saucer in each hand, "that he *is* rather handsome and charming."

"I can't say I've noticed," Burton said. "But, yes, I'll invite Styggins, if only to make my Little Bird's pet pig jealous."

Blanche giggled and reddened.

"I'll ask Monckton Milnes, too," he added.

Isabel fetched the third cup and sat down. "But none of your wretched Cannibal Club, if you please. They are far too louche."

"Agreed."

A short silence fell over them as they sipped their tea. Blanche stared at her sister and wrinkled her forehead meaningfully. Isabel put her cup down and frowned at her sibling.

"What is it?" Burton asked. "Why are you two looking daggers at each other?"

"My sister has something to tell you," Blanche said.

"Blanche!" Isabel hissed.

"Well?" Burton asked.

Isabel fiddled with the edge of her shawl, examined her fingernails, brushed her hands over her skirts, and said, "I met Hagar Burton again."

"Hagar Burton?"

"You remember? The Gypsy who used to camp on the family estate when I was a girl."

"Ah, yes."

Burton recalled that his fiancée, when fifteen years old, had befriended the Gypsy woman, who'd predicted that she'd one day fall in love with a man who bore the Burton surname.

Isabel continued, "Last June, Blanche and I went to Ascot. She was there."

"And?"

"And she read my palm."

"What did she say?"

"She asked if I'd married a Burton yet. I said no, not yet. She said, *Don't*."

"Don't?"

"She predicted that, if I put on a wedding dress for a Burton, he would—would—"

"He would what?"

"He would kill me while I was still wearing it."

CHAPTER 4

THE CANNIBALS CONVENE

THE BAKER STREET DETECTIVE
Macallister Fogg's Own Paper!
Issue 245. Every Thursday. Consolidated Press.
One Penny.
This Week: Macallister Fogg and his
lady assistant, Mrs. Boswell, investigate:
THE HORRIBLE HAUNTING OF HOWLING HOUSE!
Plus the latest installments of:
DOCTOR TZU VERSUS THE BRAIN REMOVERS
by Cecil Barry
FATTY CAKEHOLE AND THE PHANTOM PIE-MAKER
by Norman Pounder

Friday didn't dawn but merely replaced the shifting colours of the aurora with the pale yellow of a late-summer's day. Unaccustomed to his own bed, Burton awoke early and lay staring at the rectangle of his curtained window. His room was at the back of the house, overlooking the yard and mews, but the rumble of early-morning traffic—mostly delivery wagons—was noisy enough to reach him. It sounded alien and strange. No more waking to coughing lions and rumbling elephants. No quiet thrum of the *Orpheus*'s engines.

He was in London now.

But not for long, he hoped.

The Empire's capital made him uneasy. Few of the people who dwelt in its club rooms and debating chambers approved of him. He'd spent his childhood being hauled around Europe by a restless father and long-suffering mother and had, in consequence, acquired "foreign ways." He'd little patience with the complex and subtle rituals of English society, and was, in consequence, looked upon as too blunt, too challenging, too aggressive, and far too interested in matters that were better left unacknowledged.

Blackguard Burton. Ruffian Dick.

So, Damascus.

He would endure London until he was married, then he and Isabel would flee to the wide-open spaces and rather more transparent etiquettes of Arabia.

Burton pushed himself upright, let loose a deep, shuddering sigh, and reached up to touch his right eye. It was swollen and sore. What in God's name had that business in the alley been about? The Assassination of Victoria? It was two decades ago!

Giving up on further sleep, he left his bed, shaved, washed, dressed, and went down to his study. For two hours, he made inroads into his backlog of newspapers, then—when he heard Mrs. Angell moving about downstairs—rang for breakfast. By nine o'clock, he'd caught up on much of the past year's news and had consumed two kippers, two boiled eggs, four rashers of bacon, a chunk of cold ham, three slices of toast with marmalade, and two cups of coffee.

He left the house, hailed a cab, and went to Scotland Yard.

Pushing through the crowded and noisy lobby, Burton stepped up to a desk upon which a small plaque bore the name *J. D. Pepperwick*. The individual sitting behind it was the same he'd chatted with last night.

"Is Mr. Macallister Fogg available?"

"Hello there!" Pepperwick enthused. "Good morning! I hardly recognised you. What happened to the beard?"

Burton touched his drooping moustache and the small tuft of hair he'd left in the cleft of his chin. "It had to go. There were things living in it."

The clerk chuckled. "It looks like they fought to stay. That's quite a shiner you've got, Mr. Living—er—"

"Captain."

"Pardon me. Captain. Who?"

"Burton."

"No, Captain Burton, I meant, who was it you said you wanted to see?"

"Macallister Fogg."

Pepperwick removed his spectacles and blew dust from the lenses. "Hmm! Macallister Fogg. Macallister Fogg. Macallister Fogg. No, sir, I'm quite certain there's no one here by that name."

"He was standing among your people last night, watching the aurora. A shortish and bulky fellow with a large moustache."

Pepperwick replaced his eyewear and scratched his right ear. "There are plenty working here who match such a description, Captain, but no Foggs. Perhaps he was just passing by and got mixed up with us."

"Yes," Burton replied. "I suppose so. Well, it was worth a try."

"Would you like to speak with a detective?"

"About what?"

"About whatever it is you wanted to discuss with this Fogg chap."

"I didn't want to discuss anything with him. I wanted to punch him in the eye."

Pepperwick blinked rapidly. "Oh. Ha ha! Tit for tat, is it? Not quite the thing to do in Scotland Yard, sir."

"No," Burton agreed. "I expect not. Much obliged, Mr. Pepperwick. Good day to you."

The explorer recrossed the lobby and stepped out into the morning haze. The pall was much less dense today and the streets were seething with people, animals, and traffic. He hailed another cab and headed home, stopping briefly at Brundleweed's, which he again found closed.

As the carriage bumped and swayed along, Burton dozed. His bones felt cold and his flesh too warm. The crisis might have passed but he was by no means fully recovered.

A knock on the roof jerked him back to alertness. A small hatch hinged upward and the cabbie looked down at him.

"Montagu Place, boss."

"Already?"

"Yup. You've been catching forty winks. I could hear yer snoring."

Burton pushed the door open and stepped down onto the road. He passed the fare up to the man and said, "There's a little extra, for the damage to your ears."

The cabbie grinned. "Much obliged!"

He drove off.

Burton took a couple of steps then stopped. A street Arab was hawking newspapers outside his door.

"Read all about it! Sky lit up around the world! Read all about it!"

The explorer had an idea. He approached the youngster.

"I say, nipper, are you a Whisperer?"

The boy—he was no more than twelve years old, dressed in rags with a battered stovepipe hat on his tousle-haired head—pushed his chest out, stood proudly, and in a soft Irish accent declared, "Aye, sir, that I am. Any message you want to send or information you want to find, I can do it—for a small fee."

Burton fished a shilling from his pocket. "Then I have a job for you. I need to trace the whereabouts of a man named Macallister Fogg. I want to know who he is and what he does."

The boy received the coin with a broad grin and said, "Go on with ye! Macallister Fogg, is it? Are ye certain about that? You'll not be pullin' me leg?"

"I'm certain."

The boy slapped his thigh, rocked back on his heels, and roared with laughter.

"'Tis the easiest shillin' I've ever earned, so it is!"

"How so?" Burton asked.

"Would ye be willin' to invest a further penny? If ye do, I'll place Macallister Fogg in your hands in less than a minute."

The penny was brought forth, and the boy said, "Wait here a moment, will ye now?"

He left his bundle of newspapers at the explorer's feet, scampered off, and disappeared into Gloucester Place.

Burton knew how it worked. The many orphans and dispossessed youngsters who roamed the streets of the Empire had formed what amounted to a secret "communications web" through which information could pass from mouth to mouth at an astonishing speed. These "Whisperers" functioned mainly as an alternative to the post office, delivering spoken messages rather than letters—confidentiality assured—but were also what Richard Monckton Milnes called "an organic encyclopaedia" in that, where information was available, they could almost always find it. The only drawback to the system was the phenomenon of cumulative errors, or "Chinese whispers," which meant the information passed or requested needed to be as simple as possible or it would become corrupted as it travelled from child to child.

The urchin returned.

He handed Burton a periodical of cheap paper, about twenty pages in thickness, which bore the title *The Baker Street Detective*.

"What's this?" the explorer asked.

"A story paper, sir. From the newsagent's."

"A penny blood?"

"Aye, an' me very favourite one, too. I'm fair hooked on it! Fair hooked! Most o' the boys are."

Burton examined the lurid cover illustration, which showed a muscular and mustachioed man being chased through a cavern by demonic creatures. He read: *The Kingdom Beneath the Basement! Macallister Fogg at the Centre of the World!*

"I don't understand."

"Macallister Fogg is a consulting detective, sir. He works out of Baker Street, not five minutes' walk from here, though which house I don't know."

"Consulting detective?"

"Aye. Private, like. Unofficial. Not one of 'em what works at Scotland Yard."

"But . . . this?" Burton held up the penny dreadful.

The newsboy giggled. "Well, he ain't real, is he? Ha ha! He's just in story books!"

Burton clacked his teeth together in irritation. "The man I want said his name was Macallister Fogg."

"I think he was havin' ye on, sir, though there's 'em what hold that Fogg is real. If that be true and ye find 'im, can I ask ye to introduce me? I'll offer to be his assistant, so I will. Perhaps he'll take me on one of his grand adventures!"

The explorer thanked the boy, entered number 14, settled in his study, and read the periodical. It was ill-written nonsense. Plainly, whoever his assailant was, he'd called himself Fogg just to throw Burton off the scent.

He shook his head in bemusement. Laurence Oliphant, the aurora borealis, Macallister Fogg, and Hagar Burton's warning; could he really be certain he'd recovered from the hallucinatory fevers?

He went to one of his desks, picked up his notepad, and opened it. Yes, Oliphant's diagrams were real enough—those strange number-filled squares. They, at least, were something he could investigate, and of all the people he knew, Richard Monckton Milnes was the most likely to understand what they signified.

He sat, opened a bottle of ink, took up a pen, and wrote six letters. He then descended the stairs, stepped outside, and whistled at the newsboy, who came running over.

"Somethin' else, sir?"

"Thruppence for you," Burton said, "if you'll post these letters for me."

"Ah. A thruppenny bit, is it? Well now, old Stride has his sweet shop right next to the post office, so he does, and I'll not pass up the opportunity to pay him a visit. Hand over the letters, sir, an' I'll have 'em posted in a jiffy."

The money and missives exchanged hands and the boy dashed off.

Burton gave a satisfied clap of his hands, went back up to his study, and eased himself into his saddlebag armchair. He lit a cheroot.

The members of the Cannibal Club would soon convene.

He spent the rest of the day reading. By ten o'clock, his bed beckoned. He looked at his study windows and uttered a small exclamation. It was still light. Moving over to them, he pulled up a sash, leaned out, and looked up.

For the third night in a row, a coruscating radiance filled the sky.

Thomas Bendyshe raised his glass and declared, "A toast to Sir Richard Francis Burton, the man who cracked the Nile!"

"Hear hear!" Henry Murray enthused.

Burton flicked his fingers dismissively. "I'm not knighted yet."

"Pah!" Bendyshe objected. "An insignificant detail. Your good health, sir!"

"Was it worth the hardship, Burton old boy?" Charles Bradlaugh asked. "Was your expedition a mystical and enlightening experience? I mean to say, many regard the Nile as the source of life itself, don't they?"

Bendyshe added, "Personally, I regard cognac as the source, but that doesn't mean I want to visit France. Why did you do it?"

"There was no spiritual revelation involved," Burton responded. "Nor did I expect there to be. My motives were purely materialistic. I calculated that the discovery would make Disraeli and his cronies sit up and take notice of me—thus I would stand a better chance of securing a government post in one of the Arabian countries."

The members of the Cannibal Club—Burton, Bendyshe, Murray, Bradlaugh, and Richard Monckton Milnes, Doctor James Hunt, and Sir Edward Brabrooke—had gathered in the function rooms above Bartolini's Italian restaurant in Leicester Square. The chamber was furnished with leather armchairs and sofas, heavy oak tables and cabinets.

It was Sunday evening.

Yesterday morning, Burton's luggage had been delivered from the *Orpheus* to Montagu Place. As it was piled in the hallway, Mrs. Angell had thrown up her arms and exclaimed, "There's ten times as much as you took! I hope you don't have tigers in those trunks!"

"There are no tigers in Africa, Mrs. Angell."

"I'm not surprised. You've brought them all back here!"

It had taken him until midday to move all the cases upstairs and begin sorting through them. He'd then spent the afternoon relaxing, smoking cigars, catching up with his correspondence, reading voraciously, and dozing frequently. At eight in the evening, he met Isabel, Blanche, and Sadhvi Raghavendra at Jaquet's on Drury Lane, where they'd dined on the restaurant's famous à-la-mode beef.

What they'd agreed on Thursday night was agreed again: Hagar Burton's prediction must be rejected out of hand. It was patently absurd. Even Isabel, who was extremely superstitious, accepted that it would be the height of foolishness to allow such tosh to influence their wedding plans.

She and her sister were currently staying at the St. James Hotel, off Piccadilly. In a few days, they'd be returning to the family home—New Wardour Castle in Wiltshire—taking Sadhvi with them as their guest, there to engage in two months of frenzied organising and planning. November's engagement party was to be a full-blown ball such as only the country's richest Catholic family could afford.

The wedding itself was scheduled for January. Cardinal Wiseman, a friend of the Arundells', had promised that if Burton signed the Catholic pledge, a dispensation would be obtained from Rome to allow the union. As far as Burton was concerned, if ink on paper could pacify the Papists—and, more importantly, Isabel's parents—then he was happy to provide it. His atheism would be in no way sullied.

They'd left Jaquet's at eleven. The sky was clear and dark. No aurora borealis—the mysterious lights had vanished.

"Thank goodness!" Isabel had exclaimed. "Perhaps the city will quiet down now. How could anyone possibly survive a London that's active twenty-four hours a day?"

Today, Sunday, had been another of rest and recuperation. By the time Burton joined his fellow Cannibals, he was feeling considerably stronger and his skin had lost its jaundiced hue.

Now—having learned nothing from Thursday night's lesson—he was rapidly getting drunk again, only dimly aware that he was using alcohol to numb the transition from Africa to London.

"I say, old horse!" Thomas Bendyshe shouted. "This engagement party of yours—are we all invited?"

Burton refilled his brandy glass, removed the cheroot from his mouth, blew smoke into the vessel, and drank from it.

"If a horde of atheists caroused around New Wardour Castle, Isabel's mother would probably suffer an embolism," he said. "So, no, Tom, I'm afraid that, with the exception of Monckton Milnes, who knows how to conduct himself in polite society, the Cannibal Club is most definitely not invited."

"But surely her God will protect her from us?" Bendyshe protested.

"I'd rather not put it to the test."

The explorer and his friends had been quaffing, smoking, and joking for three hours. Interspersed between the ribaldry, they'd exchanged news, enjoyed Burton's yarns about the more explicit aspects of his time in Africa, and had supplemented his reading of the newspapers with their own opinions of the various developments in the world—the resolution of the Austro-Sardinian War; the commencement of the construction of the Suez Canal; the American gold rush; and, most of all, the forthcoming formation of the Central German Confederation and its official Alliance with Britain.

Finally, as "Big Ben"—the bell recently installed in Westminster Palace's St. Stephen's Tower—chimed midnight, the resolute imbibing told. Bendyshe, Hunt, Murray, Brabrooke, and Bradlaugh took to armchairs, sprawled as loose as rag dolls, and produced only sporadic drunken murmurings, which ceased as Burton started to discuss Oliphant with Monckton Milnes, who—like the explorer—possessed greater immunity to the effects of alcohol than the other men. The rest listened, barely able to comprehend the account of Stroyan's murder.

Monckton Milnes was a tall and lanky individual, rather saturnine in appearance, with the brow of an intellectual, long hair, and a preference for high collars and bright cravats. He was a wielder of influence in High Society; a writer; a poet; and a dabbler in politics. He also happened to be a keen collector of erotica and occult literature. His country manor, Fryston, in Yorkshire, contained the largest library of banned material anywhere in Europe.

Burton pulled his notebook from his pocket.

"What do you make of these? As I say, the grids and numbers were scrawled on the walls of the *Orpheus*'s observation room. There was a pentagram on the floor. Oliphant was standing in the middle of it when he slit Stroyan's throat."

Monckton Milnes took the book and examined the sketches.

"The pentagram has many associations," he muttered, "but these are magic squares, so I suspect that, in this instance, the five-pointed star represents the coalescence of spirit into flesh. The squares are employed to map the path of manifestation, the idea being that something abstract is given such a strong conceptual route into the actual that it will have the means to become as real as you or I. Hum! I must confess, they have me flummoxed. Each diagram certainly offers a sequential passage from the notional to the material, but I cannot fathom how they relate to one another. Plainly, they do, and these central numbers—ten, eight, nine hundred, and one thousand—are the key. The question is, the key to what? I have no idea, Richard."

"Are you acquainted with anyone who might know more?"

Monckton Milnes tapped his forefinger against his lips for a moment then answered, "Um. Yes. Possibly. Do you mind if I copy these pages? I'd like to send them to a Frenchman I've shared some correspondence with."

"Be my guest."

"Also, my prognosticator still sits for me, despite having retired a few years ago, but I could probably persuade her to make an exception for you. Will you see her? She might throw light on recent events."

Burton emptied his glass and shook his head.

"She's very good," Monckton Milnes said.

"I don't care for the species," Burton protested.

"Still the prejudice? What if she can actually contact Stroyan? Surely you'd listen to his account of Oliphant's ritual?"

"If I was certain it was Stroyan addressing me. But how could I be?"

"Because he'd tell you something only a spirit could know."

Burton levelled his intense eyes at Monckton Milnes. "The dead communicate directly with me, you know."

The older man looked surprised. "They do?"

"Yes, and they are telling me that you accompanied a young lady to the opening of the Theatre Royal earlier tonight, that you and she sat in the upper tier, and that you possess a romantic interest in her but did not make as much progress as you would have liked. She told you she was too preoccupied with her calling and could not at present give consideration to anything that might distract her from it."

Monckton Milnes had raised a glass of wine to his lips as Burton started to speak. He now coughed, spluttered, and gasped, "Great heavens above! You don't mean to say the spirits were watching over me during tonight's performance?"

Burton gave a savage grin. "Do you mean the actors' performance or your own?"

Snapping out of his drunken stupor, Bendyshe guffawed. "Ha ha! Poor old Monkey Milnes! It looks to me like he was the main act tonight!"

Monckton Milnes put aside his glass and squared his shoulders. "This is quite unacceptable! I demand to know who's been spying on me from the Afterlife. Reveal your source, Burton."

"And *that*," the explorer said, "is how easy it is."

"What the devil are you jabbering about?"

"Bazalgette is currently digging one of his sewers along the Strand, and I've read complaints in the newspapers about yellow dust spreading from the excavation." Burton pointed at his friend's feet. "You have such a deposit staining the edges of your boot soles, therefore you were in the area, and it must have been within the past few hours, else the dust would have been dislodged."

Hunt and Murray roused themselves and leaned forward to hear more. Brabrooke and Bradlaugh, both flirting with the point of no return, emitted crooning rumbles and gentle whistles.

"For what reason were you in the Strand?" Burton continued. "It is Sunday, so only hotels and theatres are open. One or the other, then. Of the theatres, the Royal makes a great deal about being the only one illuminated by Stroud's Patent Sun Lamp, an ingenious array of gas mantles that shine through a chandelier of cut glass. The arrangement has been much lauded by the press, though some reporters noted that it produces a waxy residue that drifts down onto the audience, especially those seated in the upper tiers. You have just such a residue on your jacket shoulders. Furthermore, when you arrived here, there were very slight indentations beneath your eyes, which suggested to me the prolonged use of opera glasses aimed downward at a stage."

"Bravo, Richard!" James Hunt cheered.

Bendyshe clapped enthusiastically and cried out, "But what of the mysterious goddess?"

Burton took Monckton Milnes by the right wrist and raised his hand into the air. "Observe! A slight green stain between our friend's forefinger and thumb signifies her presence. One can see by the hue that it is vegetable in origin, and two very slight nicks in the skin of his principal digit suggest the presence of thorns."

"I was gardening," Monckton Milnes objected.

"Is that so? Where, sir? Your gardens are a part of Fryston. Your town house has none. So no, you were not gardening, you were holding thorny stalks, the most obvious candidate being roses, which are the flowers of romance."

Monckton Milnes's shoulders slumped. "Gad! You're a confounded sorcerer. And my rejection?"

"Simple. Had you not been spurned, you would not be here."

Bendyshe, Hunt, and Murray let loose peals of laughter, which woke Brabrooke and Bradlaugh, who, being three sheets to the wind and not knowing what was going on, laughed along with them so as to not be unsociable.

Henry Murray said, "But—I say!—this business about the young lady's calling?"

"That," Burton said, "is public knowledge. In a small column in yesterday's *Daily Bugle*, one of our lesser hacks took great delight in reporting that Mr. Richard Monckton Milnes, the well-known socialite, has been courting Miss Florence Nightingale, the famous nurse. She—as was also reported— is currently raising funds for her nurses' training school at Saint Thomas's Hospital. Knowing of her notoriously single-minded disposition, I consider it highly unlikely that she would allow the distractions of a romance to interfere with her vocation."

Monckton Milnes slapped his hand to his forehead and groaned. "You are quite right. Florence stepped out to powder her nose during the interval and never returned. I sat through the second half of that bloody performance with her elderly chaperone huffing and puffing indignantly in my ear. I feel thoroughly humiliated."

With renewed boisterousness, the gentlemen of the Cannibal Club toasted failed romance, then Richard Monckton Milnes, then Nurse Nightingale, then Burton, and finally each other.

"By Gad!" Bendyshe bellowed. "My bloody astrologist warned me off port—said it'd be the death of me! If it's all chicanery, I've been denying myself for nothing! Open a bottle at once!"

The lull had passed. Thomas Bendyshe resumed his relentless foghorn-volume raillery; Henry Murray left the room to order a pot of coffee from Bartolini's but returned with a fresh bottle of brandy; Charles Bradlaugh, apropos of nothing, proclaimed that the word "gorilla" was derived from the Greek "*gorillai*," which meant "tribe of hairy women," and proceeded along a course of speculation which, had the authorities been present, would doubtless have landed him in prison; Doctor James Hunt employed his medical knowledge to mix cocktails of foul taste and terrifying potency; and Sir Edward Brabrooke propped himself in a corner with a fixed grin on his face and, over the course of thirty minutes, very, very slowly slid to the floor.

Amid the uproar, Burton quietly told Monckton Milnes, "My point wasn't to embarrass you but to demonstrate that, with a practised eye, any individual can discern a great deal about any other and pass it off as information received from the Afterlife. I suspect a little mesmerism is involved, too, just to make the victim more gullible."

"And I suppose you, being an accomplished mesmerist yourself, cannot fall under another's spell?"

"Correct."

"But surely you don't consider all spiritualists fraudulent? Why, there's practically one on every street corner. The business has been flourishing for twenty years. If they were all duplicitous, it would be the swindle of the century."

Burton was silent for a moment. Twenty years. Spiritualists had first claimed they could speak with the dead just weeks after The Assassination. Interesting.

"Certainly," he said, "I accept that a few—and I emphasise, a *few*—practitioners might actually glimpse the future or gain unusually penetrating insight into a matter, but I attribute such occurrences to an as yet undiscovered natural function of the human organism; a 'force of will,' if you like, that enables a person to sense what they cannot feel, see, hear, touch, or taste. There is nothing supernatural involved. I do not hold with the soul or spirit—a self within a self; an I within an I—that continues to exist after the body has ceased to function yet still concerns itself with corporeal matters. The very notion is utter rot. The dead, my friend, are well and truly dead."

"I cannot agree," Monckton Milnes protested. "My prognosticator's positive influence has been far more significant and widespread than I can possibly tell you. You should consult with her."

"Perhaps. Let us first see what this Frenchman of yours has to say. Refill my glass, old fellow; I'm lagging behind."

At four o'clock in the morning, having dedicated himself to catching up with the others, Burton stepped out into Leicester Square with his top hat set at such a jaunty angle that he'd taken just three paces before it fell off and rolled into the gutter. He bent to retrieve it, overbalanced, and followed it down. His panther-headed cane clattered onto the cobbles beside him.

"Now then, sir," came a stern voice. "It's not my place to lecture a fine gentleman like yourself, but I suspect you may be filled to the knocker, so to speak."

The explorer looked up and saw a police constable looking down. The man had a swollen nose. It was purple and bloodied around the nostrils.

"I topped my dropper," Burton explained.

"Dropped your topper, sir? Here it is." The policeman retrieved Burton's headgear and cast his eyes over it. "A very nice hat, that. A mite dusty now, but it'll clean up with a little brushing. Here, let me help you."

Burton gripped the outstretched hand and allowed himself to be hauled back to his feet. He bent down for his cane, stumbled, but managed to regain his footing before meeting the ground again.

"Tripped," he said. "What happened to your nose?"

"It encountered a bunch of fives, sir. There are criminals about. And you? Your eye?"

"The same. Thwacked."

"Are you a pugilist? I have it in mind that I've seen your likeness in the newspapers. Sports pages, I'll wager. You look quite the fighter."

Burton took his proffered top hat, pressed it firmly onto his head, and slurred, "There've been sketches of me in a few of the rags recently. The Nile. Africa. *Orpheus*."

"The Nile? Ah, yes! You're the explorer! Livingstone!"

Burton groaned. He squinted at the policeman's badge. "Constable Bhatti, I would be very grateful indeed if you never, ever refer to me that way again. My name is Burton."

"Right you are, sir. My apologies. No offence intended. Which way are you going?"

With a wave in a vaguely northwesterly direction, Burton said, "Thataway."

"Home?"

"Yeth. I mean, yeth. That is to say—yeth." He coughed and cleared his throat. "Yes."

"Good. Very wise. I'll call you a cab."

"No, thank you. I'll walk. Clear my head."

The constable raised his arm and whistled at a nearby hansom. "You'll take a ride, sir. I insist upon it. The streets are dangerous at this time of night. Look at my nose."

"I'd rather not. It's an unpleasant sight."

The carriage, drawn by a steam-horse, chugged across the square and drew to a halt beside them.

"What ho, Constable Bhatti!" its driver called.

"Hallo, Mr. Penniforth. I have a passenger for you. Take him to Montagu Place, please."

"Rightio! In you get, guv'nor!"

Before he could protest, Burton was bundled into the carriage by the policeman.

"Wait!" he mumbled. "I don't want—"

"You'll be fine, Doctor Livingstone," Bhatti said. "Straight home and into bed. That's an order."

"I'm not bloody Livingstone, you confounded—"

Burton toppled backward into his seat as the carriage jolted forward. His hat fell onto the floor.

"Damnation!"

He heard Constable Bhatti's laughter receding as the hansom picked up speed.

"Penniforth!" Burton yelled, knocking on the roof with his cane. "Aren't you the man who met the *Orpheus*?"

"Aye, guv'nor!" the driver called. "Small world, ain't it?"

"Not as small as all that. Would you slow down, please?"

"'Fraid not. Orders is orders. Got to get you 'ome on the double, so to speak. You needs yer sleep. Gee-up, Daisy! I calls me steam-nag Daisy, guv'nor, on account o' that bein' me wife's moniker. She has me in harness whenever I'm 'ome, so I figures it's only fair what that I have 'er in harness when I hain't."

Burton grabbed at the window frame as the carriage bounced over a pothole and hurtled around a corner. "I really don't need to hear about your domestic affairs!" he shouted. "Let me out! I demand it!"

"Sorry, yer lordship. I 'ave to do what the constable says. Wouldn't do to cross a bobby, would it! I'll let you hoff at Montagu Place."

Burton gritted his teeth and hung on.

The question came unbidden. How the hell did Constable Bhatti know where he lived?

CHAPTER 5

THE MISSING GHOST

"Men who leave their mark on the world are very often those who, being gifted and full of nervous power, are at the same time haunted and driven by a dominant idea, and are therefore within a measurable distance of insanity."
—Francis Galton

A little after three o'clock the next afternoon, at the end of the ceremony in Buckingham Palace, King George V of Great Britain and Hanover leaned close to Sir Richard Francis Burton and said, "I congratulate you. It was my pleasure to award you this knighthood. You deserve it. Are you drunk?"

Burton shook his head. "No, Your Majesty, but I may have dosed myself up rather too liberally with Saltzmann's Tincture this morning. I'm still battling the remnants of malaria. It was a choice between the medicine or my teeth chattering throughout the formalities."

"And this medicine has made you so clumsy?"

Burton glanced at the stain on the monarch's trouser-leg. "Again, my apologies. My coordination is all shot through."

"Which, I venture, is also how you came by the black eye my aide mentioned."

The explorer nodded and silently cursed Macallister Fogg.

The king grinned, revealing his cracked and uneven teeth. "You are a man of firsts, Captain. The first East India Company officer to pass all his language exams at the first try; the first non-Muslim to enter the holy city of Mecca; the first European to look upon the source of the River Nile; and the first freshly knighted man to spill wine on the royal bloomers."

Burton shifted his weight uneasily from one foot to the other and looked into the king's filmy white eyes. It was said that blind men develop a sixth sense. Did the monarch somehow know that Burton had been drinking until the small hours and was still hung-over?

"I suppose I'll be remembered, at least," he mumbled.

"You can be sure of that, Captain. Now, tell me, how many stragglers remain?"

Glancing around the presentation room, Burton saw five Yeomen of the Guard, three ushers, the Lord Chamberlain, and six of the *Orpheus*'s crew, the latter proudly wearing their medals. Isabel—soon to be Lady Burton—was loitering at the door and just managed a wave before she was politely guided out into the reception chamber.

"There are a few by the entrance," Burton said. "They are departing."

"Good. I have no objection to the post-ceremonial shaking of hands and uttering of niceties, but today there happens to be important business to attend to, and I would rather get on with it."

Reflexively, Burton gave a short bow, even though the king couldn't see it. "Then I apologise again, and shall make myself scarce."

"No! No! This business concerns you. Do you see a door off to my right? I understand it's painted yellow."

"Yes, I see it."

"Then please oblige me by leading me to it. You and I and a few others have much to discuss."

"We do?"

Damascus. There must be a situation developing in Damascus. They want to send me there post-haste.

Burton moved his left forearm up into the grip of the king's outstretched hand and escorted him to the door.

"Open it," the monarch said. "Down to the end of the corridor, then turn right."

"I wasn't informed," Burton said, carefully steering the sovereign through the portal and around a plinth that stood against the wall to the left. His host reached out and brushed his fingers against the bust of King George III that stood upon it.

"My grandfather. The longest reigning British monarch. With him it was all war, war, war. He was mad as a hatter. Some say he was poisoned."

"Was he?"

"It wouldn't surprise me, and if he was, he probably deserved it."

After a moment's silence, Burton said, "May I ask you a question?"

"By all means."

"Aside from the Royal Geographical Society, what royal charters have you issued this year?"

The king gave a chuckle. "My goodness! That's not an enquiry I could have predicted! Let's see. There was the University of Melbourne in March; the Benevolent Institution for the Relief of Aged and Infirm Journeymen Tailors in July; and I plan to issue one to the National Benevolent Institution in September. Why, Sir Richard?"

Burton started slightly at the use of his new title. He said, "The words *royal charter* were a part of an incomprehensible telegraph message received by the *Orpheus* during the aurora borealis phenomenon."

"I see. And you are curious as to the significance?"

"I am."

"Has my answer cast any light on the subject?"

"None at all."

They reached the end of the passage and turned right into another.

"Fifth door on your left," the king said. "So you weren't informed of this meeting? That's not entirely surprising. Events have been moving rapidly. Decisions were made overnight."

They came to the door.

"In we go, Captain."

Burton turned the handle and pushed. King George stepped past him into the chamber and was immediately met by one of the palace's beautiful clockwork footmen—a thing of polished brass and tiny cogwheels with a babbage probability calculator supplying its simulated intelligence. It led him to the head of a heavy table in the middle of the room. Five men, who'd been sitting around it, rose as the monarch entered. Having heard the scrape of their chairs, the king waved at them to resume their seats. "Come, Sir Richard. Settle here beside me, please."

As he moved to the table, Burton examined the room. Its panelled walls were hung with royal portraits, heavy velvet drapes had been drawn across the two windows, and bright illumination shone from a huge crystal chandelier.

He lowered himself into the seat on the king's left and struggled to maintain his composure as he recognised the other men. Opposite him, Prime Minister Benjamin Disraeli leaned back and tapped his fingernails on what looked to be Burton's African reports. Lord Stanley, sitting on the premier's right, reached for a jug of water, poured a glass, and slid it across to the explorer. Beside him, Dante Gabriel Rossetti, the minister of arts and culture, long-haired and foppishly dressed, watched Burton with curiosity.

The far end of the table was occupied by His Royal Highness Prince Albert, who'd been present at the knighting ceremony. Next to him, on the same side as Burton, the home secretary, Spencer Walpole, fidgeted restlessly.

King George turned to the footman and said, "Are we all here?"

"No, Your Majesty," the contraption responded in a clanging voice. It bent over the king until its canister-shaped head was close to his ear then chimed so softly that Burton couldn't make out a single word.

"Indisposed?" the king said. "I rather think *indolent* would be a more appropriate word. Stand outside the door, please, and ensure we're not interrupted."

The footman bowed, ding-donged, "Yes, Your Majesty," and left the room.

"Disgraceful!" Disraeli muttered. "The minister's lack of respect plummets to yet greater depths."

"We must indulge him," the king answered, with a slight smile. "His eccentricities don't undermine his value."

"Just as long as that value remains intact," Disraeli said. "Which, under the circumstances, remains to be seen."

"Forgive me," Burton said, glancing at the vacant chair between himself and Walpole, "but to whom are you referring?"

The king turned his blank eyes and answered, "The minister of mediumistic affairs."

"Ah," Burton replied. "I should have known."

A dull pain throbbed just behind his ears. His mouth felt dry, his eyes hot. The acidic aftertaste of brandy still lingered at the back of his throat. He reached for the water and drained the glass in a single swallow.

I have discomfort enough. I don't need the bloody minister of mediumistic mumbo-jumbo, too.

The king said quietly, "Well then, let us proceed. Mr. Disraeli, would you explain, please?"

Disraeli rapped his knuckles lightly against the tabletop, looked at Burton, and said, "Sir Richard, last Thursday evening, shortly after the *Orpheus* landed and while you were, I understand, at the Royal Geographical Society, Isambard Kingdom Brunel, the head of the Department of Guided Science, walked into Penfold Private Sanatorium—you know the place?"

Burton nodded. "It's where my colleague, Sister Raghavendra, worked before I commissioned her to join my expedition."

"I see," Disraeli said. "Well, Brunel walked into it and announced that, in two days' time—that is to say, this Saturday past—he was going to have a stroke."

"How could he possibly know that?"

"He received a warning from the Afterlife. The information was correct. At three o'clock on Saturday morning, he did, indeed, suffer an attack."

"Is he all right?"

"We don't know. At eleven o'clock that night, two men entered the sanatorium and attempted to kidnap him. They were prevented from doing so by two police constables. The men escaped. The constables removed Brunel from the building, telling the nurses they were taking him to a place of safety. He hasn't been seen since. We haven't been able to find or identify the policemen, and Scotland Yard's Chief Commissioner Mayne says he knew of no threat to Brunel and issued no orders to protect him." Disraeli paused, then continued, "It's not the first unexplained disappearance involving persons of significance. Two years ago, as everyone knows, Charles Babbage mysteriously vanished. In March of this year, the engineer Daniel Gooch went missing. And, last night, a man witnessed two policemen forcibly removing Nurse Florence Nightingale from outside the Theatre Royal. She did not attend her morning appointments today and her whereabouts are currently unknown."

"Nightingale!" Burton exclaimed. "She was there with Richard Monckton Milnes!"

"That fact has come to light. Commissioner Mayne has assigned a Detective Inspector Slaughter to the case. I understand he's questioning Mr. Monckton Milnes even as we speak."

"He'll not learn much. My friend thinks she ran out on him halfway through the show."

The prime minister grunted, leaned his elbows on the table, and steepled his fingers together. "Which brings us to Abdu El Yezdi."

Burton looked around the table, from one man to the next. Their eyes met his but gave nothing away.

Sudden comprehension sent prickles up his spine.

Bismillah! This has nothing to do with the consulship of Damascus! Why am I here?

He said, "Who is he?"

No one answered.

After what felt like a minute's silence, Disraeli said, in a very low voice, "We are about to discuss state secrets, Sir Richard. Is your confidence assured? I do not, at any point in the future, want to have to charge you with treason."

Burton slowly nodded.

Prince Albert spoke. "Your Majesty, Prime Minister, gentlemen—already we haff chosen to trust Sir Richard, haff we not? We must proceed. I am sure that, once all the facts before him haff been laid, the need for secrecy he will recognise."

There were murmurs of agreement.

King George nodded and addressed Disraeli. "His Royal Highness is correct. We must give Sir Richard all the facts if he is to fully appreciate the significance of what we are to ask of him. But I suggest we first review the relevant history. It will provide context."

The prime minister bowed his acquiescence.

The monarch turned to Burton. "I understand you spent your childhood outside the Empire? Where were you on the day of The Assassination?"

The explorer was so stunned to be asked that particular question again, he could hardly respond, and stammered, "I—I—I was at sea. En route from—from Italy."

"So you felt nothing?"

Burton shrugged and shook his head, then realised the king couldn't see him and said, "Nothing at all."

"Well then, um, Mr. Walpole, perhaps you would be good enough to describe your experience?"

Walpole, his face framed by whiskers and scored with a myriad of small wrinkles, straightened his back and said, in his characteristically terse manner, "Certainly. My diaries. Sir Richard, I'm rather a fastidious diary-keeper. It's a discipline I've observed since childhood. During the hour before bed, I always record the day's events and my opinions of them. I write in considerable detail, and have done so since 1822."

He paused and glanced at Burton as if expecting to be challenged. The explorer, who was feeling completely bewildered, kept his mouth closed.

Walpole continued, "In the aftermath of The Assassination, I felt the need to consult what I had written during the months preceding it. I do not know why. Perhaps I was looking for some rhyme or reason for the crime. What I read in those pages made perfect sense. I remembered everything I saw reported. Yet—" He paused. "Yet something was amiss. I found myself hunting for accounts of other events—but exactly what events eluded me. What was I searching for? Why did I feel that material was missing? I looked back over three years' worth of diaries before what I read started to feel complete."

Walpole's lips twitched as if he wanted to say more but couldn't find the appropriate words.

"Thank you, Mr. Walpole," the king said. "Yours is a typical example of what has come to be known as the Great Amnesia, which everyone inside the British Empire experienced to some degree or other. The consensus is that, during Victoria's three-year reign, events occurred that were forgotten by everyone the instant she was killed, and which have somehow left no evidence behind them." The king laid both hands palms down on the tabletop with his fingers spread. "It is also generally accepted that the Great Amnesia gave rise to the New Renaissance—a sensational outpouring of inventiveness by engineers and scientists throughout the length and breadth of the Empire."

"Led by Isambard Kingdom Brunel," Burton murmured.

"Quite right. But there is more to it than that. What very few people know is that, from its very start, the New Renaissance has been guided by a denizen of the Afterlife."

Burton pressed his lips together. A sense of unreality crept over him. The world wasn't making any sense.

The king sighed. "You'll remember that, after the queen's death, the foreign secretary of the time, Lord Palmerston, attempted to backdate the Regency Act to allow His Royal Highness—" he gestured toward Prince Albert, "—to accede to the throne. This in response to public opposition to my father, Ernest Augustus the First of Hanover, who, though the rightful heir, was believed to be as mad as his father, King George the Third." Reaching out his right hand, the monarch groped until he touched Benjamin Disraeli's forearm. "Prime Minister?"

Disraeli said, "Your friend Monckton Milnes, Sir Richard, has been rather more involved in affairs of state than you know. In 1840, a young prognosticator named Countess Sabina Lacusta approached him with the news that a spirit—Abdu El Yezdi—wished him to work against Lord Palmerston. Monckton Milnes should begin, the spirit advised, by talking to me."

The prime minister reached for the jug of water, topped up his and Burton's glasses, and took a swig.

"I was not long in politics at the time," he continued, "and had lacked focus up until Palmerston started to play fast and loose with the constitution. I'd no objection at all to His Royal Highness—" he tipped his head respectfully toward Prince Albert, "—taking the throne, but I didn't trust Palmerston's motives. I felt he was manoeuvring himself into what could easily become an unassailable position of power."

"How so?" Burton interrupted.

Prince Albert murmured, "With good health I haff never been blessed. The pressures that His Majesty bears so well would, I think, kill me."

"And if His Royal Highness had become king," Disraeli resumed, "then passed away before remarrying and fathering an heir—"

"Which I had, *unt* haff, no intention of doing," Prince Albert added.

"—there would've been no one to follow him. Britain may well have slipped into republicanism with, in all probability, Palmerston as its president."

"Ah," Burton said.

"Ah," the prime minister echoed. "So I founded the Young England political group through which to organise a campaign against Palmerston, and it succeeded in no small degree because Abdu El Yezdi persuaded Richard Monckton Milnes to secretly fund it."

There came a lengthy silence.

When Burton—who'd known nothing of his friend's involvement in Palmerston's downfall—responded to this revelation, his voice came as a hoarse whisper. "Do you mean to tell me that the history of this country has been manipulated by a—by a—by a ghost?"

"More so than you can possibly imagine," Disraeli answered. "As you know, when Palmerston was defeated, he attempted an armed insurrection, but he and his supporters—led by two men, Damien Burke and Gregory Hare—were forced into retreat. They holed up in secret chambers beneath the Tower of London, and on the thirtieth of October, 1841, a pitched battle ensued. It destroyed the Tower's Grand Armoury and caused a quarter of a million pounds' worth of damage, but Palmerston and his supporters were finally flushed out. Burke and Hare escaped. We have long assumed they fled the country. Palmerston was captured, tried as a traitor, and executed."

Disraeli regarded Burton through hooded eyes. His right forefinger tapped three times, the fingernail going *clack clack clack* on the tabletop. "In the wake of those events, Melbourne's government fell. I was elected head of the Conservative Party and, soon after, prime minister. I immediately made Countess Sabina my first minister of mediumistic affairs. Through her—and since 'fifty-six through her successor—I have received the counsel of Abdu El Yezdi. At his behest, I established the Department of Guided Science, and to counterbalance it, the Ministry of Arts and Culture. I gave Brunel access to the countess, and El Yezdi inspired him to build Battersea Power Station and the many varieties of steam transportation that our Empire so relies upon. The spirit also advised Babbage, Gooch, and Nightingale, among others. The marvellous mechanical and medical advancements we have made these past two decades are all due to his influence."

Prince Albert interjected, "I, also, by him haff been guided. The—what is the word? Sagacity?—attributed to me as architect of the Central German Confederation, *unt* of the Alliance that will be formalised on November the eleventh, belongs, in fact, to our friendly phantom."

"There's more," Disraeli said, "but that's enough to demonstrate to you how crucial this inhabitant of the Afterlife has been in our political and cultural affairs; and it was he, via the minister of mediumistic affairs, who warned Mr. Brunel of his imminent stroke."

Burton lifted his glass with a shaking hand, drank, spluttered, and said, "By God, don't you have anything stronger?"

King George smiled. "Mr. Rossetti, there's a small cabinet between the windows, yes?"

"There is, Your Majesty," Rossetti replied.

"I believe there's a bottle of port inside it. Would you fetch it, please?"

Rossetti did so, and moments later each man had emptied his glass into the water jug and refilled it with the fortified wine.

A few minutes passed while they sipped and thought and waited for Burton to regain his composure.

His heart was hammering.

It was wrong. All wrong!

Yet, he knew—instantly—that it was true. As incredible as it sounded, it made sense. It explained the unprecedented and almost supernatural progress the Empire had made during the past twenty years.

Almost supernatural?

"So," he finally said, "you fear that someone is abducting the people the ghost has advised?"

Disraeli answered, "The situation is more serious even than that. Abdu El Yezdi has consulted with us nearly every day for twenty years. On Thursday, after giving the warning concerning Brunel, he fell silent. Every mediumistic attempt to contact him has failed. In short, we are concerned that he, like the others, has gone missing."

The king reached for Burton's arm again. "I want to make you my special agent, Sir Richard. I feel you have the unique skills required for the role. I will give you authority over the police, unlimited funds to draw on, and pay far and away above what you'd receive as a consul. Say yes, then begin your first assignment—locate Abdu El Yezdi and find out why our people are being taken."

Burton snorted his derision. "Hunt a bloody ghost? In the name of Allah, I have no idea what madness has gripped you all, but I won't be a part of it!"

"Sir!" Disraeli barked. "Have a care—you're speaking to the king! Remember your place and mind your language!"

"My place is Damascus." Burton turned to address Lord Stanley. "Sir, I formally request the consulship. I am ideally suited to the post and will do the government much greater service there than I will chasing wraiths here."

"Denied," the foreign secretary snapped. "It's not available. If you want a consulship, I can offer Santos at best."

Burton curled his fingers into a fist. "Brazil? That's ridiculous. Put me where I can be of most use!"

"We are offering to do so," the prime minister said. "You can be of most use as His Majesty's agent."

"I am not—" Burton began.

The monarch interrupted. "Everyone leave. I shall speak with Sir Richard alone."

"But—" Disraeli protested.

"Out!"

The men stood, bowed, and left the room.

The king waited until he heard the door click shut then said, "You are angry."

"Your Majesty, I am to be married. I want only to settle down with my wife. She and I both feel an affinity for Syria. Isn't it sufficient that I located the source of the Nile? I'm tired of adventures and danger and—blast it!—I don't believe in bloody spooks. Enough is enough."

"What if the cause of Abdu El Yezdi's silence threatens everything your friend Monckton Milnes has helped to establish?"

Burton raised his hands to his head and massaged his temples. He was confused by the interconnectedness of apparently random events. Oliphant had killed Stroyan in the first seconds of Thursday. The aurora borealis had appeared on Thursday. Brunel's stroke had been foreseen on Thursday. Abdu El Yezdi had fallen silent on Thursday.

And The Assassination.

The Great Amnesia had been recognised just after it. The dead, including El Yezdi, had—supposedly—started communicating with the living around the same time. The New Renaissance, he'd just learned, was a consequence of that. And "Macallister Fogg" had wanted to know where Burton was on that precise date!

Why? Why? What the hell has any of this got to do with me?

"I wouldn't know where to begin," he said. "A missing ghost, Your Majesty? It's the height of absurdity."

The monarch shrugged. "In your opinion, but nevertheless, the fact is,

Sir Richard, that when I said I want to make you my special agent, I wasn't asking. If you have an issue with the concept of the Afterlife, I suggest you make the corporeal your starting point."

"How so?"

"Witnesses have described the two men who tried to take Brunel but were stopped by the police constables. We are certain they were Burke and Hare."

The haze in the Strand was saturated with yellow dust. Bright sunlight penetrated it and made the air such a blinding gold that Burton had to walk with his eyes half-closed, peering through his lashes.

The thoroughfare was almost impassable. A huge channel had been dug along its complete length, and traffic and pedestrians were forced to squeeze through the narrow spaces to either side of it. Litter-crabs were in abundance, their bulky forms adding to the chaos, their attempts to clean up the dust doing more to spread it than otherwise.

The giant ditch was plainly visible from any point along the famous street, but this didn't prevent an urchin from trying his luck. He was hollering, "A penny a look! A penny a look! See Mr. Bazalgette's sewer afore it's closed over! A penny a look! The greatest sight you'll ever behold! The eighth wonder of the bloomin' world!" and as Burton passed him, the youngster said, "How about you, sir? Won't you spare a penny to see the DOGS' latest creation? Last chance! They start rebuilding the road over it tomorrow!"

Burton dug a hand into his trouser pocket, retrieved a coin, and flipped it to the lad, who was standing on his right. As he did so, he felt fingers sliding into his jacket from the left. He viciously jabbed out an elbow and caught the pickpocket in the teeth. The man, hideously deformed by rickets and smallpox, let out a bleat and retreated into the crowd.

The explorer moved on, ruminating that the boy and man were probably in cahoots, the one distracting while the other dipped. He thought about the African natives who'd employed similar tactics to steal from his safari. What was considered crime in London was practically a sport in Africa. On that continent, hunger and want justified any action, and successful pilfering was more likely to be celebrated than punished. Here, the rich tried very hard to pretend that poverty didn't exist. To acknowledge it would be to admit that the greatest Empire on Earth was deeply faulted. Better to turn a blind eye, and make illegal the only solutions the poor could find to their dilemma.

He arrived at the Royal Venetia Hotel, located just a few doors along from the Theatre Royal, entered, and allowed a concierge to brush the dust from his clothes. Then he climbed the ornate staircase to the fifth floor and passed along a corridor to Suite Five.

Burton eyed the door for a moment before reluctantly raising his cane and rapping on it. Almost immediately, the portal swung open to reveal a clockwork man.

"I'm here to see the minister."

The mechanism bowed, moved aside, and rang, "He is expecting you, Sir Richard. This way, please. I am Grumbles, his new valet."

Burton followed the contraption through a parlour and into a large library. The room was all books; they lined every wall from floor to ceiling, teetered in tall stacks on the deep red carpet, and were strewn haphazardly over the various tables, chairs, and sideboards. In the midst of them, by the window, a giant of a man, wrapped in a threadbare red dressing gown, occupied an enormous wing-backed armchair of scuffed and cracked leather. His hair was brown and untidy, and from it a deep scar emerged, running jaggedly down the broad forehead to bisect the left eyebrow. His eyes, which followed Burton as he entered, were intensely black. The nose, obviously once broken, had reset crookedly, and the mouth—the upper lip cleft by another scar—was permanently twisted into a superior sneer. It was a face every bit as brutal in appearance as Burton's own, but the heavy jaw was buried beneath bulging jowls, and the neck was lost in rolls of fat which undulated down into a vast belly sagging over tree-trunk-sized legs. The man was so corpulent that, despite the two walking sticks propped against one of the tables, it was impossible to conceive of him in motion.

Grumbles moved to a corner and stood still, quietly ticking.

"So you've finally deigned to visit me," the fat man said. His eyes flicked toward a chair, indicating that Burton should occupy it. "It's been four years."

"I've been busy and you'd lost your mind," Burton responded, moving a pile of books aside before sitting.

"I was seriously injured, and my mind was being—shall we say —rearranged."

"As was your stomach, evidently. How could you possibly have put on so much weight in such a short period? I can hardly see you beneath all that blubber."

"Movement has been difficult for me, Dick. I never properly recovered from my paralysis, and you weren't there to help when I needed it."

"I was wounded, too, if you remember. I'd received a spear through my face. My palate was split. I couldn't speak properly, and you weren't speaking at all."

"I was listening. Do you want a drink, or are you too hung-over after getting sozzled with Monckton Milnes? I have some rather fine Alton Ale."

"Yes, I'm hung-over; and yes, I'll have a glass. Have you been spying on me, Edward?"

The minister waggled his fingers at Grumbles and pointed toward a sideboard.

"It's my job to know what people of significance are up to, though in your case, I could have guessed that it was getting drunk."

"I've become significant?"

"In so far as you haggled with the king."

"Word travels fast."

"In my direction, yes, that's true."

The clockwork man moved a small table to Burton's side and placed a glass of ale upon it. He crossed to his master and served him the same before returning to his place in the corner.

The minister raised his glass. "Enjoy it while you can. This will be a rare commodity before too long. Bazalgette will soon be digging through the East End, and the Alton Brewery's London warehouse is right in his path. The disruption will require it to be emptied of its stock for a month or two."

"I know it's one of your favourite subjects, but I didn't come here to talk about Alton Ale."

"Of course not. Tell me, then—what bargain did you make with His Majesty?"

Burton took a swig and said, "I agreed to undertake the investigation on the condition that if I find a satisfactory explanation for the ghost's silence— or can at least locate those who've gone missing—I'd be rewarded with the consulship of Damascus. My terms were accepted."

The fat man grunted. "So you've come to visit your brother to find out what his role is in all of this?"

"I knew you'd become obsessed with spiritualism and I knew you were working for the government, but I had no conception that you were so intimately involved until a few hours ago."

Edward Burton nodded. His eyes remained fixed on those of his older sibling. "Whatever you conceive, my part in it is even greater than that. For fifteen years, every government policy was passed through Countess Sabina for review by Abdu El Yezdi. It exhausted her. She retired. Now it all comes to me. I am the central exchange. The government is filled with specialists, but my specialism is omniscience. There are occasions when it would be fair to claim that I *am* the British government."

"As conceited as ever. But is the omniscience yours, Edward, or does it belong to the spook you claim contact with? Or perhaps both are sheer fantasy."

"The spirit and I are—or *were*—indivisible!" The minister tapped the side of his own head. "You don't understand. When I first heard El Yezdi, four years ago, it was as if he immediately became an integral part of my mind. I reported his absence to Disraeli last Thursday not just because, after communicating his final message, he fell silent, but because he was quite suddenly and violently torn out of me."

Burton put his glass aside and raised his hands. "Stop. Go back to the beginning. Tell me about when he first spoke to you."

"It was after my accident."

"It wasn't an accident, Edward. You were hunting elephants in Ceylon. The Singhalese consider them holy. It's no wonder they set upon you."

The minister shrugged. "A misjudgment, I'll admit. The villagers attacked me with tools, fists, and feet. My gun bearer was strangled to death. I was knocked unconscious. When I regained my wits, I was in a house in Jaffna, being nursed by two young men—Ravindra Johar and Mahakram Singh. They told me they'd stumbled upon the scene quite by chance and had dragged me away from my assailants."

He lifted his ale and took a gulp, before continuing, "Over the course of four months, they had doctors attend me. My skull had been cracked and my brain injured. I was almost completely paralysed. I couldn't speak." Edward lifted a hand and traced the scar on his forehead with a forefinger. "Then I heard him one night, inside my head, as clear as a bell. He said: *This time, you were saved. You'll recover. Pay the boys to take you to England. Have them deliver you to Penfold Sanatorium. After a few days, they'll disappear. Let them. Don't look for them.*"

"'This time'?"

Edward nodded, his chins wobbling. "Yes. I have no idea what he meant by that."

"And his voice—what was it like?"

"It was *my* voice. When Abdu El Yezdi speaks, it isn't like someone addressing you. It's more like having your own thoughts guided."

"Similar to mesmerism?"

"Yes, very much so. But I wasn't under the influence of animal magnetism. There was no one else present."

Burton mused, "Mental domination over distance?"

Edward made a noise of disagreement. "Your own prejudice prompts you to search for an explanation that doesn't involve the Afterlife. I'm sorry, Dick, but El Yezdi later stated quite categorically that he is not of this world, and I, having communicated so closely with him these past four years, am convinced beyond all doubt that he's a spirit."

Burton drew a cheroot from his pocket, contemplated it, then put it between his lips and fished for his box of lucifers.

Edward clicked his tongue impatiently and said, "Must you foul the atmosphere?"

Ignoring him, Burton lit the Manila and blew smoke into the air.

Edward sighed his exasperation, and went on, "When I was fit enough for the voyage, Ravindra and Mahakram, at my expense, accompanied me here to London. They delivered me to the sanatorium, where, as you know, Sadhvi Raghavendra nursed me back to health. As El Yezdi had warned, the boys both vanished. I never saw them again. I was unable even to thank them."

Burton retrieved his glass, gazed into the foam of his beer, and summoned the painful recollection of Edward's return to England. He'd also been in hospital at the time, and had suddenly been called to the sanatorium. With his own head swathed in bandages, he'd been escorted to a room where he'd found his brother in exactly the same state. However, where Burton's injury had deprived him of a couple of molars, left him temporarily speechless, and gouged a hideous scar across his left cheek, Edward's had threatened permanent brain damage. The two Indian lads—both gone by the time Burton arrived—had kept his brother alive, but it was Sadhvi who nursed him back to health. Having witnessed the miracles she'd worked with him, Burton immediately thought of her three years later, when he was planning his Nile expedition. He'd sought her out and, in a very unconventional move, asked her to join his team. He was surprised and delighted when she'd said yes.

"During the early days of my recovery," Edward said, "I truly thought myself mad."

"As did I," Burton replied. "You didn't say a word for three months."

"I couldn't. It was as if two personalities existed within me. I didn't know which was real. It took a long time to untangle them. Perhaps I wouldn't have been able to were it not for the Countess Sabina. She came to visit me and explained that Abdu El Yezdi had been communicating with her since 1840. She informed me that I was to take over her role. After giving an account of what it would involve, she then, to my great astonishment, ushered in Disraeli himself, who, at her recommendation, immediately appointed me his new minister of mediumistic affairs."

Sir Richard Francis Burton drained his glass, put it down, stood, and started to pace the room, carelessly kicking books aside to clear a path. He puffed furiously on his cigar. His brother watched, then signalled to Grumbles to open a window.

"Blast it!" Burton exploded. "Is it really true, Edward? Has this voice in your head been directing government policy for so long?"

"Yes, it has. Twenty years ago, Disraeli was more than willing to listen to El Yezdi. The spirit had, after all, helped him to defeat Palmerston by convincing Monckton Milnes to offer support. Disraeli's subsequent creation, at the spirit's behest, of the Department of Guided Science bore such startling fruit that it was almost impossible to doubt the spirit's benevolence. Then Ireland happened, and it made Abdu El Yezdi the government's most influential advisor."

"Ireland?"

"In 'forty-four, a man named Francis Galton presented to Isambard Kingdom Brunel a new science, which he called *Eugenics*. At its most basic, it concerns the breeding out of inherent weaknesses in plants, animals, and even in humans, and the propagation of their strengths. Galton proposed to test his theories by planting a crop of what he termed *Super Solanum tuberosum*—"

"Super potatoes?" Burton interrupted, incredulously.

"In essence, yes. He wanted to plant them in Ireland, the idea being that the plants would spread their hardiness to other crops while eliminating the fragilities that had plagued the Irish strains. Brunel put the plan before Disraeli, but Abdu El Yezdi immediately warned, via the countess, that the whole undertaking would be disastrous. He recommended that Eugenics in its entirety be made illegal. Disraeli, however, met Galton in person and allowed himself to be convinced to go ahead with the plan. It was catastrophic. The potatoes caused the entire crop, across the whole of Ireland, to fail. Widespread famine followed. Galton suffered a serious nervous breakdown and has been incarcerated in Bedlam ever since. Eugenics was made illegal, and from that point on Disraeli never again disregarded El Yezdi's advice."

Burton flicked his cigar stub into the fireplace and blew smoke from his nostrils.

"What am I to make of all this? The more I learn, the more . . . *wrong* everything feels. Everything, Edward! I'm expected to track down a man who doesn't exist!"

"But who once did," Edward noted.

The explorer stopped his pacing and regarded his brother. "When? Where? Who was he? What did he do? When and how did he die?"

The minister of mediumistic affairs shook his head. "I don't know."

"You don't know?" Burton snapped. "You've had him rattling about inside your bloody skull for four years and you've discovered nothing about him?"

"As I told you, it isn't a discussion. I feel his presence, my thoughts are manipulated into words, and I pass those words on to Disraeli. That's it."

"And his final words, aside from the warning about Brunel?"

"He gave assurance that the new unity of Italy is secure. He urged that our government establish bases in Lagos to stop the slave trade there. And—" Edward Burton examined his glass, which was now empty, and held it out to Grumbles for a refill. "And that was it." He looked at his fingernails and chewed his bottom lip. He glanced up at his brother. "There is something else, something he said a few months ago that might have some relevance to your investigation."

"It being?"

The crucial years are upon us. Soon the variations will begin to overlap.

"What does that signify?"

The minister shrugged.

Burton threw up his hands. "Riddles, obscurities, and voices in my brother's head!"

Edward answered, "You've already asked a very pertinent question—who was Abdu El Yezdi when he lived? The king selected you for this task because you have extraordinary powers of observation. I've never met another man who can learn so much about something merely by looking at it. Perhaps if you knew something of El Yezdi's appearance, you could begin to trace his origins."

Burton groaned. "Please don't suggest that I should have a table-tapper summon him out of ectoplasm."

"I wasn't going to. You met Rossetti today?"

"Yes."

"He has a friend who claims to have seen Abdu El Yezdi."

"In a vision?"

"In the flesh."

"But you insist that he's dead!"

"The man I refer to thinks not, but he has a reputation for eccentricity, so it may be nothing but waffle. Nevertheless, it's worth checking, don't you think?"

"Who is he?"

Edward took his refilled glass from the clockwork butler.

"A young poet named Algernon Charles Swinburne."

CHAPTER 6

THE ABDUCTED AND THE KILLED

"The four copper rods of Battersea Power Station extend two and a half miles into the crust of the Earth. They conduct geothermal heat into the station, where it is converted into electrical energy. With this, we thought we'd be able to illuminate London from North to South, West to East. As it happens, the electricity generated is barely enough to light even the station. The project has been a grand, extravagant, ridiculous failure. I must confess, though; I like the building. It makes a good, secure headquarters."
—From the memoirs of Isambard Kingdom Brunel.

After spending the remainder of the afternoon strolling in Hyde Park with Isabel, Burton returned home and, shortly before his evening meal, sent a letter by messenger to Rossetti. By the time he'd fished eating—Mrs. Angell insisted on serving ridiculously large portions because he was "infected with Africa and needed fattening up"—a reply had come. Algernon Swinburne was currently touring the continent and wouldn't be back until the middle of next month. Rossetti had, however, swung an invitation to Wallington Hall for Burton. This grand old manor, located in Northumberland and owned by Sir Walter Trevelyan, was a centre of artistic and intellectual endeavour due to Lady Pauline Trevelyan's fondness for creative types, whom she collected around herself and, in many cases, generously sponsored. One of her week-long gatherings was set to begin on the 24th of October, and, according to Rossetti, Burton was most welcome to attend.

Swinburne would also be there.

The explorer sent a whispered thank you to Rossetti via the Irish ragamuffin and wrote a letter to Lady Trevelyan.

Later, he wrapped himself in his *jubbah*, lolled in his armchair, and contemplated the events of the day.

The British Empire was built on foundations laid by a ghost. His friend Monckton Milnes had secretly played a major role in history; and his own brother, whose belief in the Afterlife Burton had considered an aberration caused by brain damage—and whose position as the minister of mediumistic affairs he'd regarded as a joke—was sitting slap bang in the middle of it all.

He closed his eyes and allowed his mind to wander, hoping that, from its depths, some conception would arise to inject sense into what felt like a demented fantasy.

He waited for insight.

He fell asleep.

When he awoke at six on Tuesday morning, he was still in the armchair and his muscles were stiff and sore. He grumbled when Mrs. Angell served him a too-big breakfast but ate it all and drank the whole pot of coffee before dressing and leaving the house in a hurry.

He met Sadhvi Raghavendra and Captain Lawless at William Stroyan's funeral where they all spoke movingly about their friend to the congregation. Burton struggled with his emotions as the coffin was lowered into the ground. He couldn't imagine anything more horrifying than being buried.

Afterwards, they took a cab to the RGS.

The next two days were going to be filled with geographical matters, starting with this morning's public presentation. They would, Burton hoped, be free of surprises. He'd accepted the king's commission but, right now, didn't want to think about it.

Isabel and Blanche took a break from their socialising to join the audience. Burton met them at the door and escorted them to seats at the front of the establishment's auditorium. He then retired to a back room with Raghavendra and Lawless where they reviewed their notes.

By ten o'clock, when they took to the stage, the place was packed with journalists.

Sir Roderick Murchison made a brief speech before Burton moved to the podium and gave a long, detailed, and entertaining account of the expedition, the highlight of which was his description of the moment when he, Raghavendra, Stroyan, and Herne had climbed a hill and looked down on the waterfalls from which the Nile sprang. This was greeted by such wild cheering that it was heard in Scotland Yard and echoed all the way down Whitehall.

When Burton finished, Lawless took centre stage and gave a well-received account of his flight over the eastern shore of the great lake. He was followed by Sister Raghavendra, who told of her experiences and was rewarded with a standing ovation and cries of, "Hurrah for the Lady of the Nile!"

Burton came forward to take questions. Inevitably, the journalists, ever hungry for sensation, were more interested in the murder of Stroyan than in the geography of Africa. Having learned from them that Oliphant was at present locked up in Bedlam, Burton said it was the best place for him, and concurred with the prevalent theory that Lord Elgin's private secretary had been driven mad by his opium addiction. Stroyan's death was, unfortunately, needless and meaningless.

The presentation finished at three o'clock, but the explorer spent the rest of the day with his fellow geographers going over maps and measurements, notes and specimens, and didn't leave the building until nightfall, by which time he was thoroughly exhausted and ready for bed.

There had been one significant moment.

Halfway through his speech, Burton had spotted in the audience the man who called himself Macallister Fogg. A minute later, when he looked again, that individual was gone.

Wednesday was also spent at the Society, this time presenting much more technical material to the senior committee—Murchison, Arthur Findley, Sir James Alexander, Colonel William Sykes, and Clement Markham. They spent considerable time matching Burton's maps to those made by David Livingstone of the topography to the west of the Lake Region. Central Africa was beginning to make sense. Light was finally shining onto the Dark Continent.

Two busy days, during which Burton threw himself wholeheartedly into his role as the returning hero; the man who solved the riddle of the Nile; the explorer who'd braved dangerous lands and triumphed. He relished it because he knew it was the end. No more risking his life. No further need to prove himself. One preposterous hurdle remained, then Damascus.

He rose on Thursday morning with his geographical duties behind him and a plan of action in place. Foregoing breakfast—much to his housekeeper's dismay—he left the house and plunged into the day's fog, which, though not terribly thick, more resembled soot-speckled smoke and was corrosive to the throat and eyes.

The little urchin was on the opposite side of the road with newspapers draped over his arm and piled at his feet. He was yelling, "Death of mediums! Read all about it! Twelve mediums die in a single day! Cause unknown!"

Burton crossed and purchased a *Daily Bugle*. "What's happened?"

"A great mystery, so it is, sir. Fortune tellers a-droppin' dead, an' there be no explanation for it at all."

The explorer muttered, "Odd!" He pushed the paper under his arm, bade the lad farewell, and walked on, swinging his cane.

At the corner of Montagu Place, a vendor of hot chestnuts hailed him. "Mornin', Cap'n! Glad to see you out o' the jungle!"

"Good morning to you, Mr. Grub," Burton called. "How's business?"

"Can't complain, an' if I did, it wouldn't make half a penny's worth o' difference! How you copin' with the 'orrible pong, sir?"

"Pong?"

Grub pointed downward. "Of all that muck what's swillin' below!"

Burton remembered that, beneath his feet, sewage was rising in the new tunnels, its flow constricted by sluice gates. Incredibly, after just one week, his nose had already adjusted.

"I appear to have adapted to it, Mr. Grub."

He continued into Gloucester Place, waved for a cab, and as its burly driver came into view, exclaimed, "You again!"

The hansom crunched to a standstill beside him and Montague Penniforth pushed goggles up from his eyes onto his forehead, looked down, removed a pipe from his mouth, and said, "Hallo hallo! Fancy that! It's Cap'n Burton 'imself, as I live an' bloomin' well breathe!"

"Are you following me, Mr. Penniforth?"

"Not at all, guv'nor, it's blessed chance, that's what it is; another blinkin' coincidence. Hop in. Where you hoff to?"

"The British Museum."

As he climbed into the cabin, Burton cast a searching and suspicious glance at the driver. Penniforth, though sitting, was plainly very tall and so solid he might have been carved from granite. Burton had once been described as having the physique of a bull, but even if he'd been in full health—which he certainly wasn't—he doubted he'd last long in a confrontation with this man.

Who are you, Mr. Penniforth? What are you up to?

The hansom rattled into Baker Street, navigated the traffic down to Oxford Street, then spent forty minutes traversing that hectic thoroughfare until it came to Great Russell Street. Burton passed the journey reading the newspaper. As the street Arab had proclaimed, over the course of the past week twelve mediums had been found dead, apparently from heart failure. All were discovered with a look of horror frozen on their faces, cause unknown.

The cab drew to a halt outside the famous museum.

A breeze had got up, and when Burton stepped down onto the pavement, he found the air had cleared somewhat but the temperature had risen.

He wiped sweat from his brow.

"Aye, guv'nor," Penniforth observed as the explorer counted out his coins. "It's goin' to be another scorcher. Been the 'ottest summer I can remember. Will I wait for you?"

Burton handed over payment and said, "No, that won't be necessary, thank you. But I have it in mind that we'll meet again, Mr. Penniforth." He flashed his eyes meaningfully at the cab driver. His gaze was met with a guileless grin.

"Could be so," Penniforth said. "London hain't Africa, is it? Crowded, aye, guv'nor, but small enough." He applied his teeth to one of the coins, winked, pocketed it, then took hold of his vehicle's tiller, shouted, "Gee-up, Daisy!" squeezed the accelerator lever, and went chugging away.

Burton watched him go.

He spent the rest of the morning and a good part of the afternoon sitting at a wide mahogany desk in the museum's circular reading room. He searched countless Arabian and Indian texts but found not a single reference to Abdu El Yezdi. Whomever the spirit had been when alive, he'd evidently made no imprint worth recording. Burton found that rather unlikely. Surely a ghost who managed to so affect the greatest Empire in history must, in life, have possessed enough influence to be noticed?

He was on the point of leaving when, acting on impulse, he returned to his seat and asked an attendant to bring him material relating to The Assassination.

It didn't tell him anything he didn't already know. On the 10th of June 1840, Queen Victoria and Prince Albert had been taking a carriage ride through Green Park. Eighteen-year-old Edward Oxford had stepped out of the crowd of onlookers, shot at the queen, and missed. An unknown individual, who bore some physical resemblance to the gunman, tackled him. In the struggle, the young lunatic's second flintlock had gone off. The queen was hit in the head and died instantly. The unidentified man pushed Oxford to the ground, acciden-tally killing him, then took to his heels. A police constable, William Trounce, pursued him into a thicket at the northwestern corner of the park, where he'd found him inexplicably dead, his neck broken. The man, known as "the Mystery Hero," had never been identified, his demise never explained.

Burton wondered whether the Mystery Hero and El Yezdi were one and the same. The spirit had started communicating soon after The Assassination, so may well have died around the same time. The theory had a nice symmetry to it, but unfortunately the dead man was plainly English, which made the Arabian name somewhat unlikely.

He left the museum and strolled along St. Martin's Lane to Brundleweed's. Frustratingly, the jeweller's was still closed. Burton wondered when he was going to see Isabel's engagement ring. He peered through the metal grille protecting the shop's window. All appeared in order inside—clean, with items on display and tools set out neatly on the workbenches.

He continued on to the RGS. By the time he arrived there, he was perspiring freely and cursing the absurd restrictions of so-called civilised clothing. Having worn nothing but a loose cotton shirt, trousers, and a straw hat throughout his time in Africa, his collar now felt like a noose, his jacket like a cage, and his topper like a crown of thorns.

He went into the club room, stood at the bar, guzzled a refreshing glass of soda water sans alcohol, chatted with a quietly spoken fellow member named Richard Spruce, then left the building, crossed the road, and entered Scotland Yard.

He approached J. D. Pepperwick's desk.

"Again?" the clerk exclaimed.

"Again," Burton confirmed. "Is Detective Inspector Slaughter available? I'd like to speak with him, if possible."

"Do you have an appointment, Captain Burton?"

"I have this." Burton produced a small card—issued to him by Spencer Walpole—upon which certain words were printed, a certain seal stamped, and a certain signature scrawled.

Pepperwick took it, read it, and gaped. "I say! You're an important fellow!" He hesitated a moment, then turned, reached up to a bracket of speaking tubes, lifted the lid of the one marked *D. I. Slaughter*, and pulled the tube free.

"There's a gentleman to see you, sir," he said into it. "Captain Richard—" He stopped, looked at the card again, and corrected himself. "I beg your pardon, Captain *Sir* Richard Burton." He put the tube to his ear, then a few seconds later spoke into it again. "Yes, that's right, sir, the Livingstone chap. He has, um, special authorisation." He listened, responded, "At once, sir," replaced the device, and smiled at Burton. "The inspector will see you straight away. Second floor, office number fourteen. The stairs are through there, sir." He pointed to the left.

Burton said, "Thank you," made for the indicated doors, and pushed through them. The wooden staircase beyond needed brushing and creaked as he climbed it. He reached the second floor and moved along a panelled corridor, passing closed rooms until he came to the one marked 14. He knocked.

"Come!" a voice called.

Burton entered and found himself in a high-ceilinged square room, well illuminated by a very tall window. Filing cabinets lined the wall to his left. A big portrait of Sir Robert Peel hung on the chimney-breast to the right. Two armchairs were arranged in front of the fireplace. There was a heavy desk beneath the window. Detective Inspector Slaughter, a slender and narrow-faced man with a tremendously wide, black, and bushy moustache and thick eyebrows, stepped out from behind it and strode forward, his hand outstretched.

"Sir Richard! Congratulations! The Nile! Splendid! Slaughter's the name, sir. Sidney Slaughter, at your service."

Burton, trying hard to ignore the line of white liquid that decorated the detective's moustache, handed him his authorisation, which Slaughter examined with interest before exclaiming, "Stone the crows! His Majesty's signature, hey?"

"Indeed so. I've been given special dispensation to look into the Babbage, Gooch, Brunel, and Nightingale abductions."

"Oh ho! Have you, now! Well, to be frank, I'm utterly foxed by the whole affair and would appreciate any help you can offer. Would you care for a cigar? I smoke Lord Dandy's. They don't measure up to Havanas, but they're quite acceptable."

"Thank you." Burton took the proffered smoke, accepted a light, puffed, and grunted approval.

"Drink?" he was asked.

"No, thank you."

"You don't mind if I do?" Slaughter waved the explorer into one of the armchairs before retrieving a large glass of milk from his desk. He seated himself opposite Burton and said, "I have to guzzle this blessed stuff by the gallon else my belly plays up something rotten. Acid imbalance, my doctor calls it. Stress of the job, I'd say. Who'd be a policeman in this rotten city, hey? The place is infested with villains. Anyway, the abductions."

"Yes. What can you tell me about them?"

Slaughter leaned back in his chair. "Not a great deal, unfortunately. There's been precious little progress, not for the want of trying. How much do you know?"

"Next to nothing."

Slaughter lifted his glass to his lips and drained it, adding to the snowy fringe on his moustache. "Well now, old Charles Babbage was the first. He vanished from his home on Devonshire Street, Portland Place, on the fifth of

August, 'fifty-seven. Initially, it was thought he'd made off of his own accord. He'd been under immense pressure to further refine the mechanical brains of his clockwork men and was almost certainly losing his mind."

"There's evidence of that?"

Slaughter nodded. "According to his wife, he was becoming increasingly and irrationally vexed by noise, especially that made by street musicians. He'd frequently fly into rages and harangue them from his bedroom window, and on three occasions he emptied his chamber pot over their heads."

"I've often been tempted to do the same," Burton noted.

"The point being that you didn't, hey? Also, Babbage was obsessive about his work, but apparently he was starting to apply that same mania to rather inconsequential matters. For example, he counted all the broken panes of glass in a factory, then wrote a pamphlet entitled—what was it now? Ah, yes— 'Table of the Relative Frequency of the Causes of Breakage of Plate Glass Windows.' You can see why, when he was reported missing, we were quick to conclude that he'd gone barmy and scarpered."

Burton drew thoughtfully on his cigar. "Is there anything to suggest otherwise?"

"Nothing substantial, but an elderly neighbour, Mr. Bartholomew Knock, claimed to have seen Babbage marched into a carriage by two men. I have his written statement, which you're welcome to examine, but I'm afraid it doesn't amount to much, and Knock himself died during last year's cholera epidemic."

The police detective jumped to his feet and crossed to the filing cabinets. He opened a drawer and withdrew a cardboard folder.

"Are you sure you won't take a drink, Sir Richard?"

"Perhaps a cup of tea, if it's not too much trouble."

"Splendid!"

Slaughter went to his desk, pulled out a speaking tube, whistled for the person at the other end, and said, "Have a pot of tea and a couple of cups sent up, would you? Plenty of milk, please. And give my appointments to Detective Inspector Spearing until further notice." He returned to his chair and handed the file to Burton. "I occasionally indulge in a cuppa. Plays merry havoc with the guts but it keeps the mind sharp, hey? So, where was I? Yes, Daniel Gooch, he was next to go. Like Babbage, he's one of the big DOGS. He was last seen on Friday the eighteenth of March, this year. A very odd disappearance, his. He was in charge of construction at Hydroham—you know? The undersea town off the Norfolk coast?"

"I've read a little about it."

"He was wearing an undersea suit—"

"A what?"

"It enables a man to work for prolonged periods on the seabed. Basically, a watertight all-in-one outfit, with air tanks attached. The wearer is completely covered, but for his face, which is visible through a glass plate in the front of the helmet. Gooch was sealed into such a suit, a chain was attached to it, and he was lowered into the water. An hour later, the suit was pulled back up to the boat. It was intact but empty. Gooch had vanished from inside it."

"How?"

"Exactly. How? And no one has seen him since." Slaughter frowned, his shaggy eyebrows shadowing his eyes. "Frustrating. Like all detectives, I'm allergic to mysteries. They put me on edge and make me bilious."

Burton opened the file and scanned the pages. Mostly, they contained information about the people who'd vanished rather than anything useful that might explain how or why they'd gone.

"Brunel," he said. "His case is also rather extraordinary."

"Indeed so."

There came a knock at the door and a short, white-haired woman shuffled in bearing a tray.

"Tea, sir," she said.

"Thank you, Gladys. Put it on my desk. I'll pour."

The woman did as directed and departed. Slaughter went over to the tray. "You'll want milk?"

"No. Just sugar. Four spoonfuls, please."

"Phew! You have a sweet tooth!"

"A taste I picked up in Arabia."

Slaughter served the explorer. Burton then watched with mild amusement as the detective combined just a few drops of tea with a great deal of milk and cautiously sipped the mixture.

"So," he asked the Yard man, "what exactly happened with Brunel at Penfold Private Sanatorium?"

Slaughter returned to his chair. "I spoke with a Sister Clements. She said he went there on Thursday evening and claimed he was going to suffer a stroke. The attack occurred early on Saturday morning. It was mild, but Clements was concerned it might be the precursor to something more serious. On Saturday night, at eleven o'clock, two men entered the hospital and attempted to abduct him. The nurses who tried to stop them were pretty ruthlessly rendered unconscious—"

"By what means?" Burton interrupted.

Slaughter raised a hand with the fingers held rigidly straight and made a chopping motion. "To the side of the neck."

"Not a common method for an Englishman," Burton mused.

"No. Am I right in thinking the technique is Oriental?"

"Yes. But the men weren't?"

"No, though their appearance was, by all accounts, rather grotesque. As you'll see in the report, it matches that of those infamous scoundrels and fugitives, Burke and Hare."

Burton looked back at the file and turned a page. "But they were stopped?"

"They were indeed. The question is, by whom? Certainly, no police constables were sent to the sanatorium, yet two turned up in the nick of time and a right old punch-up ensued."

"A fight?"

"Yes. And as skilled as the kidnappers might have been with their foreign chops and kicks, the two young men made good with honest bare knuckles, drove 'em off, and took Brunel away to safety. The only problem being that they didn't say where 'safety' was."

"And you're certain they weren't real policemen?"

"As I say, none was sent, none of our people reported the incident, and the men in question never identified themselves."

Burton lifted his cup, drank from it, and said, "What did they look like?"

"Young. Indian. Not unusual. We have a great many Indian men in the Force."

Sir Richard Francis Burton put his cup down, rattling it in the saucer. He looked at Slaughter and his mouth worked silently for a moment.

The detective frowned and said, "What is it? Indigestion? Tea too strong?"

Burton shook his head. "Would you—would you check to see whether there's a Constable Bhatti in the ranks?"

Slaughter arched one of his extravagant eyebrows, nodded, and went to his desk. He used a speaking tube to call the Personnel Office, made the enquiry, then returned and stood in front of Burton.

"No, Sir Richard, there isn't. Why do you ask?"

"Because late on Sunday night, I encountered a constable named Bhatti who knew where I lived, who appears to be in cahoots with a cab driver who's been following me, and whose nose was swollen, as if he'd been in a fight."

Slaughter looked surprised. "Our witness to the Nightingale kidnapping, which occurred on Sunday, said her abductors were Indian and one had a bloody nose."

The explorer got to his feet, moved to the middle of the room, and faced the other man. "Detective Inspector, there are very few people who are aware that I've been assigned to this case. My brother, the minister of mediumistic affairs, is one of them. Four years ago, two young Indians, Ravindra Johar and Mahakram Singh, rescued him from a severe beating. They accompanied him home and he was placed in the very same sanatorium from which Brunel has disappeared. They then vanished, never to be seen again."

"You think this Bhatti chap is one of them?"

"I do."

Slaughter put his hands to his stomach. "What's going on, Sir Richard?"

"Detective Inspector—I have no notion."

Burton left room 14 feeling more perplexed than when he'd entered it. If Bhatti had approached him after he'd started this investigation, it might make sense. But he'd done so the day before Burton was given the task, which suggested a foreknowledge that wasn't possible unless Edward had lied and was still in contact with his erstwhile saviours. If that was the case, what was he up to?

No. Edward was an arrogant and evasive bugger, but he was family, and as distant as they might be now, the bond they'd formed as children remained strong. Burton couldn't—wouldn't—believe that his younger sibling was doing anything untoward.

He walked along the corridor toward the stairs. As he passed the door marked 19, he heard it creak open behind him. Fingers suddenly closed over the back of his collar and a pistol was pushed between his shoulder blades. A familiar voice said, "Inside! Now!"

He was yanked into the room, whirled around, and given a violent push. The door slammed shut as he sprawled onto the floor. He rolled and looked up at Macallister Fogg.

"What the—?" he spluttered.

"Be quiet!" Fogg growled, brandishing his gun. "Tell me what you're doing here."

"Which?" Burton asked.

"What?"

"Should I be quiet or should I tell you?"

"Humph! Don't play the clever beggar with me. Answer the confounded question."

Burton raised a hand. "I'm going to retrieve something from inside my jacket. It isn't a weapon, so don't get jittery and start shooting."

"Slowly."

Reaching into his inner pocket, Burton pulled out his authorisation card and threw it to Fogg's feet. The man squatted, his aim remaining steady, retrieved it, and read it.

"By Jove!" he exclaimed. "The king!"

"Exactly," Burton said. "I'm getting to my feet now." He pushed himself up. "I suggest you put that pistol away and tell me your real name. I take it you're an actual police detective rather than a character from the penny bloods."

"I am. Detective Inspector William Trounce. I entered the lobby while you were talking to Pepperwick, saw you, waited for you to finish with Slaughter, and—" The man shrugged, pocketed his pistol, handed back the authorisation card, and gazed searchingly at Burton. His eyes were bright blue and, Burton thought, despite his aggression, good-natured in appearance.

The explorer said, "What's it all about? This habit you're developing of throwing me around is becoming quite irritating. Am I right in thinking you're the same Trounce who was at The Assassination?"

Trounce's eyes narrowed. "You saw me there?"

Burton gave a puff of annoyance. "I've already told you—I was at sea. So you were the constable who discovered the Mystery Hero?"

The detective's shoulders slumped. "There's plenty who say I killed him."

"Did you?"

"No. You did."

Burton laughed. He stopped abruptly when he saw that Trounce was serious. He took a deep breath and hissed it out between his teeth.

"All right, Detective Inspector. Why don't we, as the Americans say, lay our cards on the table? Tell me the whole story, and I give you my word of honour, I'll answer honestly any question you care to ask."

Trounce held the explorer's gaze for a second then gave a curt nod. "Not here," he said. "As far as The Assassination is concerned, I've received nothing but ridicule and suspicion inside this damned building. Will you take a pint with me?"

Burton really didn't feel like indulging, but he lifted a finger to his bruised eye and said, "You owe me one."

A few minutes later, the two men stepped out of Scotland Yard, turned left into Whitehall, and followed it along into Parliament Street. They didn't speak a word until reaching a corner, when Trounce said, "Here." They rounded it into Derby Street and, a few paces later, arrived at the Red Lion public house.

They ordered beer, settled into a relatively quiet corner, and remained wrapped in their own thoughts until the pot-boy delivered their flagons of ale.

Trounce drank half of his in a single swallow, then regarded Burton and said, "It's been the bane of my bloody life."

"The Assassination?"

"Yes."

"I was reading about it in the British Museum Library this morning."

"And I suppose you read that I chased the so-called Mystery Hero into the trees where I found him dead?"

"Isn't that what happened?"

"Not exactly. Certain parts of my report were suppressed."

"What parts?"

Trounce's left hand curled into a fist. He looked at it with a slight air of bemusement, as if it were acting under its own volition.

"I found the body, all right, but that's not all. Draped over a branch beside it, there was the strangest suit of clothes I've ever seen. A one-piece costume of shiny white material, like fish scales; a black helmet; and a pair of extraordinary boots, such as a stilt-walker might wear. Before I could take a proper look, I heard movement behind me, turned, and was immediately cracked in the head with a rifle butt. By the time I regained my wits, my attacker and the suit were gone."

"So someone else was there. No other witnesses?"

"A street-sweeper saw a man climbing over the park wall into Piccadilly. He was carrying a large bag, a jewel case, and a rifle. The description matched the man who knocked me senseless." Trounce took another swig of beer then angrily dragged his wrist across his mouth. "It was you."

Burton shook his head. "In your estimation, how old was this man?"

"Your age. No. A few years older."

"Older than my age now or my age in 1840?"

"Now. I know, I know, it couldn't have been you."

"Detective Inspector, I was nineteen and on a ship. My father, who bears no resemblance to me, was in Italy. My brother, who is three years my junior, was in India. All of this can be easily proved. The person you saw had no connection to me whatsoever."

Reluctantly, Trounce gave a guttural acknowledgement. He stared miserably into his almost empty flagon.

"I was very young—barely out of short trousers—and new to the Force. They said I panicked, reacted to events, and confused the Mystery Hero with the assassin. Some even suggested I killed him, invented the other man, and paid the witness to support my story." His upper lip curled into a snarl. "Utter bollocks! I saw what I saw!"

Burton observed unfeigned confusion in the detective's eyes. The man had assaulted him, lied to him, and accused him of a crime, yet the explorer felt himself taking an inexplicable liking to the fellow. There was something very down-to-earth about Trounce. He had passion and sincerity. He appeared trustworthy and reliable.

"Detective Inspector—" he said.

"Just Trounce. I'm off duty now."

"Very well. Mr. Trounce, I'm investigating Isambard Kingdom Brunel's disappearance—"

"Slaughter's case?"

"Yes. But there's more to it. I can't tell you what—it's a state secret. Suffice it to say, certain aspects of it appear to hark back to the time of The Assassination. For that reason, I'd rather like to meet this sweeper of yours. Is he still around?"

"Yes. He lives in Old Ford, a village to the northeast of London. Can you fly a rotorchair?"

"Yes."

"Come by the Yard tomorrow morning. I'll procure a machine for you and we'll pay him a visit."

"There's no need for you to—"

Trounce guzzled the last mouthful of beer and slammed his flagon onto the table.

"Whether you like it or not, Burton, I'm going to be behind you every step of the way. I need a solution to this accursed mystery!"

"Very well. In that case, I'll have the home secretary order Chief Commissioner Mayne to assign you to the investigation. Can you work with Slaughter?"

"Yes, he's a decent sort. You have the authority to do that?"

"I do. And if Mr. Walpole gives permission, I'll fill you in on the rest."

Trounce's eyes flashed with determination. "By Jove!" he growled. "If you can help me to clear my name, I'll be in your debt for life!"

He scowled thoughtfully.

"Is there something else?" Burton asked.

Trounce's nostrils flared slightly. "Just—just—Humph! A suggestion I made at the time. It was dismissed outright."

"Tell me."

"When I recovered my wits, I went down to the path and examined Victoria's corpse."

"And?"

"The manner in which her blood had sprayed across the carriage and ground—it looked to me like the bullet struck her in the back of her head, not the front."

Burton leaned back in his seat. "In other words, you don't think Edward Oxford killed her. You think the man with the rifle did."

"Yes. The man who looked like you."

CHAPTER 7

THE NUMBER

"The main thing is to make history, not to write it."
—OTTO VON BISMARCK

"Transform the world with Beauty!"

So declared William Morris, the leading light of the Arts and Crafts Movement; a man at the heart of Dante Gabriel Rossetti's Ministry of Arts and Culture. Without him, the machines produced by the Department of Guided Science would have been nothing but fume-breathing metal monstrosities.

"Form follows function!" the DOGS decreed.

"But form must not offend!" Morris had insisted.

So it was that the Empire's tools and various forms of transport were embellished with functionally irrelevant ornamentation; every curve and angle possessed decorative flair; every surface was engraved with patterns and cursive accents; every edge bore a pleasing trim.

Nowhere was this more apparent than in rotorchairs. From a distance, these flying vehicles resembled little more than a plush armchair affixed to a brass sled. A rigid umbrella-like hood curved over the seat; a small and complex engine was positioned at the rear; twin funnels projected backward; and six wedge-shaped wings rotated atop a tall drive-shaft above the entirety. There was something vaguely ridiculous about the contraptions until one moved closer and saw how all the disparate elements had been beautifully moulded into a unified whole by artists and designers.

Rotorchairs were elegant. They were exquisite.

Sir Richard Francis Burton hated them.

The damned things made him nervous. He had no idea how they managed to fly, couldn't fathom how they produced so much steam from so little water, and held a deep suspicion that they transcended every principle of physics. Knowing their design had been communicated to Isambard Kingdom Brunel from the Afterlife did little to reassure him.

He pushed the middle of the three control levers, following Detective Inspector Trounce's machine as it arced downward through the blue sky, leaving a curving trail of white vapour behind it. Burton pressed his heels into his foot-plate to slow his descent. His stomach squirmed as he rapidly lost altitude.

Below, the village of Old Ford rushed up toward him. It was a small and quaint little place, its houses and shops clumped together on one side of a shallow valley, with green fields facing it from the opposite side. Its High Street extended from a junction with a long country lane at the base of the hill and ran up to the top, where it bent to the right and went winding away to the next settlement. Trounce landed halfway along it. His machine hit the cobbles with a thump, a skid, and a shower of sparks. Burton brought his down more gingerly, clicked off the motor, waited for the wings to stop spinning, then clambered out and removed his goggles.

"It's like flying a bag of rocks," he grumbled. "I feared greater diligence might come at any moment."

"Diligence?" Trounce asked.

"From gravity, in the application of its own laws."

"Humph!"

They dragged their rotorchairs to the side of the road. All along the street, windows and doors were opening as Old Ford's tiny population came out to investigate the loud paradiddle that had rattled their cottages.

Nearby, outside a small dwelling, a white-haired man was leaning on a broom, watching the new arrivals.

Trounce hailed him. "Hallo, is that you, Old Carter? By Jove! You look just the same as you did nigh on twenty years ago!"

The man stepped forward and shook Trounce's hand. "By all that's holy! It's Constable Trounce, isn't it?"

"Detective Inspector nowadays."

"Is that so? Well, well. Good for you!" Old Carter looked the Scotland Yard man up and down. "Crikey, but haven't you filled out!"

Trounce neatened his moustache with a forefinger and looked at the man's broom. "Still sweeping?"

"Old habits die hard. I'm ending my working days as I began 'em, sir. I went from street-sweeper to rifleman in the King's Royal Rifle Corps, then retired from the Army and became a lamp-lighter, and next year I'll retire again to spend my twilight years keeping this here street spotless. So tell me, what brings you gentlemen to Old Ford?"

Trounce gestured toward Burton. "This is Sir Richard Francis Burton."

Burton said, "I'm pleased to meet you, Mr. Carter," and shook the man's hand.

"Not Mr. Carter. Old Carter. Everyone calls me Old Carter the Lamp-lighter. I suppose they—"

He stopped and his eyes went wide.

"Do you recognise Captain Burton?" Trounce asked. "His likeness is currently all over the newspapers."

Old Carter stuttered, "I—I—he—yes, but he looks like—"

Trounce took him by the elbow. "Could we step into your cottage, do you think?"

"Y-yes. Come. Come."

Pushing open the gate, Old Carter led them through his neatly trimmed and flowered front garden and into his one-room home. They sat on his sofa. He took a chair beside a table.

"This is about The Assassination, then?"

"It is," Trounce replied. "Is Captain Burton the man you saw?"

Old Carter looked searchingly at the explorer. "Spitting image. Except, perhaps, a few years younger."

Burton said, "Would you tell me about it—what you witnessed that day?"

"I will, but it ain't no different to what I told the constable—sorry, Detective Inspector—back at the time."

"Nevertheless."

Old Carter blinked, scratched his chin, and said, "It was about six o'clock. The junction 'tween Piccadilly and Park Lane was my patch. I was there every day from five in the morning until eleven at night. Hard work. There were no steam machines; it was all horses. For certain, the city was less crowded but there were twice as many nags as what you see now, and all of 'em doing their business in the streets. You didn't want to cross a road without a sweep to clear a path for you." He gave a slight smile. "Lucrative is the word! Aye, I earned a pretty penny keeping the muck off the toffs' boots! Anyway, come six o'clock, I'm leaning against the wall that separates the street from Green Park, when someone on the other side puts a rifle—half-wrapped in a coat—on top of it, and then a flat case, like what jewellers use. Now, I tell you, I already wanted to be a rifleman and I knew a thing or two about guns, and I swear I ain't never seen a weapon like that one afore or since. When I heard the man start climbing the wall, I was all set to ask him about it, but then I heard screams and whistles from the park and I realised something was up, so I quickly stepped away. The bloke came over the wall with a bag slung over his shoulder, took down the gun and the case, and was just about to make off when I says hello to him."

"Was he furtive or in a panic?" Burton asked.

"Not at all. More confused. Didn't seem to know up from down. Said he was having a bad day. 'Don't worry,' I tells him, 'you'll forget about it tomorrow.' Then——"

Old Carter stopped, frowned, pursed his lips, and continued, "So you know this Great Amnesia thing they talk about?"

Burton nodded.

"That's when it hit me. Right there, in the middle of the bloomin' road. Bang! I suddenly realised I could hardly remember a thing about what I'd been doing yesterday, or the day afore, or——not for the past three years, as it turned out." He shook his head in bafflement. "Anyway, our fellow made off, and that's the last I saw of him." He looked at Trounce. "Same as I told you at the time."

"Yes," Trounce confirmed. "The same."

"The rifle," Burton said. "Why did it so catch your attention?"

Old Carter looked at him searchingly and answered, "The barrel was, as I said, wrapped in a coat. Couldn't see much of it. But I saw the mechanism and it was much more like the weapons we have now than what we had back in 'forty. But smoother, tighter, more——um——*compact*, and there was a sort of tube fitted over the top of it."

"Tube?"

"Like, if you were taking aim, you'd have to look through it."

"Ah, I've seen something of the sort——it's called a telescopic sight——but I thought it a recent invention."

"It wasn't the only curious thing, Captain. There was the inscription on the stock, too. I saw it as clear as day. Remember every word of it. And all these years later, I still can't make head nor tail of it."

"Go on."

"Wait. I'll write it for you, just as I saw it."

He stood and crossed to a chest of drawers, retrieved a pencil and sheet of paper from it, used the furniture as a desk, and wrote something. He handed it to Burton. The explorer read:

Lee–Enfield MK III. Manufactured in Tabora, Africa, 1918.

Burton passed the note to Trounce, who said to the sweeper, "You didn't tell me this before."

Old Carter shrugged. "You didn't ask about the rifle, and to be honest, when we last spoke, I was shocked by the queen's murder and addled by my memory loss."

Burton plucked the paper back out of Trounce's hand and considered it.

"If Lee–Enfield is the manufacturer, I've never heard of them. Nor have I heard of Tabora, and I know Africa perhaps better than any man. It must be in the south. The only rifles made in the north are Arabian flintlocks. And this—is it an issue number?"

He pondered the words and numerals, then shrugged, folded the paper, and put it in his pocket.

"Old Carter," he said, with a wry smile. "You've added bewilderment to my perplexity, but I thank you for your time."

He stood, and the other two followed suit.

"It's queer," Old Carter said. "You so resemble the man I saw that I feel I know you."

Trounce added, "I feel the same."

"I wish I could offer an explanation," Burton said, "but during the week since my return from Africa, I've encountered more mystery than I experienced in over a year travelling those unexplored lands."

Old Carter walked his guests out, into the street, and to their rotorchairs.

"Sangappa," he said.

Burton turned to him. "What?"

"Polish. Made in India. I was just thinking—the seat of your flying machine would benefit from it. Best in the world for preserving leather."

"Could it preserve me while I'm flying the confounded thing?"

Old Carter grinned and regarded the contraption. "Aye, it's a blessed miracle such a lump can get off the ground. You'll not talk me into one, Captain. Not for all the tea in China."

"From what I've heard, tea from China might become a rare commodity. If someone offers it, I advise you not to refuse."

Burton and Trounce strapped goggles over their eyes, climbed into their vehicles, and started the engines. They gave Old Carter a wave, rose on cones of billowing steam, and soared into the sky.

Trounce set a southwesterly course and Burton followed. They were soon over the outlying districts of London, and the clear air became smudged with its smoke. Below them, factory chimneys stretched upward as if ambitious to spoil the purer, higher atmosphere.

A thought hit Burton like a punch to the head. Momentarily, he lost control of his machine.

"Bismillah!"

He grappled with the three flight rods as the rotorchair went spinning downward.

"Impossible!" he gasped, yanking at the leftmost rod until the contraption stabilised. He saw a patch of greenery below—the East London Graveyard—and made for it.

"Bloody impossible! It makes no damned sense at all!"

His vehicle angled into the ground, hit it hard, slithered over grass, slammed into the horizontal slab of a grave, and toppled onto its side. The wings broke off with a loud report and went bouncing away. Burton was catapulted out, thudded onto the grass, rolled, and came to rest on his back.

He lay still and looked up at the sky.

"How?" he whispered. "How?"

Staccato chopping cut through the air and Trounce's rotorchair came into view. The detective must have looked back and seen him go down.

Trounce landed, threw himself out of his vehicle, and raced over to Burton.

"What happened? Are you hurt?"

Burton looked up at him. "The numbers, Trounce! The bloody numbers!"

"Numbers?"

"On the rifle. One thousand, nine hundred and eighteen."

"So?"

"One thousand. Nine hundred. Ten. Eight."

Trounce threw his hands into the air. "Did you bang your head? Get up, man! What are you jabbering about?"

Burton didn't reply.

Oliphant. He had to see Oliphant.

"To secure Damascus for us, I have to first undertake a task for the government. It is a highly confidential matter—I cannot tell even you what it involves, Isabel—and I'm afraid I must ask you to refrain from visiting. I may not be able to see you again until the first of November."

Burton, Isabel, and Blanche were in the St. James Hotel tea room for

Saturday afternoon refreshments. They'd secured an isolated corner table, but, even so, Isabel's reaction—a quavering cry of, "Seven weeks, Dick?"—drew disapproving stares and a *tut* or two from the other patrons. Heedlessly, she continued, "After being parted for so long, we must be separated again? This is unendurable!"

He placed his hand over hers. "Lower your voice. The king himself has promised the consulship on this one condition. I'm confident I can complete the assignment by November, if not before. We've waited for so long, we can manage another few weeks, can't we?"

"But what is the nature of this business? Why must it prevent me from visiting?"

Burton hesitated. He wasn't certain why he was warning his fiancée away. Perhaps the suspicion that Montague Penniforth was keeping an eye on him? Or the feeling that, somehow, inexplicably, he was at the centre of the curious events that had occurred since his return?

He gave her hand a gentle squeeze.

"I once told you how I was employed by Sir Charles Napier in India—"

Blanche interrupted with a gasp and exclaimed, "How exciting! You're a secret agent again, Richard!"

"Well, I wouldn't go as far as to say—"

"No!" Isabel snapped. "I'll not have that! Last time, it ruined your reputation. You'll not risk everything you've achieved since."

Burton shook his head placatingly. "This is not at all the same sort of thing."

"Then what?"

Blanche gave a huff of disapproval. "Really, sister! If Richard has been ordered to keep his lips sealed by the king himself then you have no right to subject him to an inquisition."

"I have every right! I'm to be his wife!"

Burton's eyes hardened. "In all truthfulness," he said, "if I tell you more, I will be committing treason. Where then my reputation?"

A tear trickled down Isabel's cheek. She pulled a handkerchief from her sleeve, covered her eyes, and emitted a quiet sob.

"Please," Burton said. "Don't take on so. Consider that, with this one thing, Damascus is assured, and once we have that, we shall never be parted again."

Blanche added, "Remember how much we have to organise, Isabel. Why, we'll be so occupied, the days will fly by."

Burton gave her a small nod of gratitude.

Isabel dried her face. With downcast eyes, she said, in a hoarse whisper, "We should go up to our room now, Blanche. We have to pack our things."

"You're leaving in the morning?" Burton asked.

"Yes."

He stood and moved her chair out of the way as she rose and arranged her crinolines.

She raised her watery eyes to his.

"This commission you've been given—is there any danger associated with it?"

"Not as far as I can see," he answered. "It's a complex matter and I don't currently know how I should proceed with it, but one way or the other I'll get the thing done, and will do so as quickly as possible." He leaned forward and pecked her cheek. "We are nearly there, darling."

She smiled, though the tears were still welling. "I have waited, Dick, and I shall continue to wait. I have faith in God that He will make things right."

"Have faith in God, by all means, but have faith in me, too."

"I do."

With that, the Arundell sisters took their leave of him, carefully steered their wide skirts past the tables, and disappeared into the hotel. He watched them go and his heart sank. It dawned on him that everything he'd intended had skewed off-course and plunged into an impenetrable fog.

"O, that a man might know," he muttered, "the end of this day's business ere it come!"

It took until Monday to get the authorization for entry into Bedlam. Saturday and Sunday paralysed him with interminable emptiness. He found himself unable to work, research, or do anything else useful.

"Rest!" Mrs. Angell insisted. "Eat! Get some colour back into your cheeks. I don't know what you're up to, but you're driving yourself too hard, that much is plain to see."

He didn't rest. He paced. One thousand, nine hundred, ten, and eight were etched into the front of his mind. He couldn't stop fretting over them. He scribbled them down again and again.

One thousand. Nine hundred. Ten. Eight.

One thousand, nine hundred, and eighteen.

They connected Stroyan's murder with The Assassination. They cut a swathe through time and unfathomable events to tie Queen Victoria's death, the recognition of the Great Amnesia, the advent of Abdu El Yezdi, and the beginning of the New Renaissance to what he himself had witnessed on the *Orpheus*; him, Burton, who two people claimed—impossibly!—to have seen on that terrible day in 1840.

But how were the numbers connected—if they were at all—to the abductions? Was Burton looking at a jumble of disparate events or was there a pattern in there somewhere?

He didn't know—and if there was one thing he despised, it was not knowing.

The governmental papers arrived in the week's first post. Sir Richard Francis Burton was now, officially, a medical inspector named Gilbert Cribbins, with a specialism in institutions for the insane.

He disguised himself with a brown wig, false beard, and cosmetic paint to conceal his facial scar, and by means of two omnibuses and a hansom cab travelled southeastward through the city, crossing Waterloo Bridge into Southwark. The district was crowded with tanneries, and in the hot weather the reek was so intense that it was all he could do to keep his breakfast down. By the time he arrived at Bethlem Royal Hospital, his eyes were stinging and his nose felt clogged.

He knocked on the front gate—an imposing edifice of solid wood into which a smaller door was set—and jumped slightly when a letterbox-sized hatch slid open with a bang and a voice snapped, "What?"

"Inspection." He held his papers up to the small slot. "Government Medical Board. Let me in."

"Pass that to me."

Burton folded the papers in half and pushed them through to the guard. He waited, heard a muted expletive, then bolts scraped and clunked and the door swung a little way open.

"Step in. Be quick about it."

Burton passed into the grounds of the asylum. He faced the guard. "My good man, as one of His Majesty's medical inspectors, I require a little more respect, if you please."

The guard touched the peak of his cap. "Sorry, sir. Just bein' thorough. The escape has us all on edge."

"Escape?"

"That's why you've come, isn't it?"

Burton lied. "Of course it is."

"If you'll follow me, there's a horse and trap by the guardhouse. I'll take you to the warden."

The man guided Burton to a nearby outbuilding, gave him a hand up into a small carriage, then took the driver's seat and set the vehicle moving. The hospital grounds were extensive and well tended, and as they passed along a winding gravel path toward the imposing asylum, Burton mused that, under normal circumstances, the wide lawns would probably be dotted with patients. Now, they were empty, the inmates confined to their cells.

The trap ground to a halt in front of the entrance steps and Burton alighted. Without a word, the guard put his switch to the horse and set off back the way he'd come.

The explorer checked that his beard was properly affixed, then climbed the steps, entered through the doors, and stopped a male attendant who was hurrying through the vestibule. The man stared at him in surprise and said, "I'm sorry, sir, you should have been turned away at the gate. We aren't allowing visitors today."

"I'm not a visitor. I'm a medical inspector. Cribbins. And you?"

"Nurse Bracegirdle. How can I help you, Mr. Cribbins?"

"By fetching the warden. At once, please."

The attendant dithered. "Um. Um. Um. Er. Yes, of course. Would you, um, wait here?"

He raced away, and, as he went, whispered to himself a little too loudly, "Oh no! Today of all days!"

Burton was left alone. He looked around at the walls and saw stained paintwork, cracked plaster, and cobwebby corners. Rat droppings dotted the edges of the floor. The pervasive odour of unwashed bodies hung in the air.

Three minutes passed, then a door burst open and a pale-faced, anxious-looking man hurried in. He had closely cropped grey hair, a small clipped moustache, and very widely set brown eyes. He strode over and shook Burton's hand. "I'm Doctor Henry Monroe, the director of this establishment."

"Cribbins," Burton responded.

A nervous tic suddenly distorted Monroe's mouth and pulled his head down to the right. He grunted, "Ugh!" then said, "I'm surprised to see you here, sir. My report into Mr. Galton's escape was posted less than four hours ago."

"Galton, you say?" Burton exclaimed. "Francis Galton? The scientist?"

Monroe stammered, "Y-you're not here about the—the—ugh!—escape?"

"I'm here to interview one of your patients, Laurence Oliphant."

"Con—concerning his part in the affair?"

Burton held up a hand. "One moment. What? You're telling me that Oliphant helped Galton to break out?"

Monroe licked his lips nervously. A nurse entered the foyer. As she passed, the doctor glanced at her and, in a low voice, said, "Mr.—Mr.—ugh!—Cribbins, we should talk in my—my office."

"Very well."

Monroe ushered Burton out of the lobby, along a corridor, and into a somewhat shabby and disorganised room. He strode to a desk and, as if taking refuge, flung himself into the chair behind it. Immediately, he gained a little composure, and indicating the seat opposite said, "Please, sit. I'll explain to you the events of last night."

Burton sat.

"Oliphant!" the doctor said with mock cheerfulness. "An interesting patient. Morbidly excitable with periods of gloom. He has moments of such lucidity that one might consider him as sane as you or—ugh!—I. Certainly, his mind is organised. He keeps a little notebook, the pages of which he fills with masses of figures—numbers—added up in batches, then the totals added again, as though he were focusing some account, as an auditor would say. Then, without any obvious trigger, he's suddenly completely delusional. Rats, Mr. Cribbins."

"Rats?" Burton repeated.

"Rats. Periodically, in the week and a half that he's been here, Oliphant has been overcome by an obsessive desire to hunt and capture them. I have indulged him to see what would come of it. Unfortunately, the vermin infest every floor of this building, so he's not been starved of opportunity. You must understand that in the treatment of a lunatic one must first seek to understand the nature of the—ugh!—deep problem—ugh!—in the mind. Whatever pre-occupation dominates gives a clue to it, and more often than not, it is some—ugh!—trauma experienced in the past. Discover what, and one might perhaps help the patient to overcome the damage done to them."

Burton considered this for a moment. "You propose that madness springs from an inability to cope with a mental shock?"

"In cases of monomania, yes. There are, of course, a great many instances where the cause can be traced to a physical imbalance, but with Mr. Oliphant—he was an opium addict, you know?"

"Yes, I'm aware of that."

"Well then, I suspect he was so petrified by a nightmarish vision induced by the drug that he lost his—ugh!—mind in order to escape it. It is my supposition that the hallucination involved rats, and he is now trying to recreate it. You see, there is method in his madness."

"To what end, Doctor?"

"If he manages, independently, to reproduce his hallucination, he will achieve mastery over it. Or, to put it another way, if he can knowingly reconstruct what he experienced, he can also knowingly destroy it, thus breaking the shackles of terror that—ugh!—bind him."

Burton brushed dust from his trouser leg, nodded slowly, and said, "Very well, your theory sounds eminently plausible, but how does this relate to Galton's escape?"

Monroe's face spasmed again and his right arm jerked outward. He pulled the errant limb back to his side and held it there with his left hand.

"About fifteen years ago, Galton suffered a severe nervous breakdown and was brought here to recover. He never did. Instead, he developed an *idée fixe* concerning the transmutability of the flesh."

"Meaning what?"

"Meaning he believes animals can be artificially raised to a human standard of intelligence, and that humans can, through scientific means, be made into something akin to—ugh!—gods."

"Again—this concerns Oliphant how?"

"I'm coming to that, Mr. Cribbins. You see, Oliphant's delusion involves the conviction that a god of some sort is seeking incarnation in the flesh."

Burton recalled what Monckton Milnes had told him about the magic squares.

Monroe continued, "Since Galton's misconception concerning artificially constructed gods is—ugh!—thematically similar, I thought it might be enlightening to put the two men together. I hoped they would either cancel out each other's delusions or hasten each other toward a conclusion to their—ugh!—ugh!—demented fantasies."

"And what happened?"

"During their fourth encounter, last night, Oliphant flew into a rage and attacked his attendants. While they were distracted, Galton broke into a storage room and climbed out through its window."

Burton opened his mouth to speak but was stopped by a gesture from Monroe. "No, Mr. Cribbins, the window was not left open by accident. We are—ugh!—meticulous about security here. The fact is—it was forced from the outside."

Burton leaned forward in his seat. "By whom, Doctor?"

Monroe shrugged. "I don't know, but a ladder was left behind on this side of the perimeter wall, which means not only that Galton had help to get away, but also that whoever assisted him knew Oliphant would provide a diversion at that—ugh!—particular moment. I can't for the life of me think how such a thing could be arranged." He hesitated then added, "Although suspicion must naturally fall on Mr. Darwin."

"Darwin?"

"Charles Darwin. The *Beagle* fellow."

"What has he to do with it?"

"He and Galton are half-cousins. As one of our long-term and most docile patients, Galton was allowed to send and receive letters. Darwin is the only person he has ever corresponded with, and he did so on a regular basis. It's our policy here to monitor all incoming and outgoing post. The communication between the two men appeared purely—ugh!—scientific in nature. Darwin is apparently on the brink of publishing a theory that might alter the way we think about—ugh!—creation itself. It bears some relation to Galton's preoccupation, and I was hoping that I might gain a better understanding of my patient's fixations by reading their missives. Unfortunately, all I could glean from them is that both men are engrossed in disturbingly godless matters which make little—ugh!—sense to me. If any escape plans were discussed between them, then it was done in code and I didn't detect it."

"I should like to see those letters."

"I'm afraid Galton took them with him."

Pushing his chair back, Burton stood. "Then take me outside. Show me the window."

"Is that necessary?"

"It is."

Reluctantly, Monroe got to his feet and led Burton from the office, down the corridor, through the vestibule, and out of the building. They turned left and followed the edge of a long flower bed that skirted the foot of the hospital's front wall.

"Here." Monroe pointed to a small window set five feet from the ground.

Burton turned away from it and examined the terrain. He saw six trees huddled together nearby, providing shadows and cover; a long, squarely trimmed hedge beyond them, bordering a large vegetable garden; and more trees between that and the high wall, which they partially concealed.

"A good escape route," he muttered. "Lots of concealment."

Returning his attention to the window, he saw gouges in its frame, suggesting the application of a crowbar. He squatted and scrutinised the flower bed.

"Look at these indentations in the soil, Doctor."

"Footprints, Mr. Cribbins?"

"Yes. Peculiar ones, at that. See how square the toes are, and how small and high the heels?"

"High?"

"Revealed by the indentation. This style has been out of fashion for half a century. It's the variety of footwear that usually has a large buckle on top. I haven't seen anyone shod in such a manner since my grandfather."

"Are you suggesting that Galton's accomplice was an—ugh!—old man, sir?"

"Two men broke the window, Doctor. And it doesn't necessarily follow that because their footwear was old, so were they." Burton straightened. "Two sets of prints. Both men wore the same style of footwear. One had long, narrow feet, the other, short, wide ones. The latter individual was the heavier of the pair."

Damien Burke and Gregory Hare.

There was no doubt about it. Burton had seen plenty of newspaper illustrations of the notorious duo. Their famously old-fashioned attire, which included buckled shoes, had been the delight of *Punch* cartoonists. And Hare was shorter but far bulkier than Burke.

So, having failed to kidnap Isambard Kingdom Brunel, they'd got Francis Galton.

Why?

"I think it's high time I saw Oliphant, Doctor."

Monroe spasmed, nodded, and accompanied the explorer back the way they'd come. When they reached the lobby, he rang a bell and waited until two attendants appeared. Both were wearing stained leather aprons. Ordering them to follow, he then ushered Burton up a flight of stairs and toward the west wing of the asylum. They passed along cell-lined hallways and were assailed by shouts and screams, incoherent babbling, pleading, and curses. The odour of human sweat and excrement was worse even than the foulest-smelling of the many swamps Burton had struggled through in Africa.

More passageways, more staircases, until on the fourth floor, a door blocked their path. One of the attendants produced a bunch of keys and set about opening it.

"Ugh!" Monroe jerked. "You'll find fewer patients in this next area, but the ones we keep here are among the most seriously—ugh!—deranged and can be exceedingly violent. They'll watch our every move through the slots in their cell doors. Please refrain from making eye contact with them."

The portal's hinges squealed as the attendant pushed it open. They passed through into yet another filthy corridor. A nurse greeted them.

"This is Sister Camberwick," the doctor said. "She oversees this section. Sister, this is Inspector Cribbins of the Government Medical Board. He wishes to interview Mr. Oliphant. Is the patient quiet?"

After bobbing to Burton, the nurse replied, "He is, Doctor."

"Good. Good. Go about your duties. I'll accompany Mr. Cribbins."

She gave another bob and stood to one side to let them pass. The party moved a little farther on until it came to a cell door marked with the number 466.

Monroe addressed the two attendants. "Stay here. Come at once if I call for you." To Burton, he said, "I'll allow you as much time as you require providing he doesn't become—ugh!—agitated. If he does, I'll have to terminate the interview immediately."

"I understand."

Monroe held out his hand and one of the attendants placed his keys into it. After selecting the appropriate one, the warden put his mouth to the slot in the door and said, "Mr. Oliphant. I am Doctor Monroe. I have with me a visitor named Mr. Cribbins. We would like to come in and speak with you. Have you any objection?"

Burton heard Oliphant's familiar voice answer, "None at all, sir. Please enter freely—and of your own free will."

Monroe looked at Burton, raised an eyebrow, and whispered, "You note the inappropriate and oddly worded formality? No matter how normal a patient's behaviour may appear, such incongruous language is always a sure sign of—ugh!—defective thinking."

He turned the key in the lock and pulled the door open, revealing Laurence Oliphant, sitting on a bunk, smiling broadly, his fringe of hair and bushy beard dishevelled, his arms bound by a strait waistcoat.

"Come in, Doctor! Come in, Mr. Cribbins! I am delighted to have guests! Forgive me if I do not shake your hands. I am somewhat inconvenienced, as you'll bear witness."

They entered the cell and Monroe closed the door behind them. "I'm pleased to see that you've calmed down, Mr. Oliphant. Continue in this manner and the jacket will be removed, I assure you."

"Excellent! I'm eager to get back to work." Oliphant looked toward the window, and Burton, following his gaze, saw that what from the corner of his eye he'd presumed to be a hanging gown wasn't a gown at all, but a great mass of dead rats, woven together by their tails—as garlic is platted by its stalks—and strung from the window bars. Unable to stop himself, he cried out, "Good God!"

Oliphant cackled. "He he he! Flesh, you see, Mr. Cribbins. Dead flesh, all ready to be re-formed and given new life. It doesn't matter that it's rat flesh. Any will do. Flesh is flesh. Merely a vehicle."

"A vehicle for what?" Burton asked.

"For my master!" Oliphant suddenly checked himself. His eyes slid slyly from side to side then fixed on Burton, and he hissed, "He has the royal charter now. Drum, drum, drum! Come, come! Drum, drum, drum! They will answer the call, and then nothing will stop him. Out of Africa! Out of Africa! He'll repair this broken world of ours, and I shall be rewarded with an entire history of my very own! Ha! What shall I make of you, Mr. Cribbins, Doctor Monroe?—Paupers? Kings? Criminals? Or perhaps madmen? Ha ha ha!"

"Calm yourself, please," Monroe said. "You don't want to get—ugh!—overexcited again, do you?"

His patient's giggling stopped abruptly. Oliphant shook his head, grinned, and shrugged. "No need. Now I can wait. Now I can wait. Drum, drum, drum! Drum, drum, drum!"

The doctor turned to Burton. "Mr. Cribbins, have you any particular questions you'd like to ask the patient?"

"Just one," Burton replied. "Mr. Oliphant, the numbers one thousand, nine hundred, ten, and eight—what do they signify?"

Oliphant gave a cry of surprise, then threw back his head and let loose a peal of laughter that rapidly transformed into a scream of fury.

"What do you know?" he yelled. "Are you a spy? Yes! Yes! A spy! I'll kill you! I'll bloody kill you, you bastard spy!"

He sprang from the bed and lunged at Burton, his mouth wide and teeth exposed. The explorer dodged, was knocked back against the wall, and felt the maniac's jaws clench down on his collar.

"Attendants! Attendants!" Monroe bellowed.

Burton struggled but Oliphant seemed ten times stronger than a sane man.

"Get him away from me! He's trying to bite my throat!"

The attendants crashed in and dragged Oliphant off.

"The end!" he screamed. "The numbers add up to the end of the British Empire! Ha ha ha! The end! The end! The end!"

CHAPTER 8

CHARLES DARWIN

NOTICE

Norwood Road, Herne Hill, and Denmark Hill will be closed to through traffic until further notice. This is to facilitate the construction of Mr. Bazalgette's sewer tunnel along the course of the subterranean River Effra.
The Department of Guided Science apologises
for any inconvenience caused.
The Department of Guided Science
Making a Healthier, Cleaner, Better London.

The interview with Oliphant had been short but unsettling, and throughout the following night Burton was repeatedly shocked awake by nightmares in which he saw the lunatic's face looming out of the darkness, feline eyes blazing and muzzle-like jaws extended, displaying elongated, blood-dripping canines.

By seven in the morning he'd given up on further sleep, so washed, dressed, and went downstairs. He stepped out into the street and located the newspaper boy a little way down Montagu Place. Passing him a few coins, he said, "I need the address of a man named Charles Darwin. He's a member of the Royal Geographical Society, so you'll find it in the register there."

"Straight away, sir," the lad said, and immediately scampered off. Burton watched him approach another urchin at the corner of Seymour Place and whisper in his ear. The second youngster raced away and the Irish boy turned, grinned, and gave Burton the thumbs-up.

The explorer returned to his study. Oliphant lingered in his thoughts and made him sullen and uncommunicative during breakfast—Mrs. Angell had witnessed such moods before and served him silently and efficiently before making a rapid withdrawal—and afterward he spent the morning with a foil in his hand, practising his fencing technique against an imaginary opponent.

He forced his mind into silence, finally driving Lord Elgin's secretary out of it, and focused instead on the physical exertion, gauging carefully his own strength and weakness, and discovering, to his satisfaction, that no remnant of fever remained; he was close to his normal level of health and fitness.

At half-past eleven, he was flannelling the sweat from his face and neck when the doorbell jangled. He heard his housekeeper answer it then thump up the stairs.

"Yes?" he called in response to her knock.

She looked in. "There's an unwashed guttersnipe on our doorstep. He says he has a message for you."

"Send him up, please."

"Up the stairs?"

"I don't expect him to scale the outer wall, Mrs. Angell."

"But his boots are filthy."

Burton gave his housekeeper what she referred to as *the look*. She heaved a sigh and disappeared from sight. Moments later, a quiet tapping sounded on the door.

"Come in."

The Whisperer entered, and his eyes widened as he saw the various weapons on the wall and the foil in Burton's hand.

"You have it?" the explorer asked.

"That I do, sir. Mr. Darwin lives at Down House, on the Luxted Road, quarter of a mile south of Downe Village in Kent."

"What's your name, lad?"

"Abraham, sir. Abraham Stoker. Most folks call me Bram."

"Have you a place to call home?"

"I calls the streets me home, sir."

"Where do you sleep?"

"Wherever I can."

"Hmm! Well, here's another sixpence for you, Master Bram."

Burton took a coin from a pot on one of his workbenches and flipped it to the boy, who caught it smartly and gave a salute.

"Thank you, sir. Much obliged! Is there anything else I can be a-doin' for ye?"

"Not for the moment, thank you."

"Right you are, sir. You know where to find me." Bram saluted again and departed. Half a minute later, Burton heard Mrs. Angell cry out, "Not there! Not there! I've just brushed it!"

The street door banged. Burton resumed his training. Five minutes passed. The doorbell clanged again. Mrs. Angell reappeared at the study door, this time with a broom in her hand.

"Mr. Monckton Milnes is here. Perhaps you'd consider moving your study to the ground floor? It would save me a lot of running up and down, not to mention sweeping. I'm not as young as I used to be, you know."

Burton bellowed, "Come on up, old chap!"

Mrs. Angell grumbled, "Well! Bless me! I could have informed him in a rather more civil manner," and withdrew.

Monckton Milnes entered and announced, "Just dropping by to tell you I'm fleeing the city, old boy. The growing stink is too much for me. Gad! Have you heard? The sewage is already rising into the streets around Saint Pancras. The sooner they release the flow, the better. Anyway, I'm off to Fryston tomorrow. Fresh Yorkshire air. I've bagged a berth on the jolly old *Orpheus*. Phew! What have you been up to?"

"Practising," Burton replied. He returned his foil to its bracket over the fireplace. "Getting myself back into shape. Tipple?"

"No, thank you." Monckton Milnes dropped into an armchair. "I'm swearing off the stuff for a few days. Rossetti called on me. So, the truth is out."

"It is." Burton sat opposite him. "All these years we've been friends, and you were hiding that!"

"Not just from you. I haven't been allowed to discuss it with anyone beyond Disraeli's inner circle. One must demonstrate an ability to keep the lips firmly buttoned if one is to be trusted with secrets."

"Declares the most incorrigible gossip in town."

"It is to that reputation, my dear fellow, that I owe my success. Through the ceaseless distribution of inconsequential tittle-tattle, I have earned a reputation as a man who cannot keep a confidence, thus not a single person suspects that, in fact, I harbour some of the biggest secrets in the Empire."

"So you know the rest, I suppose?"

"The disappearances? Burke and Hare? You as king's agent? Yes, Richard. What I wasn't already aware of, I was briefed on last week. Now I understand why Florence didn't return to the theatre. My manly pride is restored but, frankly, I'd gladly give it up to know what has become of her. I'm worried sick. Have you made any progress?"

Burton regarded his friend silently then said, "Before I answer that, tell me two things. First, why me?"

Monckton Milnes gave a slight shrug. "To be the king's agent? Isn't it obvious? You have greater skills in your little finger than a dozen men could hope to accrue in a lifetime. Your intellect is ferocious; you are as strong as an ox; you can fight like a demon; and you're related to, and acquainted with, some of the principal *dramatis personæ*."

"And the decision was made the weekend after my return?"

"Yes, in an emergency meeting on the Sunday, in response to Isambard Kingdom Brunel's abduction. You and I were at the Cannibal Club at the time."

"Who suggested me for the role?"

"I understand your brother did."

"I suspected as much. Without his involvement, the coincidences are too remarkable to be credible."

"What coincidences?"

"My investigation has led again and again to The Assassination, and according to two people, I was there—except, of course, I wasn't. One of those witnesses says I had with me a rifle upon which the number one thousand, nine hundred, and eighteen was engraved. As you already know, one thousand, nine hundred, ten, and eight were integral to Oliphant's ritual."

Monckton Milnes's eyebrows rose. "By Gad! That's damned peculiar. What does it mean?"

"It means that Edward was already aware that I am somehow, unknowingly, involved in the events I'm investigating."

Burton's friend nodded as if this was a statement of the obvious. "He must have received information to that effect from Abdu El Yezdi, before the latter's sudden silence. Can you continue to doubt the existence of spirit advisors, Richard?"

Burton pressed his hands together and tapped them against his chin. "Let us just say that I now regard the subject as an avenue worth exploring. Which brings me to my second question. When Countess Sabina first approached you, back in 1840, why did you give her any credence?"

"You and I have on a couple of occasions discussed the pornographic poem *The Betuliad*."

Burton nodded. "A celebration of flagellation, author unknown. What of it?"

"The countess knew that it also exists under an alternate title—*The Rodiad*. She was also aware of the author's identity."

"Indeed! Who wrote it?"

"I did."

Burton laughed. "You deceptive hound!"

"I was just having a little fun at your and everyone else's expense. No one—absolutely no one—knew it was my work. Yet she did, and I couldn't ignore or discount her."

"Then I rescind my earlier refusal," Burton said. "I would like to meet with her. Might she be willing to see me?"

"I should think so. She's a virtual recluse these days but she still comes to me when I request it, and I daresay she'll call on you if I ask her to."

"Thank you. As to whether I've made any progress or not, I can't judge it, but there have certainly been developments, the main being that, with Oliphant's help, Burke and Hare have broken Francis Galton out of Bedlam."

"Good God! They have Galton, of all people? That man's mastery of Eugenics poses a terrible danger. Are you certain it was Burke and Hare?"

"I'm sure of it."

"What the hell are they playing at, I wonder?"

"I intend to find out."

Monckton Milnes, his face creasing with worry, massaged his forehead.

Burton said, "I'm concerned you might also be at risk. I imagine they have a bone to pick with you."

"Probably not. I strongly doubt that Palmerston's thugs are aware of the role I played in their master's fall from grace. I was very much behind the scenes."

"Good," Burton responded. "Nevertheless, I'm glad you're off to Fryston. If Burke and Hare are currently in London, then perhaps it's best that you're not."

Monckton Milnes jumped to his feet. "You're right, and I'm running late. Sorry to be unsociable but I really must dash. Bags to pack and whatnot. I understand you'll be at Wallington Hall next month. I'll see you there."

Burton rose. "Ah! You're attending, too, then?"

"I wouldn't miss it. Rossetti showed me some of young Swinburne's poetry—it's quite extraordinary. I've never read anything like it. A prodigious talent! He's going to be an absolute sensation and I'm eager to meet him. I wrote to Lady Trevelyan. She doesn't entirely approve of me—I'm rather too raffish, apparently. Nevertheless, I managed to wangle an invite. A few days there, then perhaps we can travel together to New Wardour Castle, yes?"

"Certainly."

They strode across the room. The explorer opened the door and followed his friend through.

"Incidentally," Burton said as they descended the stairs, "what of your French acquaintance?"

"No word yet—the post isn't that fast—but I'll contact you the moment he replies."

"Very well. Of course, I'll do likewise if I discover anything about Nurse Nightingale."

Monckton Milnes took his topper from the hallway stand.

Just as Burton was reaching to open the street door, a tremendous thumping rattled it on its hinges.

"Great heavens!" Monckton Milnes exclaimed. "Are we under attack?"

"It appears so." Burton turned the handle and opened the door. Detective Inspector Trounce, who was just commencing his next assault, overbalanced and stumbled in.

Burton caught him. He introduced his guests to one another, and pointed at the detective's hat. "What on earth is that?"

"Humph! Bowler!"

"Bowler?"

Monckton Milnes interjected, "It's the latest thing. All the rage with the up-and-coming. Detective Inspector Trounce is obviously quite the man about town."

Trounce removed the headgear and punched it. "Up-and-coming? More like down-and-out. I may well be a detective inspector but I'm still the village idiot as far as my colleagues are concerned."

"Fashion always evokes merriment before it catches on," Monckton Milnes observed. "My pegtop trousers had the same effect. Now every blighter is wearing them, which, I regret to say, renders them far too fashionable to be fashionable, if you get my drift."

"Eh?" Trounce said.

"Never mind," Burton interrupted. "What can I do for you, Trounce?"

"I just came by to say thank you, sir."

"No need for the 'sir.' Plain old Burton will do, or captain, if you prefer. Thank me for what?"

"For whatever you said to the home secretary. The chief commissioner has given me the—um—" He glanced at Monckton Milnes and shifted awkwardly from one foot to the other.

"It's all right. My friend works closely with the government and knows all about it."

"Oh, I see. Well then. Slaughter and I are to work the abductions case together."

"Good show!"

"I bid you good hunting, gentlemen," Monckton Milnes said. "Richard, if I find anything of relevance in my library, I shall post it to you at once." He shook his friend's hand, and the detective inspector's, stepped down to the pavement, and strolled away.

"Your arrival is propitious, Trounce," Burton said. "Can you accompany me to Kent?"

"In relation to the case?"

"Yes. Have you heard of Charles Darwin?"

"No."

"He's related to Francis Galton."

Trounce gave a start. "By Jove! A police alert was just issued for an escaped lunatic called Galton. The same man?"

"The same," Burton confirmed. "He was aided in his escape by Burke and Hare. It's possible that Darwin was involved."

"Then we must confront him at once."

"Indeed. But first, come upstairs. I've decided to take you fully into my confidence. You need to know the remaining details of the case."

Forty minutes later, as they left the house, Burton asked, "Are we to take to the air again?"

"If you don't object, and if you can manage it without destroying another of the Yard's rotorchairs."

Burton winked at Bram Stoker as they passed the little newsboy. "Object to another adventure with Mr. Macallister Fogg?" he said. "Of course not!"

They flew fifteen miles or so southeast, landed in Downe Village, asked directions, then flew another quarter of a mile south and put down in the large and well-tended gardens of Down House. The rumble of their machines' engines had hardly ceased before they were surrounded by a horde of excited children, all eagerly asking about the rotorchairs and begging for a ride.

A middle-aged woman emerged from the house and shooed away the youngsters.

"Mrs. Darwin?" Burton asked.

"Yes," she replied, prising a small boy from her skirts. "Run along, Leo. Into the house with you."

"My sincere apologies for descending upon you unannounced," Burton continued as the boy scampered off. "If we've come at an inconvenient time—"

"There's no other such in this house, I'm afraid. You gentlemen are?"

"Sir Richard Francis Burton and Detective Inspector William Trounce. Is your husband at home, ma'am?"

"He is, but I'd rather he wasn't disturbed. He's in bad health and is dealing with some rather pressing matters. What is this about?"

"Francis Galton. He's escaped from Bethlem Asylum."

Mrs. Darwin put a hand to the small crucifix that was hanging from her necklace. Her eyes widened. "Oh, Lord! Is Charles in danger?"

"I couldn't say. I know he regularly corresponded with Mr. Galton."

"Yes, he did. They are half-cousins and family is extremely important to Charles."

"And I understand they also share scientific interests?"

"I wouldn't—that is to say—Francis has ideas that—his thinking is not—is not—" She stopped and frowned.

Burton waited for her to clarify her thoughts.

"Francis has some very strange notions," she finally continued, "which my husband humours but does not approve of. I think—I think, under the circumstances—" She stopped again, then said, more assertively, "I shall fetch Charles. This news is the last thing he needs, but it would be wrong of me to keep it from him. Will you wait here? I'll send him out. A little fresh air will do him good, at least."

She left them and ran across the lawn and into the house.

"What do you make of that?" Trounce asked.

"She appears very tense," Burton replied. "More so, perhaps, than can be attributed to the mothering of so many children. Lord knows, that must place her under enough pressure, but I suspect there's some other issue at play. Did you notice how she repeatedly touched her crucifix?"

"As a matter of fact, I did. What of it?"

"My fiancée also wears the cross. I've noted her touching it to draw on her faith for comfort. Mrs. Darwin's action was quite different. There was a sort of desperation about it, as if the solace she was seeking was no longer there."

Trounce gave a non-committal grunt and nodded toward the house. Burton looked and saw a casually dressed man emerging from it, walking stick in hand. He was about fifty years old, an inch or so under six feet tall—

but a little stooped—stockily built, and bald-headed. His brows, which jutted craggily, buried his eyes in deep shadow, and his jaw, bordered by curly side-burns, might have been carved from rock, so solid was it. However, as he drew closer and the sunlight illuminated his eyes, Burton noted an intense torment in them, and realised that the man's back was bent not from physical causes but from an emotional burden.

"I am Charles Darwin," the scientist said. "Sir Richard, I regret that we've never run into one another. I have followed your exploits with much interest. My profoundest congratulations. Your solving of the Nile question is as impressive a feat as I have ever heard of."

"Thank you, sir," Burton responded. "It is indeed unfortunate that our paths haven't crossed until now—though not an uncommon circumstance within the RGS. An organisation of travellers inevitably finds its headquarters more than half-empty for most of the time. This is my colleague, Detective Inspector Trounce."

"Good day to you, sir. Colleague?"

Burton smiled. "A geographer and a policeman—a strange combination, but it so happens that I've been commissioned to investigate a certain matter, and it has thrown Detective Inspector Trounce and I together."

Darwin used his stick to indicate a path that led from his garden into the fields beyond. When he spoke again, he stuttered a little. "Sh-shall we walk? You can tell me all about it. Th-this matter concerns Francis, does it not? My wife said he's escaped."

"That's correct," Burton responded as they set off down the path. "And he was assisted by Burke and Hare."

"The—the—the traitors? B-but what has he to do with them?"

Trounce said, "That's what we were hoping you could tell us, Mr. Darwin."

They skirted a hedgerow, thick with the billowy flowers of white snake-root, and entered a meadow that had been neatly cropped by sheep. Rabbits raced away from them and vanished into their burrows.

Darwin waved his stick from side to side in an extravagant gesture of negation. "No, no, no!" he cried out. "Francis has never once mentioned the rogues. I cannot believe he has any connection with them. W-w-when they fled the country back in 'forty-one, he was still at Trinity College and so deeply involved in his research that he barely saw a soul. By mid 'forty-five, his Irish experiment had failed, he'd suffered a severe breakdown, and had been incarcerated. As far as anyone knows, Burke and Hare were somewhere on the continent during those years."

"Who funded his research?" Burton asked.

"His club."

"It being?"

"The—the—the League of Enochians."

"I've not heard of it."

"I have," Trounce put in. "It occupies a building on the corner of Mildew Street where it joins Saint Martin's Lane."

"So this club has an interest in Eugenics?"

Darwin stopped and thumped his stick into the ground. "Damn Eugenics!" Burton and Trounce looked at him in surprise, taken aback at the show of anger from a man who had thus far appeared mild in temperament.

"Francis is family," Darwin continued, "but the manner in which that bloody club encouraged him to appropriate and pervert my research is—is—is absolutely foul. I cannot forgive that he allowed himself to be so swayed."

Burton put out a hand and touched the scientist's arm. "Mr. Darwin, perhaps this would make rather more sense to me if I understood the nature of your work."

They resumed their walk. Darwin snorted. "Sir Richard, I've been attempting to articulate my theory since 1837—"

Without thinking, the explorer blurted, "The beginning of the Great Amnesia!"

Darwin peered at him curiously. "W-w-what of it?"

"I—" Burton stopped, considered, and went on, "I wonder how it affected you, that is all."

"The same way it affected everyone else. In 1840, I had to extensively review three years' worth of research and notes, and it all seemed oddly unfamiliar to me. However, it made sense, and as a matter of fact, in going through it, my enthusiasm was renewed, my ideas clarified, and I was set upon a course that led me to my current position."

"Which is?"

They reached the corner of the field and followed the path as it curved sharply to the right.

"W-w-which is that, having fully developed my hypothesis, I have, since 'fifty-seven, been writing a detailed account of it. However, a year ago, to my dismay, I received a paper from a fellow scientist—Alfred Wallace—that dealt with the very same matter. I thought I had been f-f-forestalled, but my publisher insisted that if I produced an abstract of my dissertation, it could be published before Wallace pipped me to the post. I have thus been struggling for thirteen months to condense my w-w-work. And now you ask me to explain it in a few sentences!"

Burton glanced up at the blue, cloud-spotted sky. He thought he could hear the distant clatter of approaching engines.

"I'm trying to understand why Burke and Hare took Mr. Galton from the asylum," he said, "and can only surmise that it has something to do with Eugenics. If he developed that science by subverting your own research, then I must have some grasp of your theory in order to comprehend his version of it."

Darwin stopped, poked the tip of his cane into a blackberry bush, and used it to lift a clump of overripened berries. He bent and scrutinised them closely.

"Very well," he muttered. "Let us put it this way. Our world has limited resources, thus every individual of every species is engaged in intense competition for them. Do you follow?"

"I do, sir."

"Within any given species, individuals vary in their t-t-traits. One might have better eyesight than another, or sharper teeth, or a brighter-coloured skin, or a better ability to endure cold, and so on and so forth. Yes?"

"Yes."

"Depending on local conditions, some of these traits will aid survival, while others will not. The individuals that possess the advantageous ones will generally eat better, live longer, and thus breed more successfully, passing their attributes on to their offspring. Over t-t-time, therefore, the species as a whole will retain beneficial characteristics while breeding out the weaknesses."

Darwin suddenly turned away from the bush, straightened, and faced Burton and Trounce. He raised a finger. "But, but, but! Environmental conditions are far from stable. There are ongoing geological and climactic upheavals and alterations. So it is not the strongest of the species that survives, nor is it the most intelligent. It is the one that is most adaptable to change—the one that will most quickly develop and adopt new strengths and abilities even to the point where, eventually, and if necessary, it will transmute into a new species entirely. Gentlemen, I have called this principle, by which each slight variation, if useful, is preserved, by the term of *natural selection*."

He lowered his hand and regarded them, blinking, and panting slightly after what had become an increasingly impassioned speech.

Burton heard the engines he'd noticed before draw much closer. They idled, and he looked toward Down House, convinced they'd halted at the Darwin residence.

Trounce quietly cleared his throat and said, "Um. Where does God fit into your theory, Mr. Darwin?"

The scientist winced. He set off again along the path. They walked with him.

"My poor Emma," he said. "My w-w-wife has laboured assiduously to assist me in preparing my thesis for publication, but in contemplating it, she has found, as did I, that her faith is eroded. She c-c-clings to it, Detective Inspector, whereas I—well, I cannot persuade myself that a beneficent and omnipotent God would have designedly created, for example, parasitic wasps with the express intention of their feeding within the living bodies of caterpillars. There is no other conclusion to draw than that the universe we observe has precisely the properties we would expect if there is, at bottom, no design, no purpose, no evil, no good, nothing but blind, pitiless indifference."

Burton, who'd so often drawn this same conclusion but been unable to accurately express it or identify incontrovertible evidence to support it, looked at Darwin with admiration. "Sir, if, as you said, my solving of the Nile question was as impressive a feat as you have ever heard of, then I suggest you hold your own theory to a mirror, for the elegant explanation you have just given, though you might consider it curtailed in the extreme, is enough to convince me that you are on the brink of transforming the world of man. That a human brain can produce so profound an insight is—" He stopped, lost for words.

Darwin supplied them. "Bloody dangerous."

"Dangerous?"

"You wanted to know what my half-cousin has done with my theory, Sir Richard. I will tell you. He has proposed a human intercession in the processes of natural selection. Rather than allow the successes and failures of survival to dictate the shape of species, he wants to decide for himself which strengths to breed and which weaknesses to eliminate."

"But how is that different from the actions of, say, a pigeon breeder or a cattle farmer?" Burton asked.

"It is different because he intends that it be applied to the human species. Furthermore, rather than allowing physical characteristics to develop over long periods of time and in response to the environment, he advocates surgical intervention to hasten the process of evolution."

"The warden at the hospital suggested that Mr. Galton believed that men can be made gods."

"If, by gods, you mean beings with physical and mental powers that far exceed what is currently natural to us, then yes, that is what Francis seeks."

Darwin, Burton, and Trounce all jerked their heads around toward the house.

"Was that a scream?" Trounce said.

"Emma!" Darwin gasped.

They left the path and started running across the grass. Burton rapidly drew ahead while Trounce helped the scientist along. The explorer heard children shouting and crying. Angling to the right, he rejoined the path where it entered the garden, raced past the white snakeroot flowers, and burst out of the bushes onto the lawn of Down House.

There were two steam spheres at the side of the residence, both empty but with their engines still ticking over and vapour curling from their funnels. Two of the Darwin children were lying dead or unconscious on the ground. The others were screaming in panic and running back and forth. A short, ape-like man had his arms around Mrs. Darwin, pinning her arms to her sides. She was facing away from him, and as Burton came into her line of sight, she saw him and yelled, "Get them away! Save my children! Save my children!"

Standing a little to the left of her, a second man, taller and thinner than the other, raised his right arm and pointed a green and very odd-looking pistol at the little boy named Leo. Burton, still running toward them, heard a sharp gasp—*phut!* The youngster hit the grass, rolled, and became still.

"Again," the short man snarled at Emma Darwin. "Where is your husband?"

"We have company, Mr. Hare," the taller man declared upon seeing Burton.

"Ah, so we do, Mr. Burke!"

Hare threw Mrs. Darwin aside and he and his companion turned to face the explorer. They were dressed identically in long black surtouts, black waistcoats, and knee-length breeches that gave way to pale yellow tights. Their white shirts had high cheek-scraping collars. Yellow cravats encased their necks. Their shoes were buckled and blocky-heeled.

Burton skidded to a halt in front of the taller man, Damien Burke, who said, "Good day to you, Mr. Darwin. I'm afraid I've frightened your children."

He was slightly hunchbacked and extremely bald but with a short fringe of hair around his ears that curled into enormous "Piccadilly weeper" sideburns. His face hung in a naturally maudlin expression.

Burton said, "Sorry, wrong man," and launched the heel of his hand up into Burke's chin. The cracking blow sent Palmerston's man sprawling backward and the weapon fell from his fingers. Burton had just enough time to register that, though pistol-shaped, it more resembled some sort of spineless cactus, before Hare crashed into him. The thug was immensely broad, with massive shoulders and long, thick arms. His head was crowned with an upstanding mop of pure white hair that angled around his square jawline to a tuft beneath the heavy chin. His pale grey eyes were deeply embedded in gristly sockets; he had a splayed, many-times-broken nose and an extraordinarily wide mouth filled with large flat teeth. The latter were displayed in full as Hare caught Burton around the neck, crushed his windpipe in the crook of his arm, grinned broadly, and bent him double.

Burton struggled for breath as small dots began to swim in front of his eyes. He reached down with both hands, wrapped them around Hare's right knee, and dug his thumbs in beside the two big tendons there, brutally forcing them apart. Hare screeched and fell, dragging Burton down with him. The explorer stabbed an elbow into muscle-padded ribs, broke free as Hare's grip loosened, and scrambled away from him.

He saw Darwin rushing to the fallen children and the other youngsters running to their mother.

Trounce hollered, "Burton!"

"Get the other one!" the explorer croaked, and was in the middle of gesturing toward Burke, who was getting to his feet, when Hare's fist connected with the side of his head. Blocking the follow-up—more by luck than skill, for his senses were still reeling and he was off balance—Burton thudded his knee into Hare's side and pushed himself away. He staggered to his feet and stood swaying. Hare faced him, still grinning, and assumed a fighting stance unfamiliar to the explorer but which he vaguely recognised as Oriental.

Off to the left, Trounce collided with Burke and they went down in a tangle of thrashing limbs.

Hare's right fist swept forward. Burton moved to dodge the blow but it never arrived. Instead, his opponent used the mock punch as a counterbalance, swivelled, and kicked, his heel whipping up into Burton's nose. The explorer was sent spinning backward, blood spraying around him. Without any awareness of what he was doing, he stopped himself from falling, parried a chopping hand, and—shooting out his arm—grabbed his opponent's hair. He yanked inward and delivered a savage headbutt to Hare's mouth, crushing the man's lips into his teeth. His adversary slumped. Burton twisted his grip and sank his teeth into the other's cheek, clamping hard until he felt hot blood welling. Hare shrieked and pushed him away with such force that Burton's feet left the ground. The explorer thudded down, teetered, regained his equilibrium, and spat a lump of wet flesh onto the grass.

From the corner of his eye, he saw Trounce fall. The detective didn't get up.

Burke called, "Do you require assistance, Mr. Hare?"

Hare, standing with his eyes fixed on Burton, his massive arms hanging and blood bubbling from the hole in the left side of his face, made a dismissive gesture then charged at Burton like a stampeding bull. He leaped, revolved through the air, and kicked. Burton ducked, snatched at the man's ankle, and using Hare's own momentum spun and slammed him down. Palmerston's thug tried to dodge away but Burton sprang forward and swung his boot into the man's head, once, then again, and a third time.

Hare flopped back and lay still.

Using his sleeve to wipe the blood from his mouth, Burton looked up and, though his vision was blurred, saw Mrs. Darwin collapsed with children crying over her prone form; saw Trounce motionless on the sward; and saw Burke dragging an unconscious Darwin to one of the steam spheres. He started toward the two vehicles but hadn't taken more than two steps before meaty fingers closed around his left wrist and jerked him around. He found himself face to face with the ruined features of Gregory Hare and mumbled, "Why won't you bloody well stay down?"

Hare gave a malignant hiss, raised his hand, and chopped it into Burton's forearm. A horrible crunch sounded. Burton fell to his knees as white-hot pain flared through him.

"Mr. Hare!" Burke shouted. "It is time to leave."

"I have to finish this one, Mr. Burke."

"No time to waste on irrelevancies. Come along."

Hare, with blood streaming down his neck and soaking into his clothes, glared down at Burton and said, "You'd better pray we never meet again."

He stumbled off toward the vehicles.

Burton saw Burke sit the senseless Darwin against one of the spheres, open a hatch at the rear of the vehicle, then lift the scientist and bundle him into what was obviously a storage compartment.

Hare reached the other sphere and clambered into it. With a puff of steam, it rolled, turned, and sped away from the house and onto the Luxted Road.

Damien Burke slammed the hatch shut, drew the strange cactus-like pistol from his jacket, and pointed it at Burton.

"Don't move!" he said.

Burton snarled and forced himself to his feet, cradling his broken left arm in his right.

There came that soft sound again—*phut!*—and a seven-inch spine embedded itself into the lower-left side of Burton's waistcoat.

He gingerly moved his arm aside and looked down at the quill. The front half of it was glistening with a clear substance. He took hold of the dry end and plucked it out.

The second sphere went rumbling after the first.

Tottering across the lawn, Burton bent over Trounce and felt his heart. The Scotland Yard man was still alive. One of the spines was sticking out of his shoulder. Burton pulled it out, shook the detective, but received only a groan in response.

He moved over to little Leo. The boy was also deeply unconscious but alive, with one of the needles in him.

Burton approached the other children, all gathered around their mother. He selected the eldest, a girl of about sixteen years, squatted down next to her, and put his hand on her shoulder.

"What's your name?"

"Etty," she replied, tearfully.

"Look," he said, and taking by its tip the spine that was in Emma Darwin's neck, withdrew it.

"See where it's wet?" he said. "That is what has sent your mother to sleep. Go to the other children and take out the needles, but be careful only to hold them by the dry parts. Do you understand?"

She nodded, her lower lip trembling. "Yes, sir."

"Good girl. They'll all wake up. My friend will, too." He nodded toward Trounce. "And when he does, he'll get help for you all."

"What of my father, sir?" she said.

"I'm going after him now."

Burton straightened and, despite himself, gave a yelp as he felt the broken bones of his forearm grind together. He walked unsteadily to the bottom of the garden, climbed into his rotorchair, and turned the small wheel that set the engine in motion. A minute later, the machine soared upward. He steered it, one-handed, over the house, and followed the road to the northwest: the direction in which the spheres had rolled.

It was a clear day and he could see for miles. Ahead, the road curved northward, and farther on, to the northeast. He saw the two vehicles rounding that second bend and entering the village of Downe. Burton surveyed the field-patched countryside beyond the settlement. He saw that the road exited Downe and ran on through gently undulating meadows. It was bordered on either side by woods and high hedgerows and, a couple of miles ahead, bent sharply to the left.

He pushed his toes into the rotorchair's footplate, sending the machine surging forward, and shoved the middle flight lever, which caused the contraption to drop like a stone. He cried out through gritted teeth as pain almost blinded him then yanked the lever back. The rotorchair swooped over the ground, levelling out a mere ten feet above it, and shot across the fields at terrifying speed.

As the crow flies, Captain Burton. As the crow flies.

The air forced tears from the explorer's eyes. He passed the spheres, far off to his right, drew ahead of them, and came to the sharp bend. Shielded by trees, he jerked his rotorchair to a halt, set it down in the middle of the road just beyond the curve, and momentarily passed out.

The sound of approaching engines brought him back to his senses. He coughed, spat blood, and dived out of the flying machine just as the lead sphere rounded the bend at high speed and, with no time to stop, slammed into it. Both vehicles detonated with a deafening boom and disappeared into a ball of fire. The sound tore into the far distance and left silence behind it.

Raggedly, Burton, hit by the blast, pirouetted with infinite slowness through the air.

I can't do this by myself.

He watched with detached fascination as the flame-filled world revolved majestically around him.

What of your self-sufficiency? What of your intractable independence?

Fragments of spinning metal glinted in the sunlight.

I need a different perspective. The way I apprehend things—the manner in which I and Trounce and Slaughter and Monckton Milnes view the world—it just won't suffice.

The branches of a tree embraced him, easing through his clothes and skin.

That's because the world isn't what you think it is.

Darkness swept in from all sides.

Exactly.

SWINBURNE

"Hope thou not much, and fear thou not at all."
—ALGERNON CHARLES SWINBURNE

CHAPTER 9

THE MARQUESS'S VISION

**NO!
TO THE CENTRAL GERMAN CONFEDERATION!
NO!
TO A GERMAN EMPIRE!
NO!
TO A BRITISH-GERMAN ALLIANCE!
DO NOT BELIEVE THE LIES.
EVERY GERMAN EMPLOYED MEANS A BRITISH WORKER IDLE.
EVERY GERMAN FACTORY BUILT MEANS BRITISH TRADE LOST.**

The distant chimes of Big Ben.

Burton counted them.

One. Two. Three.

Edward's voice: "Do you really suppose I'm built for standing, nurse? Find me a confounded chair. At once! You there—what's your name?"

"I'm Detective Inspector Trounce."

"What happened?"

"I'm afraid I cannot divulge police business to a—"

"No nonsense! You've seen my authorisation—I represent the prime minister. Speak or I'll have you clapped in irons, damn it!"

"Humph! Well—I—um—Sir Richard and I are investigating—"

"Yes! Yes! I know all about that. The accident, man! What caused it?"

"It was Burke and Hare, sir. They took Darwin and made off with him in steam spheres. I think Sir Richard tried to stop them by landing a rotorchair in their path. There was a collision. He didn't get clear in time and was thrown into a tree by the explosion."

"And Burke and Hare?"

"I don't know. There was no sign of them. Whichever was driving the lead vehicle was either blown to smithereens or his corpse was taken away by the other, along with Mr. Darwin."

For how long are you going to lie there? Wake up. There's work to do. The clock is ticking.

Four. Five. Six. Seven.

Doctor John Steinhaueser: "We'll move him this afternoon."

Good old Styggins.

Edward: "Is he strong enough?"

"He has the constitution of an ox. The bones are already knitting. As for the concussion—hmmm—has he spoken to you?"

"Yesterday morning. I'm not sure he was aware of it. His pupils were as big as saucers."

"What did he say?"

"He told me he'd had a heart attack."

"He said the same to me. Damned peculiar, hmmm? There's no sign of one at all. His heart is as healthy as they come."

"We can be thankful for that, at least. I need him compos mentis, Doctor. Get him back on his feet. Pour some Saltzmann's into him. He swears by the bloody stuff."

"I'll not resort to quackery, no matter that it's you who orders it."

"Pah! Principles!"

Eight. Ten. Nine hundred. One thousand.

Wake up. Wake up. Wake up.

John Steinhaueser: "Restless, hmmm? It's all right, old fellow. You're at home."

He heard the clink and clank of camel bells. The most precious moment of his life—waking in a tent in the desert, knowing he would step out and see the oasis, a tiny island amid a vast desolate nothingness, and far, far away, already shimmering in the heat of early morning, the horizon, beyond which there could be—*anything.*

He opened his eyes.

Orange light flickering on a canvas roof.

Gunshots.

This again?

El Balyuz, the chief abban, burst into the tent, yelling, "They are attacking!" He handed a Colt to Burton. "Your gun, Effendi!"

The explorer pushed back his bedsheets and stood; laid the weapon on the map table; pulled on his trousers; snapped his braces over his shoulders; picked up the gun.

He looked across to George Herne, who was also dressing hastily. "More bloody posturing! It's all for show, but we shouldn't let them get too cocky. Go out the back of the tent, away from the campfire, and ascertain their strength. Let off a few rounds over their heads. They'll soon bugger off."

"Right you are," Herne responded. Taking up his rifle, he ran to the back of the Rowtie and pushed through the canvas.

No. No. No. Stop it, you fool. There is pain enough. Why must you always return to this?

Burton checked his revolver.

"For Pete's sake, Balyuz, why have you handed me an unloaded gun? Get me my sabre!"

He shoved the Colt into the waistband of his trousers and snatched his sword from the Arab.

"Stroyan!" he bellowed. "Speke!"

Almost immediately, the tent flap was pushed aside and William Stroyan stumbled in.

He didn't. That is not what happened.

His eyes were wild.

"They knocked the tent down around my ears! I almost took a beating! Is there shooting to be done?"

"I rather suppose there is," Burton said, finally realising the situation might be more serious than he'd initially thought. "Be sharp, and arm to defend the camp!"

They waited a few moments, checking their gear and listening to the rush of men outside.

Herne returned from his recce. "There's a lot of the blighters, and our confounded guards have taken to their heels. I took a couple of pot-shots at the mob but then got tangled in the tent ropes. A big Somali swiped at me with a bloody great club. I put a bullet into the bastard. I couldn't see Speke anywhere."

Something thumped against the side of the tent. Suddenly a barrage of blows pounded the canvas while war cries were raised all around. The attackers were swarming like hornets. Javelins were thrust through the opening. Daggers ripped at the material.

"Bismillah!" Burton cursed. "We're going to have to fight our way to the supplies and get ourselves more guns. Herne, there are spears tied to the tent pole at the back. Get 'em."

"Yes, sir." Herne returned to the rear of the Rowtie. Almost immediately, he ran back, crying out, "They're breaking through!"

Burton swore vociferously. "If this blasted thing comes down on us we'll be caught up good and proper. Get out! Come on! Now!"

He hurled himself through the tent flaps and into a crowd of twenty or so Somali natives, setting about them with his sabre, slicing right and left, yelling fiercely.

Clubs and spear shafts thudded against his flesh, bruising and cutting him, drawing blood.

"Speke!" he bellowed. "Where are you?"

"Here!"

He glanced back and saw Speke stepping into the firelight from the shadows to the right of the tent. The lieutenant was splashed with blood and his left sleeve hung in tatters.

Stroyan emerged from the Rowtie and straightened, loading his rifle.

"Watch out!" Speke yelled, and threw himself in front of the other man.

A spear thudded into the middle of his chest.

No! Wrong! Wrong! This is all wrong!

A club struck Burton on the shoulder. He twisted and swiped his blade at its owner. The crush of men jostled him back and forth. Someone shoved from behind and he turned angrily, raising his sword, only recognising El Balyuz at the very last moment.

His arm froze in mid-swing.

Agonising pain exploded in his head.

He stumbled and fell onto the sandy earth.

A weight pulled him sideways.

He reached up.

A javelin had pierced his face, in one cheek and out the other, dislodging teeth and cracking his palate.

He screamed and sat up.

John Steinhaueser—handsome, blond-haired, and blue-eyed, with an imperial adorning his chin—rose from a chair beside the bed.

"Hello, old chap. Another nightmare?"

Burton, disoriented, looked around and saw his own bedroom. The after-image of flames faded. The chamber was illuminated by daylight.

"God!" he said, hoarsely. "Will they never cease?"

Steinhaueser felt the explorer's pulse. "As the pain eases up. Is it still bad?"

"Just the head."

"Let me see."

He leaned over Burton and examined the long line of stitches that snaked around his patient's shaved cranium. "Hmmm. It's remarkable. Truly remarkable."

"What is?"

"Ten days ago your scalp was hanging half-off, but it's healed just as fast as your spear wound did back in 'fifty-five. I can take the stitches out tomorrow."

"I was dreaming about it. The attack at Berbera. Speke's death." Burton realised he had no idea how long he'd been here, in his own bed. He vaguely recalled a hospital room. "What time is it? Midday?"

"No, it's ten in the morning. Lie back. Rest."

Gingerly and very slowly, Burton eased himself down.

"I could have sworn I heard Big Ben chime twelve."

"Let me look at your ribs," Steinhaueser said. "Big Ben? Not possible. The bell cracked four days ago. Hasn't made a sound since. Hmmm, good—the bones are healing nicely and the bruising is changing colour. You'll be sore and stiff for a while but it'll pass. As for the arm, you won't require the splint for much longer. Time and rest are doing their job. I'll wager you'll be able to use it in a week or so. How's your memory, hmmm?"

Burton was silent for a moment then answered, "I can't recall anything since the collision. What's the date?"

Steinhaueser pursed his lips and stroked the point of his little beard. "Friday the twenty-third of September. You've been in and out of consciousness. What about the letters to Isabel?"

"Letters?"

Steinhaueser chuckled. "You first regained some measure of wits four days after the accident. The first thing you did was demand a pen and paper. Then you composed an astonishingly lucid letter to your fiancée in which you claimed to have fallen sick with a recurrence of malaria. You wrote that you were fine and she should remain in Wiltshire."

"I did? I recall nothing of it."

"You've written twice since. You also threatened to throttle me if I told her the truth."

Burton shook his head bemusedly.

"As a matter of fact, it's not so unusual," Steinhaueser said. "I've witnessed such things before with concussion. You took a mighty blow to the head, Richard, but your eyes are far less dilated this morning, so I'll venture you're through the worst of it."

Burton wondered how much his friend knew. He tested the waters. "Remind me. What happened?"

"You were over Kent in a rotorchair and set it down in the middle of a road. Mechanical failure, perhaps?"

Burton shrugged, and winced as a pang sliced through him.

Steinhaueser continued, "A steam sphere rounded the bend at high speed and smacked into your machine. The explosion knocked you flying. Fortunately, a Scotland Yard man was on business nearby. He found you."

"And the sphere's driver?"

"No trace. Burned to ashes, I should think."

So, the truth had been covered up.

Trounce. I need to see Trounce.

"And I've been out of commission for ten days, you say? Gad! So soon after the malaria! This year is developing as many holes as a block of Swiss cheese. What have I missed, Styggins?"

"Not a great deal. You were brought home from hospital a couple of days ago. I've been living in your guest room. I had to turn a number of visitors away—Detective Inspector Trounce; Detective Inspector Slaughter; Sir Roderick Murchison; and a rather striking looking lady named Countess Sabina. She left her calling card. Strange. Look."

The doctor took a small pasteboard from the bedside table and handed it to Burton. On one side, there was printed:

Countess Sabina Elisabeta Lacusta
7 Vere Street, London
Cheiromantist, Prognosticator

On the other, written somewhat shakily by hand: *Sir Richard. Beware. There is a storm approaching.*

"Ominous, hmmm?" Steinhaueser said.

Burton sneered and shook his head despairingly. "Why do mediums always insist on the vaguest forms of innuendo? Utter rot!" He tossed the card aside. "And what of the wider world? Much happening?"

"The usual. Prussia's prince regent continues to cooperate with Albert, and has sidelined Bismarck by making him ambassador to the Russian Empire. Old Otto must be livid. In theory, it's a promotion, so he can hardly complain. In truth, it ousts him from the game."

"Good show. What else?"

"Things are hotting up in China. The French have thrown their lot in with us. Even America is caught up in it. There's been fighting, but reports are sketchy. Elgin is on his way back there already and by all accounts he's mad as hell and in no mood for compromise. His battleship, the *Sagittarius*, is nearly complete and will fly out before the year is done. Other than that, nothing to report. Are you hungry?"

"Famished."

"I'll ask your housekeeper to rustle something up, and will then leave you in her capable hands. A colleague has been looking after my practice. Now you're on the mend, I should get back to it. Don't worry, I'm not abandoning you, but I don't think you'll require my constant presence any more, hmmm?"

"Thank you, Styggins."

"Don't mention it. Frankly, now that you're back in the land of the living, I'm happy to hightail it. You're a God-awful patient and I'd rather not be exposed to your complaining, stubbornness, disobedience, and bad temper."

Burton chuckled. "Am I that disagreeable?"

"You are. Mrs. Angell will be up presently. No doubt you'll torture her horribly. I'll see you tonight. Rest, hmmm?"

Burton nodded. Steinhaueser departed.

Over the next few days, Sir Richard Francis Burton healed and grumbled and pondered and chafed and drifted in and out of sleep, Steinhaueser came and went, and Mrs. Angell fussed and cooked and cleaned and endured.

By Wednesday, the explorer had left his bed, relocated to the study, and taken root in his dilapidated old saddlebag armchair, from which he barely moved for the remainder of the week. He read, wrote letters to Isabel, and meditated. His hair started to grow back, covering the scars on his scalp. The dull ache in his arm faded. His bruises turned a dirty yellow. A seething fury developed slowly and implacably. He couldn't shake from his mind the picture of Darwin's children—some unconscious, the rest terrified.

Days passed.

On the morning of Friday the 7th of October, he received a visit from

Detective Inspectors Trounce and Slaughter. Upon seeing him, Trounce, who had a cardboard file holder in his hand, exclaimed, "I say! You look almost human again."

"You mean, as much as I ever did?" Burton quipped. He pushed himself to his feet to greet his guests.

"Brandy?" he asked Trounce.

"Thank you. That would go down a treat."

"Milk?" he enquired of Slaughter.

"God, yes! Most considerate of you. Brandy would kill me."

After Mrs. Angell had delivered the milk and the brandy had been poured, the men settled in chairs.

"Your health," Slaughter toasted.

Burton laughed. "What little of it remains!"

"I've never seen anything like it," Trounce said. "I found you hanging from a tree. I thought you were nothing but a bundle of bloody rags until you moved your head and whispered, 'Get me down, there's a good chap.' It's a blessed miracle you lived."

"I recall nothing of it. There was no sign of Burke and Hare?"

"None."

"What happened after you regained your senses in Darwin's garden?"

"I calmed Mrs. Darwin and her brood, then took to the air and immediately saw the smoke rising from the road to the north. I landed and discovered you. Unfortunately, by then our birds had flown. Who was driving the lead sphere?"

"Hare. Burke was following with Darwin in his vehicle's luggage compartment."

"By Jove, Burton, it was a damned brave thing you did."

Burton waved the observation aside, and Trounce went on, "Confound it! I took a shine to old Darwin. Whoever's behind all this will pay, so help me, they will."

Something occurred to the explorer. He reached for a cord hanging beside the fireplace and pulled it to summon back Mrs. Angell.

"Has there been any progress?" he asked the detectives.

Slaughter answered, "I've been sifting through missing-persons reports. Hundreds vanish without a trace every year, but I looked for any that involved DOGS or medical personnel. So far I've found just one of interest. A young surgeon named Joseph Lister, the first assistant to James Syme of the University of Edinburgh. Something of a prodigy, apparently, but he hasn't been seen since the nineteenth of August."

Burton sipped his brandy. "Any suggestion he was abducted?"

"None, but neither did he have any reason to take off of his own accord."

Trounce added, "We know that Isambard Kingdom Brunel and Nurse Nightingale were seized by the two Indian chaps, while Galton and Darwin were taken by Burke and Hare—who also made an unsuccessful play for Brunel. Who abducted Charles Babbage, Samuel Gooch, and possibly this Lister chap, we don't know—but whichever way we look at it, it appears that two opposing groups of kidnappers are at work."

There came a knock at the door and the housekeeper poked her head in.

"Mother Angell," Burton said. "What happened to the clothes I was wearing when I had the accident?"

"I believe the hospital burned them, sir."

"And the contents of my pockets?"

"Here." His housekeeper crossed to one of the desks, took a small tray from it, and handed it to him. She turned and stalked out of the room, muttering, "Right in front of his bloomin' eyes, it was. Up and down the stairs like a blessed yo-yo and half the time for nothing."

"Formidable woman, hey?" Slaughter murmured.

"She is," Burton agreed. "Ah ha!" He picked something from the dish and held it up.

"A tiepin?" Trounce asked.

"Burke downed you with a very queer-looking pistol. It fired spines coated with some sort of venom. They knocked you out in an instant. I received one in the gut but for some reason it had no effect. I've been wondering why. This is the answer. It was in my waistcoat pocket and the spine hit it." He stretched his arm forward and the two detectives saw the pin was topped with a small round disk of gold. There was a tiny dent in the middle of it. "I took it from Oliphant's cabin on the *Orpheus*."

"May I?" Trounce asked, reaching out.

Burton passed the pin over and the detective peered closely at the two letter-like inscriptions engraved into the metal.

"Ho! Well I never!" he said. "This is from the place Darwin mentioned—the League of Enochians Gentlemen's Club. I've been investigating it. These two symbols appear on all its literature."

"Do they, indeed?" Burton exclaimed. "So both Oliphant and Galton are members."

Trounce handed the file over. "Here, I brought you the report. You'll learn more about the club by reading it than from me trying to sum it up. One thing worth noting, though, is that it's only since March, when the founder died and a gentleman named Edward Vaughan Hyde Kenealy became its president, that the clubhouse closed its doors and became a 'by invite only' affair."

"March?" Burton mused. "Just when Oliphant joined and his behaviour took a turn for the worse. It appears we have a focus, at last. Trounce, I want you to keep a round-the-clock watch on the place. Record all the comings and goings. See if you can identify anyone who visits it."

"I'll rope in Spearing," Trounce replied. "He might be the youngest detective on the Force but he's as sharp as they come. We'll do it in shifts. Incidentally—" He hesitated.

"What is it?"

"I can't be certain, but since I started asking questions about the Enochians, I've had the conviction I'm being followed."

Burton raised an eyebrow. He thought a moment then asked, "Do you carry a weapon?"

"Not usually."

"It's time you did. In fact, I recommend that all of us keep a gun handy."

The Scotland Yard men nodded. Burton addressed Slaughter. "Your line of inquiry has been fruitful, so keep up with it. Stay focused on engineers and medical personnel. There's a common thread to all this."

"Which is?" Slaughter asked.

"Eugenics—a science that Galton developed. It strikes me that Burke's weapon might be a product of it, which suggests there's work being done in that illegal field. It would require medical knowledge and machinery."

"I see. Rightio, sir."

"Gentlemen, I'm likely to be out of commission for a few days longer. I rely on you to be my eyes and ears."

"You can count on us, Sir Richard," Slaughter said.

With that, the policemen departed and Burton settled down to read Trounce's report. The detective's handwriting looked like a spool of unravelling thread, undulating across the pages in a regular, quick, and fluid motion.

"Efficient mind," Burton mused.

He read the first paragraph, blinked, and read it again.

The League of Enochians Gentlemen's Club. Registered, 2nd January 1841. Occupied Mildew Street building the following day. Club originated in meetings held at The Hog in the Pound public house, Oxford Street. Same place where Edward Oxford had worked as a pot-boy.

"Edward Oxford!" Burton cried out. "The bloody Assassination again!" He moved on to the next paragraph.

Current membership estimated at approximately 150.

Club founder: Henry de La Poer Beresford, 3rd Marquess of Waterford (replaced as president upon his death by Edward Vaughan Hyde Kenealy). Born 26th April 1811. Inherited title in 1826, along with Curraghmore Estate in County Waterford, Ireland. Gambler, drunkard, prankster. Notorious. Nicknamed "The Mad Marquess." January 1837, moved to England and purchased Darkening Towers Estate on the outskirts of Waterford Village. (No connection with the Irish county. Vanity? Fancied himself as marquess of an English estate?) Occupied the manor from 28th February '37.

"And yet another coincidence, Trounce," Burton muttered to himself. "The start of the Great Amnesia."

Beresford killed in a horse-riding accident on the 29th of March, this year (1859). The marquessate passed to his brother, John.

The rest of the page was blank. Burton gazed at it for a moment, dwelling on the dates, then turned to the next sheet. It was Henry Beresford's criminal record: a long list of minor affrays, vandalism, drunken pranks, violent behaviour toward women, and petty thefts. The most recent of them dated from February 1837.

On the next sheet, Trounce had written:

Visited Darkening Towers, Monday 19th September 1859. Interviewed John Beresford. He claims his brother was a harmless eccentric and showed me a significant (because of its strangeness) entry in Henry Beresford's diary. Copied below, misspellings and other errors intact:

20th June 1837.

I must declare today quite the most astonishing, for this afternoon whilst I was out ryding, I was crossing the estate on my way back to the stables when my horse did shye, and upon looking down I beheld a man prone upon the ground, apparently in a dead faint, and garbed in a most outlandish costume of shimmering white. So taken aback was I that I gave a cry, and had to look and look again to be sure the vision was not some strange hellucination. When finally I concluded that it weren't, I dismounted to examin the figure more close, but as I did so, I glanced back at my horse for the briefest of moments, it being nervous, and upon returning my attention to the sward I found that no figure was upon it and the grass were un-bent, giving not the slytest indication that a thing had disturbed it.

Instantly, I douted my senses, and askt of meself wether I had seen the thing at all or was, p'raps, the victim of some trick of the light or, far worse, of some failure of the brain. The more I considered the question, the more afeared I become, specially so 'cause the impression the vision had made was fayding with un-natural rapidty, as if I were un-able to prop'ly imprint a memry of it on my mind. Indeed, I was over-come by a strange confusion, being muddled in intent, the world around me all of a sudden appearing un-familiar, as if I had been engaged in some activity and then un-expectedly snatcht away from it and robbed of my powers of recollection.

I confess that a great panic overcome me, and in a trice I re-mounted my steed and dasht home, flying through the door and yelling at Brock to take care of the nag. I raced into the study, throwed meself into the chair at my desk, and as fast as I could write, in-scribed the following onto a sheet of vellum:

"The man was tall and thin and wore a suit comprised of a single piece, white and scaley in texture, that lay flush against his skin, outlining his sinyewy form in a most overt manner, though covering it entirely from the base of his neck to his wrists and ankles, and with nary a flap, opening, button, nor hook in sight. His head was consealed by a black helmet, round and shiney and flickring all over with blue flame. A flat circlar lamp, dented and crackt, was attacht to his chest, and his booted feet were strapt into stilts, of p'raps 2ft in height."

Within minutes of setting down this slight account, the memry was reduced to the vaygest of impressions, the merest glimmering awareness that I had seed something inexplcible but knew not what.

The vellum is before me as I write, and now the description is trans-scribed into my diary, too.

Did I dream? I cannot believe so. Something strange has most certainly occurred. I feel uncannily diffrent but cannot put into further words the sensation, for there are none what fit it.

Trounce had added:

The suit Beresford describes matches exactly and without a shadow of a doubt the one I saw in the thicket in Green Park. Beresford's brother showed me portraits of the Mad Marquess but he bore no likeness to the man who knocked me cold that day.

As to the rest of the diary, after the above-copied entry, Beresford made fewer and fewer contributions to it, none of significance. By September, he'd ceased keeping it altogether. His brother informed me that the marquess, from the date of his vision, became increasingly fascinated with the 16th-century writings of Doctor John Dee and Edward Kelley. He (John Beresford) said their body of work was the subject *of Henry's meetings in The Hog in the Pound, which commenced soon after Queen Victoria's death and quickly led to the establishment of the League of Enochians. He also stated that his brother believed The Assassination to be "a moment when magic was manifest in history."*

The detective's notes moved on to the League of Enochians' current chairman:

Edward Vaughan Hyde Kenealy: Born 2 July 1819. Current address unknown (possibly resident in the club building). From Cork, Ireland. Lawyer. Called to Irish Bar, 1840, and English Bar, 1847. Extremely erratic in character. Often violent. Has apparently published poetry concerning the physical manifestation of God on Earth (have not been able to locate any of it).

The remainder of the file's contents consisted of pamphlets published by the League of Enochians prior to March. They all advertised club meetings, with titles such as: "A Discussion of John Dee's *Quinti Libri Mysteriorum*"; "On the Words of Uriel"; and "The Secret Art of Scrying." Two in particular caught Burton's attention. The first was "The Language of the Angels." Printed under the title were twenty-two symbols, each with a name. They apparently corresponded to Latin letters, the equivalents being displayed beneath. Among them were the two from the tiepin—*Ur* and *Graph*—which translated to *L* and *E*—the initials of the club.

The second pamphlet—a sheet folded to make four sides of print—was entitled "The First Call of Enoch." The inside-front page bore a long passage printed in the symbols. The facing page transposed them into Latin characters, the words looking like randomly grouped letters.

The back page offered an English translation: garbled nonsense concerning the power of angels.

However, it provided the key he needed.

He got up, crossed to one of his desks, and retrieved from it the telegraph message Christopher Spoolwinder had given him aboard the *Orpheus*.

With the pamphlet as his guide, he was able to give meaning to what had originally appeared to be gobbledegook:

THE BEAST...THE BEAST...THE BEAST...YOU SHALL BOW DOWN FOR...I REIGN OVER YOU...BORN FROM THE WRECK OF SS BRITANNIA AND...IN POWER EXALTED ABOVE THE FIRMAMENTS OF WRATH IN WHOSE HANDS THE

SUN IS AS A SWORD . . . TO REND THE VEIL . . . FROM THE FALLEN EMPIRE . . . NOW . . . LIFT UP YOUR VOICES AND SWEAR OBEDIENCE AND FAITH TO HIM . . . FOR THE ROYAL CHARTER . . . WILL DELIVER HE . . . WHOSE BEGINNING IS NOT NOR END CANNOT BE . . .

He stared into space, stunned by the implication. That telegraph machines the world over had been affected by the aurora borealis was an established fact. That the one aboard the *Orpheus* had spewed out this message, which employed a language also used by the Enochians, suggested—incredibly—a causal relationship between Oliphant's ritual and the atmospheric phenomenon.

"By God, Oliphant," he murmured. "Did you truly summon something?"

CHAPTER 10

THE COMPLEXITIES OF TIME AND ITS TRAVELLERS

"He who knows not, and knows not that he knows not, is a fool. Shun him. He who knows not, and knows that he knows not, is simple. Teach him. He who knows, and knows not that he knows, is asleep. Wake him. He who knows, and knows that he knows, is wise. Follow him."
—Isabel Arundell, from the Persian proverb

The next ten days of recovery were interspersed with visits to the British Museum's reading room, where Burton researched John Dee, the Elizabethan alchemist and occultist who'd sought to identify the purest forms and expressions of existence, primarily by communicating with divine beings. Dee claimed to have achieved this through scrying, which was undertaken by his associate, Edward Kelley. Together they'd learned—or created, Burton suspected—the language of the angels.

The hours of reading didn't provide him with any further revelations, but it gave him a solid grounding in the theories that apparently motivated Henry Beresford, Thomas Lake Harris, Laurence Oliphant, Edward Vaughan Hyde Kenealy, and the League of Enochians.

By Monday the 17th of October his bruises had vanished, his ribs healed, and his arm offered only the occasional twinge. With a loaded Beaumont–Adams revolver concealed beneath his light jacket and swinging his sword-stick as he walked, he left the house, tipped his hat to Mr. Grub the vendor, who was cooking corn on the cob on his brazier, and made his way to Baker Street. Eschewing the cabs—after so many days of inactivity he preferred to walk—he headed toward Portman Square. It was autumn but unseasonably warm and humid. The air was thick with dust, soot, and steam, and stank to high heaven. The flow of sewage through the new north-to-south tunnels was still being slowed by sluice gates, which would not be fully opened until the big intercepting tunnel was complete. Foul viscous liquid was seeping up through the streets and only flower sellers were happy about it, for it had become a necessary fashion to walk with a fragrant bouquet held to one's nose.

By the time Burton reached the square, perspiration was running from beneath his topper and he had grit in his eyes, so he stopped, sat on a bench, removed his headgear, put it down, and mopped his brow with a handkerchief.

He sat back and watched a herd of geese being guided along by a farmer and his two boy assistants, obviously on their way to market. A man on a velocipede attempted to steer his vehicle past them. His penny-farthing hit one of the birds, squashed it, wobbled, and toppled sideways, expelling steam with a hiss that matched those produced by the angry flock. The man sprang to his feet and shook his fist at the farmer. An argument ensued. Punches were exchanged. A constable arrived on the scene and separated the combatants. The velocipedist rode back in the direction he'd come, his machine clanking unhealthily. The geese were shooed on. Once the participants were out of sight, the constable picked up the killed bird, examined it, and carried it away with a satisfied grin on his face, undoubtedly anticipating a goose supper.

Burton considered the strangeness of the city. It was filled with mechanical marvels, yet England's agricultural roots were still plain to see. The place was so madly eclectic it was almost impossible to characterise.

It is off-course. It has become something it was never meant to be. It is broken.

He looked around at the square. He'd never sat here before, but a vertiginous sense of familiarity suddenly flooded through him, causing his heart to flutter.

How can you consider this natural? Velocipedes? The atmospheric railway? Steam spheres? Rotorchairs? Submarine ships? All developed within the space of twenty years? It's impossible!

He gasped and leaned forward, gripping his cane with both hands, feeling himself dividing.

The Afterlife? Mediums? Magic rituals? Madness! Madness!

"Go away!" he wheezed. "Leave me alone!"

You're moving too slowly. Piece it together, you fool. Hurry!

He heaved himself to his feet, reeled, and staggered to one side, only avoiding a fall by slamming the point of his cane into the ground. He raised a hand to his head and used his fingers to trace the long scar that parted the roots of his short hair. Just how much had the concussion damaged him?

He struggled to regulate his respiration then picked up his hat, put it on, and quickly walked from the square to Oxford Street, turning left into the busy thoroughfare.

Impatiently, he elbowed through the crowds, hurrying along, his mind awhirl. Traffic and voices roared in his ears. So did his pulse. He angrily knocked a beggar aside—detecting at once that the man's blindness was a sham—and turned into Charing Cross, following it south to Leicester Square, where he entered Long Acre, which, a few yards on, joined St. Martin's Lane. A few more paces took him to its junction with Mildew Street, and there, on the corner and opposite a building site, he found the League of Enochians Gentlemen's Club. It was an unprepossessing three-storey building with a plain portico arching over the three steps that led up to the entrance. He tried the door. It was locked. He knocked and waited. He yanked the bellpull; knocked again. No one came. Muttering an oath, he was turning away when a flier, pasted to the wall beside the door, caught his eye.

THOMAS LAKE HARRIS

America's Foremost Scryer and Summoner

Author of The Wisdom of Angels

A Lecture Entitled:

EVOCATION AND COMMUNICATION:

ON SUMMONING ADVISORS FROM THE SPIRIT WORLD.

Here: Wednesday 9th November, 9 p.m.

Open to Members and Sanctioned Guests Only.

Note to the General Public:

Mr. Harris will be giving a presentation entitled:

THE TRUTH OF SPIRITUALISM

At Almack's Assembly Rooms,

King Street, St. James's,

On Tuesday 8th November, 8 p.m.

Open to all.

Burton copied the details into his notebook, descended the steps, and walked a little farther along St. Martin's Lane until he came to Brundleweed's. Once again, the jeweller's was closed and the grille covered the window. Looking past the metal bars, he noticed changes in the window display. The tools on the benches had been moved. Plainly, Brundleweed was around; the explorer had just been unlucky in catching him.

Tearing a page from his book, he took his pencil and scribbled: *Require engagement ring at earliest possible. Please inform when convenient to call. Alternatively, deliver to me at—*

He added his address, signed the note, pushed it through the letterbox, and walked back the way he'd come. Halfway along Oxford Street, he turned right into Vere Street. Number 7 was a narrow house squashed between a hardware shop and a Museum of Anatomy. It had a bright yellow door and a tall, narrow, blue-curtained window. He lifted the knocker and banged it down three times. After a short wait, the door opened. He knew instantly that he was facing Countess Sabina.

She was of indeterminate age; either elderly but very well preserved or young and terribly worn. Her hair was pure white and pinned back in a bun; her face was angular with large, dark, slightly slanted eyes, which, like the corners of her mouth, were edged by deep lines. She wore a navy blue dress with a white shawl. Her hands were bare, the nails bitten and unpainted.

She looked at him curiously, then gave a slight start of recognition and said, "You are Richard Burton." Her voice was musical and slightly accented.

"Yes," he replied. "I apologise that I wasn't available when you called on me. I've been—" He reached into his pocket and pulled out her card, holding it up with the handwritten side facing her. "I've been wondering about this."

"Come in."

She led him along a short passageway and into a small rectangular parlour that smelled of sandalwood. At her behest, he put his hat on a sideboard, leaned his cane in a corner, and sat at a round table. She settled opposite him. Her eyes never left his.

"You do not believe," she said softly.

"In a coming storm?"

"In mediumship."

"I didn't. Now I don't know what to think. Since my return from Africa, I've experienced one strange circumstance after another, and now nothing feels as it should, and if I find that mediums are not the charlatans I've always taken them for—I mean no affront—then I shan't be at all surprised." He paused, and added, "Countess, I know all about your role in government and about Abdu El Yezdi."

Countess Sabina nodded and smiled sadly. "I am not offended by your skepticism. Perhaps I would feel the same way had my life been different. As it is, the responsibility of communicating Abdu El Yezdi's instructions fell to me, and—" She pressed her lips together and shrugged. "It weighed heavily. To be at the centre of such very rapid changes in the world, and yet to know—" She stopped again and appeared to focus inward, her lips moving silently.

"To know?" Burton prompted.

"To know, as you say, that nothing is as it should be."

"Due to El Yezdi's influence?"

"It goes far deeper than that, sir."

Burton unconsciously ran the fingers of his right hand across his jawline. The sensation he'd experienced in Portman Square was still with him. He felt disjointed, more so even than during the days of malarial fever.

A shaft of light was slanting through the gap in the curtains. Dust motes waltzed slowly through it. Burton's and the countess's shadows stretched across the floor and up onto the flock wallpaper. The room felt suspended in limbo.

"Would you explain from the beginning?" His voice was oddly hollow to his own ears. Distant. "Tell me about when Abdu El Yezdi first contacted you."

The countess took a long, slow breath, exhaled, and said, "It was when the Great Amnesia was first recognised. According to my diary, I arrived in London in 1838 to search for my cousin, who'd come here from our native Balkans the year before and had not been seen since, but that mission meant nothing to me when I read of it. The accounts of my activities during the three years leading up to The Assassination, although set down in my own hand, felt like the recollections of someone else. I was disoriented and lost. It was as if I'd gone to sleep in my own bed in the old country only to awaken in an unfamiliar room in a strange land. To make matters worse, I began to experience vivid dreams, in which another used my own voice to address me. I thought I was going mad."

She stopped, looked down at her hands, and the muscles at the sides of her jaw pulsed.

She flexed her fingers and went on, "This invisible presence introduced itself as Abdu El Yezdi. I could not converse with him, for as I say, he appropriated my inner voice in order to address me. At first, he spoke only in my dreams, assuring me that he was real, would not harm me, was my friend, but required my assistance in order to achieve a great purpose. He then started to communicate during my waking hours, though when he did so, I would inevitably slip into a trance. He told me that The Assassination of Queen Victoria was never meant to happen; that it had been caused by a man who stepped out of his own position in history and into ours."

"What?" Burton interrupted. "I don't understand. What does that mean?"

"Bear with me, Sir Richard; I shall try to explain." She ruminated for a few seconds before asking, "Will you consider that in every circumstance there is inherent at least one alternate action? For example, one can respond to an opportunity or challenge with acceptance or refusal; one can react to an event aggressively, passively, evasively, or engagingly; one can choose to walk straight on, or turn back, or go to the left, or to the right."

Burton gave a curt nod of acknowledgement.

"In a coherent world," she said, "the option selected obliterates the rest; the alternatives may exist for a little while longer, but as the consequences of the decision taken develop, those alternatives become irrelevant and inapplicable."

She waited for Burton to again indicate that he comprehended. He said, "Very well. Pray, continue."

"When the most appropriate decisions are taken—that is to say, the most appropriate within the context of the situation—a chain of consequences develops far into the future, knitting together with other chains to form a strong cohesive whole." Countess Sabina place her right elbow on the table with her forearm pointing straight upward and her hand fisted. "Like the trunk of a tree," she said, holding the pose, "from which no deviations sprout, for inappropriate decisions are either corrected by subsequent ones or their consequences lead nowhere, while the alternate decisions—the ones not taken—have no consequences at all." She lifted her arm slightly then banged her elbow back down to emphasise the verticality of her forearm. *"This is what we call history."*

Burton thought of Darwin and murmured, "You propose a sort of natural selection, wherein decisions are a response to context, and consequences evolve, and only the fittest of them survive to contribute to the ongoing narrative?"

"Good!" the countess exclaimed. "You have it, sir! You have it! But make no mistake—there are no moralities or ethics involved. An appropriate decision isn't necessarily a good or right or nice one. It is merely the decision whose consequences will survive for the longest. Time has no virtue."

"Nothing but blind, pitiless indifference," Burton quoted.

"Precisely so." Again, she raised and thudded down her elbow. "This, as I say, is the mechanism of a coherent world." She suddenly splayed her fingers wide. "But The Assassination caused history to divide into branches. There is no more coherence."

"Why?"

"Because there was interference from outside the context; from a presence that bore no relation at all to the chains of causes and effects that were active at just after six o'clock on the tenth of June 1840; from a man who's rightful place was in the far, far future."

Burton momentarily closed his eyes and tried to digest this. When he opened them, Countess Sabina was still fixed in her pose.

"A man from the future," she repeated, "who somehow travelled backward through time to observe the failure of The Assassination, only to find that his presence changed the outcome. Existence bifurcated. There were now two histories. In one—the original—Edward Oxford failed to shoot the queen. In the other—in our version—he didn't."

"Was Abdu El Yezdi the man?" Burton whispered.

"No. The traveller was a descendent of the assassin, Oxford, and was called by the same name."

"But how could Oxford have descendants? He was killed at the scene. He had no children."

"In our history, yes. In the original, no."

Burton gestured weakly for the countess to stop. She waited patiently, holding her pose, while he struggled to process the revelation. When he indicated that he was ready for more, she went on:

"The traveller was in a bind. He couldn't return to his own time, for his own ancestor was dead, meaning he no longer existed there. This paradox, along with prolonged exposure to what, for him, was the distant past, drove him insane. He died."

For a third time, Countess Sabina bumped her elbow, drawing attention back to her raised forearm and widely spread digits.

"It made no difference. The bifurcation he caused had already broken the mechanism of Time. Paths not taken and decisions not made no longer faded into non-existence but instead gave rise to multiple consequences." She wiggled her fingers. "History splits and splits and splits again, and the farther these multiplicities grow from the path the single original history should have taken, the weaker the barrier between them becomes. Picture it as a tree, if you will, whose branches extend away from the trunk and keep dividing until they blur into a mass of twigs."

Burton raised a hand in protest. "Wait. Let us suppose I accept all this. Where does Abdu El Yezdi fit into it? Who is he? What is this great purpose he spoke of?"

"I do not know who he is. He's as much a mystery to me as he is to you. But I know he's aware of you."

"How do you know that?"

"Because he told me many times that I would one day meet you, and that I must tell you to seek out the poet, who will lead you to the truth."

"You refer to Algernon Swinburne?"

She responded with a small shrug. "As for Abdu El Yezdi's purpose—his use of me, and now of your brother, as a means to communicate with the government and influence individuals—it is to prevent a war."

"A war between whom?"

"Everybody. It will engulf the planet and barely a single country will escape it. He has seen it, sir. In some histories it comes sooner, in others later, but in all of them it comes, and entire generations of men are lost. Only in ours, perhaps, will it be avoided, for Abdu El Yezdi has guided us carefully."

"Maybe so," Burton responded grimly, "but he doesn't guide us any more. He's fallen silent."

"I am aware of that." She finally lowered her arm. "It is because the storm comes. The continuing deterioration of Time has made it possible for—" a tremor ran through her and she hugged herself, "—for a man to hop from one twig to another; to break through from his own version of existence into ours. You saw the lights that turned night into day. They marked his arrival. He is in our world, and Abdu El Yezdi must remain hidden from him."

"This man is the storm? Who is he? What does he want?"

The seer shook her head wordlessly.

"Then where is he? How can I locate him?"

Countess Sabina's lips stretched against her teeth. She rocked back and forth. When she answered, her voice was hoarse and quavered. "If I reach out my mind to search, he will find me. Others have attempted it. They sensed his arrival and tried to contact him. They died."

Burton remembered the newspaper headlines—the twelve dead mediums.

"But Abdu El Yezdi has made me stronger than most," she went on. "And you are you, so I shall try."

"Wait! 'You are you'—what do you mean by that? What is my significance in this affair?"

She didn't answer. Her eyes rolled up into her head until only the whites showed. She rocked in silence and two minutes passed.

Burton sat and watched. His thoughts ran over one another. What she'd told him was more incredible even than a tale from *A Thousand Nights and a Night*, yet, somehow, he found himself totally convinced of its truth.

Countess Sabina jerked in her seat. Her head snapped back then fell forward, revealing that her eyeballs had become utterly black. She smiled wickedly and said in a deep, oily, and unpleasant manner, "Well! This is a surprise! Hallo, Burton. How perfectly splendid to see you again. You look considerably younger. So you're consulting with a genuine medium? Good chap! She's a powerful one, too. Most gratifying."

The explorer gaped. Plainly, whoever was now addressing him, it was not the countess. He couldn't credit that her throat was even capable of producing such a voice, for it sounded as if hundreds of people were speaking the same words, in exactly the same tone, and in perfect unison.

"Who are—are—" he stammered. "El Yezdi?"

"I don't know the name," the other chorused. "You don't recognise me, then? I suppose I shouldn't be surprised. We met in Africa, my friend, under rather taxing circumstances, and I gave you my word it would not be our last encounter. I've travelled far to keep that promise. Regretfully, for you, it will not be a happy reunion. I feel obliged to prove myself, you see, so where before you witnessed my failure, this time the reverse must be true."

"We've met?" Burton interrupted. "Where in Africa? When? Who are you? What failure?"

The countess emitted a nasty chuckle. "Do you play chess, Burton?"

"I have done."

"Are you good?"

"Adequate."

"Then brush up your game. I'm counted an excellent player, and as such, I'll not forecast my moves other than to tell you this: I intend to break your spirit and drive you to your knees. For certain, it would be better to kill you outright, but I possess too much respect for you to do that. I don't want you dead. I admire you too much. You could even call it hero worship. Perhaps that explains my desire to have you, above all others, as one of my pawns. I'm afraid it's a fault of mine to demean the things I love the most. But we are what we are—and I am the Beast, Perdurabo; he who will endure to the end."

The countess threw back her head and let loose a peal of laughter.

Flatly, Burton said, "I'm reminded of a pantomime I visited in childhood."

The laughter stopped. The countess regarded him.

"Oh, bugger it!" she said. "I do it every time. I don't know when to stop, Burton. Always, I stray into the melodramatic and end up looking like an ass. Let us say *au revoir* before I embarrass myself any further. I have the royal charter. I'm on my way. We shall meet soon. Say goodbye to the countess."

Before Burton could respond, Countess Sabina's eyes snapped back to normal and her head suddenly swivelled around until he was looking at the back of it. With the neck creasing and crunching horribly, the revolution continued through a complete circle, and the countess's face swung back into view. Dead, she slumped forward onto the table and slid loosely to the floor.

The next day, Burton took the atmospheric railway from London to Yorkshire, and was then driven by horse-drawn carriage to Fryston Hall. Monckton Milnes greeted his friend's unexpected arrival with surprise and delight, which quickly turned to shock when the explorer conveyed the news of Countess Sabina's death. Indeed, Monckton Milnes was so deeply affected that, for hours, he could barely speak.

Burton distracted him with an account of the prognosticator's revelations, which sent both men rummaging through Fryston's library, piling Monckton Milnes's collection of esoterica onto tables and leafing through every book and pamphlet in search of information pertaining to the evocation of spirits.

"I'm now of the opinion," Burton stated, "that what we call magic is, at root, nothing less than a science of communication between multiple realities, but I do not believe it's been well understood by its practitioners, and I think the truth of it is buried beneath an enormous heap of extraneous claptrap. We need to dig it out. If we can secure the working principles, perhaps we can employ them in such a manner as to discover where this Perdurabo has come from."

Monckton Milnes, moving toward a table with a stack of books held precariously between his hands and chin, said, "We might begin with the premise that, through ceremonial actions, rhetorical exhortations, and a deep concentration upon the symbolic meaning of magic squares, one can literally will into existence a channel between alternate histories. That, after all, is what Oliphant appears to have done."

"Quite so. But did he do it independently, or does such a feat require simultaneous rituals in both realities?"

Setting down the books, Monckton Milnes divided the tottering pile into two stable ones, then took up a volume and waved it at Burton. "And how can we account for this? *De occulta philosophia* by Heinrich Cornelius Agrippa. Published in 1533. If history didn't bifurcate until 1840, how is it possible that so many treatises about magic date from centuries earlier, before there were any realities other than the original?"

Burton, who was sitting Turkish-style on the floor with open books arranged in a circle around him, dug his knuckles into his lower back and stretched, massaging the muscles to either side of his spine. He groaned, got to his feet, and said, "I wonder—on how many occasions have you experienced what you might call a turning point in your life and felt it was predestined?" He stepped over to the fireplace and leaned with his shoulder blades against the mantle, pulling a cheroot from his pocket and lighting it.

"Many a time," Monckton Milnes replied. "Back in 'twenty-seven, when I entered Trinity College, my falling in with Tennyson and his cronies propelled me into literary circles in a manner that felt utterly precipitous yet strangely appropriate. In 1840, Abdu El Yezdi's exhortation, via the countess, that I should finance Disraeli's opposition to Palmerston, had about it a whiff of the preordained, too."

Burton blew smoke into the room's already polluted atmosphere. "I've also had such moments. Being posted to India was one. Meeting Isabel. Berbera. As a matter of fact, I feel I'm at such a juncture right now, what with this king's agent business and all."

Monckton Milnes plonked himself into an armchair. "Your point?"

"That perhaps Time isn't the unidirectional phenomenon we take it for. What if there exists, within any given history, certain moments—in the lives of individuals, of nations, of the world as a whole—that possess such potency they send out ripples in all directions? Thus, hints of a significant future event can be sensed long before it occurs, so when it finally happens, it feels as though it was always meant to be."

"How does that relate to magic?"

"What bigger moment in Time can there be than the breaking of its mechanism? Surely the ripples caused by the bifurcation of history have echoed far into the past, as well as into the future. I don't consider it inconceivable that Agrippa and John Dee and Edward Kelley and all the others who've presented their theories of magic were engaged not with what was then a feasible science, but with the foreshadowing of one that would, long after their deaths, become viable."

Monckton Milnes grappled with the concept, scratched his head, grunted, and murmured, "Sideways, too."

"Pardon?"

"Those ripples. If they extend backward and forward through time, then maybe they go sideways, too, into the alternate histories. The war the countess spoke of—you said she claimed it occurs in all versions of reality. I'm wondering whether it originates in one—perhaps the original—and the rest suffer as they are battered by the—the—"

"The resonance," Burton offered.

"Yes! Resonance! Brunel's Clifton Suspension Bridge!"

Burton frowned. "What?"

Monckton Milnes slapped the arm of his chair enthusiastically. "When an army marches over a bridge, it breaks step so as not to establish a rhythm that'll resonate through the structure and cause it to swing—potentially to such a degree that it'll collapse. Wind blowing at the right speed and angle can have a similarly disastrous effect. Brunel built dampeners into the Clifton Suspension Bridge to prevent such a phenomenon. Don't you see?"

"See what?"

"That Abdu El Yezdi is attempting the same! He's been manipulating people and events in order to dampen the resonance. He must know the causes of the war in the other histories and, in this one, just as the countess claimed, he's been trying to change them. He's making our version of history break step!"

Burton considered for a moment before answering. "In which case, I think we can discard entirely the idea that there exists an Afterlife, for it seems far more likely to me that El Yezdi is a visitor from the future."

Monckton Milnes emitted a whistle and shook his head. Sotto voce, he quoted Plato: "How can you prove whether at this moment we are sleeping, and all our thoughts are a dream; or whether we are awake, and talking to one another in the waking state?"

It was a rhetorical question, and one that perfectly summed up the sense of unreality that held both men in its grip.

On Wednesday the 19th, a telegram was delivered to Fryston. It originated from France and stated simply, *En route*. The sender arrived two days later. He was ushered into the library by the butler to be welcomed with enthusiasm by Monckton Milnes, who cried out, "Monsieur! This is indeed an unexpected pleasure. It was not my intention to wrest you from your studies. May I introduce you to my friend, Sir Richard Francis Burton? Sir Richard, this is Monsieur Eliphas Levi. In matters of the occult, no man has greater knowledge or experience."

Burton stepped forward and shook the visitor's hand. Levi was a tall, broad, and wide-faced man, with a spade-shaped beard and clear blue eyes.

He wore the robes of a monk. When he addressed Burton, he did so in a deep, booming voice. "Your recent achievement, it cause a sensation even in my own country, Sir Richard, and—*mon Dieu!*—you know how reluctant we French are to celebrate the deeds of any man not of our own nation! But *à tout seigneur tout honneur*, eh?"

Burton bowed his thanks.

Monckton Milnes instructed his butler to bring a pot of coffee, then hustled Levi and Burton into armchairs. The men settled, and Levi said, "I have no choice but to come. The information you send—oof!—*ça me donne des frissons*! So to England I travel *aller au fond des choses*—to get to the bottom of things. *Commençons par un bout.* Tell me all about it. All about it, *je vous prie!*"

Monckton Milnes looked at Burton. "Richard, I assure you, Monsieur Levi can be trusted. I recommend you hold nothing back. I will take responsibility." He then addressed the Frenchman. "But, monsieur, please understand that much of what you will hear has been classified as secret by the British government. It must not be repeated."

"I understand. *Bouche cousue!* Now, you speak and I listen. *Cela vous dérange si je fume?*"

Monckton Milnes flicked his hand in consent then looked on in amazement as Levi pulled a perfectly enormous calabash pipe from his pocket and began to stuff its exaggerated bowl with tobacco. A minute later, the Frenchman was leaning back in the chair with his eyes closed, giving every indication of being asleep but for the thick plumes of foul-smelling smoke that he puffed into the air.

Burton tried to counteract the pungent odour with one of his Manila cheroots, and while doing so, described Laurence Oliphant's ritual before going on to detail the course of his investigation, his encounter with Countess Sabina, and his and Monckton Milnes's theory.

Levi sighed and emitted a breathy whistle.

"Monsieur?" Monckton Milnes murmured.

"*Attends, je cherche!*" Levi responded. *Wait, I'm thinking!*

They sat quietly while he ruminated. Five minutes passed.

"*Bien,*" the Frenchman finally said. "*On commence à y voir plus clair!* Yes, yes! I see all now!" He reached into his pocket, produced the letter Monckton Milnes had sent him, and held up a page upon which the magic squares had been transcribed. "The four central numbers—*mille, neuf cents, dix, et huit*—I think you now comprehend, *non?* They are exactly what they appear when written: *une année!* They are 1918, fifty-nine years from now."

Levi rose and paced to a window. He gazed out of it at the clear blue sky.

"As you surmise, messieurs, these calculations they open a passage from *une réalité différente* from this, our own—but also from that world's future. Three intruders, we have! Three! But only one, he come through this way, for the lights in the sky, they are caused by the method, and they never are seen before, *non*? So, who are our visitors?" He turned to face them and raised a finger. "*Numéro un!* Edward Oxford. He arrive, I think, by means of the white suit."

"The suit!" Burton exclaimed.

"*Oui*, for it is seen in 1840 and in 1837, where it vanish in front of Henry Beresford. It is magical—it operate on scientific principles of which we have no conception."

Burton examined the glowing tip of his cigar, which was by now little more than a stub. He flicked it into the fireplace. "Then, based on his physical resemblance to the queen's assassin, I'll wager the future Oxford and the Mystery Hero are one and the same. Which means he's dead."

"*Oui, probablement* he is killed by intruder *numéro deux*. That person, he hit Detective Inspector Trounce, and he resemble you, Sir Richard. You have the countenance of an Arabian. Abdu El Yezdi is an Arabian name. So, this we add up and—*voila!*—El Yezdi is our second traveller in time. But by what method? We do not know. But he have the rifle, which tell us he come from Africa in 1918. Also, we know he stay, and is here still."

Levi sucked at his pipe for a moment. When he spoke again, it was from behind a veil of blue smoke.

"*Numéro trois.* Perdurabo. It seem he also come from Africa, 1918, but he journey through the *passage conceptuel* Oliphant create. This is very significant, for it mean he here only as *volonté*, as willpower."

"You mean he has no physical presence?" Monckton Milnes exclaimed.

"*Exactement.* Our Beast is *une personne insubstantielle*—a phantom—but *volonté*, it must have *un corps physique* to survive in the world. It mean he take possession."

"Of another person?" Burton asked.

"*Oui.* This I must study. Possibly, it is the key to his defeat, for he has the bad intentions, *non*?"

Monckton Milnes jumped up and started to pace back and forth, pulling his hair. "It's too much!" he cried out. "I feel my brain will explode! I don't know what to think or do!"

"You don't have to think or do anything," Burton said. "Your help has been invaluable, but the rest is up to me."

"*Non*, monsieur," Levi said. "Not only. I will assist. I have knowledge. This Perdurabo, his nature I must better understand. I fear what he might be, so I will research, research, research!"

Burton gave a nod of gratitude.

"And you, Richard?" Monckton Milnes asked.

"I have to locate Abdu El Yezdi. I'm certain he's an ally in all of this. The line of inquiry leads us to Wallington Hall and the poet, Swinburne."

CHAPTER 11

THE POET

"That idle clock at Westminster which may well hold its hands before its face for very shame, had cost the Nation the pretty little sum of £22,057. We never knew a richer illustration of the homely truth that Time is Money."
—PUNCH MAGAZINE ON THE CRACK IN BIG BEN, 1859

They had to wait until Monday—when they were expected at Wallington Hall—to meet Swinburne, and on that day their patience was tested further, for when they arrived they were informed that the Trevelyans and their guests were on a day trip to Tynemouth. So a steam carriage was hired, and Burton, Monckton Milnes, and Levi set off in pursuit.

They arrived at the seaside town in the middle of the afternoon, disembarked on the Grand Parade, and strolled down a sloping road to the Longsands Beach. A stiff breeze was blowing from the southwest—sultry and not at all refreshing—and the sea was agitated, bulging up and crashing noisily onto the sand.

"Strange weather," Monckton Milnes commented. He pointed to the sky inland, where inky clouds were being ripped into ribbons, curling around themselves and looking more like a gigantic swarm of insects than vapour.

There were a few individuals on the beach, but about halfway along it, strolling slowly toward the headland that sheltered Cullercoats Village, a larger group was visible. Among them, a tiny figure with long blazing-red hair was skipping about like a child, and—as Burton and his companions hurried toward the party—it detached itself from them, divested itself of its clothes, and plunged into the sea.

"*En octobre!*" Levi exclaimed.

"He'll drown for sure!" Monckton Milnes cried out.

They set off at a trot, Levi huffing and puffing, and upon drawing closer to the gathering, heard shouts and protests above the ceaseless uproar of the waters.

"Don't be a fool, lad!"

"It's too rough, Algy! Come back at once!"

"Swinburne, you lunatic! Give it up!"

Burton saw Dante Gabriel Rossetti. He also recognised William Bell Scott, the Scottish artist and poet who resided in London and was famous for his decorative embellishments to Isambard Kingdom Brunel's colossal trans-atlantic liner, the SS *Titan*. A small woman in capacious skirts and with a lace bonnet, he took to be Lady Pauline, and standing beside her, hook-nosed and with a moustache that swept around his jawline into sideburns, was her husband, Sir Walter Calverley Trevelyan. Two other men were present, both of about thirty years in age, neither of whom he knew.

"Sir Walter," he said, as he reached them, "I'm Burton."

It was Lady Pauline who answered. "Sir Richard, how wonderful! And Mr. Monckton Milnes! Welcome! Welcome!"

"I do hope you don't mind," Burton said, "but we've brought an additional guest. This is Monsieur Eliphas Levi, an accomplished occultist and philosopher."

"Not much the philosopher, I regret," Levi corrected. He took Lady Pauline's hand, bowed, kissed it, and said, "*Enchanté.*"

"Delighted," she responded. "Gentlemen, if you will forgive me, I shall make introductions in a moment. As you can see, my little Carrots is up to his usual tricks." She pointed out to sea, where the small red-headed individual was plunging through the waves. "Put him next to rough waters and he invariably jumps into them."

"By James!" Monckton Milnes exclaimed. "But he's a strong swimmer!"

Sir Walter added, "And a remarkably accomplished horseman, too, but in both disciplines he acts like a blithering idiot and takes damned silly risks!" He raised his voice to a shout. "Algernon! Come out of there and warm your bones with a swig of cognac!" Turning back to Monckton Milnes, he grinned and said, "That'll get him. Always does. What!"

The swimmer turned toward the beach, stretched out, and allowed a mountainous wave to drive him to shore. Once in the shallows, he stood, gave a squeal of delight, and loped through the water and onto the sand. Lady

Pauline averted her face and called, "For goodness sake, put on your clothes and don't do that again!"

"Fear not, dear lady!" the little poet answered. "For now I have drunken of things Lethean, and fed on the fullness of death!"

"Yes, yes," she responded impatiently. "Sir Richard, Monsieur Levi, Mr. Monckton Milnes, forgive me. Algernon is, as ever, a terrible distraction. Allow me to present the party. Gabriel, you surely know."

The minister of arts and culture greeted Burton and Monckton Milnes, and to Levi said, "Rossetti, monsieur. I'm pleased to make your acquaintance."

"William Scott," the hostess continued, and after handshakes had been exchanged, turned to a tall, slender man with curling brown hair, a somewhat asymmetrical face, and a stiff and awkward stance. "And this is Charlie Dodgson, an up-and-coming writer."

He smiled rather shyly and said, "I'm happy to—that is, pleased to make your—to meet you."

"Arthur Hughes," Lady Trevelyan went on, pulling forward a dark-complexioned individual who had very long black hair. "A talented artist and illustrator. My husband, Sir Walter. And this—" she added, as the swimmer, now fully dressed, joined them, "is Algernon Charles Swinburne, who recently toured the continent having fled Oxford University where he achieved precisely nothing, and who, apparently, is destined to be a notable poet, if he manages to stay alive long enough."

"Pah!" Swinburne screeched in a high-pitched voice. "You exaggerate wildly! About my risk-taking, I mean; not about the notability of my poetry!"

Burton looked in amazement at the little man. In aspect, the fledgling poet was extraordinary. He was in his early twenties, but tiny and childlike—barely five feet tall—with sloping shoulders that appeared far too weak to carry his huge head, the size of which was magnified by the tousled mass of red hair standing almost at right angles to it, despite being sopping wet.

Swinburne's bright green eyes met his, and he yelled, "By my ailing Aunt Agatha's blue feather hat! What a grand old time you've had of it, Burton! The riddle of the Nile solved at last! Hurrah! Hurrah! And you, Monckton Milnes! Aren't you the man with the absolutely whopping collection of erotica? I say, have you any of de Sade's work? Bound in human skin, no doubt! I hear he's *de rigueur* among the Whippinghams, Bendovers, and Lashworthies! I must indulge! I simply must!"

"Really, Carrots," Lady Pauline protested. "Do control yourself."

"Incidentally," the poet said. "Cognac. I was promised it and I demand it."

Sir Walter handed over a silver hip flask, which the little man put to his lips and upended.

"Ah! Much better!" He passed it back. Sir Walter looked at it, shook it, found it to be empty, gave a rueful sigh, and said, "You were only meant to take a sip. What!"

"My whistle required a wetting," Swinburne answered, "for I intend to recite my latest while we walk to the headland and back."

The party continued along the beach, the men holding their hats as the breeze stiffened. Swinburne skipped along, his movements jerky, his gestures excessive. "*Laus Veneris!*" he announced, and began:

> *Asleep or waking is it? for her neck,*
> *Kissed over close, wears yet a purple speck*
> *Wherein the pained blood falters and goes out;*
> *Soft, and stung softly—fairer for a fleck.*
>
> *But though my lips shut sucking on the place,*
> *There is no vein at work upon her face;*
> *Her eyelids are so peaceable, no doubt*
> *Deep sleep has warmed her blood through all its ways.*

"Gad!" Monckton Milnes whispered to Burton. "Remarkable! Remarkable!"

It was. Swinburne, though shrill-voiced, was so eloquent and evocative in his performance that his poetry became almost mesmeric, raising such an emotive response in the listeners that every other thing they sensed appeared to fuse with his strange lilting intonation, and the crashing waves sounded as if they were eulogising the words and rhythms with far-off acclamations.

Burton strolled and listened and absolutely marvelled.

The poet's praise of Venus continued until they reached the headland where the outlying cottages of Cullercoats overlooked the beach. He finished:

> *I seal myself upon thee with my might,*
> *Abiding alway out of all men's sight*
> *Until God loosen over sea and land*
> *The thunder of the trumpets of the night.*

He stopped, took a deep breath, turned to face the group, and said, "Shall we convene in the local tavern before we head back?"

"That was breathtaking, Algy!" Sir Walter said.

"A masterpiece!" his wife agreed.

"Bravo!" Levi cheered.

"A work of genius!" Rossetti declared.

"I found it incred—that is, utterly extraordinary, and, um—" Dodgson added.

Monckton Milnes stepped forward. "Mr. Swinburne, I should very much like to see about getting your work into print."

Swinburne hopped up and down and waved his arms. "Never mind that now! The tavern awaits! Come along! Come along!"

He scampered up a slope and they followed him into the village.

Eliphas Levi leaned close to Burton and murmured, "*Il est un jeune homme très doué, non?* But also very strange!"

A few minutes later, they found The Copper Kettle—which overlooked Cullercoats Bay—and settled in its lounge bar. The introductions made on the beach were now supplemented as—in conversations expertly guided by Lady Trevelyan—the men discussed their work and interests.

It was an exceptional gathering of singular personalities: Burton, magnetic, forceful, but somewhat troubled; Monckton Milnes, stylish, charming, and eclectic; Levi, perceptive and inquisitive; Rossetti, complex and a little pensive; Charles Dodgson, quiet, dreamy, and self-conscious; Arthur Hughes, brooding but penetrative in his comments; Sir Walter, passive but jocular; and Swinburne, whose enthusiasms and excitability increased in proportion to his consumption of alcohol, for which he displayed such an inordinate predilection that, three hours later, when the party departed the establishment, he required Rossetti and Hughes to hold him upright.

As they proceeded southward along the Grand Parade, Dodgson's hat was snatched from his head by the wind and flung far out to sea. "My goodness!" he exclaimed. "Where's my topper off to? It looks like—it appears that the weather is change—is taking a turn for the worse!"

Burton looked to the west and saw the dark clouds Monckton Milnes had noted earlier, now expanded dramatically and piled high into the upper atmosphere.

"*Le jour tombe,*" Levi observed.

"Straight back to Wallington, I think, gentlemen," Lady Pauline announced. "There is a storm coming."

Burton shivered at the ominous words.

At Tynemouth's coach house, Sir Walter hired the same two steam-driven landaus his group had arrived in. He, his wife, Rossetti, Hughes, and the barely conscious Swinburne squeezed into one, while Burton, Monckton Milnes, and Levi were joined by Dodgson in the other.

The carriage lurched into motion and Dodgson, who was leaning out of the window and looking at the sky, received a faceful of steam. He dropped back into his seat, coughing. "By golly, I shall never learn my lesson. These steam transports are forever puffing—that is, blowing their fumes into my face!"

"But they make the world more small, *non?*" Eliphas Levi said. "We travel so much fast *de nos jours!*"

"I am afraid—I fear they make literature smaller, too, Monsieur Levi."

"*Oui?* How is that?"

"If steam has done nothing else, it has at least contrib—added a whole new species to English literature. The booklets—the little thrilling romances, where the—the—the murder comes at page fifteen, and the wedding at page forty—surely they are due to steam?"

"*Bien sûr*, you speak of the publications for sale at the train stations, *non?*"

"I do, sir—er—monsieur. And if the Department of Guided Science succeeds in its intentions—its plans, and one day we travel by electricity, then we shall have leaflets instead of booklets, and the murder and the wedding will be—will come on the same page!"

Burton and Monckton Milnes laughed, and the latter said, "Have you read any of Sir Richard's accounts, Mr. Dodgson?"

"No, sir, I regret not."

"He stuffs into them so many appended facts, qualifiers, and opinions that your observation has given me a whole new understanding of the term 'footnote,' for if steam shortens a journey to the extent that only a booklet may be read, then Burton's volumes must require one to forgo the railway and take a very long walk!"

The landau, following the other, turned onto the coast road toward Newcastle upon Tyne. The wind gusted against it, causing it to rock.

"Have you known Swinburne for long, Mr. Dodgson?" Burton asked, grabbing at the edge of the bench to steady himself. He stifled a hiss as his arm gave a pang.

"Not at all, Mr. Burt—Sir Richard. I've not—I hadn't ever encountered him until my arrival at Wallington Hall yesterday. It is Rossetti with whom I am—that is, who I am friends with. He strikes me as—I refer to Mr. Swinburne—as a very eccentric fellow. It's a quite fantast—an amazing thing, but did you know that he cannot feel pain at all?"

"He can't feel pain? How is that possible?"

"It seems his brain is arranged—is not put together in the normal manner. Indeed, there are certain forms of pain that he even senses—interprets as—as pleasure. According to Rossetti, it has resulted in him acquiring a rather—um—um—peculiar taste for—for—for—"

"Whippingham, Bendover, and Lashworthy," Monckton Milnes offered.

"Yes."

"You mean flagellation?" Burton asked.

Dodgson cleared his throat, went beetroot-red, and nodded.

"The English vice," Levi declared. "You are a race *très drôles*!"

Monckton Milnes said, "Must I remind you that the Marquis de Sade was French, Monsieur Levi?"

"A philosopher and Utopian! In transgression, he seek to expand the mind, to allow for the establishment of Socialist thought, but you English—ha!—all you want is the whack, whack, whack of the strap!"

Dodgson crossed his arms and legs and mumbled, "Anyway, the more time I spend with—in Mr. Swinburne's company, the more I think him curiouser and curiouser."

By the time the two carriages reached the train station in Newcastle, the clouds had filled the sky from horizon to horizon. They were dark and billowing, suggesting gale-force winds at a high altitude. Even at ground level, the gusts were now whistling and howling with growing ferocity.

"It's the end of our long, hot summer," Lady Pauline commented as the party climbed aboard the Glasgow train. "And thank heavens for that. You gentlemen will never understand the infernal combination of heat and corsets. I'm certainly not the fainting type, but I came perilously close to it this season."

The Glasgow slow train—the express didn't stop near Wallington—halted at a succession of towns and villages until, at nine o'clock, it reached Kirkwhelpington, which was little more than a hamlet, lacking even a small station. Only the Trevelyan party was getting off here, and the guardsman brought from his van at the back of the three-carriage train a set of wooden steps, which he placed beneath the door to allow the nine passengers to alight.

Swinburne had by now recovered with no ill effects after his lunchtime indulgence. As the locomotive chugged away and heavy drops of rain began to slant down, he laughed, put his face to the sky, and hollered:

Outside the garden
The wet skies harden;
The gates are barred on
The summer side:
"Shut out the flower-time,
Sunbeam and shower-time;
Make way for our time,"
Wild winds have cried.

"You'll catch your death," Lady Pauline fussed, grabbing him by the elbow. The rest followed as she hurried the little poet along a path toward a large farmhouse. The wind and rain rapidly increased in fury, soaking them all.

"By God!" Rossetti shouted above the clamour. "Old England is in for a battering!"

Upon reaching the ramshackle building, they were greeted by a burly giant of a man who hustled them into a barn in which was stored one of Wallington Hall's vehicles: a very large and ornate stagecoach.

Sir Walter said, "Bless my soul, Mr. Scoggins, what weather! Can you drive us home in this downpour?"

"I 'ave no objection," the farmer replied. He eyed Burton, Monckton Milnes, and Levi. "More o' ye a-goin' back than what come out, though. Might be a tight squeeze. Would one o' the gents be willin' t' sit up top wi' me?"

"I'll do so," Burton volunteered.

Scoggins set about fetching four horses and, with Burton's help, harnessed them to the stage. He then ran to the farmhouse and returned with a set of waterproofs, which Burton donned. The passengers climbed aboard, Scoggins and Burton mounted the driver's box, and moments later the vehicle was bouncing and swinging eastward, with rain hammering against it and wind slapping at its side. Thunder roared overhead, and the countryside was one second buried in pitch darkness and the next vividly illuminated, until it achieved a vague state of permanency in the form of an after-image etched onto Burton's retina.

The journey was short—two miles—but tested them all. Those inside the stage were thrown about as it jolted through ruts and potholes, while the two men up top were soaked to the skin, even through their waterproofs.

To Burton's relief, a flash of lightning finally revealed the huge Palladian-style manor.

They'd arrived at Wallington Hall.

With one foot curled up on the chair beneath him, Algernon Swinburne was declaiming verse, introducing to the gathering his latest—but incomplete—work, *Hymn to Proserpine*. His consumption of alcohol—which had resumed as soon as they'd arrived at the Trevelyan residence, changed into dry clothes, and gathered in the large and lavishly appointed sitting room—appeared to have no effect on his performance; his voice was clear, the words enunciated with passion and style. His audience was entranced. They listened in rapt silence, but Wallington Hall itself was not at all quiet, and the recitation was accompanied by ghastly moans, sobs, screams, and howls from the chimney as the wind moved in the flue, sounding like a horde of tormented ghosts.

Swinburne finished:

> *I shall die as my fathers died, and sleep as they sleep; even so.*
> *For the glass of the years is brittle wherein we gaze for a span;*
> *A little soul for a little bears up this corpse which is man.*
> *So long I endure, no longer; and laugh not again, neither weep.*
> *For there is no God found stronger than death; and death is a sleep.*

For a short period afterward, Lady Pauline and her guests spoke not a word.

There came a loud rattle and crash as a slate was dislodged from the roof and fell to the patio outside the French doors.

Burton found himself dwelling on a line from earlier in the poem: *Time and the Gods are at strife, ye dwell in the midst thereof.*

Charles Dodgson broke the spell. "A lament, Mr. Swinburne? You regret the passing of—the death of paganism and the rise of—of Christianity?"

"When we turned our eyes to the sky," Swinburne replied, "and placed our faith in the unknowable, we ceased to worship the ground beneath our feet and all that springs from it to sustain us. See how our mighty machines now despoil it! My hat, Dodgson, I rue the day we became blinded by hope and repudiated responsibility for the world in which we live. I would rather we strive to understand what definitely is than place reliance on what probably isn't."

Arthur Hughes said, "But can you not see that the intricate beauty of this world is nothing short of miraculous? How can its creator be anything less than divine?"

"I recently met Charles Darwin," Burton interjected. "You've heard of him? *The Voyage of the* Beagle? He's formulated a rather astonishing and elegant hypothesis in which he proposes that a particular system of nature is enough to explain the extraordinary diversity and interconnectedness of life." He went on to repeat, as best he could, Darwin's summary of the theory of natural selection.

"No God need apply," Rossetti murmured.

Sir Walter opened his mouth to speak. He was cut off by a splintering crash as the French doors suddenly flew open and wind came shrieking into the chamber, overturning glasses and small tables, sending ornaments, antimacassars, and doilies flying, and causing the guests to leap out of their chairs in panic.

Burton and Eliphas Levi dived across the room and forced the doors shut.

"The latch has broken," Burton called to the others. "Rossetti, drag that chair over—we'll jam it against the handles."

This was done, and with the doors secured, they surveyed the chaos.

"I call an end to all discussions relating to God," Sir Walter proclaimed, "for whether He exists or not, we have obviously infuriated Him! What!"

Lady Pauline summoned the butler and asked him to have the staff clean up. The group then divided, with the Trevelyans ushering Rossetti, Hughes, and Dodgson to Lady Pauline's private gallery, while Burton, Monckton Milnes, Levi, and Swinburne retired to the library. There, until long past midnight while the storm raged on with ever-increasing ferocity, they discussed the merits of Darwin's theory. Even Eliphas Levi, who'd trained as a Catholic priest, agreed that it had the potential to lead mankind to a new respect and responsibility for the world and its many wonders.

Despite his growing state of inebriation, Swinburne so impressed Burton and Monckton Milnes with his unique outlook and intuitive intelligence that, by two in the morning, they'd invited him to join the Cannibal Club. Burton had taken an instant liking to the poet. They shared a similar philosophical outlook—an aversion to physical, moral, and intellectual boundaries; a fascination with the banned, the censored, and the denunciated; and a restless dissatisfaction with the mores and manners of British society—but he also detected in Swinburne an indefinable ennui, as if a normal life couldn't offer the poet even one jot of fulfilment. This, Burton understood.

The conversation had already touched on the Afterlife and the existence— or not—of the soul. Now, Burton—who'd already divulged state secrets to Detective Inspector Trounce, Detective Inspector Slaughter, and Eliphas

Levi—decided to bring Swinburne into the fold. He knew it was a risk. The little man was wild and idiosyncratic, but Burton felt an immediate trust, and he always allowed himself to be guided by instinct.

"Algernon," he said.

"Algy, please, Sir Richard. Brandy dissolves formalities."

"Very well. Then drop the *Sir*. It still feels like an absurd trimming to me. I understand you once met an individual named Abdu El Yezdi?"

"I did, and—my hat!—what a hideous creature he was, too!"

Burton glanced first at Monckton Milnes then at Levi.

"Would you tell us about it?"

Swinburne had been sitting with one leg crossed over the other, his foot swinging spasmodically. He now tucked it under himself, adopting the position that Burton already associated with the poet taking centre stage.

"It was five years ago," Swinburne began. "I was seventeen years old and eager to be a cavalryman—forlorn hopes and riotous charges!—but my father forbade it. I was holidaying with my family on the Isle of Wight at the time, and one day I decided to put my courage to the test by climbing Culver Cliff."

He addressed Levi, "Monsieur, it is a sheer face of chalk and flint, averaging three hundred feet in height."

"*Très dangereux, non?*" Levi muttered.

"Indeed so. Before commencing the climb, I swam in the sea, which was tremendously rough that day. It was the beginning of my love affair with storm-wracked waters—I've never been able to resist them since. Having survived the waves, I then made my first attempt at the rock face, but an overhanging ledge defeated me and I was forced to make my way back to the beach. I chose another route, gritted my teeth, and swore I would not come down alive again. So I climbed, and the wind, penetrating the nooks and crannies, made a sound like the Eton Chapel organ, and gulls wheeled around me and I feared they would peck out my eyes. But on I went, until, just as I came close to the top, the chalk crumbled beneath my feet and I was left dangling by my fingertips from a ledge. Thankfully, I was able to carefully gain a different foothold, and with that to secure me, hauled myself over the top and onto the edge of the Culver Downs. Gents, I was immobilised by exhaustion, on my back with eyes closed, when a voice said, 'Roll to your left, Algy, else you might find that going down is far quicker than coming up.'"

"He knew your name?" Burton asked.

"Yes. So I shifted away from the cliff edge and saw an extraordinary figure sitting cross-legged nearby."

"What did he look like? Hideous, you said?"

"Fat! He was dressed in white Arabian robes, with a *keffiyeh* covering his head. His skin was dark, his right eye blind and milky, and his teeth large, crooked, and rotten. An enormous beard flowed down over his protruding belly, and when he spoke, he moved his hands constantly. '*As-salamu alaykum*,' he said. 'I am Abdu El Yezdi. Are you satisfied now? Do you feel yourself courageous?'"

Burton frowned. "Then he was also aware of the purpose of your climb?"

"He was. And I replied, 'Courageous enough to ascend a cliff, anyway,' to which he responded, 'Courage, Algy, is not accurately measured in isolated acts of bravery, but in the ongoing ability to express your own true nature, no matter how you are judged or feted or damned.'"

"*Mon Dieu! Combien vrai!*" Levi exclaimed.

The poet nodded. "He then said, 'Listen to me, young man. Soon your courage will be tested in a manner you can't imagine. When that time comes, do not doubt yourself, for your instincts are true. Look for—'" Swinburne paused and suddenly gawped at Burton.

"What is it?" the explorer asked.

"He—he said, 'Look for the man with a scar on his face. When he comes, your travails will begin.'"

Burton reached up and with his fingertips traced the deep scar that scored his cheek. He was conscious that the poet, Levi, and Monckton Milnes were all staring at him.

A minute passed, then Swinburne went on, "The next thing I knew, I awoke, lying there, and was alone. I couldn't even remember falling asleep."

Monckton Milnes murmured, "Mesmerism?"

"Undoubtedly," Burton agreed.

"There's one more thing," Swinburne added. "I have a vague impression of Abdu El Yezdi leaning over me."

"What was he doing?" Burton asked.

"He was saying, 'Thank you.'"

CHAPTER 12

THE *ROYAL CHARTER*

PATENT
CONVEX HERALDIC JEWELLERY
**Raised Arms, Crests, and Monograms on
Watches, Studs, Lockets, Sleeve-Links, &c.**
Also, Egyptian Gold, Eudialyte Rings, Carbon Diamonds
BRUNDLEWEED JEWELLERS
Creator of the renowned "Brundleweed Necklace."
St. Martins Lane, London

The following morning, the remnants of ruined chimneys, dislodged roof tiles, and pieces of a decimated summer house were heaped against the walls of Wallington Hall, along with a huge mass of unidentifiable debris. The grounds were strewn with leaves, twigs, branches, and fallen trees. A phaeton carriage—not belonging to the estate and probably not even from Kirkwhelpington—lay crumpled beside an ornamental pond. South-facing windows had broken and rooms were in disarray. The guests confined themselves to the inner chambers while the staff cleared the mess and started repairs.

"I've never seen anything like it," Lady Pauline declared. "What a storm!"

No one had slept well. They'd risen late and breakfast was more of an early lunch. After it, Burton, Monckton Milnes, and Levi took a stroll to survey the damage. The winds were still high and the sky filled with scudding clouds.

"I think I'll head back to Fryston," Monckton Milnes said. "I'm concerned there might be nothing left of it. Will you come, Richard?"

"I'll pass, if you don't mind, old fellow. I want to spend a little more time with young Algernon. Perhaps he'll allow me to mesmerise him. As you suggested, El Yezdi certainly did so, and I'd like to peel away whatever mantle he cast over the lad's memory."

"You think there was more to their meeting, then?"

"I suspect so. I can't imagine how or why, but the poet is obviously connected with the business."

"And with you, my scar-faced friend. Gad! It's confirmed, then. The whole El Yezdi in the Afterlife idea was nonsense, and the British Empire has been manipulated for two decades by—by—"

"By a living person," Burton said. "And you find that less acceptable than a ghost?"

"I was going to say, by a foreigner."

Burton laughed. "By Allah's beard! That's far, far worse!"

"*Désastreux!*" Levi agreed.

They rounded a corner and saw a steam sphere tearing up the drive toward the house. It skidded to a halt in front of the main entrance, hissing forth a final plume of vapour before its engine fell silent. The vehicle's door hinged upward and Detective Inspector Trounce stepped out. He saw them and waved them over.

"By Jove, Burton," he cried out. "You've a lot to answer for!"

"What on earth are you doing here, Trounce? And what do you mean?"

"Chief Commissioner Mayne has issued a temporary ban on me flying police rotorchairs."

"Why so?"

"Because you destroyed two of the confounded things while under my supervision. So, what with last night's storm throwing tree trunks all over railway tracks, I had no option but to come here in this contraption. What a bloody drive! The roads are hellish!"

"I doubt a rotorchair would survive these winds, anyway," Burton said. He contemplated the metal globe and thought he heard something thudding at its rear. "But why make the journey? Has there been another abduction?"

"No, there's been a shipwreck."

Monckton Milnes, who'd walked to the back of the vehicle, said, "What have you brought with you, Detective Inspector?"

"Nothing. Not even a change of blessed clothes. Burton, the tempest grounded a ship off Anglesey at one-thirty last night. It's called the *Royal Charter*!"

Burton's hands curled into fists.

"There's something moving in here," Monckton Milnes said. He reached down to the latch, clicked it open, and lifted the door of the sphere's storage compartment.

"Great heavens!"

Burton crossed to him, looked into the vehicle, and saw Abraham Stoker curled up in the confined space.

"Would ye be good enough to help me out?" the youngster moaned. "I can't move a bloomin' muscle."

Trounce joined them and exclaimed, "A stowaway? What the dickens are you playing at, lad? Don't tell me you've been in there all the way from London?"

Burton and Monckton Milnes lifted the boy out and held him while he tried to straighten his limbs.

"Aye, that I have, Mr. Fogg. I'm sorry, but if you're off on one of your adventures, then you'll need an assistant, an' I'm just the boy for the job, so I am!"

Monckton Milnes gave the Scotland Yard man a quizzical look. "Fogg?"

Trounce groaned.

Burton told Monckton Milnes, "When he began investigating me, Trounce tried to throw me off the track by using the name Macallister Fogg, which he took from this boy's favourite penny blood."

"Spur of the moment," Trounce muttered. "And damned foolish. So now I know who's been following me. What the blazes are we going to do with the little ragamuffin?"

"We'll have him tag along with us to Anglesey," the explorer responded. "He might prove useful. He's a Whisperer."

Bram started to rub his arms and shake his legs as the blood returned to them. "Ouch! Ouch! I won't be any trouble, Mr. Fogg. I promise. And—aye!—you'll have the whole Whispering Web at your disposal, so you will!"

Trounce said, "Humph!"

"And Anglesey, did I hear ye say? Ain't that in Wales, now? It's a barren part o' the country, so it is. There are more Whisperers there than telegraph offices, to be sure."

The detective held up his hands in surrender and grumbled, "All right, all right!"

Burton surveyed the devastated grounds and the fast-moving clouds. "How the blazes are we going to travel? There are no trains, you say, Trounce?"

"All services cancelled."

"The *Orpheus*," Monckton Milnes offered. "You have the authority to commandeer it, Richard, and the airfield isn't far from here. I daresay a machine of that size can manage this wind."

A shrill voice suddenly proclaimed:

Orpheus, the night is full of tears and cries,
And hardly for the storm and ruin shed
Can even thine eyes be certain of her head
Who never passed out of thy spirit's eyes,
But stood and shone before them in such wise
As when with love her lips and hands were fed,
And with mute mouth out of the dusty dead
Strove to make answer when thou bad'st her rise.

Abraham Stoker gave a yelp of alarm. "Oy! What's that thing?"

"That thing," Burton answered, "is Algernon Swinburne."

The poet—who'd descended the front doorsteps gesticulating wildly as he recited—approached them. His hair flew about his head like a tumultuous conflagration.

"Hallo, hallo, and thrice hallo!" he cried out. "And one for the nipper, too—hallo! The *Orpheus*? Your African airship, Richard? Surely you're not leaving us already?"

"We have to fly to Anglesey, Algy. There's been a shipwreck. It has some bearing on the matters we spoke of last night."

"On El Yezdi, you mean? Then I'm coming, too!"

"There's no need for—"

Swinburne stamped his foot and screeched, "Nonsense! Balderdash! Tosh and piffle! Rot and poppycock! A shipwreck? A shipwreck? By my Aunt Betty's beastly blue bonnet! It's the very stuff of poetry!"

Trounce whispered to Burton, "Who—?"

"Later," the explorer replied. He made a snap decision. "We're wasting time. Trounce, Bram, Algy, we'll borrow the stagecoach and set off for the airfield at once." He turned to Monckton Milnes. "Fryston is on the way, I believe? We'll drop you and Monsieur Levi there. I'm afraid we'll have to abandon our plan to travel together to New Wardour Castle."

"I'll go there by train. I daresay the tracks will be cleared by next week."

"*Un moment, s'il vous plaît,*" Levi interrupted. "Is it an inconvenience if I accompany you, Sir Richard? If you are to fly on the *Orpheus*, I have the opportunity to examine the room where Oliphant make his ritual. I wish to see it, though the glass and floor are clean now, I think. *Aussi,* this *Royal Charter* affair is connected, *non?*"

Burton gave his consent, and an hour later, having packed and bade an apologetic farewell to Lady Pauline and her remaining guests, Burton and his companions were rattling northwestward in the stage. The driver made the best speed he could but the roads were hazardous, being littered with debris, and it took them two hours to reach Fryston—where they bid Monckton Milnes adieu—and another to get to the airfield.

Upon reaching the *Orpheus*, Burton hurried aboard and was greeted by a surprised Doctor Quaint, who escorted him to Captain Nathaniel Lawless's cabin.

"By James!" the airman exclaimed, gripping Burton's hand. "I wasn't expecting to see you until the engagement party. Are you recovered? You look somewhat battered, if you'll pardon the observation."

"I'm done with the malaria, Captain, but I was involved in an unfortunate accident. No permanent damage. What's the state of the ship? Can you get her into the air right away?"

"She's being fitted with armaments in preparation for the signing of the British–German Alliance—we'll be providing security at the ceremony—but I could afford to take her on a short excursion. We have no supplies aboard, though, and I'm not keen on flying in this wind. Where do you want to go?"

"Anglesey, on the west coast."

Lawless squinted. "Hmm. About a hundred and seventy miles southwest. That's straight into the gale, which'll make it simpler but slower."

"I'll need top speed, and you can forego the paperwork."

"I'm not sure you have—"

Burton thrust forward the card issued by the Home Secretary.

"—the authority," Lawless finished lamely. "Oh, you do. No paperwork, then. Good! I can't abide all the damned bureaucracy. I'll need half an hour to get the engines warmed up then we'll be off."

"Thank you, Lawless."

It was a bumpy flight, but Captain Lawless and his crew, whose loyalty to Burton was absolute, squeezed every ounce of power from the airship's mighty engines, bullying the dirigible into the headwind and exhausting themselves as they battled to keep the ship stable. At six o'clock, having made excellent time, they landed half a mile west of Moelfre Village, in Dulas Bay, Anglesey Island, on the northwest coast of Wales.

"We can't tether her here," Lawless told Burton. "The gale will tear her to ribbons. I'll take her down, you jump off, and I'll find a more sheltered spot inland."

"I can't ask any more of you, old chap. Get back to Yorkshire. I'm going to be here for a day or two, I suspect."

Lawless saluted. "Very well. As always, glad to have been of service."

Burton, Trounce, Levi, Swinburne, and Bram left the *Orpheus*, watched as it rose up and shrank rapidly eastward, then walked toward the coast. They breasted a shallow hill and were suddenly confronted by a scene of such turmoil that their hearts missed a beat.

"God in heaven!" Trounce cried out.

Below them, half a mile away, the people of Moelfre were milling about on a flat shelf of limestone, against the seaward edge of which waves of enormous size were crashing, sending white spray high into the air. Behind the crowd, a great many corpses had been laid out—Burton estimated at least three hundred—and, heedless of the risk to their own lives, the villagers were pulling more from the violent waters. Screams and shouts carried up to the onlookers.

But even such human drama and tragedy could not long distract from the spectacle being enacted a quarter of a mile out to sea where, against a bank of upthrusting stone fangs, a large steam clipper was being relentlessly smashed to pieces. Mastless and broken almost in two, it was pitching and rolling, falling apart as the sea pounded savagely against it. Even from this distance, Burton and his companions could hear the loud booms and cracks of the vessel's destruction.

"The *Royal Charter*," the explorer whispered.

Swinburne suddenly sprang forward, pulling his jacket off and flinging it aside as he bounded down the slope. "There's someone still aboard!" he shrieked.

Burton and Trounce set off after him, with Levi and Bram at their heels.

The poet yanked off his shirt.

"Collect his clothes, Bram," Burton shouted, then, "Algy! Don't be a bloody fool! You'll be killed!"

Swinburne ignored the warning, leaped onto the shelf, kicked off his shoes, ducked through the crowd, and before anyone could stop him, plunged into the sea.

"Bismillah!" Burton gasped as the raging waters engulfed the little poet. He dropped onto the wide ledge and joined the villagers, who were yelling, "*Dere nôl! Dere nôl!*" which he correctly supposed was Welsh for, "Come back!"

"There! *Regardez!*" Levi hollered, levelling a finger toward the pilothouse near the stern of the clipper's splintering deck. The structure had been almost entirely torn away and a figure was plainly visible within, propped upright against the ship's wheel.

One of the villagers, a churchman, shouted something to Burton, who—Welsh being one of the few languages he didn't speak—snapped, "In English, Father?"

The rector called to a young constable, who came over, listened to him, then said to Burton, "That man on the wreck, sir. It's the captain. Determined to go down with his ship, he is. As if we don't have sufficient deaths on our hands."

Burton anxiously scanned the turbulent waters. He saw a flash of red. He could barely believe it. Algernon Swinburne, who looked so weak and delicate, was swimming like a seal and was already halfway to the *Royal Charter*.

"How many survivors?" Burton asked, distractedly.

"Just one, may the devil take him."

Seeing Burton's shocked reaction, the policeman went on, "A member of the crew managed to swim ashore. Another followed him—a regular giant of a man, he was—and the moment he set foot on land, he took hold of his crewmate's head, broke his neck, and ran off."

Trounce said, "Constable, I'm Detective Inspector Trounce of Scotland Yard. When was this?"

"About two in the morning, sir. Half an hour after the ship ran aground. The lads from all the stations on Anglesey are searching the area. I hope they're travelling in pairs. That fellow could snap a person in half."

A cheer went up. Incredibly, Swinburne had reached the jagged rocks and was clambering up them in an astounding display of agility.

"Is he really a poet, Mr. Fogg?" Bram Stoker asked. Trounce nodded.

Burton was unable to tear his eyes from the scene. He had a lump in his throat. The red-headed figure sprang across a gap and caught at the shattered planks of the clipper's hull just as the vessel floundered laterally until its side was almost horizontal. Swinburne rose to his feet, ran forward, then dropped and clung on tightly as the ship sank down again. A horrible grinding sounded as wood fragmented.

"He's made it," Trounce gasped as Swinburne vaulted over a brass rail onto the sloping deck. "By Jove! I've never seen anything like it!"

The crowd yelled their encouragement as the poet raced toward the stern, then screamed in alarm as he was swamped by a monumental hump of water. The wave buried the ship and exploded onto the rocks, sending spray so high the wind caused it to rain over the onlookers, drenching them. For a terrible moment, the *Royal Charter* was completely lost from view, but then it reared up again and, with a shattering crash, broke completely in half. The prow swung skyward before ploughing into the ragged stone teeth. Its entire mass crumpled and flew into pieces.

At Burton's side, the village rector wailed and began to sob.

Trounce clutched Burton's arm, his fingers digging in, and the scarcely healed bone flared with pain. The explorer didn't register the shock of it at all, but his vision suddenly clarified, and every tiny detail of the destruction he was witnessing took on equal weight and significance. His knees gave way and Trounce caught him and held him upright, but the explorer was oblivious. All he knew was that, in the sternmost remains of the clipper, which was now swivelling its broken end to face shoreward, there was a figure slumped loosely against the wheel, and beside it, Algernon Swinburne.

The wreck lurched. The poet fell. He slithered across the deck and shot into the sea.

The last part of the vessel rolled over, was driven into the rocks, and fragmented.

"*Je ne peux pas le voir!*" Levi said. "I can't see him!"

"For the love of God, Trounce," Burton croaked, "let go of my arm!"

He straightened and cradled his forearm against his body.

The village constable looked around as a man approached and addressed him. He answered and, after the other had departed, said to Burton, "That was Bob Anwyl of the coastguard station. He says the tide is on the turn. There'll likely be no more bodies washed ashore. We're going to take these—" he gestured toward the many dead, "—up to Moelfre Church's hall. The county coroner is on his way. I'm sorry about your friend. He was very brave."

"And very alive!" Trounce yelled. "By God, will you look at that!"

Sure enough, Swinburne, bedraggled, exhausted, and with a package held tightly under his right arm, was climbing back onto the limestone shelf. Villagers hurried forward to help him, while others enthusiastically cheered his bravery. Burton and Trounce pushed through them. The explorer took off his coat and threw it across the poet's shoulders.

"He was dead," Swinburne panted, "and tied to the ship's wheel. Let me sit down. I'm fagged!" He collapsed to the ground. "This was in his pocket." He passed the packet up to Burton.

"I should take that, gents," the constable objected.

"I outrank you, young man," Trounce said. He indicated Burton. "And he outranks me."

The parcel was about the size of a book and was very tightly wrapped in sealskin and secured with waxed twine. Burton handed it to Trounce. "We'll examine it later. Let's get Algy dry first."

The constable whistled to a portly gentleman, who waddled over and was introduced as Bevan Llewelyn, proprietor of the Rhoslligwyspite Inn. The name might have been unpronounceable, but the prospect of ale, warmth, and comfort was enough to propel Swinburne back to his feet with a cry of, "Lead on, dear fellow! A tipple will do me a world of good!"

"You didn't swallow enough of the Irish Sea?" Trounce enquired.

Bram passed over the poet's clothes and a minute later Swinburne was hastening toward Moelfre with the rest of them trying to keep up.

"Is this him fagged?" Trounce wondered. "By Jove, Burton, but you keep some strange company!"

Bram piped up, "He's like one of 'em froons what captured ye in Greece, is that not the case, Mr. Fogg?"

"You probably mean fauns," Burton put in. "And whatever you're referring to was just a story, lad."

"To be sure, sir! *The Baker Street Detective*, issue nine hundred and eight, if I be rememberin' rightly. *The Case of the Greek Interloper*."

"I'm not Macallister Fogg," Trounce protested.

Bram grinned and gave him an exaggerated wink. "Don't you be a-worrying, sir. Me lips are sealed, so they are."

When they reached the outskirts of the village, Burton looked back and saw a long line of people, all in pairs, slowly carrying the drowned toward the little settlement. He shook his head sadly. He was no stranger to death, but had never witnessed such a terrible toll.

The Rhoslligwyspite Inn—or "Rosie with Spite," as Swinburne rechristened it, before then mutating it into "The Spiteful Rosie"—was a small but comfortable pub. It had two upstairs rooms available for guests, both of which Burton paid for. He, Levi, and Swinburne changed into dry clothes. Neither Trounce nor Stoker had brought any, so they requested that the fire be lit in one of the chambers, then stood in front of it and steamed.

They all rested. Llewelyn delivered well-filled bowls of beef stew and bottles of ale, all "on the house" due to Swinburne being regarded as a hero. Slowly, the bar downstairs filled, though its conversations were subdued. The villagers had been up all the previous night and through the day, so didn't remain for long. By eleven o'clock, silence reigned, and even the wind had worn itself out and could only manage a few pitiful whimpers.

Burton and his colleagues—minus Bram, who'd fallen asleep—gathered in the downstairs lounge, pulling armchairs around a coffee table by the fireplace. Llewelyn told them they could help themselves to beer, then locked up and went to bed.

"Damned calamity," Trounce muttered. "Worst wreck in living memory. I shall never get the image of all those corpses out of my head."

"*Il était terrible*," Levi agreed.

Burton adjusted the wick of the nearest lamp and, by its increased light, started to unwrap the package Swinburne had recovered.

"I meant to ask, Trounce—how did you know?"

"About the ship? The lifeguard station here telegraphed the Admiralty as soon as the clipper was grounded. In such cases, because a police presence is often required shoreside, the Force is always alerted. I was just finishing my shift when I happened to overhear a conversation about it. You'd already shown me the telegraph message received on the *Orpheus* during the aurora phenomenon," he tapped his head, "and things clicked, so I jumped into a steam sphere and drove all night through the storm. Thus the bags under my eyes."

"Good man," Burton said. "By James, this package is tightly swaddled!"

He unfolded the sealskin only to find a second layer beneath. This, too, was removed.

Swinburne leaned forward. "What is it?"

"The ship's log." Burton opened the book. "Somewhat damp and some of the ink has run, but the wrapping did a good job. It's readable." He spent a few minutes examining it page by page. "The captain was Thomas Taylor."

"Lashed himself to the wheel," Swinburne murmured.

"He do it himself?" Levi exclaimed.

"Yes. I could tell by the manner in which he was bound."

Burton read from the log. "Departed Melbourne on the first of August, bound for Liverpool. Three hundred and seventy-five passengers. A hundred and twelve crew. Carrying a large consignment of gold."

He turned one page after the other. "She was making good headway." He moved a few pages on, stopped, frowned, and flicked backward to an earlier point. "Strange. Algy, would you mind reading to us? Are you up to it?"

Trounce moved to object—surely the poet was exhausted!—but before he could utter a sound, Burton's eyes flashed a warning. The detective froze, then leaned back in his chair and said nothing.

"I most certainly am," Swinburne cried out. "Hand it over."

Burton passed the logbook to Swinburne, open at the page he'd selected. The poet curled his left foot up onto the chair and began to read. His voice took on the unique quality Burton had noticed at Wallington Hall, and within moments the explorer, occultist, and Scotland Yard man were entirely immersed in the account.

THE SHIP'S LOG

LIVERPOOL & AUSTRALIAN NAVIGATION COMPANY
STEAM FROM AUSTRALIA TO LIVERPOOL
UNDER 60 DAYS
THE MAGNIFICENT STEAM CLIPPER
"ROYAL CHARTER"

Thursday. 1st day of September 1859.
  8.00 a.m.
  In Doldrums off West Africa. Unable to establish exact position. Compass spinning. At midnight, the Northern Lights appeared (this far south? I've never heard of such a thing). As bright as day. No stars visible for the remainder of the night. No breath of wind. A curious atmospheric effect: all flames have died, and no match will strike. We can't fire-up the engines. I've traversed the tropics hundreds of times and have never before seen combustion suppressed this way. The men are mad with the loss of their pipes and cigars.

  3.00 p.m.
  A slight current has got up. Drifting eastward, albeit slowly. Crew short-tempered. How we all depend on our tobacco!

  10.00 p.m.
  Another night with light from horizon to horizon. The sea is like glass and so reflective we appear to be floating through clouds of shifting colours. A marvellous but very unnerving effect.

Friday. 2nd day of September 1859.
   8.00 a.m.
Still becalmed. No wind. No fire. Compass useless. Humidity tremendous, making sleep almost impossible. Second Officer Cowie reports the passengers are increasingly restless and quarrelsome. He broke up two disputes last night.

Noon
Indications that we're still moved by a current in a generally easterly (perhaps NE) direction.

11.00 p.m.
No change. Again, the Northern Lights. Passengers rowdy. More fighting. A man named Samuel Grenfell (gold miner) stabbed another, William James Ferris (storekeeper) in the arm. Has been locked in his cabin.

Saturday. 3rd day of September 1859.
   2.00 a.m.
Seaman William Draper reports he can "smell land."

11.00 a.m.
Lack of sleep overtaking all. Thank God passengers too tired for troublemaking.

Midnight
The aurora has partially cleared, now being confined to a portion of sky to the east of us, and has taken on a most curious aspect, funnelling downward onto a mountainous island just visible on the horizon. We're at 3°10 N 8°42'E. According to my charts, the island is Fernando Po. The current is pushing us toward it. Still no fire.

Sunday. 4th day of September 1859.
   7.00 p.m.
No change in our circumstance. A deep lassitude creeping over all.

Monday. 5th day of September 1859.
   Noon
Drawing close to Fernando Po. The island is dominated by a huge conical

peak, clothed in tropical forest. We're drifting toward a cove, Clarence Bay, by the charts. If we make land, we can at least lay up until the weather changes.

10.00 p.m.

Ashore. At 4.40 p.m., the *Royal Charter* touched ground just off a narrow beach, backed by steep banks of yellow clay. I led a landing party and a small crowd of people greeted us. We followed them up ladders and, beyond the top of the banks, discovered a row of buildings, newly erected by recently arrived Spanish colonists and christened Santa Isabel. Already, the dwellings are rotten and infested with vermin and their inhabitants are languid to the point of semi-consciousness, gripped by deadly ennui and disease.

After leaving the ship, we discovered that our matches were strike-able once more and we took to our tobacco with much enthusiasm, yet as soon as we stepped back aboard, no combustion was possible. Whatever the atmospheric disturbance is, it's somehow clinging to the vessel, so other than a rotating watch of seven men, the crew and passengers have abandoned her and are all put up in filthy lodgings. I fear for the women and children. This is no kind of place for them.

Tuesday. 6th day of September 1859.

2.00 a.m.

Can't sleep. There are drums thundering from somewhere inland. They've not let up for a single moment since the sun set.

11.30 a.m.

Humidity, sandflies, mosquitoes, prickly heat. This place is unbearable. The vegetation hangs limply beneath the blinding sky. Everything's still, as in death.

Wednesday. 7th day of September 1859.

9.00 p.m.

The governor of Santa Isabel, a man named de Ruvigas, has advised us to move inland to a town called Santa Cecilia, which is some 1,300 feet above sea level and less dangerous to health. Tomorrow we'll do so, remaining there until the weather improves, or until we can fire-up the ship's engines.

Thursday. 8th day of September 1859.

2.00 a.m.

The drums. On and on. I feel I might lose my mind.

6.00 p.m.

Leaving the watch aboard ship, I today led the crew and passengers inland along a steeply ascending jungle trail until we arrived, exhausted, at Santa Cecilia. The village is little more than a huddle of shacks, all raised up on poles in the centre of a wide clearing, but the inhabitants willingly made room for us in return for gifts of alcohol, tobacco, pocket watches, rings, belts, and whatever else we could afford to give them. The female passengers have set about cleaning the place up.

Midnight

The air is fresher here. The mosquitoes less numerous. But the drums are just as insistent.

Saturday. 10th day of September 1859.

3.00 p.m.

I'm remiss in my log-keeping. The days are endless, the nights worse.

Monday. 12th day of September 1859.

8.00 p.m.

We feel we are being watched. The women grip each other, their faces taut with fear. The men have become strangely quiet. I find myself checking my pistol again and again.

Tuesday. 13th day of September 1859.

3.00 p.m.

Such torpor. Sleep evades us but we slip in and out of prolonged periods of dark reverie, almost a trance, wherein we are paralysed by a sense of being examined, like pinned insects.

5.30 p.m.

From 3.00 p.m. until 5.00 p.m. every day, clouds form with astonishing rapidity and rain falls in a solid sheet. The thunder is as violent as I've ever heard. Our huts leak, and after the downpour we crawl from them soaked to the skin to dry ourselves beneath the returned sun. It's causing our clothes to rot from our backs. By all that's Holy, I've never beheld such a ragged band of miserable souls.

Friday. 16th day of September 1859.

7.00 p.m.

I dread nightfall and the commencement of the drumming. There's been so little sleep, I'm in a state of living dream. More difficult than ever to maintain this log.

Monday. 19th day of September 1859.

9.00 a.m.

Last night, I was roused by Seaman Joseph Rodgers, who was near hysterical and swearing blind that, "The devil himself is among us." It took nigh on an hour to calm him.

Tuesday. 20th day of September 1859.

8.00 p.m.

Another day has passed like an opium dream and now the drums have begun their nightly torment. A terrible sense of menace pervades the village.

Tuesday. 27th day of September 1859.

11.00 a.m.

A week has gone by in a haze, with no attention paid to this record. I remember nothing of what's passed, if anything has, beyond the repetitive torture of heat, rain, and drums, heat, rain, and drums. We've had twenty-seven days now without the merest hint of a breeze; twenty-two days on this loathsome lump of rock. Writing exhausts me.

3.00 p.m.

Something brought us here. Something is holding us captive. None of this is natural. God help us.

Wednesday. 5th day of October 1859.

11.30 a.m.

Joseph Rodgers and a passenger, John Judge, have suggested we investigate the source of the drumming. By Christ, we do something or we remain here and die of languor, so I've agreed, and will lead the expedition myself. I pray I can raise strength enough for it.

4.00 p.m.

It'll be just the three of us. The rest lie limp and vacant-eyed. A stiff climb faces us, for our hosts insist that the drummers are located in a crater, called the Pico Santa Isabel, at the top of the central mountain, which is obviously an ancient and dormant volcano. We'll set out at dawn.

Thursday. 6th day of October 1859.

7.00 p.m.

The climb is steep but not impossibly so. There's a trail with steps cut into the sheerest stretches. John Judge is a giant, Herculean in strength and endurance, but Rodgers and I are all too mortal. The heat sucks out what little energy we've been able to muster. Frequent stops necessary. No progress at all when the rains came. Nevertheless, we've covered a good distance. We'll reach the peak tomorrow. For now, Rodgers has made a little fire, which we'll huddle around while we endure the night and the damnable drums.

Friday. 7th day of October 1859.

6.30 a.m.

Not a wink of sleep. The feeling of looming menace is overpowering. We're resuming our ascent.

Saturday. 8th day of October 1859.

8.00 p.m.

Be merciful to me, O God, be merciful to me! For my soul trusts in You; and in the shadow of Your wings I will make my refuge, until these calamities have passed by.

We achieved the summit yesterday at 4.00 p.m. and stood at the lip of the crater. On the opposite side, a village, from which the nocturnal drumming no doubt emanates, has been built around about a quarter of the depression's outer edge. Its inhabitants soon spotted us, but rather than approach, they simply stared.

We paid them little attention; our eyes were pulled down to the incredible object lying amid the bubbling pools at the base of the bowl. It appeared to be the aurora borealis, somehow condensed into a globe, about two hundred feet in diameter, but with a large section missing, like a bite from an apple. As we descended toward it, details began to stand out. Though formed entirely from light, the apparition started to remind me of a steam sphere, though of gigantic proportions. There were rows of rivet-like protrusions, portholes, and the missing section was seemingly lined with broken spars and torn plating, as if exploded from within.

We climbed past pools of steaming water and sulphurous mud, stumbling constantly, unable to look away from the seething colours before us. Rodgers began to utter a prayer but was hushed by John Judge, who commanded us to listen, and in doing so confirmed what I had already noticed: that there were whisperings coming from the globe; voices, which as we drew closer gained clarity, becoming fragments of conversations, orders, pleas, and shouts. I clearly heard:

". . . advancing west. Their forces stretch from . . ."

". . . will do as I bloody well say, Private, or so help me I'll put him before a firing squad. Now get down there and tell him to . . ."

". . . isn't seaworthy and is beyond repair, sir. The long and short of it is that the *Britannia* is wrecked. If we make a last stand, it has to be here. You have to tell General Aitken there's no way out of . . ."

". . . German units to the south and west of us. Unless he can do what he says, we'll not live beyond . . ."

". . . I'm hit! Mother of God! I'm . . ."

". . . and what is left worth fighting for? Surrender, I say. It's the . . ."

". . . can't trust him to . . ."

". . . Get down! Get down! He's dead, damn it! Sweet Jesus, they aren't human! We have to . . ."

And more. These odd, panicked, desperate echoes became, unmistakably, the yammering of men caught in warfare and making a last stand against superior forces. I'm not certain how, but I was taken by the notion that their one hope had betrayed and abandoned them, and that whoever or whatever that last hope had been, it was here, now, on the island, and was the awful presence we'd all sensed.

We were but a few steps from the globe when the illumination suddenly increased until it blazed like the sun. The next thing I knew, I was on the ground and Rodgers was shaking the wits back into me. I sat up, looked around, and saw only rocks and pools and the sloping sides of the crater. The mirage was gone.

"Let's get out of this accursed hellhole," John Judge said. "I beg of ye, Cap'n Taylor, let us get back to our people."

I'd no hesitation in agreeing, and we climbed out of the crater as fast as was possible and immediately started down the path toward Santa Cecilia. Minutes later, the rain fell, and we were sent slithering wildly down the track amid mud and water. Lord knows how we survived that slide.

Night fell before we'd completed the descent but we hastened on by star-light, convinced that we were being pursued, though by what we couldn't guess. Never have I felt such stark terror!

 3.00 p.m.

We didn't realise it at the time, but there were no drums last night. We reached the village at dawn and, being fatigued beyond endurance, immediately took to our huts and, at last, slept.

 Midnight

Again, no drums. Why does this cause me such dread?

Monday. 10th day of October 1859.
 9.00 a.m.

A cannon heard from the *Royal Charter*! It can mean only one thing! Let everything that has breath praise the Lord! Praise the Lord! For He, in His infinite mercy, has given us fire! We can flee this detestable place!

 Noon

The crew and passengers trekked from Santa Cecilia to Santa Isabel and from there boarded the ship. We had to carry John Judge. He is in such a deep sleep that he won't wake.

We'll be away from here!

"My hat!" Swinburne exclaimed. He untangled his legs, stood, and moved to the bar. "They spent more than a month on that island. Wasn't the ship reported missing?"

"They were sailing from Melbourne," Burton said. "With a voyage of that length, a month's delay isn't so unusual."

Swinburne claimed fresh bottles of ale and brought them back to the table.

"What on earth was it?" he asked. "The globe of light? The aurora? It's astonishing!"

"Born from the wreck of the SS *Britannia*," Burton murmured.

Swinburne regarded him curiously. "What? What? What?"

"I'll explain later. Here, I'll pour the drinks, you continue with the log."

The poet's green eyes fixed on Burton for a few seconds then he gave a grunt, looked down at the book, and resumed.

Monday. 10th day of October 1859.
    7.00 p.m.
I will bless the Lord at all times; His praise shall continually be in my mouth. Fernando Po is receding behind us! Admittedly, the going is slow. The steam engine was designed to augment the sails, not replace them, but at least it drives us from hell and gives us hope.

Tuesday. 11th day of October 1859.
    3.00 p.m.
Crawling along. Currently at 1°34 N, 3°23 E.

Wednesday. 12th day of October 1859.
    9.00 a.m.
Passenger Colin McPhiel found dead this morning. No ascertainable cause. Have ordered corpse preserved in lime for Christian burial in God's good earth. Crew and passengers now convinced the ship is blighted. I argue against superstition, but in the name of the Almighty, I feel it myself.

    3.00 p.m.
The lassitude that immobilised us on the island is still with us. Many men, women, and children affected, in various degrees, some practically comatose.

Thursday. 13th day of October 1859.
    9.00 a.m.
Seaman Henry Evans and Second Steward Thomas Cormick both died in the night. Again, no reason apparent. Placed in lime.

    Noon
2°38'N, 13°8'E.

    9.00 p.m.
Passenger Benjamin Eckert has committed suicide by hanging. Used the last of the lime to preserve his corpse. What doom weighs so heavily upon this vessel?

Friday. 14th day of October 1859.
    7.00 a.m.
Joseph Rodgers mad with terror. Insists he saw passenger Colin McPhiel

walking the deck in the early hours of this morning. I have sent him (Rodgers), Seaman William McArthur, and Quartermaster Thomas Griffith to the hold to check on the corpse.

7.30 a.m.
They report the body is present but has been disturbed; lime scattered around the casket.

8.00 p.m.
Have put Seamen Edward Wilson, William Buxton, and Mark Mayhew on a rotating watch over the hold.

At 8°55′N, 20°39′E. Making for Cape Verde to resupply.

Saturday. 15th day of October 1859.
3.30 a.m.
Shaken from my bed at 2.30 a.m. by Cowie and Rodgers. Utter chaos in the hold. Buxton and Mayhew both dead. No marks on them, but by God, the look of horror on their faces! Edward Wilson a gibbering lunatic. Struck out wildly at all who approached him. Had to call upon John Judge to restrain the man. Corpse of Colin McPhiel stretched out on the deck, powdered with lime, a dagger embedded hilt-deep in its heart.

I'm at a loss. I've ordered the bodies of Buxton, Mayhew, McPhiel, Evans, Cormick, and Eckert cast overboard. Wilson bound and locked in cabin.

Noon
Finally, the wind has got up, but our evil luck continues, for it's driving us westward. Currently at 9°24′N, 24°18′W.

11.00 p.m.
11°21′N, 28°57′W. We'll not make Cape Verde this day.

Sunday. 16th day of October 1859.
10.00 a.m.
Passengers Mrs. C. Hodge, George Gunn, Franklin Donoughue, and Seaman Terrance O'Farrell, all dead. No indications of disease other than the severe lethargy from which they'd all suffered. By Christ, am I commanding a plague ship? Bodies thrown overboard. No energy or will for ceremony.

1.00 p.m.

Joseph Rodgers bearded me in my cabin and ranted for half an hour. He said: "Satan is sucking the souls right out of us, Captain Taylor. We'll all be dead afore this ship touches another shore."

Monday. 17th day of October 1859.

7.00 a.m.

Ten taken. Passengers: Mrs. J. B. Russell, Miss D. Glazer, P. N. Robinson, T. T. Bowden, T. Willmoth, and A. Mullard. Crewmen: Second Officer A. Cowie, Rigger G. A. Turner, Fourth Officer J. Croome, Seaman W. Draper.

3.00 p.m.

A strong southerly wind has driven us to 19°28′N, 30°14′W.

5.00 p.m.

There was a medium among our passengers, known to all as Mademoiselle Tabitha, though the manifest lists her as Miss Doris Jones. I didn't see her on the island. Apparently she spent our days there curled up in a corner of a hut and spoke to no one. Since we departed, a similar story: locked in her cabin, opening the door only to receive food from a friend among her fellow passengers. An hour ago, I was told she wanted to see me. Went down and found her seemingly in a trance.

She said, "He is reaching out, Captain. Speaking through the mouth of a woman like me."

I asked, "Who is?"

She said, "Our additional passenger. He who hides. He who feeds. He who endures to the end."

I asked, "We have a stowaway?"

To this, she giggled like a madwoman and said, in an oddly deep voice, "Let us say *au revoir* before I embarrass myself any further. I have the royal charter. I'm on my way. We shall meet soon. Say goodbye to the countess."

She reached out as if grasping something in the air and made a twisting motion, before then clutching at her chest and collapsing to the floor, stone dead. I have no explanation.

8.30 p.m.

I have had the ship searched from bow to stern. No stowaway detected.

Tuesday. 18th day of October 1859.

5.00 a.m.

Twelve more gone. I shan't list them here but will add the date of their demise against their names on the passenger and crew manifests.

Rodgers informed me that he witnessed John Judge "creeping" around the ship during the night. I approached Judge half an hour ago. He explained that he's started to keep a nightly watch. The man is not crew, but his intimidating size is such that I am glad of his vigil.

Noon

Developing storm. We are driven NNW.

Saturday. 22nd day of October 1859.

Time unknown. Daylight.

Impossible to maintain this log. Mass panic aboard. Fighting. Suicides. The death toll increases every night. Seaman Gregory Parsons attempted to lead a mutiny. Joseph Rodgers forced to shoot him dead.

We are in the stranglehold of an increasingly violent maelstrom. Compass spinning. Timepieces have stopped. Sky black with cloud. Unable to establish position.

Monday. 24th day of October 1859.

Time unknown.

Storm so intense I don't know if it's night or day.

Death. Nothing but death. Passengers refusing to leave their cabins.

Time unknown.

Rodgers has become convinced that John Judge is responsible for the evils that beset this vessel. He's going after him with a pistol. I am powerless.

Time unknown.

Not enough crew remaining to man the ship. I have to get it to port. I have to—else we're all dead.

Note.

This writ by Joseph Rodgers at Capt. Taylor's command.

The Capt. pegs us as in the Irish Sea. He is bound to the wheel so as not to be washed overboard and is set on steering us to any port we can find. I am to wrap this logbook in sealskin and return it to him, so it might be on him if we are wrecked.

Beware of John Judge. Satan took him on the island and he has preyed on us this voyage through. He walks by night and steals a man's soul from him and leaves the body dead but not dead. I saw Colin McPhiel rise and hunt for souls to replace what was took from him.

The *Royal Charter* is damned. Capt. Taylor is damned. I am damned. We are all damned. But I'll not go without a fight. I have me pistol loaded and as God is me witness I'll search this ship from bow to stern till I find Judge and send him back to hell with a bullet.

Lord have Mercy on my soul.

CHAPTER 14

THE MAN WHO SHOULD HAVE DIED

"As for a future life, every man must judge for himself between conflicting vague probabilities."
—CHARLES DARWIN

"That's the end of it," Swinburne said. "Phew! What terror! I shall have nightmares!"

Trounce exclaimed, "I'd lay good money on it being Joseph Rodgers who made it ashore and John Judge who followed and killed him."

"*La Bête est venue*," Eliphas Levi whispered.

"The Beast has come?" Swinburne repeated. "What do you mean by that?"

Burton, Trounce, and Levi glanced at each other.

The poet banged his fist on the arm of his chair. "Out with it!" he commanded. "Explain what this is all about! You—" he jabbed his finger at Burton, "—are the man with a scar on his face. Abdu El Yezdi said my travails would begin when you appeared." Swinburne lifted the logbook and waved it over his head. "If this *Royal Charter* tragedy and your interest in the Arabian are connected, then I demand to know how!"

Burton was silent for a few seconds then nodded. "Very well, but I must ask something of you first."

"What?"

"I believe the Arabian mesmerised you, and I want to do the same. Maybe I can unearth whatever he caused you to forget."

"You mean he removed something from my memory?"

"More likely he inserted something but made it inaccessible to your recollection. I'd like to know what."

"And if I allow this, you'll tell me the full story?"

"Yes."

"Then do it. At once."

Burton knew that under normal circumstances it would be impossible to put Swinburne into a trance. The poet had an excess of electric vitality. It caused him to be in constant twitchy motion and was at the root of his over-excitable personality. However, he was exhausted after his taxing swim and Burton had purposely asked him to read from the logbook to further tire him. Swinburne was drained—just as he must have been after ascending Culver Cliff—as was evinced by the relative idleness of his limbs.

Burton addressed Trounce and Levi. "Be absolutely still and quiet please, gentlemen."

He drew his chair over so it faced the poet's and leaned forward. "Algy, keep your eyes on mine. Relax. Mimic my breathing. Imagine your first breath goes into your right lung. Inhale slowly. Exhale slowly. The next breath goes into your left lung. Slowly in. Slowly out. The next into the middle of your chest. In. Out. Repeat that sequence."

As Swinburne's respiration adopted the Sufi rhythm, he became entirely motionless but for a slight rocking. Burton murmured further instructions, guiding the young man into a cycle of four breaths, each directed into a different part of the body.

The poet's mind was gradually subdued by the developing complexity of the exercise. His pupils grew wider and his face slack. Burton, satisfied that he'd gained dominance, said, "Go back to Culver Cliff, Algernon. You have just made your climb and are lying on the downs at the top. A man named Abdu El Yezdi has met you there."

"Yes," Swinburne whispered. "The fat, snaggle-toothed old Arabian."

"He's spoken to you about courage and told you to look out for a man with a scar on his face."

"Burton."

"What did he do next?"

"He shifted closer to me and looked into my eyes. He was blind in one, but the other was like a deep well, and when he instructed me to breathe in a certain manner, I felt compelled to do so. I became very drowsy. He said, 'Algy, I shall give you a verse. You will forget it until it is needed.'"

The poet raised his face toward the ceiling and recited:

Whene'er you doubt thy station in life
Thou shalt take to the tempestuous sea.
To all the four points it shall batter thee
Until you find thine own power, and me.

Swinburne looked at Burton and murmured, "What hideous doggerel."

"Did he say anything else?"

"Just, 'Thank you,' then he told me to sleep. I don't remember anything more until I awoke and he was gone."

Burton said, "I shall count backwards from five. When I'm done, you'll decide that explanations can wait until tomorrow. You'll go straight up to bed and will enjoy a deep and restful sleep. Do you understand?"

Swinburne nodded.

"Five. Four. Three. Two. One."

"My hat!" Swinburne exclaimed. "Are we to sit here all night? I can barely keep my eyes open."

"It's hardly surprising considering your earlier heroics," Burton said. "You must be knocked out."

"I am. I say—do you mind if I hit the sack?"

"Not at all. We'll talk in the morning."

The poet pushed himself to his feet, mumbled, "Nighty night, all," and stumbled from the room.

Burton turned to face his companions. As he did so, Trounce emitted a loud snore. The detective was sitting with his head against the back of his chair, his eyes closed, and his mouth wide open.

"I think he pay too much attention," Eliphas Levi observed.

"We are all exhausted, monsieur," Burton noted. "Let's get him to bed and each take to our own."

"Oui, oui. But the verse, Sir Richard? Tell me, *quelle est sa signification?*"

"What does it mean? It appears to have caused Swinburne's propensity for perilous swims but, beyond that, I really couldn't say."

Early the following morning, Bram Stoker set off in search of fellow Whisperers. Anglesey was a barren and sparsely populated island, but the lad assured "Macallister Fogg" that the web extended even to it, and if there was a working telegraph station in any of the towns, it would soon be located.

Meanwhile, the four men took a stroll along the edge of Dulas Bay. There was a stiff breeze blowing and clouds blanketed the sky, but the tempest was over. Villagers were clambering among the rocks below, calling to one another as they discovered yet more bodies.

"Ripples," Burton murmured.

Trounce looked at the still-agitated sea and said, "Hardly."

"No, old chap—I'm thinking about Time; wondering whether a disaster of this magnitude has touched other histories."

Trounce, who hadn't yet learned of Countess Sabina's revelations, growled, "Whatever you just said, it's beyond me, and if I listen to much more gobbledegook, I'll have to dose myself with bitters and return to my bed. I think I'll confine myself to the practical business of the here and now."

Burton patted the policeman's shoulder. "You're a fine fellow, Trounce."

Trounce gave a modest, "Humph!" but his chest swelled a little and he reached up and smoothed his moustache.

The king's agent again surveyed the churning waters. "I was warned a storm was coming, but I considered the omen metaphorical. I never envisioned this." He turned to Eliphas Levi. "Do you think there's been a *Royal Charter* disaster in the original history, monsieur, or is it exclusive to ours, thanks to the presence of Perdurabo?"

"My hat!" Swinburne interrupted. "I do wish you'd explain to me what the devil you're talking about!"

Burton said, "I shall do so now, Algy," and indicated a large flat stone that overlooked the bay. The group settled on it, and the explorer went through the entire affair for the poet's—and Trounce's—benefit; he missed nothing out.

Swinburne accepted the wild story with complete equanimity.

"You understand what this means?" Burton asked. "That Time is not at all as we conceive it; that our history has been manipulated; that we appear to be caught between two warring factions—Abdu El Yezdi's and Perdurabo's?"

"As any poet of merit will tell you," Swinburne replied, "at an individual level, reality is simply a function of the imagination; and at a collective, nothing but a suffocating mantle of compromise and acquiescence. That is why poets create unusual combinations of words and rhythms: to set all the possible truths free. What you have told me comes as no surprise."

"You have *une vision unique*, Monsieur Swinburne," Eliphas Levi observed. "It is one I think will prove most vital to Sir Richard."

"How so?" Burton asked.

"Because, for Abdu El Yezdi and Perdurabo, *you* are history, monsieur—a figure from the past. Perdurabo, *en particulier*, he say he know you well. If he have study you, then he will be aware of what you will do, where you will be, how you will act."

"Bismillah!" Burton cursed. "I hadn't considered that. He'll be ahead of me every step of the way."

"*Non! Non!*" Levi protested. "*Pas nécessairement.* You forget—for Perdurabo, at least, this history is not *his* history. The Sir Richard Francis Burton he have knowledge of is not the same as you, for he is expose to different challenges and opportunities and maybe he make different decisions. Perhaps he never discover the source of the Nile. Perhaps he is not the agent of the king. But there may be many similarities, so you must be very careful. *Il ne faut rien laisser au hasard, eh?* It is clear that Perdurabo mean to harm you."

Burton pulled a cheroot from his pocket. He looked down at it and saw that his hand was trembling. He suddenly sensed the Other Burton lurking. Had he now an explanation for it? Was he somehow able to discern—especially when in the grip of fever—his alternate selves?

"I understand the implication, Monsieur Levi," he muttered. "You suggest that Algy's distinctive view of the world is such that he's perfectly placed to help me second-guess myself and do the opposite of whatever my instinct or intellect dictates, for perhaps only then will I take Perdurabo by surprise and gain the upper hand."

"You speak as if going into battle," Trounce observed.

"I feel I am. I wish I better understood what against."

"You are correct," Levi said. "And this one—" he tapped Swinburne's shoulder, "—is like . . . how do you say it? Ah! *Oui!* The card up your sleeve, *non?*"

Burton regarded the little poet—who grinned happily back at him—and said, "Yes, I think you are right. And you've given me an idea."

"*Oui?*"

Burton held out his arms.

Levi looked at them.

"*La signification?*"

"I have two sleeves. And, also, I have a brother."

When they returned to The Spiteful Rosie, they found Bram waiting. He'd located a working telegraph office in Newborough, ten miles away.

"I'll hire a vehicle and leave you gentlemen for a while," Trounce said. "I must get a message to Slaughter and have him take charge of the hunt for John Judge. An island is no refuge for a murderer, so I've no doubt that he's crossed the bridge to the mainland by now."

Levi said, "*C'est nécessaire* that we examine the corpses from the ship, so perhaps you take the boy with you, *non?* Already he have seen too much death."

Trounce sighed. "Lord help me, am I condemned to be Macallister Fogg for the day?"

"You brought it on yourself," Burton said. "Consider your nursemaid duty a retribution for blackening my eye."

"Humph!" the Scotland Yard man responded. He gestured for Bram to follow, and departed.

"Why do you wish to examine the dead, Monsieur Levi?" Burton asked.

"We know the *volonté* of Perdurabo need a body, *non?* And the logbook indicate he possess John Judge."

"That is how I understood it, yes."

"I wish to perform an experiment. Perhaps some who lie in the church hall, they are his victims. A theory I must test. You will forgive me if I say nothing more about it? There is much to consider; much to research before I can be certain that what I think is correct."

"Very well. May I assist?"

"*Oui.* I will show you what is required."

After fortifying themselves with strong coffee, Burton, Levi, and Swinburne visited the High Street, where the Frenchman purchased two strings of garlic from a grocery shop and three pocket mirrors from an ironmonger's. They continued on until they reached the church hall. Burton showed his authority to the county coroner and Moelfre's rector, who were seeking to establish the identities of the many dead. "Go and rest awhile," he told them. "There are certain facts I need to establish and I'd prefer it if my companions and I were left undisturbed until we've finished."

The two men, having laboured for many hours, didn't resist, and gratefully exited the hall to fill their lungs with fresh air.

"Now, monsieur," Burton said. "What do we do?"

Levi approached the nearest body and pulled the shroud back from it, revealing the grey features of a middle-aged woman.

"*Observez.*"

Twisting a garlic bulb from its string, he crushed it in his hand and extracted one of its cloves. This he snapped in half and rubbed around the corpse's nostrils.

"Like so," he said. "And now this."

He put his thumb to the woman's eye and pulled up its lid, then held the pocket mirror in front of it. After a minute had passed, he stepped back and said, "We must the same thing do with every cadaver."

"What a thoroughly outré operation," Swinburne exclaimed. "What is its purpose?"

Levi looked down at his diminutive companion and answered, "We must identify any corpse that does not realise it is dead."

The poet hopped on one leg and jabbed his elbows outward, dancing like a puppet with tangled strings. "This is beyond the bounds!" he squealed. "It's diabolical! Give me a mirror. How can the dead not know they are dead? You're as nutty as a fruitcake! Pass the garlic. Completely batty! What should I look for?"

"*Toute réaction.*"

"Any reaction? Barmy! Bonkers! Mad as a March hare!"

Having thus expressed his doubts, the poet got to work and, with silent efficiency, moved from body to body, testing each as instructed.

It took the three of them a little over two and a half hours to complete the procedure, and at the end of it Levi proclaimed himself satisfied that none of the dead harboured any doubts as to their condition.

Swinburne leaned close to Burton and whispered, "Are you absolutely positive he hasn't a screw loose?"

"He's as sane as you and me, Algy. Well, as me, anyway. I must admit, though, I'm intrigued to know what it was all about. No doubt he'll explain when he's ready."

They left the church hall with the stench of death in their nostrils and returned to the pub where, an hour later, Trounce and Bram Stoker joined them for an early lunch.

The morning had robbed Burton and Levi of their appetites, and they picked unenthusiastically at their food. Swinburne, by contrast, ate with gusto and downed ale without restraint.

"There are no trains off the island," Trounce reported, "and services on the mainland won't resume, they say, until tomorrow. I'm afraid we're going to have to kick our heels here for another day."

Burton muttered an oath. It was the last thing he wanted to hear, but there was no other option, so he spent the afternoon impatiently reading and re-reading the log, furiously smoking cigars, and indulging in a vigorous walk along the coastline.

Levi, meanwhile, sank into such a deep contemplation that he became utterly unresponsive to conversation; Swinburne worked on his poetry and remained surprisingly sober; and Trounce and Stoker helped the local constabulary to collect the many hundreds of gold coins that were still washing ashore, and which, if the authorities accepted the rector's suggestion, would be used to help support the many women who'd soon receive the terrible news that they'd been widowed.

After what, for all of them, proved a fitful night's sleep, the detective inspector again visited the telegraph office and this time returned with the much more welcome news that although the island's railway tracks remained blocked, those on the mainland had, for the most part, been cleared of debris.

"How about I commandeer police velocipedes?" he suggested. "We could cross the bridge to the closest town—Bangor, I believe—and catch a train from there."

This was agreed, quickly arranged, and by half-past one the party was speeding eastward, with Bram balanced on Trounce's handlebars. Just over an hour later, they arrived in Bangor and, finding that lines had been cleared, boarded a small train bound for Stoke-on-Trent. By four, they'd caught the Liverpool-to-London Atmospheric Express. The pumping stations blasted the carriages along at a tremendous velocity, and with the journey punctuated by just three stops—Birmingham, Coventry, and Northampton—they were back in London by eight in the evening.

A thick fog enshrouded the city. Flecks of soot—"the blacks"—were drifting through it.

"I shall go to Chelsea," Swinburne announced. "I have my new digs at Rossetti's place on Cheyne Walk. Number sixteen."

Burton addressed Levi, who'd been unusually quiet and self-absorbed since their departure from Anglesey. "Monsieur, you are welcome to my spare bedroom, unless you'd prefer a hotel, in which case I can recommend the Saint James."

"If it is no inconvenience," the Frenchman said with a bow, "I stay with you. There is much to discuss."

"Very well. And you, lad—" Burton ruffled Bram's hair. "You're a useful little blighter to have around. What say you to permanent employment as my button-boy?"

"A page, is it?" Bram replied. "You'll not have me wearing a uniform!"

"That won't be necessary. But we'll smarten you up, and you'll take weekly baths."

"By all that's holy! You'll be a-jokin' o' course!"

"Not a bit of it. What do you say, nipper? Can you behave yourself and do as my housekeeper tells you? You'll have a proper bed to sleep in, daily meals, and plenty enough pay to satisfy your craving for penny bloods."

"Well now, since ye put it like that, I could give it a try, so I could." The boy looked at Trounce. "That is, unless Mr. Fogg is requirin' me services."

Trounce muttered, "I'll know where to find you if I need you, lad."

"Aye, that you will. It's set, then. A pageboy I'll be."

They left the station, hailed cabs, and went their separate ways.

"If Perdurabo's *volonté* has occupied John Judge's body," Burton said to Levi as their growler advanced cautiously through the pall, "then he has no need to build one. Why, then, the taking of Darwin and Galton? Why the interest in Eugenics?"

"I must research," Levi said. "I must read."

Burton grunted. "And in the meantime, I have to wait for either the police to find Judge or for him to find me."

Half an hour later, the growler stopped, the driver knocked on the roof, and they disembarked. Burton peered up at the man, who was but a shadow in the dense haze, and said, "How much?"

"On the 'ouse, guv'nor!" The cabbie leaned down until his face was visible. He pushed up his goggles, gave a grin and a wink, shouted, "Gee-up!" and sent his vehicle careening away.

"Penniforth!" Burton yelled. He started after the growler but had run only a few steps before it vanished into the gloom.

A police constable materialised at his side, stepping out of the eddying pea-souper.

"Trouble, Sir Richard?"

"No, not really. You know me?"

"Detective Inspector Slaughter has posted me to Montagu Place to keep an eye on things, sir. I understand there's some threat to you."

"I see. Well, thank you. I'll be sure to shout if I need your assistance, Constable—?"

"Krishnamurthy, sir. Goodnight."

On Friday morning, Eliphas Levi immersed himself in Burton's library while his host attended to his correspondence, which included the usual flood of letters from New Wardour Castle, plus a summons from Edward.

After composing a reply to his fiancée, Burton made his apologies—Levi was happy to remain and continue with his reading—then stepped out of the house and yelled at a hansom he vaguely perceived trundling through the miasma. He checked its driver wasn't Penniforth, then opened its door and was about to climb in when Constable Krishnamurthy called from the opposite pavement. "I'm under orders to keep guard over number fourteen, sir, but if you'd like me to accompany you—?"

"No, Constable, keep to your sentry duty. I don't expect to be gone for long."

He boarded the vehicle. "The Royal Venetia Hotel, please."

The murk made it slow going, enfolding the city in such gloom that gas lamps remained lit, hovering dimly like chains of tiny depleted suns. It took an hour to reach the Strand. The thoroughfare had returned to its normal state; the huge sewer tunnel was covered over and a new road surface laid. Bazalgette's workmen were now at Aldgate, digging their way ever closer to the East End—the "Cauldron"—and its teeming hordes of villains and beggars.

Grumbles ushered Burton into his brother's presence.

The minister of mediumistic affairs was in his red dressing gown and customary position. There was a cup of tea and a stack of documents on the table beside his armchair. He was holding a sheaf of papers, which he put down as Burton entered. "You look as if you've been trampled by a herd of cattle. It's a considerable improvement over when I last saw you."

"Thank you. I have a vague recollection of you being at the hospital. Is that what it takes to get you out of your chair—your brother nearly being blown to kingdom come?"

"No. It takes an order from His Majesty King George the Fifth, who was concerned at the possible loss of a valuable resource."

"Then I apologise for inconveniencing you."

"Accepted. Where have you been?"

"In Anglesey."

"The *Royal Charter*? It's all over the newspapers. What has that to do with the affair? Sit."

Burton neither sat nor answered the question, but instead asked one of his own. "What do you want?"

Edward took a police file from the table. "Countess Sabina. Dead. Your report is unsatisfactory, to say the least. Chief Commissioner Mayne is not happy. Neither am I. Explain."

"I answer to the king, not to you, and the report will make more sense when included with the rest of the case files."

"Then give them to me."

"They aren't written. The investigation is ongoing."

"Damnation, Dick! What the hell happened to her? You realise that, by your choice of words in this account, you've made of yourself—as far as the police are concerned—the principal suspect?"

"I didn't kill the countess, Edward."

The minister sighed, threw the file to the floor, and selected another, which he held out to his brother. "I know. Read this."

The explorer stepped forward, took the cardboard folder, and opened it. The document within was adorned with the Bethlem Royal Hospital letterhead and had been written by Doctor Monroe.

REPORT: PATIENT 466. LAURENCE OLIPHANT.

Wednesday, 26th October 1859.

I set this down in detail, for the case is the most extraordinary I have ever encountered.

At seven o'clock yesterday evening, Nurse Bracegirdle informed me that Laurence Oliphant had something of the utmost importance to impart. Having informed the nurse that I would see the patient in the morning, I was told that Oliphant was "extremely persistent and liable to have one of his violent fits" if I did not attend him immediately. Knowing Bracegirdle's judgement to be sound, I consented to the request and went to Oliphant's room, where I found him to be considerably unsettled, though perfectly rational in speech.

He said to me, "Thank you for coming, Doctor Monroe, and thank you, too, for providing me with lodgings these weeks past. I am grateful, but must inform you that the time for my departure is upon us."

"What has occasioned it, sir?" I asked, careful to humour him while neither endorsing nor contradicting his statement.

"Why, simply that I am restored to health and have much work ahead of me," he said. "I must leave here at once, this very minute, in order to fulfill my obligations."

Upon enquiring as to the nature of these obligations, I was told, "They are of a confidential nature. I am bound to secrecy. But come, you can see with your own eyes that I am perfectly sound in body and mind. I have no wish to further impose upon you."

"It is no imposition," I said, "and I cannot release you without knowing your intentions."

"Will you not simply trust that my presence is required elsewhere? Your duty is not to me, Doctor Monroe, but to he whom I obey."

The instant he made this statement, Oliphant flinched and bit his lip. He looked at me with a furtive expression on his face, then suddenly dropped to his knees and held his hands out imploringly.

"Can you not understand? I am not my own master! You have no conception of what you do by keeping me here, or, God help you, of whom you wrong. I entreat you, let me go! Let me go! I am no lunatic swayed by ungovernable emotions! I am sane! Sane! Sane!"

"Mr. Oliphant," I said sternly, "by your passion and your own actions, you cause me to doubt the veracity of that assertion. No more of this. Off your knees, now."

Reluctantly, he rose, and slumped onto his bed.

"Then I am lost," he whispered.

"Not at all, sir," I assured him. "You are well cared for, and I give you my word that I am working assiduously to understand and cure the delusions that plague you."

"Delusions!" he said, with a laugh. "Oh, you fool. It is on you now, sir. It is on you."

He fell into a sullen silence and I departed, instructing Nurse Bracegirdle and Sister Camberwick to make regular checks on him.

Not long after, a terrific storm got up, its wind, rain, and thunder so violent that sleep was impossible. I was still wide awake and clothed when, at 2 a.m., I was again summoned to room 466 by Nurse Bracegirdle, who informed me that Oliphant was suffering a serious fit. I went immediately to the patient and found him tearing apart his appalling "cloak of rats."

"Irrelevant! Irrelevant!" he screamed. "What a fool I am to think he would require this filth! Besides, I am superseded! He doesn't need me any more, Doctor Monroe. You have seen to that. I am useless to him locked away as I am. You have killed me, sir! Killed me just as surely as if you strangled me with your own hands!"

His eyes blazed and he showed his teeth and backed away as two of my staff entered bearing a strait waistcoat. "No! No! Not that! Would you now have me unable to defend myself? He'll come for me, Monroe. I know too much, and I am a medium, which means he can touch me even in this damnable place. In the name of God, leave my arms free that I may at least trace a protective sigil."

"The restraint is for your own good," I said.

He shrieked and thrashed but my two men, with help from Bracegirdle and me, were able to hold him down while Sister Camberwick applied a syringe to his neck. The sedative took immediate effect, and the strait waistcoat was put upon him and secured. When this task was done, he was left sitting passively on the edge of the bed. He quite suddenly looked up at me and whispered, "The storm heralds his arrival. He is here. God have mercy on my blighted soul, I am done."

Nurse Bracegirdle and Sister Camberwick will corroborate what happened next. I thank the Lord that I did not witness it alone, for had I done so, I would be forced to question my own sanity.

Oliphant blinked, and in that split-second, his eyes became completely black; I *refer not only to the pupils, but to the whites as well. In a deep and unfamiliar voice, which sounded uncannily like many voices in absolute harmony, he said, "I expect to be fully occupied for some considerable time, Doctor Monroe, but I shall not forget your interference. In due course, there will be a reckoning."*

The patient's head then twisted through a complete revolution, his neck popping, and he dropped to the floor, dead.

With my hand on the Holy Bible, I swear that all I have set down here is true.

The minister of mediumistic affairs reached for his cup of tea and took a sip. "The countess and Oliphant died in the same manner."

"They did," Burton confirmed.

"And do these deaths relate to the abductions?"

"I believe so."

"Explain."

Burton took a cheroot from his pocket, lit it, observed his brother's expression of disgust, and maliciously blew smoke in the fat man's direction. He then went through the case, explaining it point by point, until—before he'd finished—Edward held up a hand to stop him and said, "Enough! One absurdity after another! Gad! As a child you always had your head buried in the *Arabian Nights*, and now—"

Burton strode forward and stood looming over his brother. "The title of the book," he snarled, "is *A Thousand Nights and a Night*, and this madness we're caught up in is not from its pages. You bloody fool, Edward. You think I don't know what's passing through that Machiavellian brain of yours? You're terrified that El Yezdi has abandoned you. You're quivering in your boots at the prospect of losing your political influence. You feel yourself powerless and you fear that, if Perdurabo can reach out and kill mediums, then you—being one—might drop dead at any moment. You're such a self-obsessed bastard that you're completely oblivious to your one great advantage."

"Advantage?" Edward croaked. "What advantage?"

Burton's mouth twisted into a brutal grin. "That you're dead, brother. You're already dead."

A moment of silence.

Edward's pupils shrank to pinpricks. "What in God's name are you babbling about?"

Burton jabbed two fingers, with the cheroot between them, toward the other man's face. "The first words the Arabian ever spoke to you. 'This time, you were saved. You'll recover.'" The explorer allowed that to sink in, then continued, "This time, Edward. *This time*. The intimation being that, in other versions of history, you *weren't* saved. If Perdurabo is so concerned with me— for whatever reason—then in the future he comes from he must have consulted records of my life, which doubtless stated that I had a brother who was killed in 1856. What he doesn't know is that, thanks to Abdu El Yezdi, in this version of history I have a brother who survived; and one who has influence in every government department. As ludicrous as it may appear—considering your outrageous girth, ingrained inertia, and thoroughly objectionable personality—you, Edward, have been set up as a secret weapon."

CHAPTER 15

OF *NOSFERATU, STRIGOI MORTI* AND ARUNDELLS

"Facts are chameleons whose tint
Varies with every accident:
Each, prism-like, hath three obvious sides,
And facets ten or more besides.
Events are like the sunny light
On mirrors falling clear and bright
Through windows of a varied hue,
Now yellow seen, now red, now blue."
— SIR RICHARD FRANCIS BURTON

O n the way home, and for the umpteenth time, Burton tried Brundleweed's jewellery shop. Closed again. In four days, he would be on
his way to New Wardour Castle but still didn't have the engagement ring.
He wrote a request for it to be posted there and slipped the note through the
letterbox.

When he arrived back at Montagu Place, he tipped his hat first at Mr.
Grub, then at Constable Krishnamurthy, before stepping into number 14.

Eliphas Levi had visited the British Library while the explorer was out.

"Ranft's *De masticatione mortuorum in tumulis* and Calmet's *Dissertation on
the Vampires of Hungary*," the Frenchman announced, holding up two thick
volumes. "*Beaucoup d'aide dans la compréhension* of the creature we deal with, I
think. Much information!"

Burton blinked in surprise then moved to one of his desks and took up an
ancient and crumbling volume. Its title was printed in Sanskrit.

"The *Baital Pachisi*," he said. "A Hindu tale. I've been translating it under the title *Vikram and the Vampire*."

"Ah, *mais oui*!" Levi exclaimed. "I have heard of this story. The Baital is a great bat, *non*? It inhabit and animate the dead."

"Yes. But surely, monsieur, you don't suggest that Perdurabo is such?"

"*Non.* But these legends of the vampire, they are everywhere, in cultures far apart. We must wonder, is there a common basis—a truth at the heart of them? That truth, I think, will tell us how to defeat our enemy."

Burton carried the old book over to his armchair, gesturing that Levi should take the seat opposite. The occultist brought with him his two volumes, sat with them on his lap, and began to fill his prodigious pipe.

"Would you explain?" Burton asked.

Levi stuck his legs out and rested his feet on the fireplace's fender. He leaned his head back and puffed for a few moments, then said, "You have, I expect, experience that sensation when the presence of *une personne particulière*, it drains you, *non*? You feel exhausted by them, and you want them to go away but they stay and talk and talk and talk until you feel you have no energy left."

Burton nodded. "Many such attend the Athenaeum Club."

"*Fréquemment*," Levi went on, "these people who so fatigue others, they appear to be weak. They are indecisive and their emotions are undisciplined. *Mais non!* The truth is, their *volonté*—willpower—it is very strong, for it feed like *une sangsue*."

"A leech?"

"*Oui.* You know, the Egyptians of long ago, they think the soul it can be stored in a pot of clay. These pots, you examine them now, you analyse the clay, which have many metals in it, and you will see they are like the Leyden jar."

"I'm unfamiliar with that, monsieur. What is it?"

"*Une batterie primitive.* It hold and preserve static electricity."

"You're suggesting the soul has an electrical component?"

"Soul, *volonté*, what is the difference? I think a strong *volonté* can draw the energy from a weaker, like to drain *une batterie*, and it is from this that the legend of the vampire begin." Levi drew on his pipe and deliberated for half a minute before continuing. "Perdurabo, only his *volonté* pass through history and across reality into our world, but without a body to sustain him, he will die, so he possess this man, John Judge." Levi turned his pipe and waved its stem at Burton. "Ah! But already there is a *volonté* in the man, *non*? His own! And it, Perdurabo cannot drain completely, for it is attach to the body and keep it alive, which Perdurabo, who is not attach, cannot do. He dominate it and keep it quiet, but always struggle, struggle, struggle—John Judge, he want to be free of this parasite. It is very hard for Perdurabo, so he require much energy. He must feed on others like—how did you say? Yes—a leech."

Burton gave a low whistle. "He extracted willpower from the *Royal Charter*'s crew and passengers?"

"*Oui*. And this way he keep his own *volonté* strong. Now, Sir Richard, we are at the heart of the vampire legend, for when his victims have not sufficient *volonté* remaining, they are like the dead. Dead but not dead. *Le terme le plus approprié est 'strigoi morti'*—the un-dead."

"As with a Haitian *zombie*?" Burton asked.

"Ah, you know of that! *Mais non*. The zombie, it is but an animated corpse and must be controlled by a *bokor*—a sorcerer. The un-dead, they have just enough *volonté* remaining to know one thing—" The Frenchman paused, drew another lungful of smoke, then, with clouds of it billowing from his mouth, said, "That they, too, must feed."

"Vampire begets vampire," Burton murmured.

"*Non, pas exactement*. Not exactly! Remember, the vampire original—the *nosferatu*—it is very powerful; by its nature, it feed on and is sustained by others. Its victims, the *strigoi morti*, they have not this type of *volonté*, so they must rise at night—"

Burton interrupted. "Why at night?"

"*Parce que*, it is at night when all is concealed by darkness. The un-dead prefer this; they have an aversion to any stimulation of the senses, for this make them remember what they are not—alive! So they hunt at night, to do to others what was done to them, for they want to live again, you see? And in day, they are like in hibernation, hiding from *l'horreur* of self-awareness. Also, their prey is more easy to take at night, when sleeping."

Burton lit a cheroot, his brows furrowed as he grappled with the concept. "Can the *strigoi morti* be restored to proper life if they feed sufficiently on the willpower of others?"

The occultist shook his head. "*Il est terrible*. Blind instinct drive them to feed, but they cannot be made strong by *volonté*, as can the *nosferatu*. For the *strigoi morti*, there is only the agony of insatiable hunger, nothing else. It is the worst torture. *Mon Dieu!* The worst torture!"

They smoked in silence for five minutes, both lost in thought.

Burton murmured, "What of fangs and bloodsucking?"

"*Embellissement*, monsieur! People in the old times, they say the blood is the life, *non*? They think when the whole village is weak, it must be that their blood is taken in the night, so they dig up the dead and see the teeth." Levi pulled his lips back and ran a forefinger over his gums. "This flesh here, it quickly grow small in death and make the teeth look very long, so the people think these are the fangs that suck the blood."

Burton stood, went to a desk, and retrieved the logbook of the *Royal Charter*. He flipped through a few pages, stopped, read, and said, "So the sailor Colin McPhiel was drained of his *volonté* by Perdurabo, who'd taken possession of John Judge. He became a *strigoi morti*, and rose at night to feed on others of the crew and passengers. With Perdurabo doing the same, the un-dead would have proliferated, but for the fact that Captain Taylor ordered the corpses thrown overboard each morning."

"*Exactemente.*"

"The *nosferatu*, is it also restricted to the night?"

"In its own body, *non*. But when it occupy another, the *volonté* of the host fight hard during the day. This exhaust the parasite. Only at night can he dominate."

"And the garlic and mirror, monsieur?"

"Strong odour, it activate *le sens de l'odorat*—the sense of smell—which of all the senses is the one most connecting with memory. With *strigoi morti*, perhaps it wake the remaining *volonté* a little; perhaps make a bit of awareness; and then open the eye and hold the mirror so it see itself—a reaction of *horreur* and despair, and we know this corpse is dead but not dead."

Burton reached up and massaged his temples. "How quickly are the un-dead made?"

"By a *nosferatu*, if he need much sustenance, many in a single night. But a *strigoi morti*, it must feed again and again on the same individual to make that one un-dead, too."

"But, nevertheless, they proliferate?"

"Like the black plague."

"That, at least, might help us to locate Perdurabo. I shall alert Scotland Yard to look out for any reports that might indicate such activity. By Allah, how am I to convince Chief Commissioner Mayne that a vampire is on the loose?"

"The police, they must see it with their own eyes, I think."

For the rest of the weekend, the two men studied.

Monday, the last day of October, was the first cold day of the autumn; so much so that Burton had the fire lit and he and Levi sat around it, with books piled beside their chairs.

A letter arrived from Isabel. She reported that preparations were almost complete at New Wardour Castle and the first houseguests, her friends Mr. and Mrs. Beeton, had arrived.

Sadhvi has been of splendid assistance, and her stories of the hardships you all endured in Africa have certainly improved your standing in my parents' eyes. Perhaps they are beginning to understand, as I do, that your thorns function to preserve and protect the rarest of blooms: a courageous, honourable, and sensitive man; the only man I could possibly marry. Oh, Dick, if you could see how supportive Papa, in particular, has become; how much he has thrown himself into decorating the ballroom, organising the rooms to accommodate the guests, hiring the extra staff, planning the menus, and so forth. It has been quite simply wonderful. I must say, however, that of all of us, nobody has worked harder than Tom, our remarkable groundsman. As you know, Capability Brown landscaped the estate back in the late 1700s, and none is more "capable" of maintaining the gardens than good old Tom, but my goodness, what a task he faced after last week's atrocious storm! Trees were down, there were branches, twigs, and leaves strewn all over, fences had fallen, and even bits and pieces from the nearby villages had blown onto our lawns and flowerbeds. In his typically quiet and efficient manner, our man enlisted a force of locals and had the place shipshape and Bristol fashion in the blink of an eye. He's an absolute gem! But what a strange thing; as I sit here by the window and look out at his marvellous handiwork, I see ravens gathering by the hundreds in the trees and, in the distance, they blacken the tops of the old castle's walls. You know what a superstitious thing I am, Dick. What with that horrible omen uttered by Hagar Burton and now these wicked-looking fiends "tapping, tapping at my chamber door," I am overcome with uneasiness and a sense of foreboding. Bless my soul; your bride-to-be is a quivering bag of nerves! Perhaps it is normal. Dear Isabella says she felt the same way before she wed Sam Beeton. I should consider her happiness a far better indicator of our future than silly auguries and squawking birds!

To Burton, it was inconceivable that his engagement party was already just five days away and he'd be at New Wardour Castle by tomorrow afternoon. He was so engulfed by uncanny events that the mundane prospect of a social occasion felt strange and out of place.

He put Isabel's letter aside and opened another. It was from Buckingham Palace and signed by the king's personal secretary: *The converted stables in the mews behind numbers 13 & 14 Montagu Place have been purchased in your name. Keys enclosed.*

Mystified, Burton went downstairs, out into the backyard, passed through the door into Wyndham Mews, and crossed to the two buildings in question. In the first, he found two brand-new rotorchairs, in the second, a new steam sphere and two velocipedes. A note lay on the seat of the sphere. It read: *With compliments, His Majesty King George V.*

Burton was speechless.

At three in the afternoon, a falsetto screeching drifted up from the street below. It continued for five minutes and was followed by the jingling of the doorbell. The stairs creaked as Mrs. Angell ascended. She knocked, entered, and stood with hands on hips. "A small hobgoblin has invaded our hallway."

"Does it have red hair?" Burton asked.

"Oh, is that what it is? I thought the creature's head was on fire. I was going to throw a bucket of water over it before chasing it away with my broom."

"Resist the temptation, please, and send the apparition up. He is one of our dinner guests."

"Very well, if you think it wise."

She departed and half a minute later Algernon Swinburne bounded in.

"Swindlers!" he shrieked. "To a man! Swindlers all! To perdition with them!"

"*À qui faites-vous allusion?*" Eliphas Levi asked.

"To whom do I refer? Why, to cab drivers, of course! The villains are forever altering their charges!"

"Depending on the distance travelled," Burton explained.

"Twaddle and bosh! A cab ride is a shilling! A shilling, I tell you!" Swinburne surveyed the room. "I say! Are you planning an army or a library, Burton? Swords, pistols, a spear, and books, books, books!" He capered alongside the shelves, his eyes running over the many volumes, then let out a sudden howl of dismay—"Walt Whitman? Walt Whitman?"—and yanked a leather-bound book down. "*Leaves of Grass?* How can you possibly inhabit the same room as this mess of voluminous and incoherent effusions? My hat! You must be liberated at once!" With a violent swing of his arm, he hurled the book across the study. It hit the corner of a desk just above a waste-paper basket and rebounded, spinning with perfect accuracy into the fireplace.

"Oops!" the poet said. "I was aiming for the bin. But it's for the best. Burn, foul putrescence!" then to Burton, "Are you going to stand there with your mouth open, old chap, or offer me a brandy?"

Burton cleared his throat. "Good afternoon, Algy. How pleasant to see you again. Do come in. Make yourself comfortable. Can I interest you in a drink? Perhaps a small brandy?"

Swinburne plonked himself into the armchair Eliphas Levi had occupied before standing to greet him. "Small?"

Burton rolled his eyes and moved to the bureau. He poured the poet a generous measure, and lesser ones for himself and the Frenchman. After handing his guests their drinks, he indicated that Levi should take the unoccupied armchair. "I have a question for you, Algy. If I placed you among staunch Catholics and asked you to behave yourself, would you be capable?"

"Of politely curing their delusions?"

"No. Of keeping your mouth shut. I'm inclined to invite you to accompany me to New Wardour Castle tomorrow but not unless you can do as Monckton Milnes does, and keep your paganism to yourself. Could you give recitations for the benefit of the guests without causing them offence?"

"Sir Richard, my poems are by no means confined solely to anti-Christian declamations. If we are to celebrate your engagement, then surely verses that eulogise love and affection would be more suitable?"

"Quite so, and certainly more likely to be appreciated by the audience," Burton confirmed.

Swinburne gazed upward, his eyes taking on a dreamy expression, and chanted:

> *The shapely slender shoulders small,*
> *Long arms, hands wrought in glorious wise,*
> *Round little breasts, the hips withal*
> *High, full of flesh, not scant of size,*
> *Fit for all amorous masteries;*
> *The large loins, and the flower that was*
> *Planted above my firm round thighs*
> *In a small garden of soft grass . . .*

"Stop!" Burton commanded. "That sort of thing is also best avoided."

Swinburne giggled. "Testing the boundaries, old thing! Testing the boundaries! I have a rather lengthy piece, unfinished, but I can improvise. It tells the story of the ill-fated lovers Tristan and Isolde."

"But, *mon Dieu!*" Levi put in. "Such *tragédie—*at *une célébration?*"

"We English glory in the juxtaposition of opposing sentiments, Monsieur Levi. Nothing makes us more conscious of the glories of love than a tale of its obstruction, loss, or sacrifice," Swinburne answered.

"Ah! *Romeo et Juliet*!"

"Indeed so."

The poet knocked his drink back, gave a satisfied sigh, and said to Burton, "I assure you, I shall be the shoul of dishcretion, old shap!"

A loud hammering sounded at the street door.

"By thunder!" Swinburne exclaimed. "Thunder!"

"Trounce," Burton corrected. "He appears to have a blind spot where doorbells are concerned."

Crossing the room, he went out onto the landing and looked down the stairs in time to see Mrs. Angell admit Detective Inspectors Trounce and Slaughter.

"Come on up, gentlemen," he called.

His housekeeper glared at their police-issue boots as the two men ascended the stairs.

"Would you bring up a glass of milk, please, Mother Angell?"

"What ho! What ho!" Swinburne cheered as the detectives entered the study.

Burton introduced Slaughter to the poet and to Levi, arranged chairs, poured drinks, lit another cigar, waited until his housekeeper had delivered Slaughter's milk, then gave the group an account of his discussion with Levi.

The policemen reacted with blank faces.

Slaughter mumbled, "A vampire? Really, sir, I'm a martyr to indigestion and this manner of hoo-ha doesn't help it at all."

"I must confess," Burton said, "I'm finding it hard to swallow, too. Have you made any progress with your side of things?"

"Not a great deal, unfortunately. No further abductions and no sign of John Judge. Wherever he went after he escaped Anglesey, he's so far evaded the police."

Trounce said, "We've kept a round-the-clock watch on the League of Enochians Gentlemen's Club—a very odd place. The lights come on at night. We see shadows pass across the curtains. We've even listened at the door and heard voices within. However, no amount of knocking or shouting has solicited a response, the place remains locked, there have been no deliveries of food, drink, or anything else, and not a single soul has been observed coming or going from either the front or the back of the building."

"Puzzling. What of Edward Vaughan Hyde Kenealy?"

"I spoke to William Grove, the King's Counsel under whom Kenealy worked in defence of the poisoner William Palmer. Grove declared him a nightmare to deal with. Extremely erratic. Apparently he considers himself a direct descendent of Jesus Christ and Genghis Khan. He's a complete lunatic." Trounce glanced at Swinburne. "There's a lot of 'em about."

Burton smiled. He turned to Slaughter. "I want you to have a look at passenger lists for the transatlantic liners. A man named Thomas Lake Harris is due to give a talk at the club on the ninth of November. He's either already in the country or will be arriving soon. Get on his tail."

Slaughter nodded.

"Well, then, gentlemen," Burton said. "Mrs. Angell will be serving dinner at seven. Until then, I suggest we relax and go through the events again. Certain aspects of this affair are beginning to make sense—if 'sense' is the appropriate word for such extraordinary circumstances—but we are still faced with many enigmas. Let us, as they say, chew the fat."

Slaughter looked distraught, and Burton added, "That most definitely is not a reference to my housekeeper's cooking."

On Tuesday the 1st of November, Burton, Bram, Levi, and Swinburne travelled seventy miles southwest by atmospheric railway to Salisbury and from there a further ten miles by steam landau to the village of Tisbury and on to New Wardour Castle. After being dropped at the estate's entrance gate, they tugged at the bellpull and waited. Two minutes passed, then the large wooden portal creaked open and a slightly built man greeted them. His brown moustache was flamboyantly wide, waxed, and curled upward at the ends; his lacquered hair was parted in the middle; and he possessed grey eyes with small pupils. Though dressed in tweeds, with gaiters over his calves, he somehow managed to wear the rustic outfit with a foppish air—every button being polished and every seam perfectly stitched, without fraying or wear and tear in sight.

"Sir Richard and guests?" he asked, in a clipped and precise tone.

"Yes, good afternoon," Burton replied.

"Good afternoon, sir. Thomas Honesty, groundsman. I'll drive you to the house."

They entered, followed the dapper fellow to the lodge house, and waited while he stoked a steam carriage's furnace.

"My fiancée speaks very highly of you, Mr. Honesty," Burton said. "Your flower beds are the pride of the county. I hear you had your work cut out for you after the great storm."

"Shambles," Honesty replied. "Place in disarray. Bad timing. Had to work fast. Clear up. Big party and lots of guests coming."

They mounted the conveyance.

"Are there many already arrived?" Burton asked.

Honesty climbed onto the driver's seat. "Some, sir. Miss Raghavendra. Been here a while. Mr. and Mrs. Beeton came last week. Mr. Monckton Milnes this morning—"

"Ah, old Monckton Milnes is here already!"

"Yes, sir." The groundsman pulled a lever on the tiller and the carriage started across the grounds, steam pluming from the funnel at its rear.

"I understand the master of the house is of the Bible-thumping variety of Catholic gentleman." Burton made this statement with a loaded glance in Swinburne's direction. The poet grinned happily, held his fingers up to either side of his hat like little horns, and pulled a devilish face.

"Not for me to say, sir," Honesty answered. "Lord Gerard is a good employer. He's not here. Called away on business. Will be back for the party."

Their vehicle rounded a small grove of oak trees and New Wardour Castle came into view.

"*Mon Dieu! Il est magnifique!*" Levi exclaimed.

"Cor!" Bram Stoker added. "Would ye be a-lookin' at that, now!"

The Palladian-style manor was, indeed, a majestic edifice. Comprised of a huge main block with flanking pavilions, it was nestled among trees in a wide expanse of parkland, meadows, and lakes—a scene of exquisite pastoral beauty—that gently sloped up southeastward to a low peak, upon which, about one and a half miles away, the ruins of the old castle stood outlined against the grey sky. Even at such a distance, Burton could see the ravens Isabel had described, but more so, he could hear them. The entire estate was filled with their cawing and croaking.

"Great heavens, Mr. Honesty, you appear to have been invaded."

"The birds, sir? Often have them. Never before in such numbers. Displaced by the storm, I suppose."

Having followed a path across a wide lawn, the carriage eventually drew to a halt before the manor's entrance, a modest door beneath a very large Venetian-style arched window. Honesty jumped down and, as he did so, the door opened, a clockwork footman glanced out, ducked back in, and a moment later reappeared with another of his ilk, both following the household butler, who gestured for them to take the new arrivals' bags.

"Good day, sirs. I am Nettles. The family and guests are currently gathered in the music room. Would you care to join them immediately or shall I have the staff escort you to your rooms first?"

"I think we'd like to splash water on our faces and change out of our travelling clothes," Burton replied. He turned to the groundsman. "Thank you, Mr. Honesty."

Honesty touched his finger to his temple.

Nettles led Burton and his fellows through the elegant reception hall and into a grand rotunda, dominated by a double staircase that rose some sixty feet through the entire height of the building up to a beautiful domed skylight. Gazing in admiration at the stunning architecture and decor, the three men and disoriented boy—such surroundings were totally alien to Bram—trailed after the butler past the colonnaded first floor and onward up to the third, where they were shown to their adjoining rooms.

Nettles indicated one of the clockwork footmen and said, "Clunk will wait at the top of the stairs, sirs. He'll guide you to the music room at your convenience."

Burton, accompanied by Bram, entered his room and found soap, flannels, towels, and a basin of water on a table beneath a mirror.

"Unpack my portmanteau and lay out the clothes, would you?" he said to the boy.

Opening an inner door, he saw a small valet's room and said, "This is where you'll be sleeping, lad. The lap of luxury, eh?"

"I ain't seen nothin' like it afore, sir, so help me, I ain't. What'll I do with meself?"

"You'll attend me when I require it, which'll be first thing in the morning and just before bed, for the most part, and for the rest of the time you'll perform whatever duties the butler assigns to you. Don't worry—they will be light. As my valet, you'll be treated with the proper respect by the manor's servants, despite your youth."

While Bram got to work unpacking, the explorer washed his face and changed his clothes. He'd just finished buttoning his waistcoat when someone knocked on the door.

"Come."

Swinburne pranced in, his arms flapping.

"What a place, Richard! My hat! Your fiancée's great-uncle inhabits a palace! Are you ready? Shall we say hello to the rabid Catholics? I say, they'll offer us a drink, won't they?"

"We can but hope."

Monsieur Levi joined them and Clunk led the guests down to the first floor—where Bram left them to accompany a second footman to the servants' chambers—and along to the music room, from which the tinkle of a piano could be heard. As they stepped through the double doors, Blanche saw them first, stopped playing, and gave a cry of pleasure. Her audience turned and Isabel jumped up and ran to Burton. With her family watching, she was more restrained than usual in her greeting of him, but the explorer noticed something else, too—she was pale, seemingly tired, and had a faraway look in her eyes, as if daydreaming.

"Are you all right, darling?" he murmured.

"Yes, yes, now that you are here at last!" she replied. "I haven't been sleeping well the past couple of nights, that is all. Come and say hello to Mama and Papa."

The Honourable Henry Raymond Arundell—nephew to Lord Gerard, the 10th Baron of Arundell—was a small man with a boyish face supplemented by an oddly square-shaped beard growing from beneath the angle of his jaw; his cheeks, upper lip, and chin were all clean-shaven. His hair showed the same golden blondness his daughter had inherited. Henry Arundell held a grudging respect for Burton—an attitude not shared by his wife—and shook the explorer's hand with genuine warmth.

Mrs. Eliza Arundell was tall, like Isabel, with a face too masculine and severe to qualify as beautiful, though she was certainly handsome. She greeted Burton and his friends politely but cautiously, and looked down at Swinburne with an expression of bemusement, as if her son-in-law-to-be had ushered Shakespeare's Puck into her presence.

The rest of the family was introduced; Isabel's cousins—Rudolph, tall and somewhat bumptious in manner; Jack, short, rotund, and shy; her Uncle Renfric, white-bearded and thoroughly disapproving of, it appeared, just about everything; and Blanche's wayward husband, John Smythe Piggott, who, though handsome, carried himself with an air of superiority that Burton found thoroughly irritating.

Next, the other guests were presented, starting with Doctor George Bird and his wife, Lallah, both of whom Isabel held in high regard. "Dear George has been teaching me to fence," she told Burton.

"Indeed!" the explorer exclaimed as he shook the tall physician's hand. "Have you practised the art for long, Doctor?"

"Not long enough to hold my own against you. You're reputed one of the best in Europe."

Burton bowed his head courteously, then said to Isabel, "But why have you taken up the foil, my dear?"

"To defend you should we be attacked in the Arabian wilderness, of course!"

Burton raised an eyebrow and shared a slight smile of amusement with Bird.

Samuel Beeton was next to be introduced. Burton already knew a little about this dark-haired and good-looking man; he was a publisher and had made a fortune from Harriet Beecher Stowe's *Uncle Tom's Cabin*. His wife, Isabella—heavily pregnant—was one of his authors, very beautiful, with hair thick, black, and long, and dark, soulful eyes. When Burton took her hand, he felt an immediate affinity with her, and remembered that Isabel—who'd met her at a social function five years ago, before she'd become Mrs. Beeton—had reported a similar sensation: *I was presented to a fine lady by the name of Isabella Mayson who I took to my heart in an instant, feeling, after our initial exchange of pleasantries, as if I'd known her my entire life.*

Sadhvi Raghavendra came forward and met Swinburne and Levi, then Richard Monckton Milnes greeted his friends.

After half an hour of polite chatter with the ladies, the men repaired to the smoking room. For a brief moment, as the gents departed, Isabel was distracted when her uncle's gout caused him to give a cry of distress, and Sadhvi Raghavendra took the opportunity to lean close to Burton. "What have you been up to, Richard?" she said softly. "I see fresh scars."

"It's a long story," he replied.

"We must talk later. I'm concerned about Isabel."

His eyes held hers for a moment. "Is there a problem, Sadhvi?"

"Only that she's running herself into the ground."

He gave an acknowledging touch to her arm, then joined the men as they passed through the door, walked along the hallway, and entered the smoking room, where the usual ritual of drinks and cigars commenced.

"What is it like to be back in England's green and pleasant land, Sir Richard?" Sam Beeton asked.

"Stranger every day."

"Was Africa as savage as the stories have it?"

"Oh, absolutely so."

Monckton Milnes put in, "Richard already knew what he was letting himself in for when he went after the Nile, Mr. Beeton. He'd taken a spear through the face in a pitched battle at Berbera not four years previously."

"Ah! Now then, Burton," Bird interrupted, "tell me how you feel when you have killed a man."

Burton looked at him slyly and drawled, "Quite jolly, Doctor. How do you?"

Bird threw his head back and gave a great bellow of laughter. "Touché!" he hollered. "Touché!"

"Incidentally," Monckton Milnes said, "Steinhaueser arrives tomorrow. I daresay he'll want to give you the once-over, Richard."

"Are you referring to Doctor John Steinhaueser?" Bird asked.

"Yes—you know him?" Monckton Milnes responded.

"By repute. A very skilled practitioner, I believe." Bird regarded Burton. "Your personal physician?"

"And friend," Burton replied. "He has twice put me back together; first, after the spear wound—" he touched the scar on his cheek, "and, more recently, after I was injured when a steam sphere collided with my rotorchair." He inwardly winced, remembering that Isabel didn't know about his most recent brush with death.

Loose tongue! Dolt!

"Hah!" Uncle Renfric shouted, as—leaning heavily on his walking stick—he cautiously lowered himself into a chair by the fireplace and rested his gouty foot upon a leather pouffe. "Just as I've always said! These damnable machines are a threat to life and limb. Hah, I say! Humbug and hah! Why must everything change? Old England was in perfectly good shape before that hound Disraeli inflicted the Department of Guided Science upon us. Perfectly good! Hah!"

Swinburne, who was loitering near the drinks cabinet, screeched, "My hat, sir! Quite obviously you have never resided in London."

Uncle Renfric raised a monocle to his eye and squinted through it at the little poet. "I've not even visited it, young lady. Den of sin. And I fail to see how my geographical position has any bearing on the matter. Nor do I understand why you are present in a gentlemen's smoking parlour."

"I may be young, but I'm no lady," Swinburne replied. "And if I was, I certainly wouldn't be."

"Prattle! Prattle! What are you talking about?"

Swinburne hopped and gesticulated. "Bazalgette, of course!"

"There!" Uncle Renfric announced. "Again! Prattle! Nothing but noise! Take note of the Good Book, little missy, for it sayeth: Even a fool who keeps silent is considered wise; when he closes his lips, he is deemed intelligent. Hah! Yes! Hah!"

"Bazalgette!" Swinburne squealed. "His sewers!"

"A fit of feminine hysteria, is it? Must be the tobacco smoke. I told you, this is no place for a girl. Begone, at once!"

"Gah!" Swinburne cried out. "Don't you see? Without the DOGS we'd not have him, and without him we'd not have the new sewer system. Old England may have been perfectly good, sir, but its capital stinks something rotten!"

"Ho hah! Sense out of her, at last! Of course it stinks, missy! Of fire and brimstone, no doubt! Fire and brimstone, I say!" The old man turned his monocle, surveying the room until he fixed upon Eliphas Levi. "You, sir! You have the look of a priest about you, and I see the crucifix upon your chest."

"*Oui, monsieur.* I have train as a Catholic priest," Levi said.

"Hah! Good show! Come here. I'll have your opinion on this ungodly business of so-called scientific advancement. You are cursed with being a Frenchie, I discern, but I'll not hold that against you. Come! Come!" The old man lifted his walking stick and prodded it in Swinburne's direction. "And you, young lady, out! Out! Wrong room, wrong gender! Lord have mercy! In trousers, too! Whatever is the world coming to?"

The poet stood with mouth agape, then spun on his heel and demanded a large brandy from one of the clockwork footmen.

While Levi attended to the unenviable task of keeping Uncle Renfric occupied—and cousins Rudolph and Jack took to the billiard table with Smythe Piggott—Burton, Swinburne, Monckton Milnes, Doctor Bird, Sam Beeton, and Henry Arundell seated themselves upon three leather sofas positioned around a low coffee table.

"Speaking of Bazalgette—" Beeton started.

"I fervently wish I hadn't been," Swinburne interrupted.

"—have you heard about the adventures of the Norwood builders?"

Burton recalled reading something about it in the newspapers. "In relation to the southern part of the sewer system, I believe?"

"Yes. Bazalgette is appropriating the subterranean River Effra, as he did with the Tyburn, turning it into an outlet tunnel from Herne Hill all the way northward to Vauxhall, but his workers are in revolt due to the ghosts."

"Ghosts?" Henry Arundell asked.

Beeton nodded. "The river has its origins about a mile south of the construction site and runs past the Norwood Cemetery catacombs. The workers are convinced the upper reaches of the waterway are haunted. The poor blighters are so terrified, old Bazalgette can hardly get a day's work out of 'em!"

Burton grunted dismissively. "The average Englishman possesses the very same superstitious fears as an African tribesman, yet we claim ourselves a superior race."

"What a contrast," Monckton Milnes mused. "The irrational at one end of the river and the rational at the other."

"Rational? How so?" Doctor Bird asked.

"The river joins the Thames at Vauxhall, very close to the DOGS' headquarters. It flows from the funereal to the functional."

Bird shuddered. "Thank goodness for that. Were it reversed, we should have to rename it the Styx. Brrr! I don't like the idea of an underground river."

Nor did Burton. He had a strong aversion to enclosed spaces.

He struggled to clarify a lurking thought. Something had just occurred to him but, like the Effra, it bubbled far beneath the surface. Having failed to drag it into his conscious mind, he was left with the irritating sense that he knew something important but couldn't identify what.

Think, you dolt! Think!

CHAPTER 16

SEEN THROUGH WINDOWS

PEACE AND GOODWILL TO ALL MEN!
The 11th Hour of the 11th Day of the 11th Month

**THE COMMENCEMENT OF THE
CENTRAL GERMAN CONFEDERATION
AND THE SIGNING OF
THE TRADE ALLIANCE**

QUEEN VICTORIA MEMORIAL, GREEN PARK, LONDON

*His Majesty King George V; HRH Prince Albert;
Prime Minister Disraeli and His Majesty's Government;
Maximilian II of Bavaria; Emperor Franz Joseph I;
The Göttingen Seven; Count Franz Anton von Kolowrat-Liebsteinsky.*

A GOLDEN DAWN FOR EUROPE!
UNITY AND PROSPERITY!

Having enjoyed an extravagant dinner, Burton and his companions were given a tour of New Wardour Castle. The mansion was enormous, and had many high painted ceilings and ornate fireplaces. The ballroom, on the first floor, was perhaps eight times bigger than the one in the *Orpheus*, with Roman columns rising to a vaulted ceiling from which three elaborate chandeliers hung. A decorative balustrade circled the chamber, from which spectators could look down upon the dancing couples.

The party socialised until near midnight, then the houseguests retired to their rooms; however, shortly before they did so, Burton found a moment to converse alone with Sister Raghavendra.

"Why such concern?" he asked. "Isabel appears in fine fettle."

"You must tell her to rest," she replied. "She's so thrown herself into arranging the party that she's become overwrought and exhausted. She's hiding it well, I'll admit, but I can sense it."

"I know to trust your judgement, Sadhvi. Thank you. I'll ensure she has a leisurely day tomorrow."

When Burton entered his bedchamber, he saw that Bram Stoker had laid out his pyjamas and provided a fresh basin of water along with laundered towels. The lad was now snoring in the next room.

The explorer washed, undressed, and got into bed. He performed a Sufi meditation—one that always sent him quickly into the depths of sleep—and he dreamt.

You're awake.

No, I'm not.

You are. Get out of bed. Open the curtains.

He sat up and swung his feet to the floor, stood, and walked over to the window.

Look outside.

He took hold of the thick material, drew it to either side, stepped closer to the glass, and peered out. A half-moon was shining behind ragged, fast-moving clouds. Stars flickered, vanished, and reappeared. The landscape crawled with shadows and silver light. There was a path. It cut across a neatly trimmed lawn, ran alongside flower beds, and meandered through the inky darkness beneath breeze-blown trees.

He saw a ghost.

The window's glass was old and uneven. It distorted the vista. When he moved his head—which he did now—everything outside undulated and jumped. The wraith was there, then not there, then there again. It vanished into shadow and was then momentarily made vivid by moonlight. He struggled for a clear view of it.

A woman?

Yes. Flitting along the path, in a white gown that rippled and flapped around her.

She was moving away from the house. He watched as she darted across a wide wooden bridge spanning a stream then plunged into the gloom at the edge of a thickly forested area.

This is a dream.

If that is true, wake up.

He opened his eyes. Watery daylight was leaking into the bedroom through a chink between the closed curtains. He turned onto his side and took his pocket watch from the bedside table. It was half-past seven. He sat up, stretched, and hissed as his ribs complained, then lay back with his hands behind his head.

He struggled to bring a half-formed thought to conception. It had been there since yesterday evening, nagging at the back of his mind. Something concealed yet . . . *obvious*. Damnation, what was it?

It evaded him. However, while wrestling to bring it forth, he instead remembered the dream. Frowning, he sat up again, looked at the window, and muttered, "The Norwood ghosts," for it was obvious to him that the talk of the River Effra hauntings had invaded his sleep. He got out of bed, crossed the room, drew the curtains, and looked out. Under a grey, threatening sky, the landscape was exactly as he'd seen it under the half-moon.

He tried to recall whether he'd looked out of this window yesterday. He didn't think he had. How, then, could he have dreamt the view?

A raven flew into the glass with a loud bang. The window cracked and Burton leaped back with a yelp of surprise. The bird dropped from sight.

He put a hand to his chest. His heart was hammering. He fought to calm himself.

The connecting door opened and Bram stepped in.

"Mornin' to ye, Cap'n. Did ye drop somethin'?"

"Good morning, lad. No—a bird hit the windowpane. Startled me. Did you sleep well?"

"Aye, the sleep o' the dead. Will I be a-layin' out your mornin' suit?"

"Yes please, then go downstairs and find yourself something to eat."

An hour later, the explorer joined the Arundell family and their guests around a long dining table. A host of quietly ticking clockwork footmen served breakfast. Isabel and Doctor Bird were absent.

"She's sleeping in," Blanche said, in response to Burton's enquiry. "She had a restless night. Doctor Bird is checking on her, just as a precaution. Ah, here he is."

"She'll be fine," Bird announced, entering the room. He pulled out a chair and sat with them. "But she's very fatigued. Mrs. Arundell, I ordered her to rest today, but she's somewhat—um—um—"

"Obstinate," Eliza Arundell supplied. "Always has been. I'll go up after breakfast. If she won't listen to her doctor, perhaps she'll listen to her mother."

After they'd eaten, Monckton Milnes and Eliphas Levi took to the library to peruse the collection, while the Arundells, Birds, and Beetons retired to the music room. Burton decided on a stroll in the grounds and was joined by Swinburne. Nettles, the butler, handed them each an umbrella as they stepped out. It was raining lightly but steadily.

"You are marrying into money, Richard," the poet observed, looking back at the manor as they crossed its lawn, "and plenty of it."

"The wealth is with Isabel's Great-Uncle Gerard, Algy. Her parents are sufficiently well off but by no means rich, and the fact that their daughter is marrying a heathen means none of their pile will be coming our way. I have, I'll freely confess, felt rather guilty about that, but Isabel is adamant she wants only what I can offer."

"A dreadful headache?" Swinburne quipped.

"A life—which she regards as exotic and exciting—in Damascus."

Even as he said it, Burton felt a sudden reluctance. Bismillah! Had he become so entwined in this Abdu El Yezdi affair that the consulship had lost its allure? How could he break *that* news to his fiancée?

He pointed his swordstick at the path ahead of them—the one that led over the wooden bridge—and said, "Let's follow that."

They strode along the trail, its gravel crunching beneath their boots, the rain sizzling on their brollies, until they came to the stream.

Swinburne gazed up at the treetops. "My hat! What a ruckus those ravens are making."

Burton gave a distracted sound of agreement. He stopped and squatted, examining a patch of mud between the gravel and the wooden boards of the bridge.

"What have you found?" Swinburne asked.

"A partial print, made by a woman's bare foot. We're lucky we caught it. The rain will have it washed away soon enough."

"That's rather incongruous—a barefooted woman out in this weather."

"She was here last night, Algy. I saw her from my bedroom window. I thought I was dreaming a ghost. Apparently not. Hallo! There's Tom Honesty." Burton raised his stick and called to the groundsman, who'd just come into view ahead of them. He was dressed in waterproofs, pushing a wheelbarrow filled with cut logs, which he lowered as the explorer and his companion crossed the bridge and approached him.

"Morning, sirs. Nasty weather."

"Good morning. It is indeed. I say, Mr. Honesty, this path—where does it lead?"

"Past High Wood, sir. Through Ark Farm. Continues on to the old castle."

"We can follow it through the farm?"

"Yes. All a part of the estate."

"Thank you. I think we'll go and have a look at the ruins."

"Mind how you go, sir. Walls. Unstable." Honesty peered up at the flat layer of cloud. "Rain'll get worse, too."

The groundsman hesitated.

"Is there something else, my man?" Burton asked.

"Haunted, sir."

"I beg your pardon?"

"The castle. It's haunted."

"By whom?"

"Lady Blanche Arundell. Mistress of the castle when the Parliamentarians attacked it. 1643, that was. Her ghost walks the battlements."

"I presume the current Miss Blanche was named after her."

"That's right. Legend has it that the ghost also appears as a white owl whenever there's a death in the family."

"I hope, then, that we don't see one. Good day to you, Mr. Honesty."

Burton and Swinburne touched the brims of their hats and moved on. As they passed by the edge of the woods, the poet said, "Was your lady of the night the spook, do you think?"

"More likely it was Isabel."

"Isabel? Really? What the dickens was she up to?"

"I have no idea," Burton replied. "But as soon as I heard she had a restless night, I realised the figure I saw resembled her, though I glimpsed it only vaguely. She may have been sleepwalking. She spent her childhood on this estate, and in those fields—" he employed his cane to point ahead at the farm's pastures, "—there was often an encampment of Gypsies. She became rather fond of one of them, a woman named Hagar Burton, who predicted that Isabel would fall in love with a man who had the Burton surname."

"Fate, irreversible and inscrutable," Swinburne murmured.

"Perhaps. Of course, when Isabel and I met in Boulogne back in 'fifty-one, she immediately placed great stock in the childhood prophecy. For the past eight years, while I was overseas for extended periods, she drew much comfort from the idea that we were destined to be together. Unfortunately, earlier this year, she bumped into Hagar Burton again, and this time received an utterly preposterous but very upsetting forecast. The gypsy told Isabel that I would murder her while she was still wearing her wedding dress."

"By James! How positively macabre!"

"If someone you've had faith in for a long time told you something you cannot give any credence to, would you not suffer a degree of nervous excitement?"

"And it's to that you ascribe her sleepwalking?"

"That and her being overwrought about the party. I think she came to these fields unconsciously seeking the gypsy."

They climbed over a stile and followed the path along the edge of a sloping meadow in which sheep were sat with legs tucked under them and heads hunkered into shoulders. The animals regarded them nervously but didn't move, unwilling to abandon the dry patch beneath their bodies.

The rain fell harder.

They crossed another field, passed a small lake, and ascended a wooded bank toward Old Wardour Castle. The ancient edifice loomed over them, a massive hexagonal structure of grey stone. The Arundell family had acquired it in 1544 but a hundred years later it was partially destroyed during the Civil War. The southwestern corner was completely wrecked, its walls collapsed, what remained of them ragged, and the rest of the castle had been gutted and badly damaged. Deep cracks were visible in its moss-clad walls and piles of fallen masonry still lay all about.

There were ravens everywhere. Huddled against the downpour, they watched the two men approach, their eyes glittering blackly.

Burton and Swinburne passed beneath the remnant of a barbican and entered through an east-facing arch. They walked along a short passageway into a central courtyard upon which the rain was splashing noisily. The entrances to vaulted rooms lay to the left and right of them, and ahead a columned portal arched over the foot of a spiral staircase.

Swinburne gazed at the irregularly placed windows, the towering walls, the projecting stumps of lost floors and ceilings, and declared, "Rossetti would be transported into a state of ecstasy by this place. He'd have visions of white knights and fair damsels, of courtly manners and just crusades." He twirled his umbrella and pronounced:

In the noble days were shown
Deeds of good knights many one,
Many worthy wars were done.

It was time of scath and scorn
When at breaking of the morn
Tristram the good knight was born.

Burton looked at a dark entrance beyond which steps led down into darkness. He shivered. "You and your fellow Pre-Raphaelites might realise the romance of it but I see dank cellars, cobwebby dungeons, and claustrophobic corridors. Let's get back to the house, Algy. I have little immunity to British rain, and ruins make me melancholic."

"That's because you see in them the remorselessly degenerative attentions of Chronos," Swinburne murmured as they turned and exited the castle. "Who, we now know, is not at all as we conceive him."

An immense unkindness of ravens watched them depart.

A little over an hour later, they'd changed into dry clothes and were warming themselves by a fire in the manor's principal sitting room. They were joined by various of the other guests, including Doctor John Steinhaueser, who'd arrived while they were out and was now enjoying Blanche's undivided attention, despite the indignant presence of her husband.

Isabel was also with the party, looking wan and listless but stubbornly refusing Doctor Bird's insistence that she return to bed.

"Then humour me by drinking beef broth," the physician advised her. "It'll help you regain your strength."

"I concur," Steinhaueser said. "And chamomile tea before bed, hmmm?"

Sadhvi interjected, "I can mix a herbal brew of slightly greater potency."

"Good idea," Bird responded. "You have to sleep more deeply, Isabel. We can't have any more somnambulism."

"Ah," Burton exclaimed. "So it's confirmed? You've been sleepwalking?"

Isabel nodded. "Yes, Dick. My feet are all cut up. It seems I walked barefoot on a gravel path in the gardens. I remember nothing of it."

"Doctor Steinhaueser," Blanche said, "may I call you Styggins?"

"By all means."

Smythe Piggott cleared his throat.

"Styggins," Blanche went on, "do you agree with George that my sister's symptoms are those of a headstrong and totally unreasonable young lady who steadfastly refuses to allow anyone a say in the arranging of her engagement party, who is deaf to all opinions other than her own, and who really is the silliest thing ever?"

"Um, I don't recall putting it quite like that!" Bird interrupted.

Steinhaueser laughed. "If you're suggesting that Isabel should allow others to take some of the responsibility, then you are entirely correct."

Isabel raised her hands. "Enough, please! The work is done. I can afford to rest now."

Burton took her hand and squeezed it. "See that you do. We've waited a long time for this. I'll be demanding many a dance from you come Saturday. I expect you to be your sparkling best, is that understood?"

"It is, Dick."

The conversation moved on to other topics. Eliphas Levi was asked about his background, and talked at length about how his desire to be a Catholic priest proved incompatible with his radical beliefs, which had twice resulted in prison sentences. Uncle Renfric didn't approve of this revelation at all, and hobbled from the room muttering, "Charlatans, atheists, and criminals! Hah! I suppose I'll have the chapel to myself, at least!"

Swinburne was next to stoke the furnace of indignation. At lunchtime, he drank too much wine and mused that any flower probably enjoyed a closer relationship with the divine than even the most pious human could achieve. "What shrubbery doesn't pass the day in silent meditation upon the pure and joyous elegance of existence?" he pondered.

"The cognisance of God in all His glory is exclusive to Man, Mr. Swinburne," Eliza Arundell objected. "That is why we have dominion."

"Really, ma'am?" Swinburne drawled. "Do you include the Brahmin and the Muslim? What of the African tribesman or Australian aborigine?"

Mrs. Arundell bristled. "Outside the Church there is no salvation, sir. Those you mention will go to the everlasting fire unless, before the end of life, they have joined the one true Church of Jesus Christ, the Saviour."

Swinburne threw up his arms and squealed, "My dear lady, if a faith, in order to feel secure in itself, must condemn anyone whose opinion differs from its own, then it is a faith with no faith at all!"

"Algy, please," Burton growled. "This is neither the time nor the place."

Mrs. Arundell pushed her chair back and stood, her back stiff. "For once, I'm in agreement with my future son-in-law. If you feel it appropriate to question the beliefs held by your hosts, sir, then you are not a gentleman. I insist that you hold your tongue. If you cannot, you will oblige me by leaving this house."

With that, she turned and stalked from the dining room.

"I say!" Swinburne muttered. "I never claimed to be a gentleman."

"Pretend to be, lad," Monckton Milnes advised. "Pretend to be."

After lunch, the remaining Arundells made their excuses and left their wayward guests to their own devices.

Isabel returned to her bed. Isabella Beeton, Sister Raghavendra, and Lallah Bird settled in the drawing room.

Swinburne found a desk and set to work on his poem, *Tristan and Isolde*. Monckton Milnes and Levi buried themselves in the depths of a philosophical discussion. Sam Beeton and Doctor Bird played billiards. Burton chatted with Steinhaueser.

The afternoon passed, the rain pattered against the windows, and at seven o'clock everyone reconvened for dinner. Mrs. Arundell kept the length of the table between herself and Swinburne. Monckton Milnes assiduously regulated the poet's drinking and Burton was at his sociable best, charming the gathering with tall tales of Africa and, quite remarkably, managing to keep those tales clean and palatable. Isabel, too—having napped for four hours—was effervescent and witty, which prompted Sam Beeton to say to Burton during the post-prandial smoking, "You two belong together, that much is obvious to all."

"I never felt I belonged anywhere until I met her," Burton replied. "Now I feel I can belong any place at all, provided I am with her."

Beeton smiled and nodded. "I understand exactly what you mean, old man. Why, before I married, I was—Good Lord! What was that?"

A loud scream had echoed through the manor.

"*Les femmes!*" Eliphas Levi exclaimed.

Without another word, the men crashed out of the smoking room and raced along the hallway to the drawing room, where they found the women gathered around Lallah Bird, who'd apparently swooned onto a chaise longue.

"Stand back, please," John Steinhaueser commanded. "Allow Doctor Bird to attend his wife."

"What happened?" Burton asked.

"I don't know," Isabella Beeton answered. "She opened the curtain—" she pointed toward a nearby window, "—to see whether the moon had pierced the clouds, then screamed and fell back in a dead faint."

"It was a face," Blanche said. "I saw it, too. A terrible face!"

Smythe Piggott moved to his wife's side and put a comforting arm around her.

"I need to get smelling salts from my bag," George Bird muttered.

"Here, I have some. I always carry them with me," Steinhaueser said, handing a small bottle to his colleague. He turned as a footman entered the room. "Would you fetch a glass of brandy, please?"

The clockwork figure clanged its assent and hastened away.

Burton moved to the window and looked out. The rain was still falling and the night was pitch dark. He couldn't see a thing.

Lallah Bird uttered a small cry and pushed the smelling salts away from her face. She moaned and put her hands to her mouth. Her husband helped her to sit up.

The footman returned with the brandy, and after a couple of sips of it, Lallah's eyes fluttered open and she wailed, "I saw a man! Oh, George! A horrible brute at the window!"

"There there, dearest," Bird said. "It was probably Tom Honesty, the gardener."

"He hardly qualifies as a brute," Swinburne protested. "And at this time of night? In this rain?"

The doctor frowned at him. "I think it rather less likely that we'd have an intruder in such weather, don't you?"

"It wasn't Tom," Lallah said. "It was a—a—a monstrosity!"

"I'm going to take a look outside," Burton announced. The other men—with the exception of Uncle Renfric and Doctor Bird—immediately elected to accompany him.

While the group changed into overcoats and boots, the cousins Rudolph and Jack went down to the basement storage rooms and returned with five clockwork lanterns.

Separating into pairs, the men left the manor and spread out across the grounds. Burton, with Swinburne, first examined the lawn where it abutted the wall beneath the window, but the grass there was short, springy, and despite being wet, didn't hold a print.

They spent forty minutes in the unceasing rain.

There were no signs of an interloper.

George Bird gave his wife a mild sedative and the women went to bed. The men stayed up until well past midnight.

When Burton finally retired, he looked in on Bram and found him fast asleep. The explorer hadn't seen much of the boy—just for the change of clothes after visiting the castle and dressing to dine in the evening—but he knew the Whisperer was enjoying his time "below stairs," having become a firm favourite with the staff.

The explorer fell into a profoundly deep sleep the moment he laid his head on the pillow. He dreamt he was inside a brightly lit castle, talking to Nurse Florence Nightingale, which was curious because he'd never met her.

"You will lie still, sir, or I shall have you strapped down."

Damn and blast you, woman! I'm perfectly fine!

"You know that isn't true."

I know you're an interfering, meddlesome, infuriating shrew!

"Undo your shirt. I have to listen to your heart."

And I have to listen to whatever that blundering young dolt is thinking, which I can't do with you fussing around me like a bloody gadfly. You're a confounded distraction, woman!

"Thank you. That's the nicest thing you've ever said to me. Now shut up. You've made yourself breathless. Much more nonsense and you'll have palpitations again, which is, need I remind you, exactly what you brought me here to prevent."

Then hurry up about it and begone! The crisis is upon us. I must concentrate.

"Richard! Richard!"

Burton woke up. Someone was knocking on the bedroom door.

"Richard! Rouse yourself, man!"

Bram Stoker stepped out of the valet's room, rubbing his eyes.

"See who that is, lad," Burton mumbled. He sat up and reached for his watch. It was a quarter to eight.

Bram opened the door. John Steinhaueser, wrapped in a dressing gown, stepped in. "Richard. Come at once. Something is wrong with Isabel."

"What? Is she ill?" Burton jumped out of bed, lifted his *jubbah* from the bedpost, and hastily wound it about himself.

"She won't wake up. Her maid found her in—in—"

"In what?"

"She might be in a coma, Richard."

Burton told Bram to prepare his clothes then followed Steinhaueser out of the room and along first one corridor, then a second, until they came to Isabel's room. Her mother and father, both in night attire, were standing by the door, their faces drawn and pale.

Henry Arundell reached out and took the explorer by the elbow. "Steady, son. Doctor Bird and Sister Raghavendra are with her."

Burton looked past him and saw Isabel in her bed, her pallid features framed by outspread hair. She looked ghastly, her face as white as the sheets on which she lay, her skin translucently taut again her cheekbones, her breathing laboured and painful to hear.

Steinhaueser said, "Mr. Arundell, I should like Richard to be at her bedside. His presence may pull her out of it."

Arundell looked at his wife, who chewed her bottom lip and gave a hesitant nod.

"Very well," Arundell said. "Providing Miss Raghavendra is also present."

Steinhaueser nodded and led Burton into the room. The explorer took hold of Isabel's hand. It felt cold and limp.

"Deeply unconscious," Doctor Bird said. "But I can't fathom why." He rubbed his chin. "I hear you're well practised in the art of mesmerism, Sir Richard. Tell me what you think of this." Leaning over his patient, he used his thumb to lift her right eyelid. Isabel's pupil was fixed, directed straight ahead, the iris a pinprick.

Burton gave a guttural confirmation. "She appears to be entranced."

"Not comatose, hmmm?" Steinhaueser asked. "But the sluggishness of her pulse—is that symptomatic of a mesmeric stupor?"

"It is," Burton said, "as is, in extreme cases, catalepsy." He dropped his fiancée's hand and turned to her parents. "Mr. Arundell, I should like to call Monsieur Levi."

Before Henry Arundell could answer, his wife snapped, "I hardly think the presence of a failed priest is necessary!"

"On the contrary," Burton said, "Monsieur Levi possesses specialist knowledge. His opinion regarding this is essential."

Isabel's mother opened her mouth to respond but was interrupted by Henry Arundell, who gripped her arm, muttered, "Be quiet, dear," and said to Burton, "I shall fetch him at once, Richard."

"Thank you, sir. Mrs. Arundell, would you step in, please? I want to send Sister Raghavendra back to her bed."

Sadhvi shook her head. "I'm all right."

"No," Burton said. "Go and rest. You may be needed to nurse Isabel later."

The Sister reluctantly stood and left the room.

Eliza Arundell whispered, "Doctor Bird, is my daughter in danger?"

"I hardly know, ma'am," Bird responded. "Mesmerism is Sir Richard's field of expertise, not mine. Physically, her pulse is weak and she has the symptoms of anaemia, which in themselves are not life-threatening, but as to the cause—" He shrugged.

A few minutes later, Henry Arundell returned and ushered Levi into the room.

Immediately upon seeing Isabel's prone form, the Frenchman hurried to the side of the bed and bent over her, touching his fingertips to her jugular, lifting her eyelids, and placing a hand mirror under her nostrils so that her breath was visible upon it. He straightened and, with a grim expression, said to Burton, "Sir Richard, *nous avons un problème grave*."

"Then it is as I suspect?"

"*Oui*, I am certain. *Les symptômes*, they are unmistakable."

Burton looked down at Isabel. Almost inaudibly, he said, "Bismillah! Why didn't I recognise the signs earlier? The damnable Beast is among us."

CHAPTER 17

THE DEVIL HIMSELF

THE IMPROVED AUTO-GALVANIC BATTERY FOR NERVOUS DISEASES

Nervous Headache, Toothache, Tic Douloureux,

Lumbago, Sciatica, and all forms of Nervous Pain.

Also, for Paralysis in its various forms,

from a partial loss of sensation or motion to that of perfect Paralysis.

THE RESTORATION OF VITAL ENERGIES THROUGH THE MIRACLE OF ELECTRICITY

In thirty different languages, Sir Richard Francis Burton cursed himself for a bloody fool. Secured in the library with Swinburne, Levi, Monckton Milnes, and Steinhaueser, he fumed and paced, smoked furiously, and uttered every expletive he knew—and he knew a great many.

"I can understand him being upset that Isabel is unwell," Steinhaueser whispered to Monckton Milnes, "but why is he taking on so?"

"That's for him to explain," Monckton Milnes replied, "which he undoubtedly will do once he's calmed down, else he wouldn't have invited you to join us."

Nettles entered with a pot of coffee and set it down on a sideboard. "Will the gentlemen require anything else?"

"No," Burton barked. "Get out! We're not to be disturbed!"

Levi poured each of them a cup and, despite it still being early—eleven in the morning—also went to the drinks cabinet and retrieved a decanter of brandy.

"Hell and damnation!" Burton spat. "It's my fault. I should have cancelled the party and stayed in London; instead, I've drawn a bloody *nosferatu* here."

"*Nosferatu?*" Steinhaueser asked.

Burton flicked his hand impatiently and snarled, "Tell him."

"Richard," Monckton Milnes said, "we are still dealing with state secrets. I don't think the king had it in mind for you to freely dispense information and recruit an army."

"To blazes with the king!"

Steinhaueser looked at each of them in turn. "The king? What are you all up to?"

Monckton Milnes looked at Eliphas Levi and gave an almost imperceptible nod. The occultist took out his pipe and smoked it while quietly explaining to John Steinhaueser the nature of Perdurabo and the threat he represented.

Burton listened and slowly regained his composure. He threw his cigar into the fireplace, immediately lit another, then sat and glowered at Steinhaueser, watching his every reaction to the incredible tale.

"Is this a—a joke? A legend?" the doctor stammered. "A story?" He looked again from Levi to Monckton Milnes and from Swinburne to Burton. "Surely it's not true?"

"It's true," Burton said. "And I'll be damned if I let Perdurabo anywhere near Isabel again. I'll sit beside her the night through with a gun in my hand. But let's not wait for sundown. Styggins, how did you travel here?"

"In my steam sphere."

"Good. I want you to take it out for a spin. Drive around the local villages, talk to the bobbies, find out if there are any strangers in the district, especially any who are nocturnal in their habits. Take my valet with you. Whisperers tend to notice things the police don't."

Burton addressed Monckton Milnes. "Organise a search of the house. It's a big place with plenty of rooms, attics, and cellars where a man might hide, so be thorough. Don't miss an inch of it."

Finally, he spoke to Eliphas Levi. "Monsieur, will you join Doctor Bird at my fiancée's bedside? You best understand her condition."

"*Oui*, of course."

The men rose and set about their tasks. Burton went to his room, pulled a leather case from beneath a bed, and opened it to reveal a brace of pistols. He pushed them into his waistband and buttoned his coat to conceal them. Picking up the lantern he'd used last night, he told Bram to follow him, went downstairs, and joined Swinburne and Steinhaueser in the entrance hall. They left the house—the rain had ceased but it was a damp and chilly day—and strode to a row of low buildings that lay a few yards to the east of the mansion. Steinhaueser entered one and a few moments later they heard the unmistakable hissing and panting of a steam sphere. The vehicle rolled out and came to a halt.

Burton said, "If you identify where John Judge is holed up, don't approach him, don't challenge him, don't hesitate for a single moment—just report back here as quickly as you can."

"Understood," the doctor said. He gestured to Bram. "Hop in, nipper."

The boy rubbed his hands in delight at the prospect of a ride in the contraption—in the passenger seat rather than the storage compartment!—and swung himself into it, settling beside the doctor. He looked out at Burton. "And me, Cap'n?"

"The same. If you learn anything, get word back to me immediately."

Burton and Swinburne watched as the vehicle steamed away toward the estate's entrance gate.

"What about us?" Swinburne asked.

Burton pointed at a steam-driven landau. "We'll drive up to the old castle, Algy, and this time we're going to search it from top to bottom." Burton swallowed nervously. "Including the vaults."

They found nothing.

New Wardour Castle held none but the Arundells and their guests and servants, the surrounding villages were occupied by locals and no one else, and Old Wardour Castle was inhabited only by spiders, beetles, and ravens.

Burton had been thoroughly unnerved by the vaults. Dark, dank, and infested, they had too much of the grave about them. Years ago, in India, he'd witnessed holy men being buried alive. Many of them had been dug up days later—in some cases weeks—still living and none the worse for their experience. Others, though, had suffocated to death, their noses and mouths filled with soil and worms. The memory of it had led him to tell Isabel, shortly before his departure for Africa, that when he died, she must not under any circumstances have him buried.

"I should hate to wake up and find myself underground."

"A cremation, then?" she'd asked, unhappily. Catholics didn't favour cremations, and she secretly hoped Burton might convert some day.

"Gad, no! I don't want to burn before I have to! A mausoleum, Isabel. Above ground and with light shining in. We shall lie in it side by side."

"Oh, I like that idea, but would you mind awfully if we grow tremendously old together first?"

"I shan't mind that at all, darling."

Isabel. Isabel.

She was awake.

Sam Beeton announced it as soon as Burton and Swinburne returned to the mansion. Without bothering to change out of his dust-stained and web-bestrewn clothes, the explorer raced up the stairs and along the corridor to his fiancée's room.

Doctor Bird, Eliphas Levi, Smythe Piggott, and Blanche were with her.

"She's very weak," Bird said, "but the trance is broken."

Burton sat on the edge of the bed and took Isabel's hand. It was cold. Her eyes opened and she gave him a faint smile.

"I've been dreaming, Dick," she whispered. "I was riding on horseback across an African savannah, leading a band of wild Bedouin women. I felt such . . . freedom."

"Perhaps it was a premonition," he replied, knowing how much she desired adventure.

"A premonition. A premonition." Her eyes appeared to focus on something far away. "Yet I feel I've already been there," she said, dreamily. "Like a memory. I can still smell the spice in the air."

Burton glanced at Levi. The occultist was standing with his arms crossed over his chest and his back to the window. His brows were drawn low over his eyes, his mouth set in a grim line. Behind him, something dark moved on the exterior sill, attracting Burton's attention. It was a raven, big and black and staring implacably in at them.

Isabel whispered. "Why do I feel so feeble, Dick? Am I sick?"

He looked back at her. "Yes, dear, but we have two doctors and a nurse in the house. They'll make you well again."

"In time for the ball?"

Burton looked at Doctor Bird. The man made the slightest of gestures, indicating that he had no answer.

"Yes, Isabel, and we shall dance the night through."

"I'll need the doctors again afterward," she mumbled.

"Why so?"

"Because you dance so clumsily. My feet will be a terrible mess."

She sighed, smiled, closed her eyes, and drifted into sleep.

Blanche was clutching a Bible. She lifted it to her lips, kissed it, and placed it on the pillow beside her sister's head.

"That is wise, mademoiselle," Levi said softly. "Faith strengthens the will, and it is willpower she requires."

"But what is wrong with her, Monsieur Levi? Do you know? The doctors can tell me nothing."

"It is beyond my experience," Bird confirmed.

"She is the victim," Levi said, "of a parasite."

Blanche gasped. "What can be done?"

Burton reached across and touched her arm. "She'll recover providing we look after her. I shall sit at her side all night."

"Very well, but Mama and Papa will insist that propriety is observed, so I'll stay with you."

"No, Blanche, you sleep. Be strong for tomorrow. Sadhvi Raghavendra will chaperone."

"But—"

"She is a Sister of Noble Benevolence—her presence alone will aid Isabel's recovery."

Blanche pressed her lips together then nodded reluctantly.

"Good girl." Burton scrutinised Isabel's face. It was pale and pinched, her eyes shadowed. Standing, he said, "She must have peace and quiet and I am desperate for a change of clothing. I'll come back later. Monsieur, will you join me in the library in half an hour?"

"*Oui*, I shall be there."

Burton went to his room. Bram helped him to dress.

"I spoke to the Whisperers in Tisbury, Cap'n. There's a message for ye from Mr. Macallister Fogg."

"Trounce? What is it?"

"That Mr. Thomas Great Harris has arrived in London and is currently president at the Regency."

"President? You probably mean *resident*."

"Ah, yes, I expect so."

"And it's *Lake* Harris. Anything else?"

"Aye, they say there's trouble a-brewin' in the Cauldron."

"There always is, lad."

"You're not wrong, sir, always trouble there. But have ye ever known there to be political unrest in the blessed place?"

"Political!" Burton exclaimed. "Great heavens, no. The population couldn't give two hoots about politics, lad. They're far too busy coshing heads and burglarising to have a care about anything that might be said or done in parliament."

Bram put a brush to the explorer's jacket, sweeping specks of lint from it.

"To be sure, sir, yet the whisper is that voices are bein' raised against our Alliance with the Central German Confederation."

"East Enders protesting about international affairs? By James, I wouldn't credit them with even knowing Europe exists! What on earth has riled them so?"

"It's a regular mystery, so it is. There, Cap'n, neat an' tidy, ye are."

"Thank you, Bram. Can you keep yourself occupied for the afternoon?"

"Not half! Doctor Steinhaueser bought me the latest issue of *The Baker Street Detective*, so he did. I'm eager to discover what our friend Mr. Macallister Fogg has been up to."

A few minutes later, Burton left his valet in the grip of *The Mystery of the Master Mummer's Mummy* and joined Levi, Swinburne, Monckton Milnes, and Steinhaueser in the library where, having missed lunch, they'd been provided with a platter of cold meats, pickles, and breads, which they were picking at in a desultory manner.

"I have just resisted the urge to sneer at young Stoker's choice of reading material," Burton announced. "He's lapping up a tale of Egyptian mummies come to life. Now I find myself having to discuss, in all seriousness, a vampire in our midst. If I awake in a moment in Africa, having feverishly hallucinated everything that has occurred these past weeks, only then will life make any sort of sense." He pulled a cheroot from his top pocket, held it between his teeth, struck a lucifer, and watched the spluttering flame for a few seconds before applying it to the cigar. Inhaling the sweet smoke, he forced it out through his nostrils and continued, "But the one thing I know for sure is that my fiancée is suffering, and I won't stand for that, so I have to accept this as neither myth nor fantasy—one way or another I'm going to stop Perdurabo."

His friends remained silent, their faces perfectly reflecting Burton's stony determination.

"Monsieur," Burton said, turning to Levi, "according to folklore, a vampire is able to transform itself into an animal, or even vapour, yes?"

"Ah," Levi replied. "You think of the ravens?"

"I do."

"It is this way: Perdurabo, his *volonté* inhabit John Judge, but it is not attach to the flesh. Certain animals, they sense when that which make a man alive leave the body; they feel the loosening of the *volonté*, and it attract them, for they are scavengers. So ravens or crows or wolves or hyenas, they are seen where a *nosferatu* or *strigoi morti* is, and the superstitious people, they think transformation."

"And the vapour? Can Perdurabo enter the house in the form of steam or smoke?"

"He already show that, at least for a short time, his *volonté* can exist without *une forme physique*—vapour is a symbol of this—but he can do nothing in this state. He have to possess a man to survive and to feed off others."

Swinburne twitched and shuddered. "My hat! How can we battle such a monstrosity?"

"We must kill the body he occupy while he is still in it. Take him by surprise."

"Must I remind you all that John Judge is an innocent man?" Monckton Milnes put in. "He is a victim. Are we to murder him?"

Levi put his hands into the position of prayer and touched his fingertips to his lips. "He have been with the *nosferatu* inside for a month. It is too long. If it leave him more soon to possess another, it is possible for him to recover, but after this much time, now he becomes *nosferatu*, too. It is how the species survive and spread. To kill him is to save him."

"Is there no other way?" Monckton Milnes asked.

The Frenchman closed his eyes and shook his head.

"Gentlemen," Burton said, "not a one of you is under obligation. I am commissioned by the king, you are not. If you wish to disassociate yourself from this matter, do so now. I will not blame you. Friendships, old and new, will not be affected."

"I stand with you, Richard," Swinburne said.

"And I," Steinhaueser added.

Monckton Milnes put a hand over his eyes. "Now I fear even more for Florence Nightingale. My God, what if they took her to be—to be *food* for this damnable creature? I'm with you. Of course I'm with you."

Levi said, "Then we are together."

Burton looked at each man in turn, his expression communicating his gratitude. He asked Levi, "Do you think the *nosferatu* is liable to strike tonight?"

"It is *inévitable*. For his *volonté* to survive, it must draw from others *très fréquemment*."

"Then I suggest we rest for a couple of hours, gentlemen. Tonight, we confront the vampire."

They worked quietly and they concealed the truth. Burton knew it was more than the Arundells could accept, though he felt strongly inclined to recruit

Sam Beeton and, inexplicably and absurdly, even more drawn to confide in the man's pregnant wife, Isabella. Monckton Milnes persuaded him otherwise. "Take advice from a man who knows. In divulging sensitive information, one must consider every recipient as an insecure container. Secrets leak like water, and the more implausible they are, the more likely it is that they'll flood beyond the bounds."

He was right, of course.

To Mr. and Mrs. Arundell, Burton said, "We think the trespasser seen by Lallah Bird is still somewhere on the estate. We also suspect he's carrying the disease—or, rather, the parasite—that has infected Isabel. Swinburne, Monckton Milnes, Steinhaueser, and Monsieur Levi will patrol the grounds tonight."

Eliza Arundell looked perplexed. "This man—a fugitive?—does he threaten the household?"

"In so much that he's chosen to hide out in the vicinity, yes."

"Then I shall gather more men to help you," Henry Arundell said.

"If you'll allow, sir, I'd prefer to limit the numbers to those I've named. I should like to catch the man, so we might hand him over to the authorities. If too many of us patrol the estate, we're liable to scare him away, possibly to inflict his disease upon others."

Henry Arundell considered for a moment then nodded. "Whatever you think best."

Though they'd accepted Burton's explanation for the face at the window and for Isabel's condition, the Arundells were rather less approving of the crushed garlic bulbs Levi had liberally distributed around their daughter's bedchamber.

"What a terrible reek!" her father objected. "What in the name of God are you trying to do? Suffocate her?"

"It sterilise the atmosphere," Levi asserted. "The odour is unpleasant, but it help drive the parasite away."

Arundell wrinkled his nose. "And the crucifixes?" he asked, gesturing at the many additional crosses Levi had added to the room.

The Frenchman quoted, "'The Lord will keep you from all evil; He will keep your life.'"

Henry Arundell had blinked confusedly at this and departed, pulling his wife after him.

"Whenever Isabel open her eyes," Levi said to Burton, "she must see the cross; must be reminded of what she most deeply believe in. She not let go of it, not allow Perdurabo to steal her will to live."

Later, during a subdued dinner, Blanche asked, "Should we cancel the party, mother?"

"At such short notice?" Eliza Arundell exclaimed.

"To be frank with you, ma'am," Doctor Bird interjected, "even if the crisis has passed, I cannot envision your daughter being strong enough by Saturday."

"We'll postpone for a fortnight, not cancel," Henry Arundell said. "Which means we have nearly three hundred letters of apology to write." He addressed the butler. "Nettles, have a couple of the footmen report to my study. I believe Clunk and Tick have the best calligraphy?"

"They do, sir."

"Good. I'll compose, they can copy." Turning back to his guests, he said, "It's the fastest way. They write so rapidly their hands become a blur. We'll have the letters ready to post first thing in the morning."

After dinner, the family took to the chapel to pray for Isabel's recovery. Their guests socialised for a short time but a tense atmosphere hung over New Wardour Castle and a couple of hours after the sun had set, everyone retreated to their rooms.

Sadhvi Raghavendra joined Burton to stand watch over Isabel. They lit a wall lamp but adjusted the wick until the light was dim, so as not to disturb the patient, though she appeared to be in an extremely deep sleep.

"She is dreaming, Richard. You see how her eyes move beneath the lids? But they are not happy dreams. Her limbs are jumping, as if she is imagining herself fleeing from danger."

"Dreamt dangers are ephemeral, Sadhvi. I'm more concerned about the real."

Burton lowered himself into a chair, removed one of the pistols from his waistband, and held it resting on his thigh. Sadhvi also sat.

"I've hardly seen you today," he said. "Are you all right?"

"We Sisters are very sensitive to . . . balance."

"Balance? What do you mean by that?"

"Everything possesses a natural point of equanimity, and we have an affinity with that state, thus we sense when it is disturbed; when things become askew. What is happening to Isabel is an imbalance. Matters surrounding her are out of joint. I feel it and it distresses and tires me."

"Why didn't you say? Go to bed. I'll recruit Blanche for sentry duty."

"No. I prefer to stay." She smiled. "It reminds me of when we sat up to guard the camp on the shores of the Nyanza Lake. Africa was difficult, but it was a happy time. Already, I miss it."

Burton nodded. They gave themselves over to memories and silent companionship, breathed garlicky fumes, and the hours passed.

In a distant hallway, a grandfather clock chimed two.

Movement roused Burton and Raghavendra; they had both fallen into a light doze. It was Isabel. She was sitting up, her eyes glazed and her face slack. She pushed the bedsheets back, swung her bare feet to the floor, and stood.

"Isabel?" Burton asked.

She didn't answer or even acknowledge him.

"Sleepwalking," Sadhvi whispered.

Burton jumped up, crossed to the door, turned the key in the lock, then pulled it out and stepped back.

His fiancée swayed for a moment. She moaned softly, ran to the door, and pulled its handle. A whine of frustration escaped her. She tugged at it, twisted it, then fisted her hands and hammered them against the portal.

Burton moved behind her and took her by the wrists. "Come away from there, darling."

She struggled and whimpered; clawed her fingers and tried to scratch at the door. He pulled her back from it. Sadhvi stepped in front, reached up, and entwined her fingers in Isabel's.

"Sleep, Isabel," she murmured. "Go back to sleep."

Isabel slumped into Burton's arms. He picked her up, carried her to the bed, and laid her down. She moved restlessly. He drew the sheets up to her neck and placed a hand on her forehead.

She quietened and became still.

Burton and Raghavendra returned to their chairs. The lamp flickered and dimmed slightly. Prickles ran up Burton's spine. He checked his pistol, held it tightly, and whispered, "Do you feel it, Sadhvi?"

"Yes," she responded huskily. "A sense of—of—"

"Dread."

She nodded mutely.

Half an hour ticked by and, with every minute of it, the atmosphere in the bedchamber grew more strained, as if imbued with electricity, causing the hairs on Burton's arms to stand upright.

The flame in the lamp guttered and died.

Burton got to his feet and put his gun on the chair. He took a box of lucifers from his pocket and struck one. It didn't ignite. He tried another. Nothing.

"Stay where you are, Sadhvi," he said, retrieving the pistol.

He walked to the window and pulled open the curtains. Moonlight streamed in. He slid up the sash, then frowned and ran his forefinger around the latch. It was broken. He hadn't noticed that before.

Burton leaned out of the window to see whether Swinburne, Monckton Milnes, Levi, or Steinhaueser were in sight. He immediately saw the latter lying motionless on the lawn, but this hardly registered before movement below the window attracted his attention. He looked down and saw a big, shadowy shape clinging to the wall like a lizard. A thick, black-clad arm reached from it, the white muscular hand at its end stretching out, the splayed fingers appearing to dig into the brickwork. The figure heaved itself up.

As if from far away, Burton heard Sadhvi say, "Richard?"

He couldn't reply, couldn't tear his eyes from the uncanny form.

A face emerged from the dark hump, white in the moonlight, broad-featured, tousle-haired, with a flat nose and a wide, wickedly grinning mouth. The eyes were completely black.

John Judge.

Burton strained to move but it was like pushing through thick mud; his limbs were as heavy as lead.

Mesmerism. Break free of it. You know how.

He summoned a mantric formula and made a loop of it, mentally repeating it over and over, establishing a fast and complex rhythm. He visualised inter-locking shapes, filling his mind with convoluted geometries; and while he was doing this, the awful figure on the wall climbed closer and closer, its eyes burrowing into him, transfixing him, pinning him like an insect to a board.

Burton made an association: the hypnotic influence and the mantric chant were one and the same; the emanation from the creature below him was embodied in the serpentine designs he had visualised.

He broke the rhythm, shattered the pattern, and threw off the influence.

Leaning down out of the window, Burton pushed the barrel of his pistol against Judge's forehead and pulled the trigger. The weapon emitted a futile click.

Judge snatched it from his hand and threw it into the darkness. His arm swung forward and a gnarled fist caught the explorer on the point of the jaw. Burton's knees buckled and he fell back across the windowsill into the bedchamber.

With his senses swimming, he fought and failed to regain his feet. He was vaguely aware that Isabel was sitting up in bed again; that Sadhvi Raghavendra appeared to be paralysed in her chair; that the hulking body of John Judge was squeezing in through the window.

Burton pushed himself upright, pulled the second pistol from his waist-band, held it like a club, and faced his enemy. The mesmeric force continued to assault him, more compelling even than that demonstrated by the Brahmins and Sufi masters who'd trained him.

The fingers of Judge's left hand closed over the front of Burton's jacket and shirt. The king's agent was hauled off his feet and into the air. He lashed out with the pistol. His foe swatted it out of his grip. Burton punched at the Irishman's face. Judge weathered the storm for a moment then slapped him hard. Burton went limp.

In a familiar oily tone comprised of innumerable synchronous voices, Judge said, "The stench of garlic, Burton? The extent of your knowledge impresses me. But I'm afraid it won't work. John Judge was a good man and the reek stirs him enough to remind him of it, but he is already half-*nosferatu* and has lost the spirit to resist me. In the absence of willpower, even the most complete collection of virtues and talents is wholly worthless."

"Perdurabo," Burton mumbled. "'I will endure to the end.'"

"As indeed I shall."

The massive figure lowered Burton to the ground and released him. The explorer bunched his fists but knew it would be useless to fight. John Judge was simply too powerful to take on. Better to get as much information out of him as possible while he waited for Swinburne and the others to discover Steinhaueser. Then, perhaps together they could find a way to overpower the intruder.

"You really don't remember me?" Perdurabo asked. "It is such a pity. That, however, is the nature of existence; all the diverse versions of ourselves, the slowly fragmenting mechanisms of Time, the breakdown of natural laws." He smiled nastily. "It is glorious!"

Judge looked to his left, at Sadhvi Raghavendra sitting entranced; to his right, at Isabel, who'd fallen back onto her pillow, her glazed eyes fixed on him; then back at Burton.

"I intend to take these women from you, Burton; to wound you so deeply, you'll be immobilised by your suffering. And while you wallow in self-pity, I shall make my move and defeat the power that has blocked my path in so many different histories. When that is achieved, I shall come for you. I will take you into the future with me, into the new world I shall build, a world in which the only law is: Do what thou wilt."

He likes the sound of his own voice. Keep him talking.

"Why?" Burton asked. "Why am I of any significance?"

"Because I regard you as my predecessor, and because you, of all people, possess insight enough to understand my motives. Nevertheless, if I allowed it, you would try to stop me. Therefore, I shall not allow it. But once I am done, only you will properly appreciate the results. I am a narcissist, Burton. I confess to it. And I want your approval—that is the depth of my respect for you."

"You'll not get it."

Perdurabo shrugged. "Then let us not waste further time in discussion. Sleep."

A crushing weariness descended upon the explorer. He fought it—tried to use his Sufi training to again break the mesmeric spell—but this time it was too strong.

He collapsed to his knees, toppled forward, and was unconscious before he hit the floor.

An immeasurable period of nothingness.

A hammering on the door.

Trounce. Why does he never ring the blessed bell?

He opened his eyes and saw the rug beside his face, and beyond it, the floorboards and the gap at the bottom of the door. There were feet on the other side of it. Fists pounding on wood. Voices shouting his name.

With his mind muddled and the room spinning around him, he crawled to the portal, fumbled the key from his pocket, clumsily slid it into the lock, and twisted it until he heard the latch click. He fell back, struggling to get to his feet as Henry Arundell, Doctor Bird, Swinburne, Monckton Milnes, and Levi burst in.

Swinburne helped him to stand. "I saw him!" the poet panted. "But he ran into the darkness and I lost sight of the blighter."

"Are you all right?" Monckton Milnes asked.

Burton grunted an affirmation. He saw Eliphas Levi bent over Sadhvi Raghavendra. She was collapsed across the side of her chair, the ends of her long hair touching the floor.

An anguished moan came from Arundell. Burton looked to the bed and felt the blood drain from his face. Isabel's father was kneeling, his face buried in the sheets, his hands clutching his daughter's.

"I don't understand," Doctor Bird said. "How can it be? There's no reason for it. No cause."

Burton sagged against Monckton Milnes. "No reason for what?" he asked, an awful presentiment making his voice thin and hoarse.

Bird's eyes met his. They were steeped in sorrow.

"I'm sorry, Sir Richard. I am so sorry. Isabel is dead."

CHAPTER 18

JOHN JUDGE

"FOR THE BLOOD IS THE LIFE"
Hennessey's World-Famed
BLOOD MIXTURE

*Is warranted to cleanse the blood from all impurities,
from whatever cause arising.
For Scurvy, Sores of all kinds, Skin and Blood Diseases,
its Effects are Marvellous.*

THOUSANDS OF TESTIMONIALS FROM ALL PARTS.
*In bottles, 2s. 6d. each, and in
case of six times the quantity, 11s.*

Available at all chemists.
*Sent to any address, for 30 (bottle) or 132 (case) stamps, by the proprietor.
M. J. Shudders, Apothecary, 122 Oxford Street, London.*

Sir Richard Francis Burton stood at a window in the smoking room, facing the black night. Clouds had concealed the moon, and the darkness made the glass reflective. In it, he saw Sir Richard Francis Burton glaring back at him, vague and ghostlike but for the eyes, which burned with an accusatory fire.

He'd left the family upstairs, gathered around Isabel. The screams and wails of her mother, heard throughout the house for the past two hours, had finally dwindled to an occasional cry of despair, but they still echoed loudly in the explorer's mind. Probably, they always would.

He stared at his translucent other.

A different me in a different world, where Isabel might still be alive.

But you are in this one, where she is not.

And it is my fault.

His fault.

Perdurabo had been unequivocal: *I intend to break your spirit and drive you to your knees.* The statement, made via a medium, had felt as intangible to Burton as every other aspect of the affair—mysterious abductions; his supposed presence at The Assassination; the Mad Marquess's vision; the bifurcation of Time; Abdu El Yezdi. All of it was fantastical, and he'd approached it just as he'd approached Africa, as an observer of the unfathomable, a man willing to explore and investigate but who employed a shield of sullenness and cynicism to create an emotional distance, for exploration and anthropology demand a surveyor and the surveyed, and never the twain shall meet, else scientific credibility is lost. Burton felt comfortable with such a conceptual separation. *Too* comfortable. He had applied it to every aspect of his life.

Except Isabel.

Only she had seen past his caustically sardonic front. Only she had realised that his detachment was born not from analytical necessity but from resentment, the resentment born of uncertainty, and his uncertainty born of an upbringing that had ill-prepared him for the complex protocols of British society.

She had saved him.

She had anchored him in reality.

And now she was dead, and this reality was just one of many.

More than one world.

More than one Isabel.

He looked at his nebulous reflection and whispered, "I shall find you. Somehow, I shall find you."

Was he addressing her? Or himself? He didn't know.

In the glass, he saw the door open behind him. An ill-defined memory squirmed uncomfortably, causing him to whip around and raise his hands defensively, but rather than Laurence Oliphant, it was Levi, Swinburne, and Monckton Milnes who stepped into the room.

"*Mon Dieu!*" Levi announced. "These Sisters of the Noble Benevolence, they fill me with wonder. Perdurabo, he feed much on the *volonté* of Mademoiselle Raghavendra, but still a small flame of life remain, and it grow more strong *très rapidement*. She is not *strigoi morti*." He pulled the calabash from his pocket and stuffed tobacco into it. "Doctor Bird, he rub brandy on her lips, gums, and inner wrists, and she wake a little and say she must go into deep sleep now, to recover. She is cold and her pulse very slow, but I think she know what to do to make herself better."

The Frenchman moved over to the fireplace, leaned against the mantel, and lit his pipe. He drew on it and exhaled a thick, billowing cloud, through which he peered at Burton. "The night has been long, Sir Richard, but when the daylight come—" He glanced back at a clock by his shoulder. It was half-past five in the morning. "Then we must hunt again for the *nosferatu*."

Swinburne threw out his hands. "Where? Where? We've already searched high and low."

"The ravens," Burton said. His voice was flat and emotionless.

"Ah, *oui*!" Levi exclaimed. He addressed Swinburne and Monckton Milnes. "Sir Richard suggest they gather around John Judge to be near Perdurabo, who inhabit the body but is not secure within it. I think he is correct."

"The old castle, then?" Monckton Milnes said. He looked at Burton. "But you've been there twice."

Swinburne nodded. "We explored every part of it."

"And obviously missed something," Burton said.

Levi loosed another plume of smoke into the room. "So. At midday, when the Beast is the most weak, we go there."

"And if we find him, we shoot him?" Monckton Milnes asked.

"*Non.* To destroy a *nosferatu*, there are *méthodes spécifiques*, but I will not talk of them now, for they are not pleasant, and we must sleep for an hour or two, if we can, *non*? Best not to have the nightmares, I think."

"It strikes me that we're already caught up in one," Monckton Milnes responded. "But, yes, you're right. I'm all done in." He pushed himself to his feet and crossed to Burton, taking him by the elbow. "Come on, old man. I'll see you to your room. If you can't sleep, you can at least rest a while."

Mutely, Burton allowed himself to be guided out of the room, up the stairs, and into his bedchamber, where he sagged down onto the mattress and looked up at his friend. He whispered, "I have nothing now. Nothing."

"You have a purpose, Richard."

"A purpose?"

"Revenge."

With that, Monckton Milnes departed.

Burton lay back. He could hear Bram Stoker snoring next door. Something he'd once read—a sentence attributed to Elizabeth I—popped into his head. He spoke the words softly. "A clear and innocent conscience fears nothing."

The explorer put his hands over his eyes and clamped his teeth together.

As he battled to suppress his grief, a different emotion welled up and took him by surprise. He dragged his hands down over his face and bunched his fingers into fists over his mouth.

He was scared.

Uncle Renfric—having lost his parents to cholera, a brother to consumption, and three children to typhus—was no stranger to death. He took charge. Traditions were observed. Curtains were drawn and candles lit. Clocks were stopped and mirrors covered with black cloth. Flowers and crucifixes were distributed throughout the mansion.

Burton had slept fitfully for three hours. When he awoke, the day was gloomy and it was once again pouring with rain.

Bram, sensing that something was wrong, performed his duties efficiently and silently.

"There's been a death in the house," Burton explained. "I expect the servants will be glad of a helping hand today. They'll have to remove the decorations from the ballroom, for a start. Go and have something to eat, then do what you can to assist them."

"Right ye are, Cap'n."

The explorer joined his friends and the Birds and Beetons for breakfast. None of the Arundells was present at the table.

"We thought we might make a quiet withdrawal," Isabella Beeton told them, "but Mr. Arundell has insisted that we stay for the—the—"

"Funeral," her husband supplied. "Sunday. Today and tomorrow, the family will stand vigil. On Sunday morning, there'll be a Requiem Mass in the chapel. In the early afternoon, Isabel will be laid to rest in the family mausoleum."

"Where is that?" George Bird asked.

"It adjoins the chapel, Doctor."

"Catholic rituals baffle me," Swinburne said. "I fear I may accidentally do or say something that offends."

"Just stay out of the way," Monckton Milnes advised. "And it might be wise to avoid alcohol."

"My hat! Whatever are you suggesting?"

"I haven't known you for long, Algernon, but, if you'll forgive my impertinence, the hard stuff appears to accentuate your artistic sensibilities to such a degree that you become somewhat incomprehensible to the average man."

The poet raised his eyebrows but said nothing.

After they'd finished breakfast, Burton and his companions headed toward the library, there to plan their move against Perdurabo. In the hallway, Henry Arundell hailed the explorer, calling him over to meet two newcomers.

"Richard, may I introduce you to Father Quilty, our chaplain, and Mr. Jolly, the county coroner. Gentlemen, this is Sir Richard Burton, my daughter's intended." Arundell's voice was tremulous, his face ashen.

"My sincere sympathies, Sir Richard," the priest said. He was a rotund little man whose cheeks wobbled when he spoke. "Please be assured, the Lord is close to the broken-hearted and saves those who are crushed in spirit."

Burton heard the words as if from a great distance. He nodded distractedly and turned to the coroner.

"I apologise for my surname," Jolly said. He was an extremely tall and stooped man with a large hooked nose and a peculiar knob of hair on his chin. "It's entirely unsuited to my profession. I'll answer to Christopher, if you prefer."

"It's quite all right, Mr. Jolly," Burton said. "You've been informed there were two deaths here last night?"

"Yes, sir, I have."

"Will you look at this, please?" Burton produced the card that bore his authority and handed it over. The coroner took it, examined it, and handed it back, saying, "Am I to assume this is a police matter, then?"

"Yes. Doctor John Steinhaueser's neck was broken by an escaped fugitive."

"And Miss Isabel, sir?"

"I will leave you to assess the cause of her—of her—" Burton's mouth worked silently for a moment before he finished huskily, "of her demise."

"Then I shall examine her immediately."

Arundell waved Nettles over and instructed the butler to escort the two men first to Steinhaueser's room—to which Burton and his friends had taken the body last night—then to Isabel's. When they'd gone, he held Burton by the arm and accompanied him into the library, where Swinburne, Monckton Milnes, and Levi were waiting. He said, "I have no idea what bedevils this house, and the fact that none of you has properly explained leads me to conclude that you aren't in a position to do so—"

Burton made to speak but Arundell cut him short with a raised palm.

"No. Say nothing. I confess I have had my doubts about your character, Richard—and, to be frank, you are unlikely ever to win my wife's approval—but I don't for one moment believe you would allow my daughter's death to remain a mystery to me were you not under some obligation. I will therefore fall in with whatever explanation Mr. Jolly presents. However, I request—no, I demand—one thing of you."

"Sir?"

"If you plan to act against the fugitive—the man you say infected Isabel with a parasite, though I do not for one moment give credence to that statement—then I must be involved."

Eliphas Levi interrupted, "Monsieur, we intend to act this very morning, but what we must do, it is *très désagréable*, and it go badly against your faith. It is better that you do not see."

"I insist."

Burton said, "We believe the man is hiding out in the old castle. We plan to confront him at noon."

"Noon? Why noon? Why not now?"

"It must be at noon, or near enough. I cannot reveal why."

Henry Arundell stared searchingly at the explorer. His brows furrowed, then he shrugged. "No matter. I shall pry no further. But I will come to the castle with you."

"Very well."

"Shall I send for police assistance?"

"No, sir. The police should not witness our actions."

"Which will be?"

"An execution."

"Great heavens, man! You can't take the law into your own hands!"

"I have the king's authority to do so."

Henry Arundell took a deep breath and muttered, "This is an ungodly business."

"Yes," Burton replied. "That's exactly what it is."

An hour later, they moved to the smoking room where they were joined by Quilty, Jolly, and Uncle Renfric. The coroner reported that Isabel had died of heart failure. "The undertaker will visit later this morning to make arrangements," he said. "He's a good man. Miss Arundell will receive a first-class interment."

Renfric added, "Until then, she'll lie in our chapel. Henry, my boy, send those mechanical footmen of yours to my study. I'll have them compose the cancellation letters."

"Cancellation?" Arundell muttered. "Why, yes, of course. The party."

"What of John Steinhaueser?" Burton asked.

Jolly answered, "As you said, Sir Richard, he was murdered, his neck broken. Should I arrange for him to be reunited with his family?"

"He has none."

"Where, then, should he be laid to rest?"

"I don't think he had a preference, sir."

Quilty said, "May I suggest a small ceremony and burial at Saint John's in Tisbury? Perhaps—late on Sunday afternoon?"

Burial. Styggins, I'm sorry. I'm sorry.

"Very well. Thank you. Can I rely on you to organise it?"

"Of course."

Uncle Renfric gave a grunt of satisfaction and ushered the priest and coroner away.

Henry Arundell said, "It's a quarter-past ten."

Eliphas Levi interlaced his fingers and cracked his knuckles. "*Oui,* we must begin. First, we visit your groundsman."

"Tom Honesty? Why so?"

"*Pour faire des préparations,* monsieur. To make the preparations."

Forty minutes later, outside the groundsman's lodge, the five men stepped down from the Arundell's steam landau, each dressed in heavy boots and overcoats, each with an umbrella in hand. The rain was falling with violence. It needled against them, battering their brollies, hissing on the ground with such intensity they had to raise their voices to be heard.

Before they could knock on the lodge's door, a slim and pretty woman opened it.

"Mr. Arundell?" she said. "This is a surprise! Do you want to see Tom? Please, come in out of the rain. What dreadful weather!"

"Hello, Mrs. Honesty," Henry Arundell said. "I apologise that we've descended upon you in such numbers."

"Not at all, sir. Come in, all of you, come in."

The men closed their umbrellas, left them leaning against the door-jamb, and squeezed into the lodge's narrow, tastefully decorated entrance hall. As they did so, Tom Honesty emerged from a room at the far end, his shirtsleeves rolled impeccably up to his elbows.

"Good morning," he said.

"Not really," Swinburne muttered.

"Wet. Nasty day. Something the matter?"

"We require your assistance, Tom," Arundell said.

"Certainly. In what respect?"

Arundell looked at Eliphas Levi, who said, "You have dry logs, Monsieur Honesty? For the fire?"

"Yes, but I delivered a barrow-load to the house yesterday. You've not run out already?"

"*Non, non.* It is not for firewood. We need you to cut two stakes for us."

"Stakes?"

"*Oui.* About two feet long and three inches thick with one end pointed and sharp."

"May I ask——?"

"It is better if you do not. Also, we require—how are the words?—*un maillet lourd.*"

"A heavy mallet," Burton said.

"*Oui.* And an axe."

A puzzled expression crossed the groundsman's face. "Very well. Parlour. Fire. Dry yourselves. I shan't be long."

Honesty worked quickly and efficiently, completing his task in less than ten minutes. He rejoined them and handed the stakes and mallet to Levi, and the axe to Monckton Milnes.

"Tom," Arundell said, "have you been to the old castle recently?"

"Checked it after last week's storm. Not since."

"We suspect a dangerous fugitive is hiding out in it. Might he be in the priest hole? Is it still accessible?"

"Priest hole!" Swinburne exclaimed. "My hat! We saw no such thing when we searched the place."

"Many of the old Catholic homes and castles have a hidden priest hole, Mr. Swinburne," Arundell said. "It would defeat the point of them if they were easily detected."

"Where is it?" Burton asked.

"Beneath one of the vaults. There are two removable stone steps concealing the entrance, though for the life of me I can never remember which they are."

"I'll come with you. Show you," Honesty said.

Burton opened his mouth to say no but suddenly felt an unaccountable trust in the groundsman, and before he even realised it, nodded his agreement.

"To the castle, then," Arundell said.

They waited for Honesty to change into waterproofs then ventured back out into the downpour and into the landau. The groundsman climbed up to the driver's box and sat next to Burton.

The rain made conversation impossible, crashing down like an Indian monsoon, obscuring the path ahead and causing the vehicle to skid across the waterlogged gravel. Burton grappled with the tiller, which shuddered and jerked in his hands, and was thankful when Honesty reached across and took a hold of it, too, adding his own strength to the explorer's. Between them, they managed to navigate along the same path that Burton and Swinburne had twice traversed, passing over the bridge, alongside the woods, through Ark Farm, and up the mound to the ruins.

The men disembarked—each carrying a clockwork lantern—and squinted through the torrent at the grey, jagged walls, the tops of which were still black with ravens, all hunched together and motionless. Henry Arundell led them into the short entrance passage, where they stopped to shelter for a few minutes.

"Oof!" Levi exclaimed. "The reputation of your English weather is most deserve, I think!"

As if to underline his assertion, there came a sudden flash and a deafening detonation. The thunderclap echoed through the atmosphere and was immediately followed by another, sounding as if the air itself was being torn apart.

"*Le Diable*, he know what we intend," Levi muttered. "But we must do what we must do. Monsieur Honesty, you will lead us to the priest hole?"

"Yes, sir. This way."

He led them out into the hexagonal courtyard. They splashed across to an arched doorway and into the room beyond, a large square chamber with two small windows at its far end. A dark opening—a door made irregular by the collapse of its lintel—gave access to downward-leading steps. Swinburne wound his lantern and handed it to Honesty, who, holding it before him, descended.

Burton knew the castle's beetle-infested wine vaults lay below, and even though he'd already visited them, his horror of darkness and enclosed spaces caused him to hesitate at the top of the steps.

Lightning flickered and thunder shook the castle to its foundations.

"All right, old thing?" Monckton Milnes asked quietly.

The explorer gave a brusque nod. He moved forward, brushing spiderwebs out of the way.

At the bottom of the stairs, Levi said to the others, "Perdurabo, he feel our presence but he have no power over the body of John Judge in daytime. To us, the man will appear to be in deep sleep, but inside him, it is all strain and fighting. If we kill Perdurabo but not John Judge, Monsieur Judge will become *nosferatu*. If we kill Judge but not Perdurabo, our enemy will flee into another. So we must kill both at once. My directions, you must follow them exactly, or all is lost." The occultist turned to Henry Arundell. "It is best that you remain here. This thing we do, it offend the Catholic faith."

"But are you not yourself a Catholic, Mr. Levi?" Arundell objected.

"It is so, but this, it is like the exorcism. Rome is aware of the procedure, but it not like to acknowledge that it exist and sometime is necessary."

"The man killed my daughter, sir. I'll not be excluded."

"*Bien.* And you, Mr. Honesty—show us the steps, *s'il vous plait*, then return to the carriage and wait for us."

Honesty turned back the way they'd come and started up the stone stairs. After he'd climbed seven of them, he faced the group, squatted, and pointed at the last two steps he'd passed. "These. I'll need help to lift them."

Burton moved to assist. A gutter, about two inches wide and six deep, ran to either side of the stairs. Honesty slid his fingers into it and jerked his chin toward the opposite side. "If you feel, sir. Concealed handhold." Burton did as directed, curling his digits into a cavity he detected in the stone. The groundsman said, "One, two, three, lift." They pulled, Burton's arm gave a stab of pain, and the two steps came free. Thunder boomed outside.

The two men placed the heavy stone trapdoor on the lower steps and looked into the dark and narrow tunnel they'd exposed. Four feet wide and four high, it sloped downward into blackness. Burton felt himself trembling.

"Thank you, Mr. Honesty," he said huskily. "Leave us, please."

Honesty looked from one man to the other, shifted indecisively, then turned and departed.

Burton gritted his teeth, glanced back at his companions, then dropped to his knees, picked up his lantern, and, holding it out before him, crawled into the tight passageway. He immediately saw that it opened into a larger space about fifteen feet ahead. He shuffled forward, his heart thumping, and the others followed.

When he emerged and stood up, he found himself in a surprisingly large chamber with a vaulted ceiling. Its walls were chalked all over with sigils, their contorted shapes suggestive of forbidden knowledge and banished gods, and in an arched recess in the far wall, a big stone crucifix had been desecrated with an obscene diagram. At the foot of the cross, in the middle of a roughly drawn pentagram, John Judge lay stretched out on an altar. Burton walked over and looked down at the man. Shadows danced and slid across the figure as the others entered the room, their lanterns swinging. The light made the sigils appear to writhe restlessly.

"My hat!" Swinburne whispered.

"Blasphemy!" Arundell gasped.

"Won't our presence here wake him?" Monckton Milnes asked, gesturing at the prone figure.

Levi said, *"Non. Observez!"* And, leaning over Judge, slapped his face. Instinctively, the others took a hurried pace backward, but their caution was unwarranted; the big Irishman didn't respond to the stimulus at all.

"Now we begin," Levi said. He pulled a garlic bulb from his pocket, put it on the altar, and crushed it with the head of the mallet. Scraping up the juicy, piquant vegetable matter, he smeared it liberally around Judge's nostrils and lips.

"What are you doing?" Henry Arundell asked.

"I make him uncomfortable."

"Is that wise?"

"C'est nécessaire. See!"

Levi swung his lantern over Judge's face. The man's eyes had started to move agitatedly beneath the closed lids. He groaned and his fingers twitched.

"The *volonté* of John Judge is disturbed by the *odeur terrible*, by the bad stink. It struggle, and Perdurabo must battle to stay in control. See! It get very difficult!"

Judge's limbs were now shaking and jerking as if gripped by an epileptic fit.

"The two who inhabit this body," the Frenchman said, "they are now *entrelacé*—intertwined—and so die both at once when we do what we must do."

Burton drew a pistol from his waistband and aimed it at Judge's head. Levi reached out and grabbed his wrist. *"Non! Non*, Sir Richard! That is not the way!"

"Why not?" Burton growled. "A bullet in his damned brain will do for him, surely!"

"It is the *volonté* that must be first *immobilisé* and then destroyed. The *volonté* occupy not just the head but the whole body. The *méthode appropriée*, it is *spécifique*. There is much wisdom in tradition, even if we do not fully comprehend."

Burton slipped his gun into his pocket. "All right. Let's get on with it. Show me what to do."

"We do it together."

Levi took hold of John Judge's shirt and ripped it open, exposing the man's chest. He pulled one of the stakes from his jacket and held it with its point touching the sailor's skin, directly over the heart.

"Take the mallet," he said.

"You can't mean to—?" Henry Arundell blurted.

"Leave!" Levi snapped. "Go! Do not be witness to this!"

Arundell stayed put.

"Monsieur," Levi said to Burton. "One stroke. Very hard."

The explorer hefted the mallet. He looked from one man to the other, then swung the tool up and, putting every ounce of his weight behind it, swept it down.

In mid-swing, everything happened at once.

A deafening crash of thunder reverberated through the castle.

John Judge's head rolled sideways.

His eyes opened and flicked from total black to white with a blue iris. They looked past the men to the priest hole's entrance.

The mallet impacted against the stake, driving it straight through Judge's body.

A piercing scream rent the air, merging with the echoing thunderclap.

Judge bucked. He coughed a fountain of blood.

Burton and his companions, momentarily confused, suddenly realised the scream had come not from Judge, but from behind them. They swivelled around and saw Thomas Honesty standing at the mouth of the passage. His eyes were wide, his face filled with horror. He screamed again, turned, and plunged into the tunnel.

"*Imbécile!*" Levi cursed. "He too curious!"

John Judge gave a final twitch and went limp. Blood dribbled down the sides of the altar. Henry Arundell gazed at it, aghast.

The Frenchman extended his arm toward Monckton Milnes. "The axe. *Immédiatement!*"

Monckton Milnes blinked, as if coming out of a daze, and handed it over.

Without hesitation or explanation, Levi raised it and sliced it down onto Judge's neck. Three times he chopped, and on the third, the corpse's head came away and rolled to the floor, making a horrible knock as it impacted against the stone.

"Holy mother of Christ!" Arundell moaned. "God forgive us! God forgive us!"

"We eradicate the unholy, Monsieur Arundell," Levi said. "It is barbaric and horrible, but it is the Lord's work. Now we must take the remains upstairs and burn them."

Arundell and Monckton Milnes crossed to the upward-sloping passage and crawled out through it. Swinburne followed, carrying the severed head. Burton and the occultist, with great difficulty, then manoeuvred the corpse through the crawlspace.

After they'd replaced the removable steps and ascended to the square room, they put the dead man in the middle of its floor. Levi took the clockwork lanterns, broke each one open, and poured the oil from them onto the body. He struck a lucifer, threw it, and stepped back as the remains of John Judge ignited. "We not leave until it is nothing but ash," he said. "But we wait in another room, *non*? The air will be very bad in here."

The courtyard was half-flooded, the rain bucketing down, lighting and thunder still crashing overhead. They ran across to a doorway on its opposite side and into a high-ceilinged hall. It was dusty but dry, and they sank onto its floor and leaned against its walls and tried to process what they had just done.

Arundell buried his face in his hands. "Was I just party to murder?"

Levi answered, "*Non*, monsieur. It is difficult to understand, but John Judge was already dead. *En fait*, he was worse than dead. We have saved his immortal soul."

"I shall never make sense of this." Arundell looked pleadingly at Burton. "Please, Richard, I have come to regard you as family—tell me we have done the right thing."

"We have," Burton responded. "That creature—for he wasn't a man—took my fiancée from me. Deprived you of your daughter. Others would have died at his hands."

"*Non!*" Levi exclaimed. He banged his fist against the floor. "Not die! Not die! This is the *horreur vraie*—the true horror—of it. His victims do not properly die. They become un-dead—*strigoi morti*! They must each be disposed of as we have today disposed of Perdurabo—at very least, burned to nothing. If they are not, their terrible condition, it will spread like the plague. That is why I ask for two stakes."

It took some seconds for his meaning to register.

"God, no," Arundell moaned. "Surely you don't mean to say—you aren't suggesting—you can't—"

All of a sudden, Burton couldn't breathe. He grabbed his throat with one hand and clutched at the air with the other. "Bismillah!" he choked. "Please! Not that! Anything—*anything*—but that!"

Levi shook his head sadly. "*Je suis désolé*, but it must be done. We have set John Judge free. Now we must do the same for Mademoiselle Isabel."

CHAPTER 19

BY THE HAND OF THE MAN SHE LOVES

"Prophet!" said I, "thing of evil!—prophet still, if bird or devil!—
Whether Tempter sent, or whether tempest tossed thee here ashore,
Desolate yet all undaunted, on this desert land enchanted—
On this home by Horror haunted—tell me truly, I implore—
Is there—is there balm in Gilead?—tell me—tell me, I implore!"
Quoth the Raven, "Nevermore."
—EDGAR ALLAN POE, "THE RAVEN"

They found Thomas Honesty fussing frantically over the engine of the landau. "It won't start! It won't start!" he cried out. He recoiled away from them as they approached, brandished a pocketknife, and yelled, "Stay back! I saw what you did! Murderers!"

"Don't be a bloody fool!" Henry Arundell barked. "It's not what it seems, I can assure you. Move over! You've opened the inlet valve too wide—no wonder she won't start. Come on, out of the way! We're getting soaked to the skin!"

Honesty pressed himself against the side of the carriage, his eyes flitting anxiously from man to man as they climbed into the vehicle's cabin.

The engine coughed and grumbled.

Arundell exclaimed, "Got it!" and joined his companions, pulling the groundsman inside with him.

Swinburne and Monckton Milnes didn't enter, but climbed up to drive the vehicle, setting it into motion as soon as the passenger door had been pulled shut.

Eliphas Levi raised his voice over the rumbling of the rain on the wooden roof. "Monsieur Honesty, there is no danger. That man, he was the fugitive Monsieur Arundell told you of, and Sir Richard here is an agent of His Majesty the King. You witness a thing very terrible, but not murder. *Non!* Not murder!"

"What, then? You drove a stake through the man's heart!"

"*Oui*, it was necessary, but to explain, ah, that is a difficult thing."

"Not now," Arundell interrupted. "In the name of God, not now! I can't stand any more of it." He pulled a handkerchief from his pocket and wiped his face. "Tom, we are all traumatised. Rest this afternoon and come to the house before the church service tomorrow morning. We'll give you a full account."

Honesty looked searchingly at his employer's face then gave a reluctant nod.

The landau slid and rocked its way along the path, stopped at the lodge, where the groundsman got off, then continued on to the manor, and into the vehicle shed.

An hour later, the men, having washed and changed into dry clothing, met in the smoking room. They'd missed lunch but had no appetite for anything but fortifying brandies and comforting cigars and pipes.

Burton was withdrawn, his thought processes paralysed, an intolerable constriction gripping his heart, but in his room he'd swallowed half a bottle of Saltzmann's Tincture, and now, when he downed a brandy in a single gulp, its warmth permeated out from his stomach and didn't stop. He felt it course through his arteries, branch off into the veins, spread through the capillaries, and bleed into the surface of his skin, spreading and flattening and reconnecting him with the exterior world.

Like Time. Dividing, dividing, dividing, until all its many filaments become indistinguishable from one another, the consequences of decisions—made and unmade—taken to their ultimate limits then conflated, unconstrained by context, fully perceptible from every possible perspective.

The unity of multiplicity.

A new mode of being.

The empty glass slipped from his fingers and shattered on the floor.

He realised he was standing by the fireplace and the others were looking at him.

"Sorry," he muttered. "Clumsy."

Henry Arundell rang for one of his clockwork footmen and instructed it to clean up the fragments.

"You and me both, Richard," he said. "My hands won't stop shaking."

"A shock prolonged, it is very damaging," Levi said. "So we must proceed *intrépide*—undaunted—though it hurt us bad. We act fast and cure this disease before it spread far."

Swinburne said, "What should we do, monsieur?"

Levi addressed Arundell. "Your family, they are in the chapel, *oui*? Standing vigil over Mademoiselle Isabel?"

"Yes."

"Just before dark come, you must remove them."

"That won't be difficult. They'll need to eat and sleep." Arundell raised his hands to his head and dug his fingers into his hair. "But, Mother of God, no! I know the deviltry you intend, sir, and I'll not have my daughter's body so violated without absolute proof that she's become the thing you claim!"

Burton interjected, "Despite everything I've seen, I agree. You'll not lay a finger on her, Levi, not unless she—" He swayed and grabbed at the mantelpiece for support. "Not unless she rises before my eyes."

Levi considered the bowl of his pipe. "Then we must witness more *horreur*, *que Dieu nous protège!*" He addressed Arundell. "In my room, monsieur, there is a tall floor mirror. You have many such in the house?"

"One in every bedroom."

"*C'est fortuit.* Will you have them all put in the chapel? *C'est nécessaire.*"

"Very well."

Arundell's haunted eyes fixed upon the objects beside the occultist's chair: the second stake, the mallet, and the axe.

He poured himself another brandy.

At six o'clock, Arundell went to the chapel to relieve his family of their vigil, telling them he would sit through the night with his daughter.

His wife, Blanche, Smythe Piggott, the cousins Rudolph and Jack, and Uncle Renfric joined Burton, Swinburne, Monckton Milnes, and Levi in the dining room. The Birds and Beetons joined them, having spent much of the day since breakfast sitting with Sadhvi Raghavendra, helping to write letters, taking down the decorations, and arranging flowers all over the house.

The meal was a perfunctory affair. Halfway through it, Mrs. Arundell made tearful apologies and retired to her room, and afterwards the family members were quick to disperse, all exhausted by their grief.

Blanche hung back, clinging to Burton's arm. "Richard—that this should happen at such a time. I am so sorry."

"We've both suffered a dreadful loss," he replied. "I wish I could somehow comfort you, Blanche, but it's all I can do to keep myself standing. I don't know what words I can offer."

"I have my faith and my Bible. At times like this, religion proves its worth. I would be comforted if you would finally realise the value of it, too."

His eyes met hers and she flinched at the smouldering anger in them. He said, "I'm afraid, if anything, I'm being pushed rather in the opposite direction."

A tear rolled down Blanche's cheek. She took his hand, squeezed it, and left the room.

Burton turned to his companions. "Let's get this over and done with."

They waited for Levi to retrieve the tools then followed Burton out into the hallway and along a number of passages to All Saints Chapel, which was incorporated into the west wing of New Wardour Castle, being undetectable from the outside. Semicircular at both ends, almost a hundred feet long, forty wide, and forty high, it was remarkably sumptuous, painted white with gold fittings and decorated with many paintings and vestments.

Leading the group along the aisle between the pews, Burton approached the chancel. He saw Henry Arundell sitting beside an open coffin, which was on a catafalque in front of the altar. The explorer mounted two steps and looked down into the casket.

The chapel fell away, as if rapidly sinking into a dark chasm. He felt hands grabbing him beneath the arms; heard Monckton Milnes's distant cry of, "Richard!"

There was deep shadow, a confusion of memories and sensations. He smelled the spice-laden air of Zanzibar; listened to parakeets bizarrely cursing him in English; saw his reflection in the facets of a black gemstone; tasted blood.

Nurse! By God! Don't lose him!

Stand aside, sir. Move! At once!

Is it another attack? His heart?

Will you please get out of my way? How am I supposed to do my job with you breathing down my neck?

He opened his eyes, looked up at Swinburne, and said, "It's all right. Just a momentary dizziness. Not my heart."

"No one thought it was," the poet answered.

"I heard them say so."

"No. You must have imagined it. The shock hit you hard—you fainted."

Burton sat up and looked at Henry Arundell. "Why, sir? Why is she in her wedding dress?"

"It's what she would have wanted, Richard. In the eight years since she met you, she desired only to be your wife. She talked about it incessantly. We thought it appropriate that she be interred in the dress."

With help from Swinburne and Levi, Burton got to his feet and looked into the coffin again. Isabel lay motionless, white, with silver coins covering her eyes and her hands crossed over her chest. A rosary was wound about her fingers.

He said to Levi, "For pity's sake, monsieur, we can't do it. She's at peace."

"*Pardieu!* I wish it to be true!" the occultist replied. He pulled a hand mirror and clove of garlic from his pocket. "We test, *oui?*"

Reluctantly, Burton nodded.

"Wait!" Arundell snapped. "What are you doing?"

"Sir," Burton said, "please allow Monsieur Levi to proceed. There will be no defilement at his hands—you know I would not allow it."

Arundell frowned but conceded.

Levi broke the clove and placed it on Isabel's upper lip. He waited for two minutes, then removed the coins from her eyes, pulled up the left lid, and held the mirror before it.

Silence.

The men stood motionless, holding their breath.

Burton looked at Levi and opened his mouth to speak.

Isabel cried out. Her arms flew up, knocked the mirror away then flopped back down. She moaned and became still.

Henry Arundell let loose a despairing wail and fell backward against the side of the chancel. He slid to the floor, cradled his head in his arms, and wept.

Burton felt the heat drain from his body. "It happens to all corpses," he whispered. "The muscles contract. Air escapes. They spasm and emit noises. I've seen it many times."

Swinburne rounded on him and took a hold of his arms. "Richard, you know it's not the case. And you know what must be done. But you don't have to be here; you don't have to witness it. Go. I'll help Monsieur Levi."

"Help him what?" Arundell shouted. "Drive a stake into my daughter's heart? No! No! No!"

Levi held out his hands placatingly. "*Je comprends.* But if we delay, the *horreur* you feel now, it is nothing to what will come."

Arundell angrily wiped the tears from his cheeks. "You're leading me down the path to hell, sir."

"I seek only salvation for your daughter."

"I forbid you to touch her!"

Levi's shoulders slumped. "Then we have not the choice. We wait. You have the floor mirrors?"

Arundell pointed toward the pulpit. The mirrors were stacked against it.

"Messieurs," Levi said to Swinburne and Monckton Milnes, "will you assist? They must be put in a circle around the coffin, facing it." He asked Arundell, "You will allow this?"

The slightest of nods gave him permission and in short order the task was completed. The occultist then walked the length of the nave and turned the key in the chapel's entrance door.

There were crucifixes of various sizes mounted on stands around the chamber. As Levi returned to his companions, he selected five of them—each about a foot high—then distributed them among the men, keeping one for himself.

"*Si vous avez raison,*" he said to Burton and Arundell, "if you are correct, I am very happy. But—*je regrette*—you will soon see the wickedness of the *nosferatu*. Close to midnight, Isabel will rise. These crucifixes will remind her of her faith. She see herself in the mirrors. She recognise that she is *strigoi morti*. This, I hope, is sufficient to overcome her hunger. She seek the oblivion of the grave. We help her achieve it."

"O compassionate God," Arundell whispered, "I plead with thee, send your Holy Spirit to soothe my suffering!"

No more was said.

The men waited.

An hour passed.

At ten minutes to twelve, Isabel groaned.

Arundell cried out. In a jabbering voice, he yelled, "*Gloria Patri et Filio et Spiritui Sancto!*"

His daughter shrieked and sat up. Her hands flew to her face, the palms facing outward, the fingers clawed.

"Most blessed glorious Eternal Holy Trinity adorable unity in the Glory of Your majesty in the splendour of Your power!" Arundell babbled.

Isabel's eyes opened. She hissed like an angry cat. The men—except Arundell—raised their crucifixes. Her father screeched, "Exalted unto the ages of ages! *Kyrie eleison! Kyrie eleison! Kyrie eleison!*"

As if it cost her no effort at all, Isabel climbed out of the coffin, her white dress flowing around her. She looked at each of the men in turn, her pupils pinpricks, her lips drawn so far back that her teeth appeared almost fang-like.

On his knees, Arundell jabbered, *"Kyrie eleison Jesu soter unice eleison! Kyrie eleison Jesu soter unice eleison! Kyrie eleison Jesu soter unice eleison!"*

Isabel darted toward Burton but jerked to a stop when he brandished his cross in her face. Her hair came loose and fell wildly about her. She whimpered. "Dick, please! Love me! Love me!"

Hearing her speak, Arundell screamed, "She's alive! She's alive!"

"No!" Levi shouted. "She is un-dead! *Strigoi morti!* Do not let her touch you!"

"Isabel!" Arundell pleaded. "Daughter!"

She turned on him with a throaty growl, and seeing the dead sheen across her eyes and the savage hunger in her face, he moaned and fell backward, clutching the crucifix to his chest. *"Kyrie eleison! Kyrie eleison! Kyrie eleison!* Holy Holy Holy Lord God Pantocrator who is and was and is to come!"

"Isabel, *regardez-moi!*" Levi barked. *"Regardez-moi! Dieu le commande!"*

She spun, cringing away from the crucifixes, and snarled, "Give me my life!"

"Il est allé," Levi said. "It is gone. *Regardez!*" He reached to the mirror beside him and adjusted it to face her.

Isabel stared at her reflection. She lifted her hands and looked with an air of puzzlement at the rosary that was entangled in her fingers. She touched the cross that dangled on a silver chain around her neck.

"What has happened to me?" she croaked. "Why am I—why am I—?"

She looked at Burton and saw the dread in his eyes.

"No!" she pleaded. "No, no, no, no!"

Henry Arundell toppled sideways to the floor, unconscious.

Levi stepped forward. "Back!" he commanded. "The Lord God Almighty awaits you. You must be sanctified and delivered unto Him!"

She retreated, confused, panicked, emitting an animalistic keening, and bumped against the table. Her eyes fixed on Burton. "Help me!"

The explorer stumbled into the side of the chancel. He dropped his crucifix and gasped for air.

"Paix éternelle, Isabel," Levi said. "Eternal peace shall be yours."

With her eyes fastened immovably on Burton, Isabel hoisted herself onto the table and clambered into the coffin. She sat gazing at him for a few seconds then lay back.

Levi approached the casket. He leaned over it and held the crucifix before her face. In a low, crooning voice, he recited:

Go forth, Christian soul, from this world
in the name of God the almighty Father,
who created you,
in the name of Jesus Christ, the Son of the living God,
who suffered for you,
in the name of the Holy Spirit,
who was poured out upon you.
Go forth, faithful Christian!
May you die in peace this day,
may your home be with God in Zion,
with Mary, the virgin Mother of God,
with Joseph, and all the angels and saints.
May you return to your Creator
who formed you from the dust of the earth.
May holy Mary, the angels, and all the saints
come to meet you as you go forth from this life.
May you see your Redeemer face to face.

She closed her eyes and became still.

"Sir Richard," Levi said quietly. "Come here."

Algernon Swinburne looked at Burton, who was immobilised, then stepped over to him, slipped an arm around his waist, and pushed him forward, guiding him to the side of the coffin.

"Feel for the pulse," Levi ordered.

Burton did so, moving like one of Arundell's clockwork footmen.

"You detect it?" Levi asked.

"No," the explorer responded hoarsely. "There is none, and her skin is cold."

"As in death?"

"Yes."

Levi addressed Monckton Milnes. "The tools, monsieur, they are by the lectern. Fetch them, *s'il vous plaît.*" He turned to Burton. "It is very terrible, what we must do, Sir Richard. *Pardieu!* To have to ask it of a man! But, you comprehend, *non*? You understand how she must be released?"

The explorer nodded wordlessly.

Monckton Milnes passed the stake to Levi, who positioned it over Isabel's heart. With his other hand, the occultist took the mallet and held it out to Burton. "It is best by the hand of someone she loves."

Like a mirage seen in the Arabian Desert, everything around Burton was visible but a long way off, indefinite and impossible to grasp. He observed but was utterly detached; was conscious but empty of thought. He knew Swinburne was prising the axe from his fingers; heard Levi say that burning would not be necessary; watched him sprinkle holy water onto Isabel's remains then close the coffin and seal it; stood frozen while the others took the floor mirrors and stacked them against a wall.

Flowers were placed on the casket. All signs that anything untoward had occurred were removed. Henry Arundell was revived and reassured that his daughter was now with God. He knelt and prayed and prayed and prayed. The men waited for him to finish. By the time he did, he appeared to have achieved some degree of inner peace and said, "I will stand vigil over my daughter for the rest of the night. It is my duty."

Monckton Milnes and Swinburne took hold of Burton and guided him out of the chapel. They trailed after Levi, back into the main house where, at the foot of the spiral staircase, they found Clunk, the footman, lying spreadeagled on the ground. His canister-shaped head had been twisted off and was ten feet away, under a small decorative table.

"What the blazes?" Swinburne uttered.

"There are spots of blood on the floor," Monckton Milnes observed.

Burton pulled himself from their grasp. His senses clicked back into focus. He said, "I hear someone in the sitting room."

Leading the others, he strode across the vestibule and entered the chamber where he found, on chairs and sofas around the fireplace and wrapped in dressing gowns, Blanche, Smythe Piggott, Lallah Bird, Samuel and Isabella Beeton, and Bram Stoker. Sam Beeton was holding a bloodied handkerchief to his nose. His right eye was blackened and swollen shut. Smythe Piggott, obviously in considerable pain, was cradling his left wrist.

"It was the gardener, Cap'n!" Bram Stoker blurted the moment he saw Burton.

"Tom Honesty? What was? What has happened?"

"He attacked us," Sam Beeton said, his voice muffled by the cloth. "The man might be small but he's dashed strong!"

"What? Wait! Start from the beginning."

"He woke the boy up." Beeton nodded toward Bram.

"Aye, sir! Shook me awake, so he did, and he looked like the devil himself. He said, 'Congratulate your master. Tell him it was an admirable attempt and we shall meet again.' Then he left the room, an' I was so afeared, I ran an' knocked on the bedroom doors until I woke Mr. Beeton."

Beeton resumed the account. "The lad was hardly making sense, but I gathered there was an intruder of some sort, so roused Doctor Bird and Smythe Piggott. We caught Honesty descending the stairs with Sister Raghavendra over his shoulder. We tackled him but he fought like a madman. Knocked us about like a damned prizefighter. I called for one of the footmen to stop him—"

"We saw what happened to it," Burton interjected. "Are you telling me he's made off with Sadhvi?"

"Yes. We couldn't stop him."

"Cap'n," Bram put in. "His eyes, they were black as tar."

Burton swung round to Eliphas Levi, who cursed, "*Quel désastre!* The *nosferatu*, it must transfer to this man in the instant before John Judge die. It *dormant* in the groundsman until night come. We fail! *Merde! Merde!* We fail!"

The explorer snapped at Beeton, "When?"

"Ten, maybe fifteen minutes ago. Bird, the cousins, and some of the staff are out looking for him, but it's still pouring with rain, so—" His words trailed off. He pulled the handkerchief away from his face but immediately reapplied it as blood dribbled from his nose.

Burton ran from the room. He crossed to the front door, yanked it open, and stepped out. The rain pounded against him. He could hardly see a thing.

"Doctor Bird!" he bellowed. "Doctor Bird!"

A voice sounded to his left. "Here!"

Burton set off toward it but had taken only a few steps before the doctor emerged into view and shouted, "He made off in Steinhaueser's steam sphere. I thought to follow in one of the other vehicles but they'll never keep pace with it. Besides, in this bloody weather, he'd evade us in an instant. Hell! We've lost Sister Raghavendra, Sir Richard. But why in heaven's name has he taken her? What's come over the man?"

Burton swiped a fist through the air and yelled his frustration.

Great-Uncle Gerard, the owner of New Wardour Castle, returned in time for a weekend of funerals, grief, and rain. Burton was introduced to him but hardly realised it. His thoughts had folded in on themselves. Events were enacted around him but failed to register.

Swinburne was the first to penetrate this state of fugue. "I don't think she'll be welcomed by the family," he said, "but I have it in mind to send for one of the girls from Verbena Lodge."

Burton blinked and mumbled, "What are you talking about?"

"A dolly-mop. The vigorous application of a switch to your rear end, Richard. If you must be whipped into action, I'm just the man to arrange it."

The explorer sighed and massaged his forehead with the heel of his hand.

"You can't afford another day of mourning," Swinburne went on relentlessly. "It may be considered a little premature, but it's time to leave. This Catholic desolation is not for you. It's stultifying. Closed curtains and bloody flowers stinking up the house. Black crepe everywhere. You need to get back to London. Whatever madness you're caught up in, it has no regard for etiquette, and every minute you spend here is another minute of peril for Sister Raghavendra. Have you given up on her?"

Burton's eyes finally slid into focus. "Of course not, but how—where—?"

Swinburne threw out his hands, stamped his foot, and screeched, "Almack's! Almack's! Have you forgotten? That American fellow is speaking there tomorrow night! We must go!"

"Tomorrow? Today is the seventh?" Blank despair suddenly gave way to grim determination, and Burton examined the knuckles of his right fist, as if assessing their potency for destruction. "Will you find Bram, Algy? Tell him to pack our bags. I must say my goodbyes."

Midway through the morning, the guests departed. The Arundells had presented Burton with a new pocket watch. A lock of Isabel's hair—cut while she was dressed for the vigil—had been inset inside its lid. He accepted it with gratitude and such an acute tightening of the chest that tears blurred his eyes.

Burton, Swinburne, Levi, Bram, and Monckton Milnes travelled together by steam landau to Salisbury, where Monckton Milnes parted from them, bound for Fryston.

After bidding him farewell, the rest booked passage on the atmospheric railway.

Sitting in the carriage, Burton peered out at the massive bellows, which were slowly inflating. In a few moments, they'd constrict, sending the train rocketing forward to the next pumping station.

As had occurred frequently these past few days, he suddenly sensed that something had eluded him. This time, after a moment's thought, it slotted into place.

"The bloody poem," he murmured.

"Poem?" Swinburne asked.

"Abdu El Yezdi's. I still haven't fathomed it."

"Battersea Power Station."

Burton started. "What?"

"I thought you must have it. After all, it's as plain as the nose on your face."

The poet recited:

> *Whene'er you doubt thy station in life*
> *Thou shalt take to the tempestuous sea.*
> *To all the four points it shall batter thee*
> *Until you find thine own power, and me.*

He concluded, "Station, sea, batter, power, and four points. Bleedin' obvious!"

Burton muttered, "It is, and I feel an absolute dolt."

A warning bell jangled and the guardsman's voice sounded through a speaking tube. "Brace for departure, please. Brace for departure."

The passengers sat back in the forward-facing seats and waited for the countdown bell's three clangs. They came. Outside, the bellows squeezed shut. The train shot forward as if fired out of a cannon. Bram Stoker hollered his delight.

London, Burton thought. *And vengeance.*

THE BEAST

"Character is destiny."
—HERACLITUS, *FRAGMENTS*

CHAPTER 20

THE TWELFTH MESSENGER OF GOD

NOTICE
PREVENTIVES OF CHOLERA!
Published by order of the Sanitary Committee,
under the sanction of the Medical Council.
BE TEMPERATE IN EATING & DRINKING!
Avoid Raw Vegetables and Unripe Fruit!
Abstain from COLD WATER,
and above all from ARDENT SPIRITS.
If habit has rendered them indispensable,
take much less than usual.

T hey were back in the capital by mid-afternoon.

"I need to meditate," Burton said. "I have to repair the damage done to me. I cannot function like this—my heart is ruling my head. We're all exhausted, too. I suggest we reconvene tomorrow. Let us face the enemy refreshed."

"Smashing!" Swinburne exclaimed. "I shall have Betsy thwack some sense into me, else this sensation that I'm stuck in the pages of one of Bram's lurid penny dreadfuls is liable to continue." He crossed and uncrossed his arms. "My apologies, Richard. That was insensitive of me. This is all rather too real."

"It is, Algy. Go to your dolly-mop if you must, but don't overindulge. We have much to do tomorrow."

The poet left them while Burton and Levi continued on to Montagu Place. There, the occultist immersed himself once again in the library. Burton sent a summons to Detective Inspector Trounce via the Whispering Web then went up to his bedroom and gulped down an entire bottle of Saltzmann's Tincture. The cure-all coursed through his veins and turned him into the vacuum at the heart of a swirling storm of light; caused his anguish to flare into countless possibilities; made his isolation branch into infinite multiplicities; but it did not bring back Isabel.

He slumped in his armchair—barely aware of the occultist, who was reading at one of the desks—and for two hours stared at one of the windows, perceiving it to be stacked upon itself, like a pack of cards, as if present over and over.

Shuffle them, select one, and look out at a slightly different world.

He heard a carriage draw up outside.

Watch it. See its door open. Isabel steps out and pays the driver. She crosses to number 14 and yanks the bellpull.

She didn't ring. She knocked, a strident hammering. It broke the spell.

The explorer let out a small cry, as if wounded.

"Monsieur?" Levi said.

"Dreaming," Burton muttered. He rubbed his eyes, stood, and went out onto the landing.

The front door was open and Mrs. Angell was arguing with Trounce.

"You could be King George him-bloomin'-self, but you'll not set foot in this 'ere house until you scrapes yer blessed boots."

"My dear woman, I've practically scraped 'em thin! I have no desire to arrest you, but if you don't stand aside, so help me, I'll—"

"It's all right, Mrs. Angell," Burton called. "Let him in, please."

"With all that muck around his soles?" she protested.

"Leave your boots in the hallway, old man," Burton advised. "You can warm your feet by my fire."

Reluctantly, Trounce did as instructed and started up the stairs.

Mrs. Angell glowered at his feet and muttered, "An' them stockings ain't none-the-cleaner neither!"

The police detective hurried into the study, greeted Levi, and gave a gasp of relief when Burton closed the door behind him.

"By Jove! I feel like I'm committing a felony every time I set foot on your carpets. Have you seen the streets? The sewers are so backed up the filth is overflowing into 'em! What am I supposed to do, walk on stilts?"

"You'll just have to be patient, like everyone else," Burton responded. "Wasn't Bazalgette supposed to have opened the sluice gates by now?"

"He was, but the riots have slowed him down. The tunneling has been halted beneath the Alton Ale warehouse in the Cauldron. Do you mind if I smoke?"

"Not at all. The rioting is really that serious?"

"The whole district has gone barking mad."

Trounce sat down, took a cigar from his pocket, and toyed with it irresolutely, turning it in his fingers and passing it from hand to hand. "I heard about—about—I'm not much good at—at—well, I'm sorry that—about what happened to—um—Miss Arundell. Are you—are you all right?"

"I've not properly dealt with it yet. Let me get you a brandy. I'll tell you the whole story."

Over the next half-hour, Burton and Levi gave an account of the events at New Wardour Castle.

The explorer's mind played tricks. With every incident he reported, the Saltzmann's caused him to sense all the alternatives that might have occurred, as if each event had produced echoes, every one a slight variation of the original.

Having listened in silence, Trounce said, "This is so far beyond my ken it might as well be a fairy tale. I have no idea how to proceed."

"By keeping your ears open for any reports of the dead coming back to life," Burton said. "Perdurabo will continue to feed, and so will his victims. These *strigoi morti*—as Monsieur Levi refers to them—are going to proliferate, and rapidly. They can't go unnoticed for long."

"They hunt at night," Eliphas Levi commented.

Trounce grunted. "Humph! Very well. May we return to sane matters?"

Burton gestured for him to continue.

"There have been no further abductions reported," the police detective said, "but something else has come to light. I remembered you saying Eugenics was at the heart of all this, and that it requires medical knowledge and machinery. Four days ago, equipment and supplies were stolen from the chemical laboratories at the University College on Upper Gower Street. It prompted me to go through the records. It turns out there have been a spate of such burglaries all around the city over the past two months. It looks to me as if someone has been gathering the means to create their own laboratory, and an extravagant one, at that."

Burton said, "Ah! I wonder where."

"I've put out a general order for our constables to keep their eyes peeled, but our resources are stretched thin at the moment. We've had to divert a lot of men to the East End."

"What's happening there? It's political agitation, I heard."

"It is, and it's worsening every day. We've managed to keep it out of the rags so far—fortunately newspapermen are too cowardly to set foot in the Cauldron—but Chief Commissioner Mayne is concerned that when the story breaks, as it inevitably will, it might stir up trouble in other parts of the country. Look at these."

Trounce reached into his jacket and pulled out a number of leaflets, handing them to Burton. They were each printed on one side only; black ink on cheap paper.

"Apparently, they're all over the area," the Scotland Yard man said. "Pasted to lampposts, doors, window shutters—thousands of them."

Burton examined the first, struggling to bring his eyes into focus.

The Germanic States Must Be Destroyed!
Oppose the Confederation! Oppose the Alliance!
Save British Jobs!
Save British Pride!
Save the British Empire!

He turned to the next.

German Trickery!
Do not believe the lies you have been told.
Prince Albert is German.
He is working for German interests not for British.
The Central German Confederation wants our trade.
It is greedy for our territory and for our influence.
Resist those who promote this foreign power and undermine our own.
Fight for Britain! Fight the enemy among us!

Burton made a small exclamation and held one of the leaflets up to the light. He snapped his fingers, went to a desk, returned, and handed a pamphlet to Trounce. "You remember this?"

"'The Language of the Angels.' Yes, of course, it's from the League of Enochians Gentlemen's Club."

"Look at the paper, Trounce. It's the same brand, and printed with the same ink."

"By Jove! Are the Enochians spreading this sedition? Then we've got them. We have cause to raid their headquarters."

"We do, but hold off. Such tactics will get us nowhere. Is Thomas Lake Harris still at the Regency?"

"Yes. I have Spearing keeping a round-the-clock watch on him."

"I intend to approach him tomorrow night—see if he'll take me into the club as a guest. I daresay I can find out more from posing as a friend than if we storm the place swinging truncheons at them."

"Messieurs," Levi said, "this hate of the Germanic countries, it link again the Enochians to Perdurabo."

"The—what did you call him?—*Nefertiti?*" Trounce asked.

"*Nosferatu.*"

"How so?"

"You recall Captain Taylor of the *Royal Charter*—he report voices in the crater where Perdurabo take possession of John Judge. They suggest a battle against German forces, *non?* Too, Countess Sabina, she claim that Abdu El Yezdi try to prevent a war."

"With a united Germany, you mean?" Burton asked.

"Oui. It explain why all this business occur at this moment in time, with the Alliance, you see?"

Burton nodded. "I think you're right. I'd venture that, while Abdu El Yezdi has manipulated the government to broker peace and avoid a conflict, Perdurabo is using the Enochians to provoke the war early, before Germany has the manufacturing power it would gain from the Alliance."

"*Exactement!*"

Trounce scratched his head. "Provoke it by stirring up the Cauldron? That's a stretch. The place is a hive of criminals and paupers—what influence do they have?"

"They have the weight of numbers," Burton responded. "Plus a lack of education and a grudge against the better-off. Mobilise that, and you have an army eager to fight, whatever the cause. Besides, I suspect this—" he waved one of the leaflets, "—is just the beginning."

"I know you can't sit still at the best of times," Burton whispered to Algernon Swinburne, "but this is beyond the bounds. Will you please control yourself? You're attracting attention."

"I can't help it. Betsy has a very strong right arm. You should've come with me to Verbena Lodge, Richard. The madams are the strictest in London."

"I've spent the day in peaceful meditation, Algy. I find it preferable to having my arse striped."

Behind them, a portly woman leaned forward and hissed, "Shhh!"

Swinburne rolled his eyes at Burton, as if to say, *Good grief, somebody actually wants to listen to this balderdash!*

The balderdash in question was spouting from the mouth of Mr. Thomas Lake Harris, who was standing on a podium in Almack's Assembly Rooms addressing a crowd of about three hundred, Burton and Swinburne among them.

He was a tall man, with low black eyebrows, a long black beard, and a sallow countenance. His eyes blazed intensely as he declaimed, "At this moment, drew near a Spirit who represented a Mercury or messenger, though indeed as to form he was beautiful as fabled Endymion. He appeared in the flower of his youth, and moved as if borne on the breath of the swift electric atmosphere. I heard a sound as of melodious voices, and in a moment beheld a multitude gathered together, assembled by proclamation; the character of which was, that news from Earth was permitted to be uttered through a man who, as to his body, was a resident of the natural world, but who, as to his spirit, was elevated into their society. These spirits all appeared to be in the acknowledgement of one Lord God. The beginning of all things they acknowledged to be not in Nature, but in the Divine Ability of One Eternal Spirit."

"Hogwash, phooey, and bunkum," Swinburne muttered, imitating Harris's American accent. "How much more of this has my sore bum to endure?"

"You've no one to blame but yourself," Burton noted.

Swinburne giggled. "Swish! Thwack! Swish! Thwack! Utterly delicious!"

The woman behind him leaned forward again and said, "Sir, if you persist in talking through Mr. Harris's presentation, I shall have little choice but to apply my umbrella to the top of your head."

"Madam," Swinburne responded, "I should prefer the other end, and a weapon with a little more bite."

"Well!" the woman exclaimed indignantly. "I never did!"

"No matter, for Betsy already has!"

Burton pushed his companion to his feet. "Come on, Algy. I think we've heard enough from Mr. Harris for now."

"I'd heard enough five minutes after he started," Swinburne complained as they edged through onlookers to the side of the auditorium. They moved along the wall until they came to a door, passed through it into a side hall, and followed it to the double doors that opened into the club bar.

A couple of minutes later, they settled at a table, each with a pint of beer.

Burton took a long draught. The previous day's dose of Saltzmann's had worn off, leaving him thirsty.

"I've arranged with the manager for us to meet Mr. Harris when he finishes," he said. "We'll wait here. I find a glass of beer much easier to swallow than all that hokum about angels."

"Not half," Swinburne enthused.

"I hope he'll be our key to unlock the Enochians' door, but as soon as we've had a poke around enemy territory, we'll then do the same at Battersea Power Station, as a matter of urgency. I trust you're set for a long night."

They'd consumed two pints each by the time the audience filed out of the assembly room. The bar began to fill up with club members and was soon noisy and wreathed in tobacco smoke.

Almack's manager entered with Harris, spotted Burton, and ushered the American over. He introduced them, then made a polite withdrawal, his presence being required elsewhere.

"Well now," Harris said, in a nasal New York accent, "the Nile, hey? That's quite something, Burton; yes, sir, it sure is! I gotta tell you, I'm a big admirer of yours. I've read your books, an' you don't beat about the bush like the rest of the English. I like a straight-talkin' man. You're a fella after my own heart."

"Thank you, Mr. Harris. Would you join us for a beverage?"

"Sure, I'd be happy to. Whisky. A large one. All that speechifyin' has left me dry."

Burton called a pot-boy over and ordered the whisky and two more beers.

"I'll take a beer as well," Harris put in.

"And I'll have a whisky, too," Swinburne added.

"Say, Swinburne, what business are you in?"

"I'm a poet, sir."

"Is that so? I do a little in that line myself. Whaddya think of this?" Harris spread his arms wide and recited, in too loud a voice:

> To God be praise! This happy work is done:
> It spreads towards man the Solar Angel's pinions.
> My mind conceived this poem of the sun
> Long years ago, when all the world's dominions
> In clouds of fantasy were veiled; while death
> Held empire in man's universal breath.

Swinburne glanced at Burton. "That's—um—very interesting, Mr. Harris. Am I then mistaken in my assumption that limericks are the principle form of verse in America?"

"Limericks, sir?"

"Quite so. *A spiritual man from Rhode Island, had an uncanny knack to beguile and, seduce lovely women, and leave their heads swimmin', but he—*"

"Mr. Harris," Burton interrupted hastily, "I'm intrigued by your thesis concerning the nature of angels. Have you been contacted directly?"

"Yup. I'm blessed with vivid dreams, Burton. Blessed is the word. The Lily Queen has revealed much of the true nature of existence to me."

"Ah, yes, the Lily Queen. She is your wife, if I'm not mistaken?"

"My spirit wife, sir. She exists in Lilistan, the interspace inhabited by the angel folk, and has so far borne me two celestial children."

Harris had turned to face Burton. Behind his back, Swinburne waggled a forefinger against his temple, stuck his tongue out, and crossed his eyes. Burton tried to ignore him, a task made easier by the arrival of fresh drinks.

"Good health, sir," Burton toasted.

"Yours, too," Harris responded. He downed the whisky in one, picked up his pint, and half-emptied it in a single swig. "You see, Burton, we ain't alone in the universe. All the planets that circle our sun are inhabited by spiritual beings, and there are Lunarians on the far side of our moon who remember Oriana, the world where evil originated, an' which the moon once orbited."

"I see," Burton said.

"This was revealed to you during dreams?" Swinburne asked. "Do you perhaps take anything to help you sleep?"

"It was, an' I don't. The thing of it is, if a man could attune himself to the rhythmic chord that leads the harmonic vibrations between these worlds, why, he could live forever. Immortality, Burton! How does that sound, hey?"

"Quite difficult to grasp."

"Incomprehensible," Swinburne agreed. "My hat! You appear to have finished your beer already, Mr. Harris. As have I. Shall we order another?"

"Sure, but what say you we get out of this place?" Harris said. "Never mix work with pleasure, that's my motto. This place is work. Meetin' you gents is a pleasure."

"The Red Lion on Derby Street isn't far from here," Burton said. "Shall we?"

This was agreed, and the trio settled up at the bar, retrieved their hats, coats, and canes from the cloakroom, and exited into King Street.

The day had been cold and damp, with rain-heavy clouds filling the sky. Now the atmosphere was saturated with water—too thin to be classified as rain, too thick to qualify as mist. Street lamps flared, particles of their orange light seemingly borne aloft by the droplets and sent swirling around the three men as they passed along St. James's Street and turned left into Pall Mall.

"I should very much enjoy hearing you speak again," Burton said to Harris as they entered Whitehall. "I understand you'll be addressing the League of Enochians Gentlemen's Club tomorrow. Do you think I might attend?"

"Phew!" the American exclaimed. "If it was up to me, for sure, but the Enochians are an exclusive set, Burton, an' as their guest, I ain't got the right to invite another."

"I understand." Burton waited until a loudly clanking steam-horse had passed by, then went on, "May I ask how you were approached by them?"

"By the Enochians? I got a letter last May from a fella named Laurence Oliphant. An insightful guy—he'd seen the importance of my philosophy and wrote that he recognised me as the twelfth messenger of God."

"Received in America in May," Swinburne muttered. "So probably posted in March or thereabouts."

"The Enochians' president, Doctor Kenealy, then arranged for me to come here."

They arrived at the Red Lion, found a corner table, and ordered more drinks.

For the next three hours, Burton plied Harris with alcohol and gave every indication that he was fast becoming an ardent admirer of the spiritualist, artfully hiding his true opinion that the man was a conceited—and only partially sane—nincompoop.

It was near midnight before Harris succumbed to the considerable amount he'd imbibed. Burton picked his moment, then asked, "What are the arrangements for tomorrow? Perhaps I could have dinner with you before you go to the Enochians' Club?"

"'Fraid not. I have to meet a fella named Count Sobieski outside Saint Martin's Church at eight o'clock. Gotta work on my presentation beforehand. Perhaps another night, though?"

"Very well," Burton said, silently vowing to be at the church, too, unseen, ready to follow Harris to what he suspected was a secret entrance to the club.

He nudged Swinburne. "Are you still with us, Algy?"

"Yesh," the poet slurred. "But I shushpect I might have had one too mummy—money—many."

"We should get you home. You, too, Mr. Harris. It sounds as if you have a busy day ahead of you."

They stood and fumbled with their coat buttons; picked up, dropped, and retrieved their hats; tripped over their canes; and stumbled out into the night.

As they emerged into Whitehall, Harris pointed at St. Stephen's Tower and exclaimed, "Would ya look at that! The clouds are so low you can barely see the clock. Say, though, what's the story? Ain't that the famous Big Ben? I've not heard a chime all night."

"The bell's cracked," Burton explained. "They made the hammer too big. I believe they're currently adjusting the mechanism to strike the hour on the quarter bells while the main one's repaired. It's the second—" He cried out and whipped his hands up to his eyes, half-blinded by the flash that suddenly burst from the top of the tower. A thunderous detonation smacked against his ears. Peering past his fingers, he saw a ball of flame pushing bricks and masonry away from the edifice. Without thinking, he knocked his companions back into the shelter of Derby Street. Debris started to rain down around them; bricks and concrete thudding and shattering on the roads and smashing through windows; metal and glass clanging and clattering; pieces of flaming wood falling like comets. The noise pummelled them, jumbling their senses, then thick, black dust came at them like an avalanche, enveloping and blinding, filling their mouths and nostrils.

Half a brick ricocheted off the side of Harris's head. The American slumped into Swinburne's arms, his weight carrying the poet to the ground.

Burton crouched over them, trying to shield them with his body. Small fragments of stone thudded into his back and bounced all around. He pressed his palms to his ears but the cacophonous sound of destruction penetrated his skull, so harsh that he bellowed with the pain of it.

Finally, silence fell, only gradually giving way to individual sounds: screams; cries of alarm; shouts; police whistles; the rattle of small stones still raining down.

The explorer uncurled and stood, powder cascading off him. He coughed and spat.

"Are you hurt, Algy?"

"No, but you could pull this great lump off me."

Burton lifted Harris from the poet and laid him on his back.

"Is he dead?" Swinburne asked.

"No. Knocked cold."

"He'll be disappointed. The Lily Queen might have been expecting him."

"The angels will have to wait. Brush yourself down and help me carry him. We'll take him to the Regency."

They hoisted the American to his feet and got beneath his arms to support him. He was so limp he might as well have been boneless, and the difference in height between Burton and Swinburne, along with the poet's inability to walk in a straight line, made the operation extremely awkward. However, they managed to drag him out onto Whitehall, where they stumbled to a halt and gazed in horror at the scene.

The top half of St. Stephen's Tower had gone and what remained was a shattered and burning stump. Even from this distance, they could feel the heat of the flames. Black smoke and dust were billowing through the streets and debris was strewn everywhere. Fortunately, the lateness of the hour meant there were fewer people about than usual, but nevertheless many individuals could be seen staggering aimlessly, their faces slack with shock.

Burton and Swinburne half-carried, half-dragged Harris northward past the government buildings, then turned right into Whitehall Place in order to rest on the steps of the Royal Geographical Society. They watched policemen and detectives pouring out of Scotland Yard.

"Excuse me, sir. Do you know that gentleman? Is he badly hurt?"

Burton looked up to find a young, round-faced, and sandy-haired man standing beside him. "He's a visiting American. Thomas Lake Harris. He's out for the count but not badly wounded, as far as I can make out. Who are you, sir?"

"Detective Inspector Spearing."

"Ah, then I suppose you've been following us? I know you were ordered to keep an eye on this fellow. It's all right, Spearing—I'm Burton."

"Oh, I see. Detective Inspector Trounce has told me all about you, of course. Can I be of assistance?"

Swinburne piped up, "You could tell us what the blazes has happened!"

"This is my colleague, Mr. Swinburne," Burton explained.

"I have no idea, sir," Spearing said. "They've been making repairs in the clock tower, but I can't credit them with using anything capable of causing such a blast. What are you going to do with Mr. Harris?"

"We're taking him back to the Regency Hotel."

"You'll need a ride. Here, let me lend a hand. We'll take him through to the back of the Yard. You can commandeer a police vehicle." Spearing paused, then said, "You won't crash it, will you?"

"I appear to have gained a reputation," Burton noted ruefully.

They lifted Harris and carried him across the road, treading carefully to avoid the scattered rubble.

"Through here," Spearing said, leading them into a narrow alleyway.

At the back of the police headquarters, in a large courtyard lined with stable-like buildings, Spearing left them, entered one of the structures, and a few moments later steered out a steam-horse-drawn brougham. He jumped down from the driver's seat. "I'd take you myself, sir, but I think it's a case of all hands on deck at the Yard."

"I quite understand. Help me get him into the cabin, would you?"

They lifted Harris into the vehicle. The detective pointed to an open gate and said, "That opens onto Northumberland Street."

"Thank you, Spearing."

The policeman saluted and hastened away.

Swinburne climbed in beside the American. Burton took the driver's seat, gripped the tiller, and guided the machine out through the gate and to the left, in the direction of Trafalgar Square. It was slow going—there were lumps of masonry in the road and rapidly expanding crowds of people, all gathering to gaze at the destruction.

When they reached the square, Burton made to steer into the Mall, intending to follow it westward, but Swinburne thumped on the roof and screeched, "Stop! Hey, Richard, stop, I say!"

The explorer pulled over and the poet jumped out and scrambled up beside him.

"I've been looking at his face," Swinburne said breathlessly, "and it's given me an idea. Let's take him to your place."

"Why?" Burton asked, puzzled.

"Because his bone structure is similar to yours. With whitened skin, a false beard, and a few other cosmetic adjustments, you could pass yourself off as him."

"You intend to hold Harris prisoner, Algy, while I go off to meet this Count Sobieski fellow?"

"Yes! Why not become the twelfth messenger of God?"

Burton considered the poet's enthusiastic countenance.

"Just how drunk are you?"

"Hah! Considerably!" Swinburne smiled. "How else could I have come up with such a ridiculous scheme?"

"It *is* ridiculous," Burton agreed. "And I rather like it."

CHAPTER 21

THE LEAGUE OF ENOCHIANS
GENTLEMEN'S CLUB

The sewer tunnels are constructed from brick and stone and range from six to twenty feet in diameter. The smaller of them are round in section, the larger egg-shaped, with the narrow end downward, which serves to increase the flow and prevent silt from building up. The main interceptor tunnels run from west to east. North-and-south-flowing sewers run into them, the waste being diverted away toward the mouth of the Thames, rather than flowing straight into it. Each tunnel is fitted with many iron sluice gates, some of massive proportions, which can be manually raised or lowered by means of geared mechanisms, and which are used to regulate the flow and, on occasion, to block it, so that sections of the tunnels can be inspected and, if necessary, repaired.
—From MR. BAZALGETTE'S UNDERGROUND MARVEL,
THE *DAILY BUGLE*

Burton leaned on his cane and snapped open his new pocket watch. His eyes lingered on the lock of Isabel's hair before registering the time. Ten-past eight. Count Sobieski was late.

Earlier that afternoon—it was now Wednesday the 9th of November—Trounce had called again at Montagu Place, finding Swinburne already there with Burton and Levi. The detective inspector was dishevelled and tired, and grateful for a brandy and water. "Seven killed last night and more than a hundred injured. It was a bomb. A big one, too. Three hours after it went off, a chap walked into the offices of the *Daily Bugle*, introduced himself to the night editor as Vincent Sneed—thirty-two years old, a chimney sweep—and made a full confession. He recently cleaned the flues at the Whitechapel Bell Foundry, where Big Ben was cast, and stole a spare set of tower keys from there."

"But his motive?" Burton asked. "Why commit such an atrocity?"

Trounce had pulled a notebook from his pocket, extracted a sheet of paper from it, and passed it to the explorer. "The statement he made to the newspaper man."

Burton read it, handed it to Swinburne, and said, "They don't strike me as the words of a sweep."

"I thought the same," Trounce muttered.

"My hat!" Swinburne exclaimed. "What could possibly warrant such an outpouring of hatred? Smash the German Alliance? Hang Prince Albert as a traitor? Assassinate Bismarck?"

"That last is an oddity in itself," Burton observed. "Bismarck is out of the picture. Why include him?"

"Why any of it at all?" Trounce asked. "According to Sneed's apprentice—a lad named William Cornish—the man has never once before expressed a political opinion."

"Has he said anything more?"

Trounce took up his bowler from beside the chair and punched it in frustration. "That's the problem. He can't. He's dead."

"Dead?"

"Inexplicably. We put him in a cell, intending to question him this morning, but at dawn he simply stopped breathing. The coroner was unable to identify the cause."

Eliphas Levi exclaimed, "*Mon Dieu! Où est le cadavre maintenant?*"

"Eh?"

"The corpse," Burton translated. "Where is it?"

"In the mortuary."

The explorer and occultist exchanged a glance.

"Trounce," Burton said, after a momentary pause, "I have to use my authority to issue you with a direct order."

"On the basis of that statement, should I expect an unusual one?"

"Yes. Take Monsieur Levi to the mortuary and do exactly as he tells you. It's probable that Sneed is *strigoi morti*. He may have been acting under the spell of Perdurabo."

"I find it hard to believe any of this."

Levi murmured, "I show you. You will believe."

"Think of it as a disease," Burton advised. "John Judge carried it aboard the ship from Fernando Po. If Sneed has been infected, as I suspect he has, he'll appear to die in daylight but will rise at night. While active, he'll be highly infectious."

Trounce scratched his chin. "Then Perdurabo, in the body of Thomas Honesty, is hiding out among the anti-German activists in the Cauldron? Infecting them? Is that what you're suggesting?"

"It is. Or, at very least, he's made of the district a hunting ground. Tonight, Levi will accompany you to the East End. Take young Bram, too, but keep him away from any trouble. The Whisperers have a strong presence in the Cauldron—there are more street Arabs there than anywhere else in the city. Use Bram to collect information from the district. Look for signs of the un-dead." He turned to the Frenchman. "You will advise, monsieur?"

"*Oui.* We find them and do what must be done."

Burton said to Trounce, "Come with me."

They went upstairs to the room where Burton's half-unpacked African crates were stored. Thomas Lake Harris was bound to a chair in the middle of it with his head bandaged and a gag in his mouth.

"What the blazes?" Trounce cried out. "Who's this? What are you playing at?"

"It's Mr. Harris, the American spiritualist Detective Inspector Spearing has been following. He's due to give a lecture at the Enochians' Club tonight. I intend to masquerade as him and go in his stead."

"But—but—by Jove! Is he one of them? Has he done anything wrong?"

"Nothing, unless you count his incessant spouting of sheer nonsense."

"But you can't keep him here like that! Hell's bells! I know the king gave you special dispensation, but this is indefensible."

"The security of the Empire is at stake."

Trounce pointed at the prisoner. "From him?"

"No."

"Then you have to let him go."

"It would be better if you took him into police custody for the night. It's for his own protection—he's in danger of associating with bad people."

"By the looks of it, he's already done so."

"I didn't thump him over the head, Trounce, he was hit by a falling brick. As for his current incarceration, it inconveniences him, that's all. It's necessary."

"Humph! I'll put him in a police cell, but I don't approve of this. The law is the law. You have to realise where the boundaries lie."

"Need I remind you of our first encounter? You adopted a false name and assaulted me in an alleyway. Hardly legal, I'd venture."

"I judged it a necessary ploy."

"As I do this."

With that, Trounce had departed, accompanied by Levi and a very verbosely indignant Thomas Lake Harris, whose last words to Burton were, "You'd better pray the Lily Queen never gets her hands on you, you goddam snake in the grass!"

Burton spent the next few hours applying makeup and false hair, transforming himself into a convincing approximation of the American. He and Swinburne then rode his velocipedes to Upper St. Martin's Lane, where the poet was now waiting for Burton in the Queen's Arms.

Outside the church, Burton put away his timepiece and gazed at a litter-crab as it lumbered past. The already bad weather was worsening and rain was starting to fall again, the water steaming from the machine's humped back.

Trafalgar Square was congested with traffic. The din was such that he initially failed to hear the individual who stopped behind him and said, "Mr. Harris?" The man reached up and tapped him on the shoulder. "Mr. Harris?"

Burton turned to see a short, ferrety fellow, whose lack of teeth caused his bearded chin to be much closer to his nose than was natural.

"Yes. You are Count Sobieski?"

The man bowed. He didn't look like a count. His clothes were baggy and unwashed. He smelled bad. His breath reeked of stale gin.

In a Russian-accented voice, he said, "Follow me, please."

He led Burton toward the Strand but turned left before reaching it and plunged into the network of narrow streets and alleys behind the eastern side of St. Martin's Lane. They turned left, right, left, and right again, then stopped at a gate. Sobieski pushed it open, crossed a yard, and unlocked the back door of one of the shops lining the main street. Burton followed his guide inside, to the end of a short corridor, and through another door into a workshop. There was a large safe in one corner and a number of workbenches, all scattered with tools. He recognised the place instantly, and a mystery was solved. He was in Brundleweed's jewellery shop. Plainly, the old man was either captive or done away with.

With difficulty, Burton pushed the thought of his engagement ring aside. He couldn't allow the pain it brought with it.

"This way," Sobieski murmured. He opened a door and descended a narrow staircase, emerging into a mildewed basement, empty but for broken packing crates, a rusty iron bedstead, and an old chest of drawers. The far wall had a hole cut into it. There was a dark passage beyond.

Burton's heart began to thud.

Bismillah! Must I venture underground again?

The Russian lifted an oil lamp from the chest of drawers, lit it, and stepped through the ragged gap. The explorer trailed after him and said, in an American accent, "Say, Count, this is a mighty strange tour you're takin' me on. What's the game?"

"Just a little patience, please, Mr. Harris," Sobieski replied. "This is a secret route into the clubhouse. All will be explained when we get there. Not far to go now."

The passage was short. It opened into the side of a clay-walled tunnel through which one of London's many subterranean rivers flowed, its brown surface heaving and frothing as it sped past.

They went to the right and carefully shuffled along an outward-thrusting shelf, moving upstream. It was slippery, and Burton, using his swordstick for balance, imagined himself sliding from it into the water and being carried into darkness. His corpse, he supposed, would be ejected into the Thames, which—now that he considered it—wasn't very far away.

They hadn't gone far before the damp chill permeated the explorer's bones. His left forearm started to ache.

The lamplight slid over the clay walls. Parts of the roof had been shored up with wooden struts. Their shadows swung disconcertingly beneath the illumination, giving the impression that the tunnel was slowly collapsing. Burton paused and closed his eyes, trying to control his shaking.

Sobieski had stopped just ahead, at the foot of a ladder. He looked back, said, "Come," and started up it.

Burton's respiration was rapid and shallow, hissing unsteadily through his teeth. He straightened, opened his eyes, cursed himself, and followed.

The count pushed open a trapdoor and disappeared through it.

Quickly, Burton ascended. He crawled thankfully out into a room furnished with coat-, hat-, and umbrella stands, plus rough mats and stiff-haired brushes. Taking the cue from his companion, he used the latter to clean the mud from his boots.

"I'll take you to Doctor Kenealy, sir."

Sobieski opened a door and ushered the explorer through, across a wood-panelled hallway, and into a plushly appointed sitting room.

Two men got up from leather armchairs and faced the newcomers.

"Thank you, Count," one of them said. "The others are awaiting you in the temple chamber."

Sobieski left the room, closing the door after him.

"We're honoured to have you with us, Mr. Harris. Come, sit. I am Doctor Edward Hyde Kenealy, president of the League of Enochians. This is my advisor, Mr. John Dee."

Dee be damned! Damien Burke, more like!

"I'm mighty glad to be here, gents," Burton said, continuing to imitate Harris's accent. He shook the proffered hands, sat in the indicated chair, and nodded when Burke offered him a glass of red wine.

"I trust you're enjoying your visit to London," Kenealy said.

"I'd sure like it more if the rain stopped fallin'."

Kenealy smiled. He had a wide face outlined by an enormous bush of dark hair which curled down into a shaggy beard. His upper lip was clean-shaven, his nose flat, his small eyes half-concealed by round pebble-like spectacles.

"The tears of the angels, Mr. Harris. They weep for the civilised world."

"They lament the rise of evil men," Burke added, "don't you agree, Mr. Harris?"

"Well now," Burton drawled, "I don't know nothin' about that. What men do you mean?"

"The ones who believe that Europe should cower in the face of Germanic ambition, sir," Kenealy said. "The men who promote appeasement and cooperation, blind to the danger."

Burton took a sip of wine. He saw fanaticism in Kenealy's eyes, ruthlessness in Burke's.

"Danger?"

Kenealy leaned back in his seat, crossed his legs, steepled his fingers, and said, "A discussion for later, Mr. Harris. First, I have a confession to make. We have brought you here under false pretences."

Burton was inclined to raise an eyebrow, but both of them being false, decided not to risk it, and instead said, "How so? You'll still want to hear my presentation on the invoking of angels?"

"As a matter of fact," Kenealy responded, "we Enochians are already very proficient at summoning. We have regular communication with an angel named Perdurabo, who has taken a great interest in your work, sir, and now wishes to address you directly."

Burton gripped the arms of his seat, giving every indication of barely suppressed excitement. "That's real interestin'. This Perdurabo asked specifically to speak with me, you say?"

"Yes, Mr. Harris, which is why we're inviting you to join us in a summoning ritual. No doubt you noticed that the person who escorted you here, Count Sobieski, is, shall we say, not the most sophisticated of men. He does, however, possess one redeeming quality, it being that when he's under the influence of certain drugs, he becomes a powerful medium. Channelling Perdurabo is too stressful for most—it can cause the heart to burst—but in Sobieski we have a strong vessel through which the angel can speak for a prolonged period."

"About what?" Burton asked. "Have you received information about Lilistan?"

"Lilistan?"

"Sure! The interspace between the planets, sir, where the angels dwell."

"Ah, I see. Perhaps Perdurabo has reserved such revelations for you alone."

Damien Burke said, "Are you willing to join us for the ritual, Mr. Harris?"

"Mr. Dee, I sure am. Yes, sir!"

Burke stood and bowed, "Then, if you'll excuse me, I'll go and prepare the chamber."

Burton watched the man leave and wondered what had happened to Gregory Hare. Had he survived the collision on the outskirts of Downe Village? It was difficult to imagine so.

"Will you tell me somethin' about your organisation, Mr. Kenealy?" he asked. "Its history?"

"Certainly. The Marquess of Waterford founded it in 1841, three years or so after an angel visited him in the grounds of his estate. The marquess came to believe that angels hold the key to the advancement of mankind."

"Advancement? In what way?"

"Spiritually, Mr. Harris. Beresford—the marquess's name was Henry Beresford—didn't regard angels as messengers of God. In fact, he regarded the belief in God as a repudiation of responsibility. The human race, he said, should be accountable only to itself. It should feel shame for its many mistakes and pride for its many achievements, abandoning the notion of an unknowable divine plan, to which these things are so often attributed. As for religion, he wanted it dismantled, for it is nothing but a primitive form of politics, enabling an elite minority to control and feed off the masses."

"This Beresford fella sounds like an astute guy, but what did he think angels are, then?"

"The liberated spirits of humans, sir. He attempted to make the Enochians the seed of a movement he named 'Libertarianism.' This had as its basis the philosophies of the Marquis de Sade, which he perceived as the means through which we can cast off the church-imposed moralities that quash the natural expansiveness of the human spirit. We don't require a supreme deity, he proposed, because we ourselves, like the angel he saw, can become godlike."

"You say 'attempted'? So he didn't succeed?"

"He didn't. It went wrong about ten years ago, when Beresford tried to recruit a group of influential artists led by a man named Dante Gabriel Rossetti. Rossetti rejected his philosophy and instead formed the Pre-Raphaelite Brotherhood, which went on to produce many paintings linking human dignity with Christian religious themes—a direct challenge to Beresford's ideas. Rossetti was then made the government's minister of arts and culture. From that position, he was able to influence the Home Office, instigating the repression of Libertine activity. Many Enochians were arrested on charges ranging from lewd behaviour to being drunk and disorderly, but the biggest loss was that of Mr. Francis Galton."

"Who's he?" Burton asked.

"A scientist. He joined the Enochians early in 'forty-four and immediately shook things up by introducing to Beresford the idea that angels—he designated the species *Supreme Man*—must develop at some point in future history, and if they are godlike in their abilities, then they should be able to penetrate the barrier of time, if not physically then certainly mentally. Beresford had long been fascinated by the works of the sixteenth-century occultist John Dee—"

"Dee?" Burton interrupted. "The same name as the gent who just left us?"

"Yes, Mr. Harris. I often wonder whether such coincidences indicate some deep pattern in the substance of time, don't you? Anyway, as I was saying, the marquess was already well versed in the theories of Dee, who was much obsessed with the summoning of angels, and so responded with great enthusiasm when Galton suggested that angels could communicate from the future. This idea provided a new impetus for the Enochians, and the art of summoning became its primary focus. Indeed, very quickly, the club achieved its first contact with Perdurabo, who, via a mediumistically talented member, instructed Galton in great detail with regard to a new science called Eugenics. This, it was hoped, would give Galton the means to artificially hasten the transformation of man into Supreme Man. Unfortunately, disaster followed. The medium suffered heart failure, and there was no one strong enough to channel Perdurabo again, so Galton was forced to proceed without further assistance from him. The experiments went wrong, Eugenics was banned by the government, and the experience caused Galton to lose his sanity."

Burton adjusted his face into an expression of concern and confusion. "Hold on there! Are you sayin' that my knowledge of the interplanetary realm is nothin' but hogwash? That angels ain't the supernatural beings I take 'em for?"

Kenealy made a calming gesture and smiled. "Not necessarily, sir. It might well be that you have insight into the nature—or perhaps I should say, *super-nature*—of future humans."

Burton said, "I guess. So what happened?"

"After Galton? Not a great deal, unfortunately. From the mid 'forties, the Enochians lacked a medium strong enough to summon Perdurabo—or any other entity, for that matter. There was no progress until the start of this year, when I was approached by Mr. Dee and his companion, Mr. Kelley, who had with them Count Sobieski. They informed me that someone wanted to communicate with me from the Afterlife. I consented to a séance, during which Perdurabo took possession of the count. He revealed his true nature— not a spirit from Beyond but, as Galton had suggested, a being from the future—and told me Henry Beresford's time on Earth was nearly done and that I should move to take over the running of the League of Enochians. New and influential members would join to support me, he said. Well, I was a lawyer at the time, Mr. Harris, and my career was in tatters after my decision to defend the poisoner William Palmer, in which undertaking I'd failed miserably, so I was very much enthused by this new opportunity. During January and February I started to wrest control of the Enochians from Beresford, and in March was greatly assisted by a man named Laurence Oliphant, who is Lord Elgin's private secretary. Oliphant's interest in summoning was inspired by your work, sir, which is how I became aware of you and the enormous contribution you might make to our cause. On the evening of the twenty-eighth of March, Dee, Kelley, Oliphant, Sobieski, and I conducted a séance during which Perdurabo again possessed the count. He informed us that the marquess would die on the morrow and we must now prepare for an undertaking of inordinate significance, upon which humanity depended. He then asked for private audiences, first with Dee and Kelley, then with Oliphant, and finally with me. During mine, he informed me that each of us was being set a task, which we must not discuss with each other. My own was the simplest: I was to close the Enochians to further membership, establish a secret route into the clubhouse, prevent intruders from entering, and follow whatever instructions Dee and Kelley issued. For this, he said, I would be amply rewarded."

"Incredible!" Burton exclaimed. "Such specific communication with a supernatural being is far beyond what I've experienced. They've come to me in dreams and imaginings but—phewee!—never in the flesh, so to speak."

"Tonight, sir, we intend to remedy that. Tonight, Perdurabo will address you directly, if you are willing."

Burton picked up his wine glass and drained it. "For sure!" he cried out. "For sure! But, say, did it happen? Did the marquess kick the bucket the next day?"

"He did. He fell from his horse and broke his neck."

The door opened and Damien Burke stepped in. He said, "It's all prepared."

Kenealy stood. "I hope you'll forgive my deception, Mr. Harris. I feel positive your presentation would have fascinated us all, but I trust the experience we offer you instead will prove more edifying even than the applause of an admiring audience."

"Tactfully put, Mr. Kenealy," Burton said as he got to his feet. "You have in me an eager subject."

"Then let us go at once to the temple chamber."

Kenealy and "Dee" conducted Burton out of the room and along a hallway. It was hung with paintings, all depicting the manifestation of angels.

They came to double doors, which Dee pushed open to reveal a large square room hung with purple drapes into which sigils had been embroidered with silver thread. A circular table stood at its centre, with twenty-four chairs arranged around it, twenty-one of them occupied by men dressed in white robes. Burton noted that Sobieski held a position of prominence, his chair being throne-like and raised higher than the rest. Kenealy instructed Burton to take an empty seat directly opposite the medium. He and Burke then sat to either side of the count.

As he settled, Burton examined the tabletop, which was inset with a silver pentagram with a border of engraved Enochian letters. Seven candles were arranged in a circle in the middle of the pentagram. Inside them, an extremely complex symbol had been painted—using what appeared to be beeswax— around the base of a large crystal ball.

Kenealy clicked his fingers. A man stood and moved around the chamber extinguishing the lamps until the only illumination was that provided by the candles. He returned to his seat.

Gesturing toward the crystal ball, in which the beeswax symbol was peculiarly reflected, Kenealy said, "Please devote your attention to the *Sigillum dei Aemeth*, Mr. Harris. You must fixate on the speculum, for through it Perdurabo will show you visions of the future; of what must be if we fail in our great cause."

Burton gazed at the glass ball. The twisting and distorted lines of the symbol—the *Sigillum dei Aemeth*, as Kenealy had called it—confused his eyes, and the more he looked, the more aware he became that they were somehow pushing him into a trance-like state. He allowed it to happen, but at the same time devoted part of his mind to a Sufi exercise, establishing a "fenced-off" segment of consciousness, which, he hoped, would be resistant to external influence.

Count Sobieski said, "It begins. It is fast tonight. Perdurabo is eager to speak. *Geh londoh mica olz busd gohed.*"

The assembly chanted, "*Exarpe, bit to em, he co ma, na en ta.*"

The hairs at the back of Burton's neck stood on end. The temperature suddenly dropped and the atmosphere of the room prickled his skin.

The men to either side of Burton took hold of his hands. All around the table, the Enochians formed a chain in this manner.

Damien Burke said, "*Ra asa i Raphael.*"

Kenealy said, "*Sobo el i Gabriel.*"

The man to Burton's left leaned close to him and whispered, "Pronounce aloud: *Baba ge i Michael.*"

Burton did as he was told. "*Baba ge i Michael.*"

Sobieski jerked in his seat and his head lolled forward. He murmured, "*Od luca el i Perdurabo.*"

The gathering intoned, "*Mi cama, un al, i alpo re, o i veae, dasa ta, bia he, asa peta, ta!*"

Burton felt the reassuring presence of the pistol in his waistband.

The count loosed a long groan. He slowly raised his head. His eyes glinted in the candlelight. They were black from edge to edge.

"Faithful," he said, "I give you my thanks. Much has already been achieved."

The voice was as Burton had heard twice before, glutinous and comprised of innumerable but perfectly concerted parts.

"The great work has commenced," Perdurabo said. "The flow of events is being adjusted and corrected in preparation for my incarnation in corporeal form and your ascendance to a new mode of existence."

Sobieski's dreadful eyes settled on Burton. "You are the American, Thomas Lake Harris?"

"Yes, I am."

"I'm most gratified by your presence. I have a special place reserved for you in the new world that is to come, Mr. Harris. You will occupy a position of honour and influence. You shall be as a king among your brethren. Look into the shew-stone, please, that I might unveil to you that which we work to avoid."

Burton turned his attention back to the crystal ball. The lines and shapes within it moved as the candles flickered. He felt himself drawn in and didn't resist, though he was careful to strengthen the part of his mind he'd separated. Gradually, the confusion of angles and surfaces coalesced around him, until he felt himself embedded in the midst of a vision.

"Africa," Perdurabo said. "Mr. Harris, a war of indescribable ferocity is coming, and this is where it will end."

Incongruously, amid the rolling savannahs that were unveiled in Burton's mind, a city sprawled; a metropolis of British character, spread out in the shadow of a tall green-topped column of rock. Burton recognised the geological structure immediately. It marked the position of Kazeh, the Arabian outpost where the *Orpheus* had taken on supplies before flying east to Zanzibar. But the city? That most certainly hadn't been there.

"Tabora," Perdurabo said. "The last bastion of the British Empire. You are looking at the future, Mr. Harris, the year 1918. The final days of a war that will grow out of unbridled German ambition."

Burton observed a vast ring of cannons—many of them poking out of heavily armoured vehicles—surrounding the city and bombarding it relentlessly. Refugees were fleeing in droves, thousands being brutally cut down by relentless gunfire. Burton saw men, women, and children falling.

"Death," Perdurabo said. "Nothing but death. Here comes the final blow."

The vision swung dizzyingly around Burton until he was looking into the sky. There was something there—a machine or creature? He couldn't tell. It bore some similarity to a dirigible but also to a gigantic pea pod, with a tulip-like flower pulsating at one end, driving it along.

"A weapon of such terrible potency that it will obliterate the last vestiges of the British—a demise which has been, in this future, long overdue. It is the consequence of mistakes made in the present."

The perspective changed. Burton watched as a gigantic steam sphere powered out of Tabora. He saw on its side the name SS *Britannia*. Behind it, a blinding white flash suddenly burst from the city. When the glare receded, it revealed an ugly yellow cloud boiling into the atmosphere.

"There are many possible futures," Perdurabo said, "but the war comes in all of them. Generations are annihilated, and we have only ourselves to blame."

The cloud, billowing into the shape of a vast mushroom, fell away into the distance and was lost from view as the vision followed the escaping steam sphere.

"Your own country will suffer, too, of that you can be sure. The German Empire will become greedy for America's many resources. I have shown you the end of the British Empire. America will be next."

The scene blurred and reshaped itself. Now the SS *Britannia* was lying motionless and damaged on the floor of a wide shallow crater.

The Pico Santa Isabel. Fernando Po.

The steam sphere wavered, became a transparent globe of shifting colours, and was suddenly a crystal ball, on a table, with a complex symbol reflected in it.

Burton looked up at Count Sobieski. Perdurabo addressed him through the Russian's toothless mouth.

"The future you have just witnessed is disastrous not only for our countries, but for the human race. It will set back our natural development and long delay the emergence of individuals like myself—a new species that has dominion over nature and even time itself. It is of utmost importance, therefore, that we alter the present in order to avoid its catastrophic consequences. Do you agree?"

"Yes," Burton said.

"Very good. As I am sure you are aware, the British government is about to enter into an alliance with a newly formed Central German Confederation. This will give the Germanic states a new cohesion and the means to create a powerful manufacturing base. The seed of German expansionism is being planted right now. We can't allow it. The Germans must be weakened, not strengthened."

Burton was aware of an acute mesmeric influence needling into his consciousness. He didn't resist, but retreated into the protected area of his mind, and from there said, "I can't doubt what you say. Hell, when a man sees something like that with his own eyes, he ain't gonna sit back an' do nothin'."

"Then you'll join our crusade against this abomination? You'll undertake a task for us, one that will save your country from the horror you've just witnessed?"

"For sure."

"Good, Mr. Harris! Very good! Your task is a simple one. Are you aware of a man named Abraham Lincoln?"

"Yup! Who isn't?"

"A year from now he will be elected as president of your country. His opposition to slavery will cause the Southern states to rebel and plunge America into a bloody civil war. The British Empire can ill-afford a potential ally to be so distracted. Thus we have to reshape history. The conflict must be avoided so America is free to join us in an incisive attack on Germany. There is only one way to achieve this, Mr. Harris, and you are the key."

Perdurabo paused. His black eyes glittered.

Burton said, "Tell me what to do."

"You must return to America at once and shoot Abraham Lincoln dead."

CHAPTER 22

ABDU EL YEZDI

"I had during the fever-fit, and often for hours afterwards, a queer conviction of divided identity, never ceasing to be two persons that generally thwarted and opposed each other."
—RICHARD F. BURTON, *THE LAKE REGIONS OF CENTRAL AFRICA*

Burton was led out of the League of Enochians Gentlemen's Club by the same route through which he'd entered, guided by a man named Doyle, who ducked back into Brundleweed's without having uttered a single word.

The explorer could feel the aftermath of Perdurabo's mesmeric influence and was strongly inclined to book passage to America, there to assassinate Abraham Lincoln.

He liberated the enclosed portion of his mind. It flooded into the rest and drowned the insistent suggestion. Lincoln would be safe from him, and from Thomas Lake Harris, too.

It was half-past midnight by the time the explorer met Swinburne outside the Queen's Arms. The pub had just closed and the poet was leaning against a lamppost, careless of the rain that was pattering on and around him, quietly reciting poetry to himself. The velocipedes were standing at the side of the road.

He looked up as the explorer approached. "Hallo! Hallo! You're still in one piece, then? Was it worth it?"

"Most definitely. Are you sober?"

"Horribly. It's a thoroughly objectionable state. What next?"

"How awake are you? We haven't had much sleep recently."

"Wide."

"To Battersea Power Station, then. I have the measure of our enemy. Let us now meet our mysterious ally, if that he be."

"Rather!" Swinburne enthused.

They mounted their vehicles, started the engines, and went rattling down St. Martin's Lane. The streets were mostly empty and quiet but for the hiss of rain, so they rode side by side while Burton described what had occurred in the club.

"You have to warn Disraeli," Swinburne said. "The signing ceremony is not even two days hence, and is surely Perdurabo's target. The entirety of the British and German governments will be gathered in Green Park. The royal families, too. He could kill them all in one fell swoop."

"How, though?" Burton pondered. "The event will be wrapped in the tightest security possible. Even if he has an army of assassins at his disposal, they'd never get past the guards, and the *Orpheus* will be hovering over the park, too, bristling with her new guns."

Crossing Trafalgar Square, they steered into Whitehall and parked their penny-farthings. While Swinburne guarded them, Burton entered Scotland Yard. Pepperwick was off duty and had been replaced by the night clerk. The man examined the explorer's authorization then said, "Can I help you, sir?"

"Are Detective Inspectors Trounce or Slaughter on duty?"

"All our officers are on extended duty tonight due to the unrest in the East End, but I think I saw Detective Inspector Slaughter come in a few minutes ago. Hold on a minute."

He turned to the speaking tubes, selected the one connected to Room 14, and through it confirmed Slaughter's presence.

"Go right up, sir."

Burton found Slaughter in his office nursing a pint of milk. His clothes were dirty, his jacket sleeve torn, and a large bruise marked the left side of his forehead.

"Bloody chaos!" the policeman announced as the explorer entered. "The Cauldron is boiling over. Half the population is frightened out of its wits and fleeing north into Hackney, and the other half is ranting about Germanic perfidy and pushing westward into the city, apparently intent on smashing its way to parliament. We're trying to hold them back but they're like wild animals."

"The League of Enochians Gentlemen's Club is at the root of it," Burton said.

"So Trounce told me. Can't we raid the place?"

"You can. Have your men knock down the doors. You'll find an underground tunnel connecting the club to the basement of the Brundleweed jewellery shop, so be sure to go in that way, too. Arrest them all."

"By George!" Slaughter exclaimed. "If we can stop 'em from fanning the flames, that'll be something. I'll organize it at once. We'll have the Enochians behind bars before the night is done."

Burton rejoined Swinburne and they set off down Millbank. The reek of the Thames assaulted their nostrils.

The Vauxhall Bridge tollbooths were closed at night, so they traversed the river unimpeded and turned right by the Belmont Candle Factory onto Nine Elms Lane.

The rain intensified. Both men were wet through, and Burton felt ice clawing out of the ache in his left forearm and invading his flesh.

Please! Not a fever. Not now.

The four tall copper rods of Battersea Power Station glimmered ahead.

"'To all the four points it shall batter thee,'" Swinburne quoted. "I hope Abdu El Yezdi is waiting for us. I shall have to take him to task over that childish doggerel."

"Indeed," Burton agreed. "Had it been rather more sophisticated, I might have got the message a little sooner. As it was—though it was staring me in the face—I couldn't see the wood for the trees."

A stretch of wasteland extended from the base of the station, separating it from the Royal Navy Air Service Station. It was too uneven to drive across, so they dismounted, turned off the engines, and pushed their penny-farthings along. The whole area was illuminated by the lights of the airfield, which even at this time of night was a hive of activity, with ground crew working in and around a truly gargantuan rotorship that dwarfed even the mighty *Orpheus*.

"The *Sagittarius*," Swinburne said.

"So that's the fist Elgin will use against China," Burton exclaimed. "Bismillah! The size of it!"

"It's the biggest warship ever built. Rossetti thinks Elgin will employ it to destroy the Summer Palaces."

"If he does, it'll go down in history as one of the worst acts of vandalism ever committed," Burton said. "And having looked into Elgin's eyes, I feel quite certain he's capable of it."

Swinburne pointed at the power station. "It's all lit up but the gates are shut. Shall we knock?"

"I'd rather reconnoitre before we present ourselves. Let's see if we can find an alternative means of entry."

They leaned their vehicles against the building and examined the huge gates. A normal-sized door was fitted into the right-hand portal but it was firmly bolted. Starting off around the perimeter, they looked up at the lowest windows, which were far too high to reach, even had Swinburne stood on Burton's shoulders.

"Impregnable," Swinburne muttered. "This is what Old Wardour Castle must have been like before it was ruined."

The comment prompted Burton to peer at the upper reaches of the structure. As far as he could tell, there were no ravens squatting atop it. That was a good sign.

After completing a circuit of the station and seeing no possible way in, they stood again outside the gates. Burton looked at his companion, shrugged, moved to the small door, and hammered upon it with the head of his cane. The portal swung inward immediately. A pistol was poked into his face.

"Give me that swordstick and put your hands over your head," Krishnamurthy said, "and step in. You, too, Mr. Swinburne."

"Not a constable, then?" Burton growled. "I should have known."

The two men did as instructed, passing through into a large quadrangle. Montague Penniforth loomed out of the shadows. "Sorry, guv'nor," he said, and frisked Burton. He removed the pistol from the explorer's waistband. Swinburne was subjected to the same treatment.

A third man, Bhatti, also brandishing a pistol, closed the door behind them. "If you'll pardon the language, Sir Richard," he said, "about bloody time. What kept you?"

"Perdurabo," the explorer answered. Then, "Ravindra Johar and Mahakram Singh, I presume?"

"Yes, sir, though we go by Shyamji Bhatti and Maneesh Krishnamurthy these days. How is your brother?"

"Fat and obnoxious but alive—thanks to you."

"I'm glad to hear it. Perhaps we can be reunited at a later date. I'd very much like to see him again. For now, though, we can't afford to lose another moment. Will you start toward the big doors, please?"

Burton looked across the open space and saw the station's inner entrance. He set off, with Swinburne on his left and Bhatti on his right. Krishnamurthy and Penniforth trailed behind.

"You can lower your guns," he said.

"All in due course," Bhatti replied.

Swinburne shrilled, "Are we on the same side or not?"

"We are, Mr. Swinburne, but this meeting has been a long time coming and we need to feel confident that neither of you will do anything silly. We're cutting it very fine indeed—there's no room for any monkey business."

"Would've been a lot better if'n you'd turned up a few weeks ago," Penniforth rumbled. "If I 'ad me own way, I'd 'ave thrown you into me cab an' driven you here the moment you stepped off the bloomin' *Orpheus*."

Krishnamurthy said, "Now, now, Monty. You know perfectly well that time has its shapes and patterns, and Sir Richard had to come here of his own accord."

"Yus, but—lord love a duck!—he's almost too late, ain't he!"

"Perhaps that is what's necessary," Bhatti said as they stopped outside the doors.

"My hat! What the blazes are you blathering about?" Swinburne cried out.

"Patience, my friend," Krishnamurthy said. He reached up and twisted an odd-looking combination lock back and forth until a click sounded. He pushed the doors open. Burton squinted as an incandescent light assaulted his eyes. As his vision adjusted to it, he saw a cathedral-sized chamber, from the roof of which hung big glass globes. The light radiated out from them, as if they each held captive lightning.

"This way," Bhatti said, and led them in and across a vast floor crowded with baffling machinery. There was no steam here; it was all electricity, fizzling, crackling, and popping; sending writhing bolts from one megalithic device to another, filling the place with the tang of ozone.

From among the coils, towers, dials, and showering sparks, a man emerged and approached. Short, plump, and blond-haired, he was dressed conservatively but for an extraordinary contraption slung around his shoulders and buckled over his chest and waist; an extra pair of arms, mechanical and intricate, multi-jointed, and with a number of different tools arranged at their ends. Two thin cables ran from the harness up to either side of his neck. They appeared to be plugged directly into his skull, just behind his ears. The artificial arms moved as naturally as his fleshy ones.

"Daniel Gooch!" Swinburne exclaimed.

"Yes," the man said. "And you must be Algernon Swinburne. I'm very pleased to meet you. And you, too, of course, Sir Richard." He addressed the others. "Lower your guns, chaps. Our guests are doubtlessly far too curious to cause us trouble." He looked at Burton for confirmation and received it in the form of a brisk nod. To Bhatti, he said, "Shyamji, would you tell him? I expect he'll want to prepare."

"Rightio." Bhatti hurried away.

"This way," Gooch said, gesturing to the right with a metal limb. "Let's get out of this noise."

They followed him past a bank of flashing lights, around a dome-shaped contraption of glass and silver rods, and through a central area of workbenches.

"Are you a captive, Mr. Gooch?" Burton asked.

"No. I'm free to leave whenever I want to."

"You disappeared from an undersea suit."

"Yes. One of those." Gooch pointed to the right where bizarre outfits were hanging from a rail; padded rubbery affairs each criss-crossed by harnesses and draped beneath globular metal helmets that had porthole-like openings in their fronts. "It was planned. The suit they raised was not the same one I was wearing. I was collected from the seabed by a prototype submarine boat and brought here. Through this door, please."

He ushered them into a room furnished with bookshelves, leather arm-chairs and couches, expensive rugs, a grandfather clock, and tasteful pictures and ornaments. It could have been the sitting room of a manor house, were it not for the tall metal box mounted on wheels in one corner.

A figure, sitting at a desk, rose as they entered. Constructed of polished brass, it resembled one of Charles Babbage's clockwork men, but was consid-erably bulkier, possessed six arms, and was more extensively engraved with decorative designs. The front of its head was beautifully fashioned to resemble a human face, though, being immobile, it more resembled a death mask.

Burton recognised the features.

"Brunel!" he blurted.

"Sir Richard," the mechanism clanged. Its voice sounded like a blending of handbells and a church organ. "Thank goodness you've come at last! I wanted to fetch you but *he* wouldn't allow it."

With much whirring and ticking, the metal man stepped forward and extended a gauntlet-like hand. Bemusedly, Burton shook it and said, "'He' being Abdu El Yezdi?"

"Correct. He has a baffling obsession with the timing of events. Ah! Algernon Swinburne. It is good to see you. I am Isambard Kingdom Brunel."

"In a suit of armour?" Swinburne asked.

Brunel produced a tinkling noise that might have been laughter. He tapped the side of his head. "As a matter of fact, I'm nothing but electrical impulses. Unfortunately, my body suffered a stroke and breathed its last this September past. During my final hours, Shyamji Bhatti and Maneesh

Krishnamurthy brought me to Charles Babbage and Daniel Gooch, who had this mechanism already prepared for me. My consciousness was transferred into a number of black diamonds of a rather unique nature. They were fitted into a babbage probability calculator—to all intents and purposes an artificial brain—so I live on, I'm happy to say, and in a considerably stronger body."

"I need a drink," Swinburne said. "This is a lot to take in."

"I envy you. I've missed my cigars and brandy terribly since becoming mechanical. Well, it's dashed late, and there's much to discuss, but I'm sure a tipple won't do any harm. Daniel, would you do the honours? Gentlemen, take a seat, please. Our host will join us presently."

Burton, Swinburne, and Krishnamurthy settled in armchairs. Brunel pulled the wooden chair he'd been sitting in away from the desk, turned it around, and carefully lowered himself into it. "I'm still getting used to weighing a ton," he chimed. "I keep breaking chairs, and if I use an armchair, I have difficulty getting out of it."

Gooch distributed brandies to all but the engineer, then sat and said, "As you just heard, Babbage is among our little band. Nurse Nightingale is, too. None of us has been harmed and we all remain here of our own free will."

"Are you certain of that?" Burton asked. "I find it hard to believe that Nightingale would abandon Saint Thomas's Hospital."

"I'm certain. She recognises priorities."

"Anyone else with you?"

"Plenty of engineers and scientists, Sir Richard, but I expect you're referring to other people who've been reported missing, in which case the answer is no."

"We are all working for Abdu El Yezdi," Brunel put in. "A situation that will, I fear, soon end."

"Why?"

"He's dying. He suffered a serious heart attack on the first of September, and a number of minor ones since."

"The first of September?" Burton said. "The day the aurora borealis appeared."

When my friend William Stroyan had his throat cut by Laurence Oliphant.

"And the day a disruptive presence arrived in our world," Gooch added.

Brunel said, "The point is, he is extremely frail, Sir Richard, and has very little time remaining. He has much to tell you, but it will exhaust him, so, please, could you refrain from challenging him?"

Burton sipped his brandy. "I shall do my best. May I smoke?"

"Be my guest," Brunel said, and emitted an airy whistle that somehow resembled a forlorn sigh.

After lighting his cheroot, the explorer addressed Krishnamurthy. "For how long have you and Mr. Bhatti known the Arabian?"

"Arabian?"

"El Yezdi."

"Ah. He approached us in Ceylon, early in 'fifty-six, and told us when and how your brother was going to be attacked. If we saved him, he said, he'd ensure Edward would pay our passage to England. It was an opportunity too good to miss, but we nearly *did* miss it—we arrived a little late, and your brother was almost killed."

"Nevertheless, I'm in your and El Yezdi's debt," Burton said.

The door opened and Bhatti entered, followed by a stooped and elderly man. Burton instantly recognised Charles Babbage and stood to greet him.

"What's happening?" the scientist snapped in a querulous tone. "Where are the helmets? Why am I dragged from my work? Interruptions! Always interruptions! Don't you realize how close I am to completion?"

"Sir Richard and Mr. Swinburne have arrived," Brunel said.

"About bloody time!" Babbage glared at Burton. "I've done the calculations, sir. The probabilities don't lie. You no doubt received all the required information seventeen days ago. Why did you not act upon it? Why have you delayed?"

"Charles," Daniel Gooch said, "you know full well that random elements must be factored in."

"Random be damned! Any man with a clear head can steer the correct path. Random is just another word for muddled thinking!"

Brunel clanged, "I fear we shall embark upon another of our inexhaustible debates if we pursue this any further. You know there's no time for that, Charles, so please recalculate and join us. Would you care for a brandy?"

Babbage disregarded the question. His brows lowered over his eyes and, ignoring the gathering as if it weren't there, he lowered himself into a seat, mumbling, "Recalculate. Recalculate. Another bloody divergence. Let's see now—" He raised the fingers of both hands to his high forehead and began to tap them upon it, as if pressing lots of small buttons in a specific but inscrutable sequence.

Swinburne leaned close to Burton, rolled his eyes, and whispered, "First Harris, now Babbage. Cuckoo!"

Bhatti helped himself to a drink and sat down just as the door opened again. Nurse Florence Nightingale entered, pushing a three-wheeled wicker bath chair. She positioned it in the middle of the room, facing them all, then stood by its side.

Burton couldn't take his eyes off the man sitting in it.

Abdu El Yezdi.

He was swarthy-skinned and sharp-cheeked, with a dark left eye and a milky right. His nose was large and hooked, and his long grey beard flowed down over a very fat stomach. Dressed in the robes of a sheik, he exuded magnetism and authority, but as Burton took in the details, it quickly became apparent that the man was also deep into his final days, if not hours; his hands were shaking, there was a blue tinge about his lips, and he was struggling to breathe.

When he spoke, his voice was thin and weak.

"Algy, it is good to see you again. Are you well?"

"Yes," Swinburne answered. "But I wasn't sure whether I'd dreamt you or not."

"Culver Cliff? No dream."

The impenetrable eyes flicked to Burton and considered him for what felt to the explorer like a minute, though it was probably seconds. "And you. You have lost—have lost—" His respiration faltered. He gasped in air, waved Nightingale away when she bent toward him, and went on, "You have lost Isabel."

Burton nodded wordlessly.

"The pain you feel. You deserve every bit of it. Bloody fool."

"Sir," Brunel quietly rang. "I don't think—"

"Shut up, Brunel, I'm speaking. So, Burton, who else has died while you've been flapping about like a headless bird?"

Burton glared at the Arabian and snarled, "Why, exactly, must I account to you, sir?"

"Because I know a great deal more than you do, dolt."

El Yezdi addressed Krishnamurthy while gesturing toward the wardrobe-like wheeled box. "Maneesh, show him."

Krishnamurthy stood and walked over to the odd item of furniture, which was about a foot taller than him, and dragged it out of the corner. He positioned it beside the bath chair, then twisted a catch and slid the front panel aside. Two white suits were hanging inside, both one-piece affairs that would cover a man completely but for the head, hands, and feet. The material was white and had the texture of fish scales. Each had a circular disk attached to the chest and a cloak descending from the shoulders. Two shiny black helmets rested on the floor of the box, along with two pairs of boots attached to two-foot-high stilts. The outlandish costumes differed only in that one was fire-scorched and its helmet dented, while the other was in pristine condition. Without a doubt, Trounce had seen one of those outfits hanging from a branch in Green Park back in 1840, and the Mad Marquess had also glimpsed one momentarily in the grounds of Darkening Towers three years earlier.

Babbage jumped up from his seat. "There they are! Why? Put them back in the workshop at once! I have to finish!"

"Settle down, Charles," Abdu El Yezdi said. "They'll be returned to you presently."

The old scientist muttered an incomprehensible protestation and sat down.

El Yezdi returned his attention to his guests. "You are not looking at two suits. You are looking at the same suit, which is present twice."

"What? What? What?" Swinburne shrilled.

The Arabian chuckled, revealing large crooked and decayed teeth.

"And this outfit, which is here in duplicate, will not be created for another three hundred and forty-three years."

"More brandy!" Swinburne screeched. "At once!"

Bhatti, smiling, passed the decanter.

El Yezdi went on, "It is from the year 2202—an almost inconceivable date, I'm sure you'll agree—and though there is nothing visibly mechanical about it, it is, in fact, a machine."

"One that enables its wearer to travel through history," Burton said. "And that wearer was Edward Oxford, descended from the man of the same name who shot Queen Victoria."

"Good! The late Countess Sabina didn't speak to you in vain, then?"

"Of course not."

"She was a good, good woman, Burton. So far, she has sacrificed herself twice for me."

"Twice? So far? Do you intend, at any point in this conversation, to make sense?"

El Yezdi gave a bark of amusement, coughed, then recovered himself, rubbed the heel of his right hand against the middle of his chest, winced, and continued, "Oxford travelled back to watch his ancestor at work. It went wrong. His presence caused The Assassination—which should have failed—to succeed. Worse, his forebear was killed, and in an instant there could be no descendants, which meant Oxford had no ancestors and no longer existed in the future he'd come from." The Arabian shook his head sadly. "The situation didn't get any better. While fleeing the scene, his suit was damaged by young Constable Trounce. When he leaped away through time, it misfired and sent him to 1837 and Darkening Towers, where Henry Beresford took him in."

"Your statement differs considerably from the accounts of both Trounce and Beresford," Burton objected.

"I know. I'll come to that. During Oxford's subsequent weeks on the estate, while he attempted to make repairs, he dropped many hints about the future world. The marquess communicated these to Mr. Brunel, who, with his extraordinary inventiveness, turned them into the machinery we see around us today, much of which should never have existed."

"Wait!" Burton exclaimed. He turned to the brass figure. "You knew Beresford, Brunel?"

The engineer clanged, "No, I didn't."

Swinburne gave a screech of confusion.

"Then how——?" Burton said.

"Be patient, Sir Richard," Daniel Gooch advised.

Abdu El Yezdi was grinning, obviously enjoying himself at Burton's expense. He said, "May I continue?"

Burton answered with a slight motion of his hands.

"Beresford and Oxford concocted a plan. If Oxford could locate the woman his now-dead ancestor would have married, and if he could impregnate her, then perhaps he might become his own great-great—I don't know how many greats—grandfather. In other words, he might re-establish the line of descent and his own eventual existence in the year 2202."

"That's utterly insane," Swinburne objected. "Pure gobbledegook!"

"Beresford always was half-loopy," the Arabian responded, "and Oxford's predicament sent him right over the edge, too. Nevertheless, they put the plan into action, and though the suit wasn't properly repaired, it carried Oxford far enough into the future to do what he intended. So he started leaping through time in and around 1861—a little over a year from now—and while hunting for the right girl, he was spotted again and again, becoming known as Spring Heeled Jack. Perhaps it would have stopped there—with nothing but rumours of a mysterious stilted figure—but unfortunately Henry Beresford had learned too much, and when he told Francis Galton and Charles Darwin about the time suit, they became obsessed with using it to create their own futures, which they regarded as little more than Petri dishes such as are used in experimental biology."

Burton interrupted, "I've met Darwin. He struck me as a decent sort."

"A man is the sum of the opportunities he accepts and the challenges he does battle with," El Yezdi said. "Change those, and you'll have a different man."

"Personality adapting to the environment," Burton mused.

"Precisely. So history was sent careening off course by Oxford, and no one would have realised were it not for the investigations undertaken by Sir Richard Francis Burton and his companion, Algernon Swinburne."

Burton looked at Swinburne. The poet looked back.

"In 1861?" Burton said. "In our future?"

"After a fashion," the Arabian answered. He turned to Nightingale. "Florence, help me to my feet."

"You're not strong enough, sir. This charade is quite ridiculous."

"Stop quibbling and do as I say!"

Nightingale bent and took him by the elbow.

Krishnamurthy whispered to Burton, "He does so enjoy his dramatics."

El Yezdi gained his feet and stood unsteadily. He glowered at Burton as if expecting a challenge. When none came, he reached up to his mouth and pulled out a set of dentures, which he threw carelessly aside. His real teeth, exposed, were much smaller and in far better condition. Unbelting his robe, he shrugged it off and allowed it to fall to the floor, revealing padding strapped around his middle. Nightingale helped him remove it, until he was standing in trousers and shirt—a deep-chested and broad-shouldered man, whose stomach was paunchy with age but not fat.

He yanked the false beard from his face—a neatly trimmed white Van Dyke adorned his chin—then took hold of his nose and twisted off the theatrical putty that had made it so hooked. The milky eye followed; a thin saucer of smoked glass that fitted over the pupil. He slipped the *keffiyeh* from his head. His hair was short and white, the oddly glittering lines of a tattoo on his scalp visible through it. Finally, he used a handkerchief to wipe his face. Makeup came off, showing him to be in his mid-sixties or thereabouts.

Swinburne yelled.

Burton jumped to his feet, stepped back, fell against his armchair, and thudded onto the floor. With his eyes fixed on the old man, he scrambled backward until his shoulders hit the wall. His mouth worked but no sound came out. He couldn't tear his eyes away from the long, deep scar on the man's left cheek.

There could be no doubt about it.

Abdu El Yezdi was Sir Richard Francis Burton.

CHAPTER 23

CATACOMBS

"Believing as I do that man in the distant future will be a far more perfect creature than he now is, it is an intolerable thought that he and all other sentient beings are doomed to complete annihilation after such long-continued slow progress."
—CHARLES DARWIN

Burton's thoughts refused to coalesce. He was still numb.

After Abdu El Yezdi revealed his true identity, the meeting had ended. The old man was exhausted, Burton was paralysed by shock, and everyone else was badly in need of sleep. It was a little past four o'clock in the morning when Krishnamurthy escorted the explorer and poet to rooms prepared for them.

"I'll wake you at nine," the faux-constable said.

Burton possessed little awareness of his own actions. He undressed and got into bed. Sleep came fast—a response to trauma and fatigue—but he awoke just four hours later and lay staring at the ceiling, attempting to think coherently.

His mind fixated on the image of his own face, aged, worn, sick, and with eyes steeped in sadness and anger.

"Is that what I am to become?" he whispered.

He remembered the sound of camel bells, a tent in an oasis, the desert, a far-off horizon, and the promise of what lay beyond it.

One day, he would be physically incapable of exploration and discovery.

A momentary flicker in infinity, then we are gone.

Time is implacable. Time is cruel.

He got up and was washed and dressed by the time Krishnamurthy knocked at the door. The Indian led him to a dining room where he breakfasted with Swinburne, Daniel Gooch, and Florence Nightingale. The latter reported that El Yezdi was still sleeping and would be left undisturbed until he woke of his own accord.

"He's very frail, Sir Richard," she said, "and last night's performance was ill-advised."

"How long has he got?"

"His heart is damaged. It could be a matter of hours."

"Bismillah! Am I to witness my own death?"

"Is he really you, though?" Swinburne asked. "He's from a different version of our world, and as he said, change the opportunities and challenges that a man encounters and you'll change the man."

Gooch said, "I recommend we postpone the philosophical pondering. Finish eating, gentlemen; Mr. Brunel has more to tell you."

Half an hour later, he accompanied them to the famous engineer's office, where Krishnamurthy and Bhatti were waiting.

As he entered, Burton noticed that Brunel had a large canister affixed to his back.

"It's a battery," the mechanical man explained. "Unlike the common clockwork servants, my body is powered by electricity. It has internal batteries but they require recharging every forty-eight hours, and this—" he jerked a metal thumb over his shoulder at the cylinder, "—does the job."

Brunel gestured toward the armchairs. They settled, and he took the middle of the floor, facing them. In his clanging voice, he said, "You have met yourself, Sir Richard, but that other you was formed amid a tangle of particular circumstances that will occur in the near future—but in a world we do not inhabit. In the past of that world, a different Isambard Kingdom Brunel knew Henry Beresford, the Mad Marquess. Here, I never met the man. This idea—that there are multiple variants of our history and we are present in all of them—is difficult to comprehend, yet we must accept it as true if we are to understand our enemy."

Burton murmured, "I'm hardly in a position to oppose the notion."

"Indeed not. So, allow me to tell you a little more about the world the other you came from—"

"Please refer to him as Abdu El Yezdi," Burton interrupted. "It will be less confusing."

"Very well. In 1861, he killed the future Oxford, out of whose meddling these multiple histories were born. The following year, another man from the future tried to influence events. He was a Russian named Rasputin, who sent his spirit body back from 1914 in order to reshape the events that were leading to a war. El Yezdi killed him, too."

"He appears to be rather violent," Swinburne noted, with a glance at Burton.

"He's had to be," Brunel said. "And it's taken its toll."

Burton shifted uneasily in his chair. He lit a cheroot and raised it to his mouth with a trembling hand.

"In 'sixty-three," Brunel continued, "El Yezdi himself became what you might call a *chrononaut*. He was thrown into the future, into 1918, where a world war had decimated the British Empire, which was making its last stand in a city called—"

"Tabora," Burton croaked. "I witnessed its destruction last night."

Brunel chimed, "How?"

"In a vision, forced upon me by an entity that calls itself Perdurabo."

"Ah. Aleister Crowley."

"Who?"

"In the war that threatens, there will be three great powers, all mediums of startling potency. In Germany, a man named Friedrich Nietzsche; in Russia, the aforementioned Rasputin; and for the British Empire, Aleister Crowley, who calls himself Perdurabo. He is a traitor and a madman. He has come among us to undo all the good work Abdu El Yezdi has done."

"The manipulation of history," Swinburne said. "To avoid the war?"

"Yes. After witnessing the conflict in 1918, El Yezdi attempted to repair the damage that Oxford had done to the mechanism of time. He traveled back through history to 1840, to the scene of Victoria's assassination. When Oxford arrived from 2202, El Yezdi killed him—again. As it turned out, he also found himself responsible for Queen Victoria's death."

"The killing shot came from the rifle," Burton whispered, remembering Trounce's observation that the bullet had hit the monarch in the back of the head.

Brunel's brass face turned so that he appeared to be looking straight at the explorer. "You will quickly learn to appreciate, Sir Richard, that where time is concerned, paradoxes proliferate and are impossibly baffling to any mind—with the exception, perhaps, of Charles Babbage's. El Yezdi's multiple murder of Oxford is far from being the most difficult of them to comprehend. The oddest is that, because El Yezdi prevented Oxford from being thrown back to 1837, three years of history suddenly vanished."

"The Great Amnesia," Burton said. "The Mad Marquess must have written about his encounter with Oxford at the precise moment history changed. His diary entry is an anomaly."

"Oxford being thrown into 'thirty-seven, then *not* being thrown in 'thirty-seven, caused yet another branch to split from the original history—it is the one we inhabit—and El Yezdi was trapped in it. He'd already lived forty-two years in his own time, he spent four years in the future, and now he was back in 1840, aged forty-six, with his nineteen-year-old counterpart already there."

"Me," Burton said. "I always put it down to the effects of fever, but I think I felt his presence."

"There is a resonance between versions of anything that possesses a multiple existence," Brunel said. He rapped the side of his metal head. "The diamonds in which my consciousness resides, for example, are present many times over. Their resonation accentuates—even bestows—mediumistic abilities. It is how El Yezdi contacted Countess Sabina and through her began to shape a British Empire that would never go to war against Germany."

The engineer said to Burton, "You have, quite literally, made history."

Burton muttered, "And Perdurabo—Crowley—wants to destroy it."

"He doesn't believe the war can be avoided, so intends to ignite it earlier, before Germany can prepare. Once the conflict is won, he'll make himself ruler."

"Of Germany?" Swinburne asked.

"No, Mr. Swinburne, of the world. He has to be stopped."

Burton suddenly jumped to his feet. "Do you have a map of London, Mr. Brunel?"

The electric man nodded and looked at Gooch, who crossed to a cabinet and returned with a rolled map. He unfurled it on Brunel's desk, weighting the corners with a book, inkpot, spanner, and magnifying glass.

Everyone gathered around it.

Burton looked at the grandfather clock. It was eleven. He tapped a finger on the map. "Green Park. In exactly twenty-four hours, it will host a gathering of dignitaries from Britain and the Germanic states. The Central German Confederation will be formalised and our Alliance with it signed. Undoubtedly, Perdurabo will strike at the ceremony."

"He'll never get past the security," Brunel said.

"He might intend to overpower the police and King's Guard by force of numbers."

"Has he an army?" Krishnamurthy asked.

"He has the Cauldron. Aleister Crowley currently exists only as parasitical willpower—a *nosferatu*. His victims become un-dead and are proliferating throughout the East End. He has power over them, and is using them to whip up fear and anti-German sentiment in the local population."

A gruff voice came from the doorway. "Willpower, you say?"

They turned. Nurse Nightingale was guiding Abdu El Yezdi's bath chair in through the door.

"My associate, the French occultist Eliphas Levi, calls it *volonté*," Burton said.

His older self grunted an acknowledgment. "If Crowley is here only in such a form, we can be certain that his plans involve more than just a strike against the fledgling German Empire."

"You refer to his need for a body?"

"I do. He is obsessed with the idea that medical and scientific intervention might hasten a man toward a state of godhood. He will attempt to achieve that."

"A Supreme Man," Burton muttered.

"Or as Nietzsche will have it, an *Übermensch*."

"Artificially constructed?"

"I imagine so. I understand Galton escaped from Bedlam. Whatever he may have been in the original history, I've already seen him demonstrate just how thin is the line between genius and insanity. I have no doubt he's been recruited by Crowley to create a physical structure in which our enemy's *volonté* can be permanently housed."

Burton nodded. "He also has Darwin and a talented surgeon named Joseph Lister, though they're almost certainly being held against their will. And—" He hesitated.

"And what?" his other snapped.

"And he took one of the Sisters of Noble Benevolence."

El Yezdi closed his eyes and clutched the sides of his chair. "Not—not Sadhvi Raghavendra?"

"Yes."

"Damnation! Are you incapable of protecting anyone?"

"You," Burton snarled, "are better placed to answer that question. How many have you allowed to die, old man?"

El Yezdi sucked in a breath and placed a fist over his heart. His lips drew back over his teeth.

"Stop it!" Nightingale commanded.

Burton held up his hands placatingly and took a step backward. "The point," he said, "is that the presence alone of one of the Sisters accelerates healing. That, and the thefts of laboratory equipment and chemical supplies from locations all over the city, suggests that you're right."

Krishnamurthy said, "So he's set up a laboratory of some sort? Where? In the Cauldron? That seems unlikely. The whole district is a cesspit of crime and grime."

Burton noticed that Swinburne was becoming increasingly agitated, his limbs twitching and jerking spasmodically. He asked, "Algy?"

"Are you all blind?" the poet suddenly screeched, jumping into the air and swiping an arm at them. "My giddy aunt! Can't you see it?"

Abdu El Yezdi chuckled. "How I've missed you, Algy! What revelation have you for us?"

"You!" Swinburne yelled, jabbing a finger at El Yezdi, "And you!" He pointed at Burton. "We've deduced what Crowley is here for, but you both appear to have forgotten what he did first, the moment he arrived. He came after you. He killed Isabel to hurt you. My hat! He even told you outright that he wants you at his feet. Why? Obviously because he considers you his biggest threat."

The two Burtons looked at each other. The younger of them said, "So?"

"He didn't kill you," Swinburne said. "Surely, therefore, he hasn't discounted your possible interference. Wherever he is, it must be somewhere he thinks you'd never go."

"Which is where?" El Yezdi asked.

"Underground, of course! You hate it! You're claustrophobic. Surely Sir Richard Francis Burton will forever be associated with wide-open spaces. Never with caves or vaults or tunnels! We've already seen Perdurabo hiding beneath Old Wardour Castle, and his people using the river under Saint Martin's Lane. Doesn't that give us an indication of his methods? And what better opportunity to make use of such than now, when Bazalgette is burrowing beneath the city and opening up ages-old subterranean thoroughfares?"

Brunel clanged, "But surely, if Crowley and his allies are using the sewer tunnels, the workers would have encountered them?"

Swinburne let loose a piercing shriek and danced around the desk, gesticulating wildly. "They have! The Norwood builders! The Norwood builders! Ghosts! The River Effra!"

"Hmm," Daniel Gooch said. "It's true, our workers have downed tools and are refusing to construct the tunnel any farther than Herne Hill." He put a finger on the map. "The mouth of the Effra is a little east of Battersea, here, beside Vauxhall Bridge. The river runs beneath Kennington, Stockwell, and Brixton. That length of it has been enclosed in a brick tunnel, but beyond, up past Norwood to its source, the river is so far untouched."

"And it flows right past Norwood Cemetery," Swinburne declared, "which is famous for its extensive vaults and catacombs."

"You think Crowley has set up a laboratory in them?" Bhatti asked.

El Yezdi slapped the side of his chair. "By Allah's beard! I learned a long time ago to listen to Algy!" He waved a hand at Burton. "Go! Investigate!"

Burton glanced at the map. His face whitened. "Through five miles of tunnel?"

"Bhatti and I will take the tunnel, Sir Richard," Krishnamurthy said. "You and Mr. Swinburne fly rotorchairs to the graveyard and enter the catacombs from above."

Burton couldn't hide his relief. El Yezdi snorted disdainfully. The explorer glowered at him then turned to Brunel. "Will you send someone to fetch Detective Inspector Trounce and Eliphas Levi? If we're to hunt the *nosferatu*, I'd like those two with us."

"I'll send a rotorship to Scotland Yard at once."

Brunel departed. Krishnamurthy crossed to a cabinet, opened it, and started to remove weapons from it.

Swinburne looked at El Yezdi. "The Swinburne you knew—was he like me?"

"Yes. A couple of years older."

"What became of him?"

The old man thought for a moment then replied, "I've learned to consider time an organic thing, Algy. We are all entwined in it, we are all subject to it, and the choices we all make define its ever-developing patterns and rhythms. The Swinburne I knew came to understand its intricacies perhaps better than any other living person. I will not tell you his eventual fate—I don't want to influence your behaviour—but I know he grew to be happy and content with his lot."

"I don't suppose I can ask for anything more than that," Swinburne said, and declaimed, *"For in the days we know not of did Fate begin weaving the web of days that wove your doom."*

"In the days we know not of?" El Yezdi exclaimed. "No, no. Fate is weaving today, Algy! Today!" He suddenly became quiet, and his eyes appeared to focus inward. "So be careful," he muttered. "Don't get tangled in the skein, as I did." He turned to Nightingale. "Take me to my room, nurse."

She wheeled him out.

Burton visibly relaxed.

"Difficult?" Swinburne asked.

"Sharing a room with my dying counterpart? Yes, Algy. Difficult."

Bhatti and Krishnamurthy had armed themselves with a brace of pistols apiece. They passed revolvers to Burton and Swinburne. "It will take us a minimum of two hours to traverse the tunnel," Krishnamurthy said. "Let's say three, to be safe, as the upper reaches won't be easy. We'll leave immediately. Give us a head start. We should try to time it so we arrive in the catacombs simultaneously."

Burton shook both men by the hand. "No rash actions," he advised. "I want to get the measure of Crowley's forces, nothing more. Keep your heads down. We'll observe, evaluate, and return. Once we know exactly what we're facing, we'll plan our next move."

The two Indians secured their weapons in their waistbands and left the room.

Burton and Swinburne waited with Daniel Gooch for Trounce and Levi's arrival. After an hour had passed, they divined that Brunel's men were having difficulty in locating the duo. Undoubtedly, the detective and occultist were caught up in the commotion in and around the East End.

"We'll proceed without them," Burton decided. "Bhatti and Krishnamurthy must be near halfway through the tunnel by now. Let's go."

Gooch led them through the station and out into the quadrangle where two rotorchairs had been prepared. They mounted the machines, pulled goggles over their eyes, and started the engines. Gooch gave them a thumbs-up as they rose on columns of steam and soared into the rain-filled air.

The cloud cover was thick, dark, and low. Remaining below it, they flew across the Royal Navy Air Service Station, past a network of railway tracks and rail yards, and out over the streets, homes, tanneries, and workhouses of Wandsworth. Angling southward, they passed over Clapham and Streatham. To his left, Burton saw Herne Hill. He guessed Bhatti and Krishnamurthy had reached and passed beneath it, and were by now following the river along the ages-old course it had cut through the area's dense clay. The thought of it made him clench his teeth.

The rain suddenly intensified and lightning flashed. The clouds had taken on a curious formation, appearing to be twisting and circling around themselves.

A mile or so farther south, a wooded hill hove into view. Burton steered toward it, flew over it, and saw gravestones and mausoleums huddled amid the trees. He kept going, before landing in the yard of an inn a little to the south of the burial ground.

Swinburne's machine thumped down beside him.

"Phew!" the poet cried out as the rotors slowed and stopped. "I'm wet to the bones!"

Burton removed his goggles and disembarked.

A man with an umbrella stepped out of the inn and pointed at a large wooden shed on the other side of the yard. "Hallo, gentlemen! You can park 'em in there, if you like. There's a fee, though, unless you want to put up in the inn, of course."

Burton paid and, to Swinburne's evident dismay, refused the offer of a hot toddy. "There's no time for indulgences, as you well know," he told his companion as they dragged their rotorchairs into the shelter.

"If my insides aren't warmed soon, I shall come down with a cold," the poet grumbled.

"If Aleister Crowley has his way, you'll likely suffer far worse," Burton said. "Do you think a world beneath his heel will be fit for a poet?"

Swinburne gave a cry of protest and punched at the air. "Certainly not! Let's get the dog!"

Exiting the yard, they crossed a road, turned a corner, and followed a puddled lane along to the boundary of the graveyard. High pointed railings, designed to deter resurrectionists, enclosed the hill, but after following them around, the two men came to a secured back gate. Burton pulled a set of lockpicks from his pocket. "I've had these since India," he said, applying them to the portal's keyhole. "They were presented to me by Sir Charles Napier when he made me his agent. I've only used them once before."

"Breaking into an enemy's hideaway to reconnoitre?" Swinburne asked.

"No. Into a nunnery for a romantic assignation."

The poet squealed his delight then gave a cry of alarm as thunder boomed overhead.

"Great Scott!" he cried out, pointing at the sky. "Look at that!"

Directly above them, the clouds were swirling around a central point from which lightning crackled and sizzled.

"The eye of the storm," Burton said. "Ah! Got it!"

The locked clicked and he pushed the gate open.

They entered the cemetery and started along a path through the trees. The steeple of the Episcopal Church could be glimpsed through the branches and, as they rounded a bend, the building itself came into view. A man in a heavy overcoat was sheltering beneath the arch of its front door. He saw them, stepped out, and shouted, "I say! Can I help? Are you looking for a particular tomb? Not a good day for it! It's tipping it down!"

"You work here, sir?" Burton asked as the man approached.

"Um. Um. Yes, I'm the sexton. May I ask who you've come to visit?"

"We're here to see the catacombs, Mr.—?"

"Oh. Solomon. Yes. Well. Yes. They are rather splendid."

"How do we enter them?"

"Ah. Er. I suppose—yes. I could show you. They're dry, I'll say that for 'em."

"Thank you."

"This way, then."

Solomon walked back to the church door, opened it, and waved them through. He followed then guided them to the right, skirting around the base of the wall, along the outer aisle, and forward into the right-hand transept. He indicated an arch at the top of descending stone steps. "The entrance. Um. Shall we?"

"Lead the way," Burton responded.

Solomon took a clockwork lantern from his pocket. Its light flared. He started down the stairs with Burton and Swinburne behind.

"No priests, Mr. Solomon?" Swinburne asked. "The church seems awfully empty."

"Um. Um. Not much call for it on a rainy weekday, I suppose, sir. The vicar is out visiting the sick and elderly, I should think. Ah, here we are."

They'd arrived at a wooden door, which Solomon pushed open. Its creak echoed hollowly. Burton's mouth suddenly felt dry. He reached into his pocket and pulled out his own lantern, opening it, winding it, and holding it high.

"Oh, good," Solomon mumbled. "That'll help."

The sexton led them into the catacomb; a tall, long, and narrow vaulted passage of elegant brickwork with three arched doorways on either side, each opening onto narrower but longer corridors. Coffins lay in wall niches, and decorative wrought-iron gates opened onto small bays and loculi in which individuals and families had been interred.

"Shall I light the wall lamps, sir?" Solomon asked.

"Please," Burton replied. The chill air penetrated his damp clothes and caused him to tremble. Shadows shifted as if creeping furtively away from the visitors.

The duo moved forward, staying close to Solomon as he passed from one wall-mounted lamp to another, applying a flame to each. As the illumination swelled through the passage, Burton felt the presence of the dead crowding around him. He crossed to an arch and raised his lamp, revealing a long, straight corridor.

Silence reigned.

Solomon watched as the explorer and poet passed among the coffins, examining every nook and cranny of the vaults. "Who are you looking for?" he asked.

Burton stopped and regarded the sexton, then gave an exasperated sigh, crossed to him, and punched him in the face. Solomon fell back against a gate, regained his balance, and launched a fist at his assailant. Burton pulled his chin back, avoiding the blow. He slammed his knuckles into the man's stomach. Solomon doubled over and vomited.

"Hold the lamp, Algy."

Swinburne took the proffered lantern and asked, "Have you taken a dislike to him?"

Burton took Solomon by the hair and swung him up, around, and face-first into the wall. He grabbed the sexton's left hand and brutally forced it between his shoulder blades. Solomon screamed with pain.

"Idiot!" Burton spat. "Walking around with that pin in your coat lapel."

"Pin?" Swinburne enquired.

"He's an Enochian. It's their club insignia."

"Oh, I see." The poet ran forward and administered a hard kick to the side of Solomon's knee. "Speak!" he screeched.

"Ow!" Solomon yelled.

"Where is Perdurabo?" Burton demanded.

"I don't know what you're talking about!"

Swinburne kicked him again.

"Ouch! Stop it!" Solomon cried out.

"There's more to these catacombs than meets the eye," Burton snarled. "Start talking."

"Go to hell!"

A loud snap sounded. The sexton screamed.

"You have nine digits remaining," Burton said. "I'll continue to break them one by one."

"Please."

Burton took hold of the man's forefinger.

"No," Solomon whimpered. "All right. All right. There are more catacombs."

"Where?"

"Under the Dissenters' Church."

"So take us to it."

"God! Ease up! Don't break my fingers. I—I play the piano."

"I have very little interest in your pastimes, Solomon."

"Just don't hurt me. We don't have to go to the church. A secret passage connects the two catacombs. Over there." He nodded his head toward the far end of the main corridor.

Burton pulled him away from the wall and, without releasing the man's hand, pushed him along to the indicated spot. Swinburne followed. With his right foot, Solomon nudged a brick at the base of the wall. It had an eye carved into it. "Push this."

Swinburne bent and did so. There was a soft clunk.

"Give the wall a shove," Solomon said.

The poet put his shoulder against the brickwork. A square section of it swung inward.

"Much obliged," Burton said. He twisted the sexton around and delivered a left hook to his jaw. Solomon crumpled to the floor. The explorer rubbed his forearm and muttered, "The damned thing still hurts. What do you see, Algy?"

"A long, dusty corridor. It's rather narrow, I'm afraid."

Burton took the lantern from the poet and, holding it before him, squeezed into the passage.

"Quietly does it," he said, and pushed ahead.

The path sloped downward.

Sooner than Burton expected, a blank wall barred his way. He couldn't move forward. Swinburne, behind him, was blocking the route back. He stopped, felt trapped, and for a moment was unable even to think.

"There must be another hidden switch," Swinburne whispered.

His voice broke Burton's paralysis. The explorer lowered his lantern and immediately saw the eye design near the base of the wall. He crouched and, with his right hand, took the pistol from his waistband. With his left, he turned off the lamp, reached into the darkness, and placed his fingers against the brick.

"Not a sound, Algy," he hissed.

He pressed—*clunk!*—then reached up and pushed against the barrier. It gave a little, clicked, and swung inward to reveal a dimly lit vault.

Burton leaned forward and peered out. There was no one in sight but light was streaming past a corner to his left and he could hear voices. He crawled from the secret tunnel and straightened. Swinburne emerged and stood beside him. They exchanged a glance, then—bending low and moving on tiptoe—crept past coffin-filled alcoves and gated bays toward the illumination.

A weird shadow convulsed and quivered across the wall opposite the end of the passage, as if cast by a tangle of struggling bodies. Burton and Swinburne froze and stared as a part of it extended and uncurled, and they recognised a hand. It possessed too many fingers and the limb it was attached to had three elbows.

A voice echoed, "Is something wrong, Mr. Hare? You appear to be agitated."

A dreadful gurgling voice responded, "I sense something, Mr. Burke. A presence."

"Check, but don't be long. The storm is almost at its height. Your assistance may be required."

The shadow lurched. Parts of it unfolded. Other parts coiled.

Seven clawed talons curled around the corner of the wall.

Burton tried to raise his pistol but was transfixed by a dreadful fascination. Swinburne, too, was rooted to the spot.

With terrifying swiftness, the source of the shadow floundered into view and rushed at them. There was a brief glimpse of thrashing multi-jointed limbs; of an incomprehensible knot of arms and legs and boneless appendages; of many black, glittering eyes and a hideous fanged maw; then it was upon them, and Burton felt himself gripped, crushed, and smothered.

He yelled, fired the pistol, and blacked out.

CHAPTER 24

THE TRANS-TEMPORAL MAN

"In Magick, on the contrary, one passes through the veil of the
exterior world (which, as in Yoga, but in another sense, becomes
'unreal' by comparison as one passes beyond), one creates a subtle
body (instrument is a better term) called the Body of Light; this
one develops and controls; it gains new powers as one progresses,
usually by means of what is called 'initiation': finally, one carries
on almost one's whole life in this Body of Light, and achieves in
its own way the mastery of the Universe."
—ALEISTER CROWLEY, *MAGICK WITHOUT TEARS*

Burton opened his eyes and saw, inches in front of them, orange light
wavering across white silk padding. Something was burning his hand.
He moved it and recognised the shape of his clockwork lantern. He realised
that he and it were inside a coffin.

Buried alive.

With a yell of terror, he slammed his hands into the lid. It came loose,
slid aside, and fell away with a loud crash. He threw himself out of the box
and tumbled to the floor, panting wildly, his fingers digging into the crevices
between flagstones, clinging to physical existence.

Panic slowly loosed its claws and his senses stabilised. He glanced around.
He was in one of the bays; its iron gate closed, chained, and padlocked. There
were five coffins occupying the shelves; the one he'd been in, three that were
dusty and cobwebbed, and another that appeared new. From inside the latter,
he heard movement.

Burton pushed himself to his feet, took hold of the coffin's lid, and eased it open. Swinburne was inside. The poet blinked and mumbled, "I'm famished. What's for breakfast?"

"It's not morning, Algy. We're in the catacombs."

Swinburne sat up, his eyes widening. "By my Aunt Tabitha's terrible touring hat! I dreamt a horrible monster!"

A familiar chorus of voices said, "No dream, Mr. Swinburne. It was Gregory Hare."

Burton turned. Perdurabo—still inhabiting the body of Thomas Honesty—was standing on the other side of the gate, his eyes black and his mouth twisted into a nasty smile. There were beads of sweat on his forehead. He said, "You caused him considerable damage, Burton; left him a bruised brain inside a burned and mangled carcass. You have my gratitude."

"Gratitude?"

"Growing a new body from material harvested from corpses is a complex business even in 1918, where it's a well-established science. My people have had to cobble equipment together from what they could find here in your primitive time. Our first creation was an utter mess, but Mr. Hare, who would otherwise have died, allowed us to transfer his consciousness into it, which kept it alive and thus allowed us to examine its faults and perfect the technique." He held an arm out to the left, and from that direction a shuffling and dragging sounded. The abomination that had captured them flopped into view. Its many eyes glittered. Its profusion of knees and elbows angled chaotically. Its long, many-jointed fingers twitched and trembled. A large nodule at the side of its misshapen core split wetly open to reveal long, uneven fangs.

"Good afternoon, Sir Richard," it bubbled. "Had I known it was you at Down House, I would have broken your neck rather than your arm."

"Hello, Mr. Hare," Burton replied. "You're looking well."

Swinburne gave a screech of amusement.

"Let me have him," Hare said to Perdurabo. "I'm hungry."

His master waved him away impatiently. "Later. I want him to witness my rebirth. Go and check the other catacomb, Mr. Hare. He may have brought more men with him."

Reluctantly, the creature scrambled away, its talons clicking and scraping across the floor.

Perdurabo wiped his face with his sleeve and closed his eyes. He swayed slightly, appearing to lose himself momentarily.

"You're pale," Burton said. "Weak. The hour, I suppose."

The black eyes met his. "Indeed so. It is difficult for me to move this body during the daylight hours. Tom Honesty is a good deal stronger than he looks. He's a very uncomfortable vehicle, Burton. I shall be glad to be rid of him."

Perdurabo turned his attention to Swinburne. "I'm honoured to make your acquaintance, Mr. Swinburne. In my history, you are regarded as England's finest romantic poet. I have admired your work since I was a boy." He stopped, frowned, and continued, "It is curious, though—during the final days of the war in Africa, I sensed a vague but omniscient presence which I could never identify. You exude the same charisma. Have you travelled to the future, sir?"

"Knowing I'd find you there?" the poet responded. "Most certainly not."

Perdurabo threw his arms wide. "Ah. Such are the convolutions of time. What is true of this history is not necessarily the truth of another. Confessions and denials mean far less when every possibility gives birth to a new reality." He closed his eyes again and put his head back. Dreamily, he continued, "I can feel them; all those futures. Division after division; an infinity of causes and consequences blurring together. Time itself is evolving, my friends, and mankind must review his relationship with it if he is to survive."

"The 1918 you came from," Burton interrupted, "it is not a part of this world's future. Why did you cross into an alternate past? And of all of them, why this one in particular, Crowley?"

At the use of his real name, Thomas Honesty's eyebrows shot up. "You know more than I anticipated! How?"

"I have my resources."

"And are hardly likely to give them away. Very well. I understand. You play a very good game, but in vain, I'm afraid, for there is but one of you—" the abundant tones of his voice suddenly intensified and separated from one another slightly, so, even more, it sounded as if a crowd was speaking all at once, "—while I am manifold."

"And tedious," Swinburne added.

Perdurabo glared at the little poet, then laughed. "Oh, Mr. Swinburne!" he cried out. "I shall enjoy killing you!"

He staggered slightly and hissed, "Damn this bloody groundsman! Will he not stop fighting me?"

"Answer the question," Burton demanded.

"Wait." Crowley put his fingertips to his temples, screwed up his eyes, and concentrated. Half a minute later, he sighed, dropped his arms to his sides, and smiled. "Why this history? For two reasons: it is the only one in which Bismarck has been sidelined and Germanic nationalism quelled to the point where a surprise attack can, in a single stroke, put paid to their ability to wage war; and it is the only one in whose future I don't exist."

"For the latter reason alone," Swinburne interjected, "it is surely the best of them."

"It's a vacuum," Crowley continued. "For whatever reason, it appears my parents do not meet in this version of reality. My absence means I can gather all my myriad variations here without stepping on my own toes, so to speak." He jerked a thumb over his shoulder. "We shall be unified in a single body."

Burton looked past him and for the first time properly took in the chamber beyond.

The catacombs beneath the Dissenters' Church were bigger than the neighbouring tunnels—wider, taller, and evidently more extensive. From the confines of his cell, which was at one end of the main gallery, Burton could see many more passages branching off from it. The general topography he took in automatically, but it was the scene in the central corridor that engaged his full attention. The floorspace was crowded with machinery, chemical apparatus, vats, surgical beds, and a network of pipes and wires. It was all as exotic and arcane as the paraphernalia he'd seen in Battersea Power Station but, unlike the equipment there, this had a central focus: a throne upon which a body— naked but for a loincloth—was strapped.

"The Supreme Man," Crowley said. "Humanity evolved. Designed according to Mr. Darwin's extrapolations, created by Mr. Galton's methods, and maintained by Mr. Joseph Lister's genius."

The figure was, Burton estimated, about seven feet tall. Its skin was bluish-grey, stretched over lean muscles and a rangy skeletal structure; long-limbed, narrow-hipped, broad-shouldered, and deep-chested; a body that obviously possessed both strength and speed. The head, though, was disproportionately big, with a massive cranium that swelled up and back from a small, oddly delicate face. The cheekbones were fine and angular; the nose comprised of two vertical slits; the mouth small and lipless; and the jaw pointed. The eyes were closed, slanted, and very large.

The body was completely motionless, not even breathing.

"It holds such a brain, Burton; a central sorting house for all the many Aleister Crowleys. My perception will gain clarity across every strand of time. Where you must make a single choice whenever life offers you options, I'll be able to take every course of action and see all the possible consequences at work."

There were people moving around the throne. Burton saw Charles Darwin and a man he recognised from portraits as Francis Galton. There were four Enochians, though he felt certain others were present but out of sight.

The muffled rumble of thunder penetrated the ceiling. Crowley looked up at it and gave a nod of satisfaction. A woman emerged from one of the side passages and approached.

"Sadhvi!" Burton shouted. "Are you all right?"

Sister Sadhvi Raghavendra ignored him and said to Crowley, "We cannot delay any longer, Master. The storm is at its height. Mr. Burke has gone to the steeple to raise the mast."

Burton noticed that her eyes were glazed. She was in a trance.

Crowley addressed his captives. "I must take my leave of you for a little while. I'm glad you both came. I want you to see this." He turned away and followed Raghavendra toward the machinery.

Swinburne nudged Burton in the ribs and whispered, "Look at the far end of the corridor. They've dug a hole through the wall. Do you suppose that leads to the River Effra? Perhaps Bhatti and Krishnamurthy are in the shadows there."

The explorer felt for his pistol and wasn't surprised to find it gone. "Unarmed," he muttered. "But I still have these." He glanced up, saw that Crowley, Galton, and Darwin were examining a piece of equipment, and pulled the lock-picks from his pocket. "Keep your eyes on that opening, Algy. Maybe we can join Bhatti and Krishnamurthy in a concerted attack."

He set to work on the padlock.

"Now would be a good time," Swinburne murmured, "while neither Burke nor Hare are here."

Focused on his task, Burton asked, "What are our captors up to?"

"They're fitting some sort of device to their creation's head. Like a crown but with wires extending from it and connected to an ugly metal contraption. By George! They need to let William Morris loose on all this machinery. It's hideously utilitarian."

Burton felt the ground vibrate beneath his feet again. He heard a distant roar.

"The instruments are measuring the storm," Swinburne observed. "Dials and lights are responding to every crack of thunder."

"This weather is no more natural than that which gripped the *Royal Charter*," Burton noted. "The science of the future has given Crowley mediumistic control of atmospheric conditions."

"That seems more like magic."

"So does any science before one understands it."

The padlock clicked.

"Ah! Bingo!"

He looked up and saw Francis Galton adjust something on the crown-like apparatus before moving over to a sparking and hissing stack of metal disks.

"Burton," Crowley called. "Pay attention. In a few moments you'll witness the advent of a new species of human. I have referred to him as Supreme Man, but I think perhaps there's a better designation."

"Supercilious Man?" Swinburne suggested.

"You're beginning to irritate me, Mr. Swinburne."

"I do hope so."

"Trans-Temporal Man!" Crowley announced. "Let him be born! Do it now, if you please, Mr. Galton."

Galton took hold of a lever and pulled it. Burton and Swinburne raised their hands before their faces as the catacomb was suddenly filled with lightning. Electricity leaped from machine to machine, snapping and cracking, spitting and hissing; so bright they could see it even through their eyelids. Bolt after bolt arced into the crown, and the figure beneath it jerked and spasmed in its restraints.

For thirty seconds, they were blinded and deafened by the din, and their skin crawled as the air itself was filled with static. Then, rapidly, the tumult subsided and as Burton unshielded his eyes there came a final flash, which momentarily illuminated the mouth of the hole in the wall, revealing the faces of Bhatti and Krishnamurthy.

The two men ducked back out of sight.

"Prepare yourself," Burton whispered to Swinburne. "On my word, we'll rush out and cause as much damage as possible."

"It breathes!" Crowley cried out. "It breathes! See, Burton—I have made a new life!"

Through the bars of the gate, the explorer examined Crowley's creation. Its wide chest was rising and falling in steady respiration.

"Lister!" Crowley barked. "Examine it! Examine it, man!"

A young fellow, remarkable for his high forehead and bushy sideburns, stepped into view. He listened with a trumpet-shaped stethoscope to the tall figure's heart, took its pulse, then pressed an instrument to the side of its head and pushed a button. The artificial man groaned, then became still as Lister stepped away.

"It's ready," he said.

Crowley nodded his satisfaction. He stepped to the throne and stood face to face with his creation. Putting his hands to either side of its head, he used his thumbs to push open its eyelids, revealing the black eyeballs beneath. He gazed into them and said to one of the Enochians, "This will take a few minutes. Do not disturb me. When the transfer is complete, this body I currently inhabit will collapse. Imprison it. I intend to make Thomas Honesty suffer for all the trouble he's given me."

He became silent and motionless.

Lister, Darwin, Galton, Sister Raghavendra, and the Enochians stood back and watched, oblivious to all but Crowley.

"Quietly," Burton hissed. "We'll move around behind them. Grab something to clock the Enochians over the head with."

He eased open the gate and slipped out into the passage. Swinburne followed. Bhatti and Krishnamurthy cautiously emerged from the burrow at the other end of the catacomb. They'd obviously watched and waited for Burton to make the first move. He signalled to them to keep to the right, where they wouldn't be seen unless someone turned around.

The explorer inched past a quietly buzzing metal structure, squatted, and put up a hand to signal Krishnamurthy to halt. The young Indian nodded, then looked horrified, raised his pistol, pointed it at Burton, and fired. The report was tremendous in the enclosed space. Burton felt the bullet brush past his ear and thud into something behind him. He turned. Hare loomed over him. Swinburne hollered as a ten-fingered hand clamped his forearm, yanked him into the air, and hurled him spinning into a wall. Burton dived toward a length of pipe he saw on a workbench, intending to employ it as a cudgel. Hare's great weight thumped down onto him before he reached it. He was aware of shouts and screams. More shots resounded through the chamber. A stone surface slammed into his face. He was flung upward, hit the ceiling hard, and dropped onto a table. It collapsed beneath him. Tools clanged across the floor. Burton tried to rise but the heel of a foot smashed into the side of his face. He went down again, felt himself lifted, and was enveloped in a crushing embrace.

Through blurring eyes, he saw Thomas Honesty fall back from the throne and collapse to the floor; saw the Enochians drawing pistols; saw everyone scattering for cover. Reports rent the air as guns fired.

Burton felt himself turned and forced down, back first, onto a knotted limb. His spine was bent to its limit then pushed beyond it. Pain flared. With his one free hand he punched, grabbed, and clawed, but to no effect. He couldn't breathe, couldn't think.

The agony increased. His vertebrae crunched. Darkness narrowed his vision as if he were sinking into a well.

He groped for his jacket pocket, found the opening, slipped his fingers into it, and retrieved the lock-pick.

Momentarily, there was nothing, then Burton's senses returned as he sprawled backward onto the floor, felt a tremendous release, and looked up at the bellowing and thrashing monstrosity standing over him. The lock-pick was deeply embedded in one of Hare's many eyes.

The explorer rolled out of reach and tried to take measure of the chaos around him. Swinburne was nearby, grappling with Francis Galton, the two men rolling on the floor, screaming and shouting as they punched and wrestled.

One of the Enochians was down with a bullet in his shoulder, but two more men, who'd been working in one of the side tunnels, had raced out and were taking pot-shots at Bhatti and Krishnamurthy, pinning them in a corner behind a barrel-shaped contraption.

Crowley's mesmerised captives clung to the ground, making themselves as small as possible. Sadhvi Raghavendra was nearby, crouching beside a thick column of bundled cables. Burton crawled toward her. Bullets ricocheted around him.

The Trans-Temporal Man opened his jet-black eyes. He turned his head and shouted at one of the Enochians, "Get over here and unstrap me. At once!"

"Sadhvi!" Burton called. He put his hand to the side of her jaw and turned her face until she was looking dazedly at him. "Break loose! Don't let him control you."

The explorer radiated mesmeric authority. It was a technique he'd practised many times, attempting to dominate and influence through the eyes alone—but he'd only ever succeeded with it after preparation and in silent and calm environments. How could it possibly be effective in the midst of a pitched battle?

"Feel his presence in your mind," he shouted above the din, "and step aside from it. Step aside, Sadhvi. He has no control over you."

She frowned and blinked in confusion. All of a sudden, she and the column and the wall behind it jerked away from Burton and rapidly receded. For an instant, his disoriented mind struggled to comprehend what was happening, then he realised something was gripping his ankle and dragging him away from her. He snatched at a table leg. The furniture overturned, sending short lengths of pipe clanking onto the flagstones. He grabbed one, rolled onto his back, and used it to club Gregory Hare. The creature's hold loosened. Burton kicked himself free, staggered to his feet, reversed the pipe in his grip, and holding it at one end with both hands, stabbed it downward into to misshapen mass of Hare's body. It pierced the mottled skin and sank into flesh. Hare emitted an ear-splitting noise, like the whistle of a locomotive, and shoved Burton away, sending him reeling into a workbench.

Swinburne kicked free of Galton, charged at the thrashing creature, and launched himself into the air, landing amid the flailing limbs and applying his full weight to the pipe. It sank deeper. Blood fountained from its end.

Krishnamurthy bellowed across the chamber, "Get away from it, Swinburne!"

Before the poet could oblige, a knotted fist caught him on the point of the chin. His head snapped back and he toppled to the floor, skidding across it, leaving a smear of Hare's blood behind him.

Krishnamurthy immediately jumped from cover and loosed a volley of shots. Burton, on his knees, felt the bullets drilling through the air above him and heard them thump into Hare's body.

Hare shrieked and tumbled backward.

The explorer yelled, "Straight to hell with you, Gregory Hare!"

Beyond the floundering creature, Damien Burke stepped into view, having returned from the Dissenters' Church. He calmly took in the scene, pulled the odd-looking cactus pistol from his pocket, and shot a spine into Swinburne, who was struggling to his feet. The poet sagged back to the flagstones.

Burke turned his attention to Burton. The explorer scrabbled away from him but felt a sharp pain in the side of his neck. He reached up and plucked a spine from it. His senses began to swim. He sagged onto his side and, with dimming vision, watched as one of the Enochians unstrapped Crowley. The Trans-Temporal Man rose from the throne and shouted, "Enough of this!"

The gunfire stopped. Burton heard revolvers clicking fruitlessly. Those machines that were still sparking fell silent. Nothing that required ignition functioned.

Crowley vaulted over a bench, pounced on Krishnamurthy and Bhatti, and knocked their heads together. They folded to the floor.

Burton tried to rise but the strength was draining from him.

"Mr. Burke," Crowley said, "check the cell. I want to know how Burton got out of it."

An Enochian snatched up a large spanner, strode to the explorer, and stood over him. "Shall I kill him, Master?"

"Certainly not. Empty his pockets, and be thorough about it."

Burton was unable to offer resistance as his clothes were searched. It took all his concentration just to cling to consciousness.

"I think he picked the lock," Burke reported.

Crowley bent and hauled Krishnamurthy up by his collar. He dragged him toward one of the bays. "Find whatever he used."

"A locksmith's tool," Burke replied. "Mr. Hare has it in his eye. He's dead. May I kick Burton in the head, Mr. Crowley?"

"Yes, Mr. Burke, but I'd be obliged if you'd avoid doing any critical damage."

Groggily, Burton pushed himself up on his elbows and looked at Burke as he approached.

"You killed my partner," Burke said.

Burton sneered and slurred, "Think nothing of it. It was my pleasure."

A boot smashed viciously into his jaw.

Awareness came, departed, and returned. Hazy shapes moved, and voices drifted in and out of cognition. Slowly Burton realised that the cold, flat surface pressing against the side of his face was a flagstone. Blurs coalesced and gained edges. He saw a barred gate.

He was back inside his cell, with the five coffins, but without Swinburne. Instead, he found Thomas Honesty sprawled beside him.

The explorer stifled a groan, rolled over, and sat up. The cell swayed around him. He held his head in his hands and fought the urge to vomit.

I'm tired. So bloody tired. How much more of this madness can I take?

As much as is necessary to get the job done.

Then Damascus.

Except he didn't want Damascus any more.

He gritted his teeth, raised his head, and looked at Honesty. The groundsman's eyes were open but glazed, his face slack.

Burton reached out, shook him by the shoulder, and croaked, "How are you feeling, old chap?"

"Where am I?" Honesty slurred.

"That's a long story. What do you remember?"

The man rubbed his eyes. "Nothing. Saw you murder John Judge. Nightmares. Have I—have I been in the Cauldron? Why do I think that? I recall—no—I don't know. By God, I feel weak."

Burton got to his feet. His head was aching abominably and his lower left molars felt loose. Half-dried blood caked his moustache, lips, and the left side of his face. His arm was throbbing.

He looked through the gate. Crowley's people were clearing the central passage, moving the machines and equipment into the side corridors. The twisted, multi-limbed carcass of Gregory Hare lay where it had fallen, with blood pooled around it. The Trans-Temporal Man was sitting cross-legged on a table and appeared to be meditating.

A voice hissed from the cell to the right. "Sir Richard, are you with us?"

"Is that you, Krishnamurthy?"

"Yes. I'm sorry, sir—that didn't quite go to plan."

"My fault. I shouldn't have got caught in the first place. Is Algy with you?"

"No, just Bhatti."

Swinburne's voice came from the left. "I'm here. What shall we do?"

"Watch and wait."

Sister Raghavendra, perhaps hearing the whispering, looked up and saw that Burton had revived. She walked over and checked the padlock. "If you attempt to escape again, Sir Richard, you'll be shot in the kneecaps. The Master wants you alive but he has no reservations about causing you immense pain. Tomorrow you will serve not a primitive government, but a visionary leader."

"A despot!" Burton snorted.

She winked at him. "Benign. All those who support him will be artificially advanced to a new stage of physical and mental development."

"And those who oppose?" he asked, puzzled by the wink.

"They will provide manual labour or die." Raghavendra leaned closer to the bars and, in barely audible tones, said, "I'm free of him but he doesn't realise it. Stand ready, Richard. I'll do what I can." Aloud, she added, "Do not cause further disruption. If you attempt anything, your friends will be killed in front of you."

"What's he doing?" Burton mouthed, nodding his head in Crowley's direction.

"He's settling into his new form. Its brain has been designed to accentuate his mediumistic connection with his alternate selves but it will take him time to learn how to use it. I have to leave you now, else I'll rouse suspicion."

She moved away.

Burton watched her go then turned back to Honesty and squatted beside him, peering into his eyes. "You were possessed, Mr. Honesty. I shall try to explain."

For half an hour, the explorer spoke quietly and rapidly, describing the *nosferatu* and how, like a parasite, it had lodged in John Judge before transplanting itself into Honesty. He told how Honesty had been used to create *strigoi morti* in the East End, their presence causing panic, and how that panic had been channelled into rioting by the Enochians' seditious anti-German campaigning.

"Un-dead," Honesty mumbled. "And me? Oh, God! Am I *strigoi morti*?"

"I don't think so. Perdurabo can't feed off the *volonté* of a body he inhabits and didn't occupy you long enough to transform you into a *nosferatu*, but when we're through with all this, we'll have Monsieur Levi examine you to make sure."

Burton pointed past the bars of the gate at Crowley's new form. "Our enemy has his own flesh now," he said. "There's no other presence inside it to resist him the way you did, which means he can move around in daylight as easily as any of us. He's intent on attacking the British and Germanic governments when they gather in Green Park tomorrow morning."

"Attack how?"

"I don't know. We'll have to—"

A low whistle from Krishnamurthy interrupted him. He moved to the corner of the cell and murmured, "What is it?"

"I was listening. I know how he intends to do it."

"Tell me."

"For half the length of the River Effra, where the new sewer tunnel encloses it, there's a wide brick shelf running alongside the water. For the rest of the way—the upper reaches—the shelf narrows and is of hard clay, but between those two stretches there's a short section where the clay has been cut away and shaped ready for the next section of brickwork. The workmen have dug a large niche into the wall there for storing their tools and materials. Bhatti and I encountered two Enochians by it. We overpowered them and found they'd been guarding a wheeled trolley on which rested a big barrel-shaped affair. We took a closer look. I'm certain it was a bomb, Sir Richard—a bloody huge one. If Crowley drops it on Green Park, it'll leave nothing but an enormous crater."

Burton was silent as he digested this. Then, "Drop it how? He'll never get past the *Orpheus*. It would take—" He stopped. His eyes widened. "Bismillah!"

"Sir?"

"He's going to hijack the *Sagittarius*!"

CHAPTER 25

THE BATTLE OF VAUXHALL BRIDGE

"No one knows the secret of the Sisterhood of Noble Benevolence. They work with the diseased but never fall sick. They move among criminals but never fall victim. They surround themselves with sinners but never fall from Grace. These women appear blessed. Good fortune favours them. Some say they emanate some manner of mediumistic defence. Others say that God protects them. All I know is that I wish I was one of them, and I would have given anything to have had them with me during the dark days of the Crimean War."
—NURSE FLORENCE NIGHTINGALE

Hours passed. The prisoners alternated between short naps and watching as Crowley's people tended to their wounds, loaded their weapons, packed away equipment, and prepared to move.

Swinburne said to Burton, "How can Crowley possibly take the *Sagittarius*?"

"You're forgetting," Burton replied, "even if Detective Inspector Slaughter's raid on the Enochians' clubhouse has succeeded, there were only twenty or so members in it, which—if Trounce got his figures right—leaves well over a hundred unaccounted for."

"Ah, a sizeable raiding party."

"Exactly, and the airfield isn't expecting an attack. With Crowley's ability to quash gunfire, they could wrest control of the ship before anyone realises what's happening." Burton rubbed his aching arm. "The *Orpheus* has been fitted with weapons but it wouldn't stand a chance against that battleship."

"Confound it!" the poet cursed. "We have to get out of here!"

"We still have hope," Burton noted.

"In what form?" came the dubious reply.

"Sadhvi Raghavendra."

However, four more hours went by before Burton was able to speak to the Sister of Noble Benevolence. She had slept for a period before reappearing at the far end of the passage, only to then vanish into the tunnel that led to the Effra. After an agonising wait, he saw her return to the catacomb. Many more minutes dragged by before she moved close enough for him to attract her attention.

He clicked his fingers.

She glanced at him, then strode over to a tangle of wire, picked it up, and started to unravel and coil it, giving the appearance of industriousness while edging closer to the cells, turning her ear to the explorer.

"Sadhvi," he whispered, "are you familiar with the hidden passage that connects to the catacomb beneath the Episcopal chapel?"

She gave a barely perceptible nod.

"You have to escape through it and make your way to Battersea Power Station. Warn Isambard Kingdom Brunel of Crowley's plan."

"I don't know his plan," she breathed. "There's a bomb. I have no idea what he intends to do with it."

"I believe he'll transport it through the Effra tunnel to the river's outlet beside Vauxhall Bridge. From there, he'll take it along the bank of the Thames to the Royal Navy Air Service Station. He and his people will attack the airfield and seize the *Sagittarius*. They'll use the ship to drop the bomb on Green Park. Tell Brunel and Detective Inspector Trounce to ambush the Enochians at the bridge."

Sadhvi nodded. "I'll try."

"We'll cause a rumpus so you can get away while the attention is on us."

At the far end of the passage, Crowley suddenly stretched, uncrossed his legs, and slid from the table.

"Good!" he announced. "I feel stronger."

Raghavendra moved away from the prisoners.

"Galton, report!" Crowley snapped.

"It's dawn, Master. We're almost ready to move. Our fellows will be gathering."

"We have a few minutes to spare?"

"Yes."

"Good. Mr. Burke, you have my permission to proceed. Gather around, please, everybody."

Damien Burke's naturally woebegone features twisted into a wicked smile. He picked up a six-foot length of finger-thick cable, approached the prisoners, took keys from his pocket, and unlocked the gate to the left of Burton and Honesty's cell.

Crowley and his people formed a semicircle halfway along the central catacomb, leaving a wide cleared space between them and the cells.

Swinburne screeched, "Get off me, you brute!"

Burke reappeared, dragging the poet by his long scarlet hair. He shoved him forward, sending him staggering into the middle of what, to Burton, was starting to look unpleasantly similar to an Indian fight pit.

"Mr. Swinburne," Crowley announced. "You rather irritated me earlier and you also have the misfortune of being one of Sir Richard Francis Burton's truest friends. He values you highly."

"Nonsense!" Swinburne responded. "He hasn't known me for more than a few days."

Crowley laughed, revealing small, pointed teeth. His big, slanted, black eyes gleamed. He opened his long, muscular arms wide and declaimed:

> But him we hailed from afar or near
> As boldest born of the bravest here
> And loved as brightest of souls that eyed
> Life, time, and death with unchangeful cheer,
>
> A wider soul than the world was wide,
> Whose praise made love of him one with pride,
> What part has death or has time in him,
> Who rode life's lists as a god might ride?

"My hat!" Swinburne exclaimed. "That was rather good, though horribly recited. Not yours, obviously."

"No, Mr. Swinburne, not mine. Yours. You will write it in 1890. It is entitled 'On the Death of Richard Burton.' You see—you shall become very good friends indeed."

Swinburne turned to face Burton and raised his eyebrows.

Burton gave a slight shake of the head, as if to say: *Don't provoke him!*

"So," Crowley said, "much as it pains me to do so—for I admire you greatly—I shall hurt you in order to hurt him. And perhaps in future you will think twice before mocking me."

"I wouldn't put money on it," Swinburne replied.

Burke lifted the cable, whirled it around his head, and cracked it onto the poet's back. It tore through Swinburne's jacket and sent him to his knees.

"Ow!" he cried out. "Bloody hell! Ha ha! Yes!"

Burke pulled back his makeshift whip and sliced it down again. It slapped across Swinburne's shoulders, shredding his outer garments.

"Argh! He he he! Ooh! I say! Golly, that smarts!"

Thomas Honesty moved to Burton's side and gripped the bars of the locked gate. They watched grimly as Burke set about the poet, his lash striking again and again. Swinburne hopped and skipped about. He fell and got up, fell and got up, all the time squealing and crying out as his clothes and skin were flayed.

"By God!" Honesty groaned. "How can he stand it?"

"Yow!" Swinburne screeched. "Oh! Oh! Oh! Eek!"

"He's enjoying it," Burton murmured. He saw Sadhvi Raghavendra surreptitiously backing out of the semicircle.

"Enjoying? Are you mad?"

"His brain doesn't function as a normal man's. He feels pain as pleasure."

"Yikes!" Swinburne yelled. "Ha ha ha! Blimey!"

"Pleasure?"

Sadhvi slipped into a side corridor and was gone.

"Yes, Mr. Honesty. He's in raptures. Look at him."

Swinburne was laughing hysterically, tears of unbridled joy streaming down his cheeks.

"More!" he shrieked. "Put your back into it, old thing!"

Burke snarled and slashed. The cable wound around Swinburne's waist then fell away, taking a strip of his shirt with it.

"Stings!" he squawked, and, turning around, pushed down his trousers and showed his buttocks to Burke. "Tally-ho, old chap! Let loose! Swish! Swish!"

Burke obliged, flying into such a rage that the slashing cable became almost invisible to the eye.

Crack! Crack! Crack!

"Yaaah! Ooh ooh ooh, yes! Ouch! Ouch! Ha ha!"

Uttering a yell of frustration, Burke sprang forward, took Swinburne by what remained of his collar, yanked him around, and shoved him hard toward the coffin bay in which Burton was held. The poet crashed against the gate and clutched at the bars. He looked at the explorer, winked, grinned, and said, "My hat, Richard, what a dose he's giving me!"

The cable smacked across his back.

"Oof! Yow! Has Sadhvi got away?"

"Yes. Go for his eyes, Algy. He's dangerous. We need him out of the picture."

Crack!

"Ouch! Ouch! Ouch! I'll see—"

Crack!

"Ha ha ha! What I—"

Crack!

"Aaah! Eek! Oh oh! Can do!"

Crack!

The poet staggered back from the gate. The whip slapped against his shoulder blades and curled around his chest. He immediately raised his arms and pirouetted, winding the cable around himself and dancing closer to his assailant. Furiously, Burke jerked at the line, trying to yank it away from the poet. Swinburne timed it perfectly—just as Burke pulled, he jumped. Their combined strength sent him leaping high. His knees impacted against Burke's shoulders and as the thug lost balance and went down beneath him, Swinburne fell on top with his thumbs over the man's eyes and his full weight behind them.

Burke's howl of agony shattered the spell, and as Swinburne rolled away from him, everyone started moving. One of the Enochians drew a pistol. Crowley snatched it from his hand, paced forward, and smacked the weapon into the poet's mop of hair. It clunked against Swinburne's skull and he went limp.

The Trans-Temporal Man straightened and looked down at Burke, who was writhing on the ground emitting scream after scream with his hands clamped to his face and blood welling between the fingers.

"Unfortunately, Mr. Burke, you're no use to me at all in that state." He pointed the pistol, shot Burke through the heart, then turned to Galton and said, "Put Swinburne back in the cell. I'll deal with him at my leisure. It's time to get going."

The unconscious poet was returned to the bay beside Burton's. A few minutes later, the Enochians locked Darwin and Lister into another before gathering at the tunnel mouth and filing out through it. They didn't appear to notice Raghavendra's absence.

Aleister Crowley approached Burton and with a cruel smile said, "I forgot to tell you, Isabel was perfectly delicious. How are you bearing up without her?"

Burton stared at him silently for a moment, then said, "She and I once talked about how we'd like to be laid to rest. We settled on a mausoleum. I now realise my post-mortem circumstances will be quite different."

"Really?"

"Yes. I shall spend eternity in hell with my hands clamped around your throat."

Crowley laughed. "After what I intend for you, that is quite probable. I'm going to work my way through all those you hold dear, Burton. Swinburne first, then Monckton Milnes, Thomas Bendyshe, Charles Bradlaugh, Edward Brabrooke—oh, I know them all. You'll watch them die slowly and painfully until your life is desolate." He clapped his hands. "But such amusements are for tomorrow. First I have a couple of parliaments and royal families to kill. Wait here. I'll return for you. Perhaps we can lunch together."

He turned away and walked toward the tunnel.

"Why, Crowley?" Burton shouted after him. "Why me?"

The Trans-Temporal Man looked back, blinked his unnerving eyes, and deliberated for a moment before answering. "In truth? Because you're the only person I fear."

He departed.

Burton slammed his hands against the gate. "Damn him! Damn him!"

He heard a crash from Krishnamurthy and Bhatti's cell.

"What are you doing?"

"Trying to kick my way out," Bhatti called. "Unsuccessfully. All I've managed to do is hurt my blasted foot. For the love of God, do we have to remain here with no idea of what's happening?"

Burton signalled to Honesty and they put their shoulders to the gate. The heavy wrought iron didn't budge. The explorer spat an oath and began to examine every inch of the cell. He looked for loose bricks, for a removable flagstone, for a means to lever the barrier from its hinges; he found nothing.

Swinburne groaned.

A voice hissed, "Are they all gone?"

"Trounce!" Burton exclaimed. "Is that you? Yes, we're alone. How did you find us?"

Detective Inspector Trounce stepped into view, a revolver in his hand. Eliphas Levi and Montague Penniforth followed behind him.

"We waited at the power station," the policeman said. "When you didn't return, we came looking for you. We'd just descended into the other catacomb when Sister Raghavendra appeared. She's gone on to warn Brunel. Is it true? There's a bomb?"

"It's true. Get us out of here."

"Here, let me, guv'nor," Penniforth rumbled. He stepped forward, gripped the gate near its hinges, put a foot against the wall, and heaved. While he pulled, Burton and Honesty pushed, and after a few seconds of straining, the gate suddenly gave, its hinges breaking free of the brickwork in an explosion of red dust.

The giant cabbie applied himself to the other cells, and in short order all the prisoners were liberated.

"*Mon Dieu!*" Levi cried out upon seeing Swinburne, who emerged a ragged and bloody mess.

"It's all right, monsieur," the poet said. "I'm stinging all over, but it's perfectly delicious." He reached up and gingerly felt a large lump on his head. "Apart from this."

"And you, Monsieur Honesty?" the Frenchman asked. "*Comment allez-vous?*"

"Regaining some strength," Honesty answered.

"*Très bon!* Your weakness is to be expected, but Perdurabo, he possess you only for a few days. You will soon recover, I think."

"We have to get to the power station at once," Burton said.

Krishnamurthy addressed Trounce and Levi, "If you don't mind loaning Bhatti and me your revolvers, sirs, we'll set off back along the Effra. While you attack the Enochians from the front, we'll surprise them from the rear."

The police officer and occultist handed over their weapons and ammunition. Krishnamurthy and Bhatti saluted, said, "Good luck all," and departed.

"We'll leave Darwin and Lister," Burton said, looking at the scientist and surgeon, who were sitting blank-eyed in a cell. "They're still under Crowley's mesmeric spell but have obviously played their part for the moment, else he wouldn't have left them here. We'll send someone to pick them up."

He led the remaining group to the secret passage and through to the other catacomb. As they proceeded, Trounce explained, "The violence and hysteria in the Cauldron are out of hand. We managed to prevent the rioters from marching westward but they won't be contained for another night. The whole city is threatened. As for the less infuriated residents, we've evacuated thousands. They're all scared to death."

"There are many *strigoi morti*," Levi added. "You are correct about Vincent Sneed, who destroy Big Ben. He is one. I stake and behead him. But your boy, Bram, he have nearly a hundred more reports of un-dead. At night, the East End is their place of hunting. In day, they sleep in the cellars and dark places. How we destroy them all, *je ne sais pas*. It seem impossible."

They emerged into the vaults, passed Solomon, who was lying handcuffed on the floor—"I'll send a constable for you," Trounce promised—climbed the stairs to the church, and ran out into the morning rain, which was falling steadily from a leaden sky.

"Our rotorchairs are at the cemetery entrance," the detective stated. "I told Sister Raghavendra to take one. There's not enough left for all of us."

"I'll find one o' me mates what's in the business of cabbyin'," Penniforth said. "I'll get to the station in a jiffy. Anyways, I much prefers wheels to wings." He touched the brim of his cloth cap and raced away.

"We have our machines parked nearby," Burton said. "Mr. Honesty, you come with us. You and Algy are slightly built. His rotorchair will bear you both."

The party split in two, and ten minutes later four rotorchairs soared above the rainclouds and sped northward.

It was early and cold and Burton had no recollection of his last full night's sleep. Every part of him hurt: bones aching; flesh bruised; emotions savagely suppressed. He still hadn't properly grieved. Isabel's death was like a knife that couldn't be removed lest the blood start flowing. It stabbed him through the heart but he would not—must not—acknowledge the damage. Not yet.

Don't think of Isabel.

Don't think of William Stroyan.

Don't think of John Steinhaueser.

Think only of Aleister Crowley—of killing him.

Ahead, the tips of the four towers of Battersea Power Station poked out of the clouds. Burton sent his flying machine down into the wet shroud. The rain drummed against him. He plunged out of the vapour. To his left, the bulk of the *Sagittarius* humped up from the airfield. Visibility was poor, but as far as he could make out, there weren't many people around it. If Crowley had an army of a hundred, he could hijack the battleship with ease.

Drawing to a halt above the power station's quadrangle, the explorer eased his machine to the ground. As its rotors slowed to a stop, the other chairs descended, Swinburne's slamming down heavily thanks to its additional weight.

The men ran to the entrance and were met by Daniel Gooch.

"Sister Raghavendra has told us what's what," he said. "We've gathered our forces—about fifty men. Come and arm yourselves."

"El Yezdi?" Burton asked as they stepped into the immense workshop.

"Fading fast. I'm afraid these are his final hours, Sir Richard. Do you want to see him?"

The explorer hesitated then said, "There's no time."

A technician approached and handed him a Beaumont–Adams revolver and box of bullets. Trounce, Levi, Swinburne, and Honesty received the same.

"Are you up to it?" Burton asked the groundsman.

Honesty's grey eyes took on a steely glint. "Fit for retribution."

"Good man. And you, Algy? You look all in."

The poet jerked his limbs restlessly and objected, "Not a bit of it. Don't let the blood and ragged clothing fool you. I'm up for a scrap. Like Honesty here, I have a score to settle."

"We all do." Burton turned as clanking footsteps approached. Isambard Kingdom Brunel chimed a greeting. Each of the brass man's six arms had a large multi-barrelled weapon bolted to it. He held one up and clanged, "Invented by one of our American associates, Doctor Richard Gatling. It loads automatically and has a very rapid rate of fire. Are you ready?"

"Yes."

Brunel said to Gooch, "Have the men gather at the gates. On the double, please, Daniel."

"We'll head east along Riverside Walk," Burton said. "It's the most sheltered route between here and the mouth of the Effra."

"You think that's the way Crowley and his people will come?" Trounce asked.

"I can't imagine them strolling along Nine Elms Lane."

The policeman grunted his agreement.

Brunel's DOGS, all armed, streamed from the building. The mechanical engineer led Burton's party out to join them.

Burton addressed the little army. "We're facing enemies of the Empire, gentlemen. Don't hesitate to shoot to kill."

From behind him, a voice said, "You mean *lady* and gentlemen."

He turned to find Sister Raghavendra outfitted in men's clothing and holding a revolver in each hand.

"You've played your part splendidly, Sadhvi—and thank you—but this next isn't for you."

"Oh dear," she said. "My mistake. I'll remain here, then. Perhaps I can knit you a scarf or embroider a doily or two while you're fighting the insane tyrant who mesmerised me and forced me to assist him."

Swinburne giggled and said, "Madam, may I declare my everlasting love?"

She ignored the poet. "Are you going to be a brute and stand here arguing, Richard, or shall we get on with it?"

The explorer gave a slight smile then turned and shouted, "Let's go!"

The crowd filed through the gates and crossed the waste ground, moving along a rough path that led down to Riverside Walk. Here, they headed to the right, passing the Southwark and Vauxhall waterworks.

Even in the rain, the stench of the river was dreadful. "By Jove!" Trounce grumbled. "We have to get the Cauldron under control if only so Bazalgette can finish digging through it. The sooner his sewer system starts operating, the better."

An idea flirted at the periphery of Burton's mind then eluded him.

Too tired. Can't even think straight.

They crossed a small dock at the side of a flour mill and continued on past a pottery, a coal wharf, a row of saw mills, and a brewery. When they reached Brunswick Wharf, Gooch pointed one of his mechanical arms at a large edifice beyond which, made vague by the downpour, Vauxhall Bridge could be seen extending across the choppy Thames. "That's the Belmont Candle Factory."

Eliphas Levi murmured, "*Mouvement*, messieurs."

Burton squinted through the rain. "Men. Standing at a doorway. Not many."

"I'll go," Brunel said. "They can't harm me."

He raised his Gatling guns and strode forward, his metal feet thudding on the wood of the platform that extended from the wharf and along the river-facing side of the factory. In his bell-like tones, he shouted, "Vacate the area, please. Your lives are at risk. Leave at once."

The many windows of the building suddenly flew open, guns poked out, and a hail of bullets clanged against him, sending sparks flying. The men standing outside the factory ran into it.

"Enochians!" Swinburne yelled. "An ambuscade!" He ducked into cover, took aim, and returned fire.

Brunel aimed his six weapons and let loose. His guns roared, flames shooting from the barrels, and the building's facade spat thick clouds of dust and glass as his bullets gouged across it, ruining brickwork and shattering windows.

While the enemy was thus distracted, Burton and his fellows took shelter, positioning themselves behind crates, barrels, and the equipment used to offload cargo vessels.

Brunel's guns whirred to silence. "Give yourselves up. Put down your weapons and come out with your hands in the air."

Faintly, they heard someone shout, "Hold your fire!"

Silence fell. They waited.

"What are they up to?" Trounce muttered.

"We're sending someone out to parley," an Enochian yelled.

"This feels rather too easy," Burton muttered. "But let's hear what they have to say."

A door opened and a man stepped out. He held a white handkerchief aloft and walked toward Brunel, who levelled his guns at him and warned, "No sudden moves, if you please."

"That's Count Sobieski," Burton observed. "Did Slaughter raid the Enochians' club, Trounce?"

"He did. He got Kenealy and sixteen of his fanatics, and found old Brundleweed and his family being held captive in one of the upstairs rooms."

"Hmm. Some got away, then; Sobieski among them."

The count stopped just in front of Brunel and said, "Withdraw. We'll allow you to go in peace."

"You don't appear to understand," Brunel clanged. "It is you who are trapped."

"It's true. Those guns of yours have us pinned down."

"Then you understand you have no choice."

"There's always a choice," Sobieski said. "We can surrender, or we can get rid of you."

"You will find the former easy, the latter very difficult."

"Do you think so?"

Sobieski lowered the handkerchief and raised his other hand. There was something in it. Burton jumped to his feet and yelled, "Brunel, it's a trick!"

The count pressed down his thumb. He exploded. Isambard Kingdom Brunel was thrown high into the air. Bits of him were ripped away. He cart-wheeled out over the Thames, trailing flames and smoke behind him, hit the water, and sank like a stone.

Guns started blazing from the factory windows. Bullets chewed into the wood of the wharf, ploughing up splinters. Three of the DOGS were hit; two killed outright, the third clutching his neck and coughing blood.

"Return fire!" Gooch bellowed.

Burton dived back into cover, aimed his revolver, and started shooting.

For the next fifteen minutes, the battle raged, a constant barrage of bullets hitting the wharf and the factory, the noise deafening, the air filling with smoke despite the continuing rain.

Burton glanced to his right at Sister Raghavendra. She was standing, with a revolver in each hand, in plain view of the enemy, blazing away and seemingly oblivious to the bullets that zipped past her. As he'd done many times before, he marvelled at her courage and her luck.

"Stalemate!" Trounce observed. "But we only have to keep them holed-up in there for another ninety minutes or so and the win will be ours. The ceremony will be over."

"Blast it, chaps! Something is very wrong about all of this," Swinburne objected stridently. "It doesn't make any sense at all. Where is Crowley? Why are we able to use our weapons when he can so easily prevent their functioning?"

"Might Krishnamurthy and Bhatti have him cornered in the tunnel?" Trounce mused.

"I'm going to find out," Burton said. "Are you with me, Algy?"

"Of course I am!"

"Keep them busy," Burton said to Trounce and Gooch.

Gesturing for Swinburne to follow, he ran the length of the wharf and along the side of a warehouse until he emerged onto Wandsworth Road, where a crowd had gathered. Five constables immediately pounced on the two men and tried to tear the pistols from their hands. Burton remembered that Crowley had emptied his pockets, and his identity card was back in the catacombs.

"Stop!" he yelled. "We're with the police! Detective Inspector Trounce! Slaughter! J. D. Pepperwick!"

"Pepperwick?" one of the policemen said. "I know him. Who are you? What's going on? Who's shooting?"

"I'm Burton. Sir Richard Francis Burton. Keep these people back, Constable—?"

"Sergeant, sir. Piper."

"Detective Inspector Trounce is on the wharf, Piper. He's leading an assault against a group of men who're intent on bombing the ceremony in Green Park."

"The devil you say! A bomb?"

"Can you spare one of your fellows? We're out to nab their leader."

"I'll come myself." Piper turned to the other policemen and barked, "Tamworth, you're with me. Lampwick, Carlyle, Patterson, you keep this crowd back, is that understood?"

He received a saluted response.

"Lead on," he said to Burton.

Following the road, they skirted the front of the factory to the corner of Vauxhall Bridge. Here a set of concrete steps led down to the riverside and the outlet of the Effra. They found another gun battle raging there—Krishnamurthy and Bhatti, crouched behind a bulwark, were exchanging shots with men in the building.

Burton, Swinburne, and the policemen stayed low and ran to the two Indians.

Bhatti, bleeding profusely from a furrow on the side of his head, said, "Hello, fellows! They're stubborn blighters! How many men do you have? Enough to rush the place?"

"They have double our number," Burton answered. "But if we hold them in there, their plan is scuppered. Have you seen Crowley?"

"No sign of the hound. Is he with them?"

Burton frowned and turned to Swinburne. "You're right, Algy. Something is badly amiss."

He flinched as a bullet whined past his ear. Krishnamurthy returned fire before muttering, "I'm low on ammunition."

Sergeant Piper addressed Constable Tamworth. "I'll not tolerate a blessed shooting match on my beat. Run to the station, lad, and round up everyone you can. We'll get into that building, forlorn hope or no."

Tamworth took to his heels. Bullets drilled into the ground behind him.

"*Modus operandi*," Swinburne murmured.

Burton looked at him. "Pardon?"

"*Modus operandi*. Crowley's every move, right from the start—the murder of your friend Stroyan—has been undertaken in the context of your existence."

"He said he was scared of me."

"Yet he steadfastly refuses to kill you. Why?"

"I don't know."

"Because by disposing of you, he'd rid himself of the cause of his fear but not of the emotion itself. It isn't enough for him. Fear has such a power. He wants to conquer it. Take control of it. Turn it into a strength. That is why you must live. That is why he must have you at his feet. Only then can the Supreme Man feel truly supreme."

Burton recalled Doctor Monroe's theory concerning Oliphant's obsession with rats.

"Crowley is blinkered," Swinburne went on. "He can only think to counter *his* greatest fear with *your* greatest fear."

"By God!" Burton whispered. "He's still underground."

"Yes."

Krishnamurthy shook his head. "We walked the complete length of the tunnel, Mr. Swinburne. There was no sign of the bomb or of Crowley. Wherever he is, he's not by the Effra."

"There are other tunnels."

What had been lurking at the back of Burton's mind suddenly blossomed into comprehension. He punched his palm, shouted, "Bismillah!" then looked at Sergeant Piper, and—acting on impulse—pointed at the whistle hanging around the policeman's neck and barked, "Give me that!"

"What?" the policeman asked, puzzled.

"Your whistle, man! Now!"

Piper pulled the chain over his head and handed it to the explorer.

Burton took Swinburne by the arm and drew him toward the road, shouting back to the others, "Stay put! Keep them immobilised!"

"What are you doing?" Bhatti shouted after him.

"Saving the bloody Empire!" Burton yelled. "If it's not too late!"

CHAPTER 26

THE ELEVENTH HOUR OF THE ELEVENTH DAY OF THE ELEVENTH MONTH

"Frater Perdurabo."
(I shall endure to the end.)
—ALEISTER CROWLEY

B urton was enclosed twice over—first by the heavy undersea suit, and second by the claustrophobic sewer tunnel. Despite the mephitic reek rising from the thick, fast-flowing sludge in which he was immersed up to his knees and which threatened to suck him down at any moment, he'd left the faceplate of his helmet open.

His jaw was clamped shut, his eyes moved anxiously, and his chest was rising and falling with short, sharp breaths. He waded ahead, dragging behind him the long, weighty chain attached to the suit's harness. With every step, his fear increased. He wrapped his gloved right hand around his swordstick—secured against him by one of the harness's straps—and pulled at the chain with his left.

The light from the small lamps on either side of his headgear projected forward, illuminating about twenty feet of the tunnel, but beyond the radiance the brickwork plunged into absolute darkness. Burton couldn't throw off the sensation that he was slipping down the throat of a gigantic beast.

One foot in front of the other. Keep your balance. Don't think about how this has to end.

The Enochian gunmen had been a subterfuge, a diversion. Crowley never intended to take the *Sagittarius*. When Burton realised this—thanks to Swinburne's insight—he'd raced back to Battersea Power Station, where Montague Penniforth was waiting and wondering where everyone had gone.

Rushing into Brunel's office, the explorer consulted Bazalgette's maps of subterranean London and discovered that, a few yards north of the Effra's outlet, under Vauxhall Bridge, a small maintenance tunnel spanned the bed of the Thames. It gave access to the big west-to-east intercepting sewer, which ran parallel to the north bank of the river. Crowley need only have wheeled the bomb through it, turned left into the sewer system's artery, and half a mile along its length he'd have come to what used to be the mouth of the Tyburn. That subterranean waterway, now enclosed by Bazalgette's incredible brickwork and reduced to a trickle by a massive sluice gate, ran southward all the way from Hampstead.

It passed directly beneath Green Park.

There was no time for planning. The politicians and royal families were already gathering around the Victoria Memorial. No time, even, to speak with Abdu El Yezdi, who was, according to Nurse Nightingale, taking his final breaths.

Burton adopted the first scheme that came to mind—it had occurred to him in an instant while he was still with Krishnamurthy, Bhatti, and Piper—and after hastily grabbing the required equipment, he, Swinburne, and Penniforth boarded one of the DOGS' small rotorships and sped northward. There was a wide exclusion zone around the park—no flying machines permitted except the *Orpheus*—and they possessed no means with which to signal Captain Lawless, so they'd angled to the west, flying in a wide arc over Belgravia and Hyde Park before landing in Berkeley Square. Here, after roughly pushing protesting pedestrians out of the way, they'd lifted an iron manhole cover, revealing the rungs of a ladder. Burton, donning the undersea suit, had issued instructions then descended into the darkness of the Tyburn tunnel, where he found himself in front of the giant sluice gate. It was impeding the swollen waters and accumulated sewage from a wide swathe of northern London, but was very slightly raised, and viscous filth was spurting from its base with tremendous force. The thick liquid would have knocked the explorer flying had he not been tethered by the chain to the windlass they'd picked up from the Royal Navy Air Service Station. Penniforth was attending to the apparatus, above ground, slowly unwinding it to allow Burton's passage through the tunnel.

He'd walked half a mile—barely any distance at all—but it was the exact length of the chain and felt like ten times as far to Burton, who was increasingly exhausted by the weight of the links as they accumulated behind him.

Buried alive. By God, would the nightmare never end?

He struggled to concentrate—balance, step, move—but couldn't. His mind kept throwing up disjointed images: Isabel, the African savannah,

John Speke, the Kaaba at Mecca, and the distant Mountains of the Moon. He became confused. Had he bypassed the mountains or visited them? Was Speke dead or alive?

He was cold. Fatigued beyond measure. Scared. He needed Saltzmann's Tincture. Required its honeyed warmth in his veins.

A choir of voices said, "I can hear you. Stay back if you value your life."

"Crowley," he called. The word echoed into the darkness.

"Burton! Is that you? Escaped? Bravo, man! Bravo! I certainly didn't expect you. Come forward, by all means."

The explorer splashed on and rounded a bend. His lamps illuminated a tall, freakish figure bent over a trolley on which a large cylinder rested.

Crowley's weird eyes assessed him and the thin-lipped, needle-toothed mouth twisted into a mocking grin. "Look at you! I wish I'd thought of donning such an outfit. I'm calf-high in stinking effluence."

"And possess a cranium full of it," Burton added.

"Now now, Sir Richard. I would have thought you above such petty insults."

"Give it up. I'll not let you explode the bomb."

"How do you intend to stop me? I have twice your strength and the device is on a timer. Twenty minutes from now—boom!—the new world begins."

"The new?" Burton sneered. "There's nothing new about the subjugation of a population to a madman's lust for power. Sulla did it. Caesar did it. Genghis Khan, Attila the Hun, Bonaparte—need I go on?"

"Please don't. I bore so very easily."

"The event above us—*that* is the birth of a new world, Crowley. It is the avoidance of war; the establishment of a permanent peace; the beginning of a stable Europe."

Crowley waved his hand dismissively. "You're a fool, Burton. I was born sixteen years from now, in 1875, and saw forty-three years of history develop before I travelled back to this time. You have no conception of the scale of the conflict I lived through. It devastated nation after nation; killed whole generations; gave rise to evils beyond anything you can possibly imagine. The Germans rampaged across the globe like a plague of locusts, murdering every man, woman, and child who stood in their way, and millions who didn't. They have to be stopped."

"What happened in your history will not happen in this."

"It will. Certain events occur, in varying forms, in all the histories— sometimes earlier, sometimes later, but they are inevitable. Perhaps we might term them *evolutionary*, for through them the community of mankind alters and develops, and the business of living takes on a different character. The war *must* come. But the British Empire has to win it."

"I'll not accept that the business of living is dependent upon the business of death for its development."

"Life and death have always been indivisible. The one is undertaken in the shadow of the other."

"So you're doing mankind a favour by blowing up innocent people?"

"Politicians are never innocent."

"Perhaps not, but what of their wives and children?"

"What is the suffering of hundreds compared to the suffering of millions?"

"That's the idle argument of one who entirely lacks compassion. No such should be allowed power."

"*Allowed*, Burton?" Crowley said disdainfully. "I require no permission. I am a superior human. I'm aligned with every possible version of myself. I'm attuned to the ebb and flow of time. I accept its opportunities and relish its challenges. I see all the possibilities, all the choices, and all the outcomes. You oppose me for what you believe will be the consequences of my actions, but I *see* those consequences, and I know them to be preferable to the alternatives, for I have seen those, too—lived through them!"

Burton drew the rapier from his cane. "You'll not meddle with history, Crowley. Not in this world. It is not yours. It's—" Burton stumbled over the final word, and finished lamely, "—mine."

Bismillah! How could he argue against Crowley when he himself was guilty of interfering with the natural course of events? His elder self, Abdu El Yezdi, had been manipulating for two decades!

He stood hesitantly, the sword-tip wavering.

There was no moral high ground.

This confrontation was suited only to the sewers.

"I can't begin to describe," Crowley said, "the depth of my disappointment. You aren't what I imagined at all. I thought you far-sighted—a man who pushes to the limits then looks beyond them—but you are blind. Worse, you can't string together a cogent objection. You oppose me out of nothing but indignation. You are of the species *Vegrandis humanus*—a diminutive human, and nothing more. Bring your blade to me. I no longer require you at my feet. I shall put you out of your misery."

Burton snarled, splashed two steps forward, and jerked to an abrupt halt. He heaved at the chain, but it had reached its limit; he could proceed no farther.

Crowley threw his head back and roared with laughter. His multiplicity of voices echoed up and down the tunnel. It sounded as if the whole world was mocking Burton.

"You can't even do that! Pathetic creature!" Crowley leaned over the bomb and examined a dial. "Ten minutes remaining, Burton. Then, at the eleventh hour of the eleventh day of the eleventh month, my reign will begin. Here—" he pushed the trolley forward a little, "—a fighting chance. If you amount to anything more than a man who scrabbles around looking for river sources and fabled mountains, you'll have defused the bomb by the time I reach an access hatch and climb out of here."

He turned and started to walk away.

Burton sheathed his rapier, reversed it, and holding it by its end tried to hook the trolley with its handle. He stretched and strained but just couldn't reach. The trolley was a mere half-inch too far from him.

Crowley stopped and looked back. His skin was a pale purple in the lamplight. His black eyes were pitiless.

"I thought not," he said. "Just an explorer."

He continued down the tunnel.

"No!" Burton barked. He slid his cane back into his harness. "I haven't been an explorer since you murdered Isabel Arundell."

Crowley halted and swung around. "Then what?"

Burton straightened. "I am Sir Richard Francis Burton, the king's agent." He lifted the police whistle hanging from the cord around his neck, put it to his lips, and blew it as hard as he could. Its high-pitched shriek reverberated deafeningly in the confined space. He dropped it, slammed shut his helmet's faceplate, and quickly turned the butterfly screws that locked it tight.

From far behind him, a loud clank sounded, followed by a deep, reverberating boom.

Crowley frowned. His mouth moved but Burton couldn't hear what he said.

The sewage flowing around Burton's legs suddenly rose to his waist, causing him to stagger. A rumbling turned into a roar. Unable to resist, Burton turned and looked back. A wall of brown sludge, moving at breathtaking speed, shot down the tunnel and slammed into him. It knocked him off his feet, enveloped him, and whirled him up into the middle of the channel. The harness pushed into his ribs harder and harder as the great weight of accumulated water, urine, excrement, animal waste, and filth of every imaginable description pressed against him and thundered over and around him. The noise was deafening, the pressure agonizing, the terror unendurable. He was battered up and down and from side to side, physically anchored by the chain but mentally swept away, feeling himself drowning in the depths of madness.

Hold on.

I can't.

If I can, you can. Death has come for me, but it isn't your time. I'll stay with you until the crisis has passed.

Abdu El Yezdi?

I am you.

Help me.

Endure this. It is but a few minutes in eternity. Your role in the narrative is not done.

What?

The future beckons. It depends on you.

I don't understand.

Soon you will embark on a new expedition.

Burton screamed as the harness cut into him. His ribs creaked. He couldn't breathe. The surging liquid banged him against the ceiling. He was petrified that the helmet might break like an eggshell.

Listen to Swinburne. I have left you many resources, but none is more valuable than the poet. Trust his instincts above even your own. He has a vital role to play.

Please. Make it stop.

Know this: Edward Oxford is waking from his slumber.

Oxford is dead.

No. Spring Heeled Jack will return. But our brother is in a position of influence. You must become his Abdu El Yezdi. Through him, you can keep this world safe from the stilt-man. Play the card well.

No. No. No.

There is so much more I want to tell you. I'm sorry.

Sorry?

For so much. I pray you don't suffer as I have. But peace will come to me now.

I'm dying. Bismillah! I'm dying.

No, you are not. But I am. Blessed release! I can see it. I can see it.

What? Tell me!

The roof of the tent. The dawn light upon the canvas. It's beautiful. So beautiful. I'm going to step out.

No! Don't leave me!

I have to. I want to look across the desert. I want to see the horizon again.

Please.

I hear the camel bells . . .

Burton's back bumped into something solid. He felt himself drawn sideways. He realised that his left hand was pressed so hard against his swordstick—still secured by the harness—that it had cramped and he couldn't move his fingers. The heels of his boots scraped across a corner. He was rising.

Foul gunk drained from his faceplate. Light shone through. Gravity tugged at him. Brickwork slid past, sinking downward.

He saw the round edge of a manhole, felt hands slide under his armpits, was hauled up, and was suddenly lying on his back looking up at a grey sky.

Fingers moved over him. The helmet turned. It was pulled away. He gulped in a huge breath of air.

"Wotcha!" Montague Penniforth said. "Cripes, I think me arms are goin' to fall off! I 'ad the very devil of a time windin' you in."

"You stink worse than the Thames!" Swinburne exclaimed.

Burton didn't respond. His eyes were fixed straight ahead. He was paralysed.

"Richard? Richard? My hat! What's wrong with him?"

"Oof!" Penniforth grunted. "Sorry about this, guv'nor." He leaned down and slapped Burton's face, hard. He did it again.

The world crashed back into place.

"Stop," Burton croaked. "Help me up."

Careless of the muck that covered the king's agent, Penniforth heaved him to his feet and set about undoing the undersea suit's fastenings.

"Are you all right?" Swinburne asked.

"Yes."

"I opened the sluice gate as soon as I heard the whistle. Did I flush him away?"

"You did. And the—" Burton was interrupted by a deep detonation that resounded across the city, shaking windows and causing screams and shouts of consternation. A colossal ball of flame and black smoke rolled into the eastern sky. "Bomb," he finished. "Damnation. I hoped the sewage would disable it." He shrugged out of the evil-smelling suit.

"That's the Cauldron," Swinburne said, watching the distant smoke mushrooming over the city. "The flood must have pushed the bomb down to the intercepting sewer and all the way there."

"The eleventh hour," Burton murmured. "The end of Crowley. The signing of the Alliance."

Swinburne jumped into the air and yelled, "Hurrah!"

Burton looked up at the *Orpheus*, drifting nearby high over Green Park. "Perhaps I should have Lawless take me back to Africa," he muttered. "For a rest."

They returned to Battersea Power Station and were met by Nurse Nightingale. "He has passed," she said. "Do you want to see him, Sir Richard?"

"Look upon my own corpse? No, Nurse, I could not bear to do that."

Sadhvi Raghavendra, Thomas Honesty, and Daniel Gooch arrived with the DOGS trailing behind. One of Gooch's mechanical arms was swinging loosely, having been damaged by a bullet. Many of his men were clutching wounds.

"They surrendered," he said. "Detective Inspector Trounce is rounding them up. Krishnamurthy and Bhatti are helping. Galton was among the Enochians. No doubt he'll go back to Bedlam. Crowley?"

"Drowned and blown to pieces," Burton replied. "I'm sorry about Brunel."

"Oh, he'll be fine. We'll dredge him up and put him back together again. His consciousness will be intact, preserved in the diamonds."

The king's agent nodded and turned to Nightingale. "Will you see to Algy? He's putting a brave face on it, but he's been pretty badly knocked about."

"There's nothing wrong with me," the poet protested, "that a swig of brandy won't put to rights."

Nightingale regarded his tattered form and said, "You need alcohol rubbed into your wounds, not poured down your throat."

"Will it sting?"

"Yes, a lot."

"Then I insist on both."

While the nurse got to work, assisted by Raghavendra, Burton washed, borrowed clean clothes, and departed the station in a rotorchair. He flew across the river and followed it eastward. Ahead, the Cauldron was ablaze and thick plumes of smoke were curling into the air. Just when it was needed most, the rain had stopped, and with nothing to oppose the conflagration, it was spreading with alarming rapidity.

He set down in the yard at the back of the Royal Venetia Hotel and was a few minutes later knocking on the door of Suite Five. Grumbles answered and chimed, "Good morning, sir."

Burton ignored him, pushed past, and entered his brother's sitting room. Edward, as ever, was in his red dressing gown and creaking armchair. He looked up from a piece of paper and said, "Ah, it's you. I'm supposed to be at the ceremony but I'll be damned if I—Great heavens! What on earth has happened? You look positively ghastly. Grumbles, give my brother some ale."

Burton suddenly felt so fragile that he barely made it to a chair. He collapsed into it and weakly accepted the glass from the clockwork man. He mumbled, "Unlike Swinburne, I regard it as a little early in the day for alcohol," before downing the pint in a single, long swig.

"That was my last bottle and I don't know when I'll lay my hands on more," Edward said, somewhat ruefully. He looked his sibling up and down and shook his head despairingly. "Gad! Every time you set foot in this room you look worse than the last. Has your current state anything to do with this?" He held up the note he'd been reading when Burton had entered. "It arrived a couple of minutes before you. Apparently the detonation that shook the city a little while ago was an explosion. A very large one. In the East End."

Burton rubbed his side and winced as his ribs complained. "Yes, I know," he said hoarsely. "It marked the end of the case. Abdu El Yezdi is dead, and I was right—you are a secret weapon, Edward, but not for the purpose I envisioned."

The minister's face paled. He laced his fingers together, rested his hands on his stomach, and regarded his sibling, waiting silently for further explanation.

Burton told the whole story.

For three days, the conflagration raged through the Cauldron. The bomb had exploded beneath the Alton Ale warehouse and its flames rapidly jumped from dwelling to dwelling, consuming the wooden shacks and slumping tenements, destroying everything between Whitechapel and the Limehouse Cut Canal, Stepney, and Wapping. It was the worst blaze the city had experienced since the Great Fire of 1666, and just as that disaster had rid the city of the plague, so this one cured it of the infestation of *strigoi morti*. The un-dead burned to ash in their hidden lairs, unable to escape in the daylight. Many innocents also perished, but the death toll was far less than it might have been due to the mass exodus of the previous days.

"I suppose it will work out for the good," William Trounce mused. He was sharing morning coffee with Burton, Swinburne, Levi, Sister Raghavendra, and Slaughter in the study at 14 Montagu Place. Five days had passed since the death of Crowley. "The district can be rebuilt. Better housing, what!"

"Brunel has an idea for a new class of accommodation," Burton said. "Something he calls a *high-rise*."

"What is it?" Swinburne asked.

"I don't know, but the name suggests a variation of the old rookeries."

"Lord help us," Trounce put in. "Are we going to pile the poor on top of one another again?" He shook his head. "Never let the DOGS run free. They have no self-control."

"Monsieur Trounce," Levi said, "have the police discover *le cadavre* of Perdurabo?"

"No, and we probably won't. The crater where the Alton Ale warehouse stood is still smouldering—too hot to get anywhere near—and anyway there'll be nothing left of him, I'm certain." The detective frowned and sipped his drink. "By Jove, a strange coincidence, though. Do you know who owns the Alton breweries?"

"*Non*. Who?"

"The Crowley family. Three of them were killed by the blast."

Burton raised his eyebrows. "Are you suggesting one of them might have been Perdurabo's ancestor?"

"It's possible. The surname isn't particularly common."

"So Aleister Crowley chose to invade our history because he didn't exist in its future, and in doing so he became the reason *why* he didn't exist."

"That makes my head hurt," Trounce groaned.

"A paradox," Swinburne announced gleefully. "I like it. There's poetry in it."

"We must prepare ourselves for further such ironies and enigmas," Burton said. "The king has approved Edward's proposition. My brother is now the minister of chronological affairs and we, along with Brunel, Gooch, Krishnamurthy, Penniforth, Bhatti, and Babbage make up his clandestine department."

"I suggest we add Thomas Honesty to our ranks," Trounce said. "He's applied to join the Force and I'll certainly push for his acceptance. He's a good chap."

Sister Sadhvi added, "I suppose the poor fellow finds the prospect of groundskeeping rather tame after what he's been through."

Detective Inspector Slaughter gazed into his glass of milk and muttered, "He should be warned that Scotland Yard will play havoc with his innards."

Despite the presence of the clock on the mantelpiece, the king's agent reached into his waistcoat pocket and pulled out his chronometer, which had been retrieved from the Norwood catacombs when the police liberated Darwin and Lister. He opened it and looked at the lock of hair in its lid.

In some histories, Isabel was still alive.

Somehow, there was a modicum of comfort in that.

He said, "They'll be here at any moment."

No sooner had he spoken than carriages were heard pulling up outside. Eliphas Levi rose and crossed to the window, peered out, and said, "*Oui, ils sont arrives.*"

The party put on their coats and hats and left the house. Burton carried with him a Gladstone bag. There were three steam-horse-drawn growlers outside, and a hearse. Montague Penniforth was driving the lead vehicle, which held Nurse Nightingale, Daniel Gooch, Shyamji Bhatti, and Maneesh Krishnamurthy.

Burton and his fellows climbed into the empty carriages and the procession set off. It turned into Baker Street and followed the thoroughfare down to Bayswater Road, then proceeded westward all the way to Lime Grove before steering south, crossing the river below Hammersmith, and heading west again toward Mortlake.

The journey began amid the density of the Empire's capital—the vehicles wending their way slowly through the pandemonium of the packed streets—but ended in a quiet and quaint village on the edge of the metropolis; a place where little had changed over the past two decades.

In Mortlake Cemetery, Burton was pleased to discover that the stonemasons he'd hired had applied themselves to their commission with expertise, though he'd given them precious little time for it and the job wasn't yet complete. Nevertheless, when finished, it would be the tomb he'd requested: an Arabian tent sculpted from sandstone with such realism that its sides appeared to be rippling in a breeze. Set in a quiet corner of the graveyard, it stood thirteen feet tall on a twelve-by-twelve base, and had a glass window in the rear of its sloping roof so the inside would always be light.

It was, he thought, rather beautiful, and most importantly of all, it was above ground.

They carried a coffin from the hearse and placed it inside the mausoleum. Burton took a string of camel bells from his bag and hung them—gently tinkling and clanking—from the front point of the structure's roof. Swinburne recited a poem he'd composed for the occasion.

They laid Abdu El Yezdi to rest.

MEANWHILE, IN THE VICTORIAN AGE AND BEYOND . . .

PRINCE ALBERT OF SAXE-COBURG AND GOTHA (1819–1861)

In the months following his marriage to Queen Victoria in February 1840, Albert was not popular with the British, who harboured a deep suspicion of Germans. However, when Edward Oxford attempted to assassinate the queen in June 1840, Albert displayed remarkable courage and coolness, which won the people over. Shortly afterward, the Regency Act was passed to ensure that he would gain the throne in the event of Victoria's death.

ISABEL ARUNDELL (1831–1896)

Isabel and Richard Francis Burton met in 1851 and, after a ten-year courtship, married in 1861. Isabel was convinced they were destined to be together due to a prediction made during her childhood by a Gypsy named Hagar Burton.

GEORGE FREDERICK ALEXANDER CHARLES ERNEST AUGUSTUS (1819–1878)

If Queen Victoria had died in 1840, Ernest Augustus I of Hanover would have succeeded to the British throne, to be followed, upon his death in 1851, by his son, George V. Queen Victoria's long life meant this never happened, and

George V instead became King of Hanover. He was deposed when Prussia annexed the country in 1866 and spent the remainder of his life in exile.

CHARLES BABBAGE (1791–1871)

By 1859, Charles Babbage had already contributed to the world his designs for a "Difference Engine" and an "Analytical Engine" and was concerning himself more with campaigns against noise, street musicians, and children's hoops. His increasingly erratic behaviour had perhaps been signalled in 1857 by his analysis of "The Relative Frequency of the Causes of Breakage of Plate-Glass Windows."

THE BATTERSEA POWER STATION

The station was neither designed nor built by Isambard Kingdom Brunel and did not exist during the Victorian Age. Actually comprised of two stations, it was first proposed in 1927 by the London Power Company. Sir Giles Gilbert Scott (who created the iconic red telephone box) designed the building's exterior. The first station was constructed between 1929 and 1933. The second station, a mirror image of the first, was built between 1953 and 1955. Considered a London landmark, both stations are still standing, but derelict.

SIR JOSEPH WILLIAM BAZALGETTE (1819–1891)

A civil engineer, Bazalgette designed and oversaw the building of London's sewer network. Work commenced in 1859. The system is still fully functional in the 21st century.

ISABELLA MARY BEETON (NÉE MAYSON) (1836–1865)

Isabella Mayson married the publisher Samuel Orchart Beeton in 1856. In September 1859, they were expecting their second son (the first had died two years earlier). Mrs. Beeton became famous as the author of *The Book of*

Household Management, published in 1861. Four years later, she died of puerperal fever, aged just 28.

BIG BEN

Big Ben is the nickname of the Great Bell in the Elizabeth Tower at the Palace of Westminster. The tower—originally named St. Stephen's, then just "the Clock Tower"—was completed in 1858. The bell is the second to be cast, the first having cracked beyond repair. The replacement was made at the Whitechapel Bell Foundry. It first chimed in July 1859 but cracked in September and was out of commission for three years.

HENRY BERESFORD, 3RD MARQUESS OF WATERFORD (1811–1859)

Nicknamed "the Mad Marquess," Beresford's drunken pranks made him the prime suspect during the Spring Heeled Jack phenomenon of the Victorian Age. He was killed in a horse-riding accident in 1859.

JAMES BRUCE, 8TH EARL OF ELGIN (1811–1863)

From 1857 to 1861, Lord Elgin was High Commissioner to China, during which time he organised the bombing of Canton, oversaw the end of the Second Opium War, and ordered the looting and burning of the *Yuan Ming Yuan* (Old Summer Palace). In 1860, he put his signature to the Convention of Beijing, which stipulated that Hong Kong would become a part of the British Empire.

In 1859, Lord Elgin and his secretary, Laurence Oliphant, were in Aden, en route to London, when Burton and Speke arrived at Zanzibar, having completed their expedition to Africa's Central Lakes. Elgin offered to convey them home aboard his ship, HMS *Furious*. In the event, with Burton being too sick to travel, it was only Speke who accepted the offer.

ISAMBARD KINGDOM BRUNEL (1806–1859)

Brunel was, by 1859, the British Empire's most celebrated civil engineer, responsible for building the bridges, tunnels, dockyards, railways, and steamships that revolutionised transport during Victoria's reign. On 5th September 1859, he suffered a stroke and died ten days later, aged 53.

EDWARD JOSEPH BURTON (1824–1895)

Richard Francis Burton's younger brother shared his wild youth but later settled into Army life. Extremely handsome and a talented violinist, he became an enthusiastic hunter, which proved his undoing—in 1856, his killing of elephants so enraged Singhalese villagers that they beat him senseless. The following year, still not properly recovered, he fought valiantly during the Indian Mutiny but was so severely affected by sunstroke that he suffered a psychotic reaction. He never spoke again. For much of the remaining 37 years of his life, he was a patient in the Surrey County Lunatic Asylum.

CAPTAIN SIR RICHARD FRANCIS BURTON (1821–1890)

On 4th March 1859, Captain Richard Francis Burton and Lieutenant John Hanning Speke arrived at Zanzibar having completed their two-year expedition to the Central Lake Regions of Africa in search of the source of the Nile. While Burton recuperated, Speke sailed for London and there took the honours for the expedition's success, thus beginning a feud that would last for five years and end with Speke's death. Burton's career would never recover. By 1861, he had married Isabel Arundell and accepted the consulship of the disease-ridden island of Fernando Po. He was not knighted until 1886, just four years before his death.

THE CANNIBAL CLUB

In 1863, Burton and Doctor James Hunt established The Anthropological Society, through which to publish books concerning ethnological and anthropological matters. As an offshoot of the society, the Cannibal Club was a dining (and drinking) club for Burton and Hunt's closest cohorts: Richard Monckton Milnes, Algernon Swinburne, Henry Murray, Sir Edward Brabrooke, Thomas Bendyshe, and Charles Bradlaugh.

ALEISTER CROWLEY (1875–1947)

Aleister Crowley, called by the press of his time "the wickedest man in the world," was an influential occultist, author, poet, and mountaineer. He was a great admirer of Sir Richard Francis Burton and Algernon Swinburne.

CHARLES ROBERT DARWIN (1809–1882)

After decades of work researching and developing his theory of natural selection, Darwin had only partially written up his thesis when, in June 1858, he received a paper from Alfred Russel Wallace that outlined the same hypothesis. For the next year, Darwin, suffering from ill-health, rushed to produce an "abstract" of his work, so that he, rather than Wallace, might claim to be the theory's architect. *On the Origin of Species* was finally published on 22nd November 1859. It was an instant best-seller and has become one of the most influential books in history.

BENJAMIN DISRAELI, 1ST EARL OF BEACONSFIELD (1804–1881)

Having already succeeded as a novelist, Disraeli entered politics in the 1830s. In 1835, he outlined the principles for the Young England political group, which sought to advance an idealised version of feudalism, supported the idea of an absolute monarch, and promoted the raising of the lower classes. The group lasted until 1847. Disraeli achieved greater prominence in the mid 1840s, when, in light of the Great Irish Famine, he led opposition to the repeal of the Corn Laws. In 1852, Lord Derby appointed him chancellor of the Exchequer. His subsequent budget led to the fall of the government. Nonetheless, Disraeli occupied the post again from 1858 to the middle of

1859, before eventually becoming prime minister throughout 1868, and again from 1874 to 1880.

CHARLES DODGSON (1832–1898)

Better known as Lewis Carroll, by 1859 Dodgson was contributing stories and poetry to various magazines and had become friendly with the Pre-Raphaelite artists, including Gabriel Dante Rossetti. He'd also become acquainted with the Liddell family, whose daughter, Alice, would inspire his greatest work, *Alice's Adventures in Wonderland*.

SIR FRANCIS GALTON (1822–1911)

The half-cousin of Charles Darwin, Francis Galton was an anthropologist, eugenicist, explorer, geographer, inventor, meteorologist, and statistician. Darwin's *On the Origin of Species* inspired him, in 1859, to dedicate the rest of his life to the research of heredity in human beings.

Fifteen years earlier, in February 1844, 22-year-old Galton had joined the Freemasons. He rose through the Masonic degrees from Apprentice, to Fellow Craft, then to Master Mason, over the course of just four months. The records of the Grand Lodge state that: "Francis Galton, Trinity College student, gained his certificate 13th March 1845."

Also in 1845, he suffered a severe nervous breakdown.

SIR DANIEL GOOCH (1816–1889)

After training with a number of companies, including the one run by Robert Stephenson, Daniel Gooch was recruited in 1837 by Isambard Kingdom Brunel for the Great Western Railway. He became one of Britain's most eminent railway engineers, and later played a major role in laying the first successful transatlantic telegraph cable.

THE GREAT IRISH FAMINE

Potato blight struck Ireland in February of 1845. It caused mass starvation and disease, leading to an exodus between 1845 and 1852, when thousands of Irish citizens emigrated.

THOMAS LAKE HARRIS (1823–1906)

An American mystic and self-styled prophet, Lake preached in London in 1859, claiming his inspirations were received from an angel named the Lily Queen, to whom he was married. He dedicated one of his books, *Lyra Triumphalis*, to Algernon Swinburne. In the late 1860s, Harris created the Fountain Grove community in California—essentially a cult—which Laurence Oliphant joined. Oliphant gave all his money to the community and worked as a farm labourer, not properly splitting from the group until 1881.

G. E. HERNE (?–?)

Herne was a lieutenant in the 1st Bombay European Regiment of Fusiliers, who, prior to his participation in Burton's disastrous Harar expedition, was distinguished by his surveys, photography, and engineering projects on the west coast of India. He was not involved in Burton's expedition to the source of the Nile and was never consul at Zanzibar.

JOHN JUDGE (?–?)

An Irish survivor of the *Royal Charter* wreck. Described as being "of Herculean size," he was in the forecastle when the ship broke on the rocks and was washed out to sea. Fortunately, he managed to catch hold of a spar and made his way to shore.

EDWARD VAUGHAN HYDE KENEALY (1819–1880)

Best remembered for his scandalous behaviour during the Tichborne trials of 1873, Kenealy was a barrister, writer, and self-proclaimed prophet.

ELIPHAS LEVI, BORN ALPHONSE LOUIS CONSTANT (1810–1875)

Levi was a French occultist and ceremonial magician who published his first treatise on magic in 1855. He was a major influence on Aleister Crowley.

RICHARD MONCKTON MILNES
1ST BARON HOUGHTON(1809–1885)

Monckton Milnes was a poet, socialite, politician, patron of the arts, and collector of erotic and esoteric literature. He was a supporter, not opponent, of Lord Palmerston. For many years he courted Florence Nightingale, who turned down his marriage proposal on the grounds that marriage would interfere with her dedication to nursing. Monckton Milnes is thought to have created the name Young England for the political group led by Benjamin Disraeli.

SIR RODERICK MURCHISON (1792–1871)

One of the founders of the Royal Geographical Society and its president for a considerable period, including during 1859, when the Society was granted a Royal Charter.

LAURENCE OLIPHANT (1829–1888)

An author, traveller, diplomat, and mystic, in 1859 Oliphant encouraged John Hanning Speke to claim the honours for the discovery of the source of the Nile, thus betraying Burton, whose expedition it was. In the subsequent years, Oliphant was instrumental in keeping their feud alive. During the late 1860s, he fell under the influence of Thomas Lake Harris.

JOSEPH ROGERS (1829–1897)

Born Guzeppi Ruggier in Malta, Rogers was a seaman aboard the *Royal Charter*. When the ship ran aground in October 1859, he managed to swim ashore, dragging a rope with him. He was injured in the attempt, but his efforts allowed a bosun's chair to be rigged, providing a lifeline for thirty-nine passengers and crew. Rogers was awarded the RNLI Gold Medal for bravery.

THE *ROYAL CHARTER*

The *Royal Charter* was a passenger ship which, during the great storm of 1859, was wrecked on the northeast coast of Anglesey with a loss of approximately 459 lives. A 2,719-ton iron-hulled steam clipper, she had auxiliary steam engines for use in windless conditions, making her a fast vessel, able to complete the Liverpool-to-Australia voyage in as little as 60 days. On 26th October, she was completing the journey from Melbourne when the storm struck.

THE *ROYAL CHARTER* STORM OF 1859

On 25th and 26th October 1859, the British Isles were battered by the most severe storm of the 19th century. It caused the deaths of more than 800 people. 100mph winds wrecked 133 ships and badly damaged another 90.

THE ROYAL GEOGRAPHICAL SOCIETY

The Royal Geographical Society was given a Royal Charter—official sanction—by Queen Victoria in 1859.

LORD JOHN RUSSELL (1792–1878)

An English Whig and Liberal politician, Russell was twice prime minister, serving in that capacity from June 1846 to February 1852, and from October 1865 to June 1866. In 1859, he was secretary of state for foreign affairs in Lord Palmerston's government.

JOHN HANNING SPEKE (1827–1864)

In 1854, John Speke joined Burton's expedition to Harar, which was attacked at Berbera. He was captured and severely wounded, but survived and, in 1857, accompanied Burton on an expedition to discover the source of the Nile. In '58, while Burton lay ill, Speke discovered and named Lake Victoria, which he claimed as the source. The following year, encouraged by Laurence Oliphant, he raced back to London ahead of Burton and took full credit for the discovery, despite that he was a junior officer under Burton's command. The two men engaged in a five-year-long feud, which was to culminate in a confrontational debate in September 1864. On the eve of the event, Speke died of a gunshot wound while out hunting. Some biographers claim this was an accident, others suggest suicide.

DOCTOR JOHN FREDERICK "STYGGINS" STEINHAUESER (?–?)

Steinhaueser met Burton in India in 1846 and soon became one of his most valued friends. He later served as resident civil surgeon at Aden, and treated Burton and Speke after they were both seriously injured on the coast of Berbera in 1855. Burton subsequently asked him to join the quest for the source of the Nile, an invitation Steinhaueser was keen to accept but, in the end, was forced to turn down. In 1860, he and Burton travelled together around America. This is one of the most obscure periods of Burton's life. Not long afterwards, Steinhaueser died, quite suddenly, of a brain embolism.

COUNT SOBIESKI (1833–?)

Real name Michael Ostrog, he was a Russian-born fraudster and thief. In 1889, he was named as a suspect in the Jack the Ripper killings, but was later discovered to have been in a French prison at the time of the murders.

THE SOLAR STORM OF 1859

Also known as the Carrington Event, this was the most powerful solar storm in recorded history, which caused, on September 1st and 2nd of that year, the largest recorded geomagnetic storm. Aurorae appeared around the world and telegraph systems failed, shocked their operators, caused spontaneous fires, and in some cases mysteriously sent and received messages despite having been disconnected.

ABRAHAM "BRAM" STOKER (1847–1912)

Born in Dublin, Ireland, 12-year-old Stoker was still at school in 1859. In adulthood, he became the personal assistant of actor Henry Irving and business manager of the Lyceum Theatre in London. On 13th August 1878, Stoker met Sir Richard Francis Burton for the first time, and described him as follows: *"The man riveted my attention. He was dark and forceful, and masterful, and ruthless. I have never seen so iron a countenance. As he spoke the upper lip rose and his canine tooth showed its full length like the gleam of a dagger."* Stoker's novel *Dracula* was published in 1897.

WILLIAM STROYAN (?–1855)

A lieutenant in the Indian Navy, Stroyan was a talented astronomer and surveyor. He was killed by a spear-thrust, on the coast of Berbera, during Burton's ill-fated expedition to Harar in 1855.

ALGERNON CHARLES SWINBURNE (1837–1909)

During 1859, Swinburne was temporarily rusticated from Balliol College, Oxford, for having publicly supported Felice Orsini's attempted assassination of Napoleon III. He spent much of the year at Wallington Hall, mixing with Lady Pauline Trevelyan's intellectual circle. It was not, however, until December 1862 that he joined Lady Pauline and her guests on a trip to Tynemouth where, according to William Bell Scott, the poet recited the as yet unpublished *Hymn to Proserpine* and *Laus Veneris*.

HENRY JOHN TEMPLE, 3RD VISCOUNT PALMERSTON (1784–1865)

Lord Palmerston lost his seat in government when Lord Melbourne was defeated in the general election of 1841. Though out of office for five years, he returned as foreign secretary under Lord John Russell and served in that capacity until 1852, when he became home secretary in the Earl of Aberdeen's government. In 1855, he became prime minister. International intrigues forced him to resign three years later, but after just twelve months he was re-elected and served as a very popular premier until his death in 1865.

THE TOWER OF LONDON

In October 1841, a serious fire destroyed parts of the tower, including the Grand Armoury.

LADY PAULINE TREVELYAN (1816–1866)

An English painter, Paulina Jermyn Jermyn was married to Sir Walter Calverley Trevelyan in May 1835. She made Wallington Hall in Northumberland a focal point for Victorian artists and intellectuals, counting among her frequent guests Swinburne and other members of the Pre-Raphaelite Brotherhood.

ABOUT THE AUTHOR

Mark Hodder is a time traveler of limited capacity. He is restricted to forward momentum and cannot alter his speed, which is set at the breakneck pace of sixty seconds per minute. Despite these constraints, he is able to achieve the feat without mechanical assistance, though he fears this may change if he goes too far.

Mark's voyage began on November 28th, 1962—embarkation point: Southampton, England—and has currently reached the year 2013 and Valencia, Spain. So far, the experience has not resulted in any ill-effects, other than a phenomenon wherein increased familiarity with the sensation of time travel has caused Mark's mind to falsely report an ongoing increase in velocity.

Entertainments enjoyed during the excursion have included vast amounts of reading, writing, and studying; a good deal of contact with other time travelers; various degrees of involvement with radio, television, and film production; and an immoderate amount of eating and drinking.

Mark was at one point skilled in the operation of a bow and arrow (location: university) but has since transferred his attention to more complex technologies. He has employed the latter to create accounts that might possibly continue onward in some form after the cessation of his journey. They are: *The Strange Affair of Spring Heeled Jack* (winner of the Philip K. Dick Award, 2011); *The Curious Case of the Clockwork Man*; *Expedition to the Mountains of the Moon*; *A Red Sun Also Rises*; and the volume you are currently holding in your hands, viewing on your device, listening to, or having streamed directly into your mind.

The aforementioned works are not instruction manuals, and Mark would like to remind his fellow time travelers that, in cases of emergency, they should consult with one another at the earliest opportunity.